Copyright © 2023 by Valerie Gomez
All rights reserved.

No part of this publication may be reproduced, distributed, or transmitted in any form or by any means, including photocopying, recording, or other electronic or mechanical methods, without the prior written permission of the publisher, except for the use of brief quotations in a book review.

This is a work of fiction. All names, characters, and incidents portrayed in this book are fictitious. Any similarities to any persons (living or deceased) or situations, either real or imagined, are purely coincidental and not intended by the author.

Print ISBN: 979-8-9884748-0-7
Ebook ISBN: 979-8-9884748-1-4

Cover art and interior illustrations by the author.

Editors:
Amy Spalding, *getyourbookon.com*
Peter Senftleben, *peseditorial.com*
Jessica Smith, *reedsy.com*

Accuracy reader:
Rose Thomson, *rcthomson.com*

*To my sister, for your ability to make me laugh,
especially in the most inappropriate situations.
And for teaching me to always be myself.*

AUTHOR'S NOTE

Thank you for taking the time to read *Cover Story*. While my book is a work of fiction, both main characters' personalities and journeys are inspired by my own experiences. The idea for this book came from my own background as a magazine art director. I am Mexican American. I have anxiety and frequent panic attacks. I also have a fear of horses.

This book contains detailed scenes of panic attacks, which mirror my own. No two people experience anxiety in the same way, and while panic-induced vertigo isn't as common as other symptoms, it's one that affects me, which is why I included it.

Content warnings: sexual activity, anxiety, panic attacks, homophobia (remembered, not current).
Trigger warnings: on-page panic attacks, suggestion of conversion therapy (off-page, remembered), one instance of physical abuse (off-page, remembered).

If someone in your life tells you they're concerned about your mental health, please listen to them. You are not alone.

Cover Story

VALERIE GOMEZ

CHAPTER 1

DAX

Fifty.
Forty-nine.
Why are the lyrics to Eminem's "Lose Yourself"—the ones about sweaty palms and mom's spaghetti—playing in my head right now? Right fucking now?
Forty-eight.
I can do this. I've done this dozens of times before. I signed up for this.

I'm standing near the stage in the back of RockPaperScissors—a small club in Manhattan's Lower East Side that usually hosts lesser-known musical acts, but holds a comedy night once a week—waiting for Charlie, the club's owner, to call my name.

I'm an actor, not a professional stand-up comedian, but I've been doing sets here on and off for the last two years. It started out as an exercise to help me get more comfortable performing in front of people, but has evolved into a way for me to unwind. I rarely get anxious when I'm about to go onstage, and I can't pinpoint what makes tonight any different. When I step off the stage, that's a different story, and definitely not something I should be thinking about at the moment. I need to get my thoughts back on track.

I continue to count down from fifty in my head to center myself. I only make it to thirty-eight before Charlie introduces me.

"Up next," his voice booms, "regulars to our weekly comedy night will recognize our next guest. Let's give it up for Dax Ximénez."

I take a deep breath and step onto the stage.

"Thanks, Charlie. Hello, and thanks for coming out here tonight.

"I used to be an IT consultant for a very well-known tech company. I won't say the name of the company—" (Someone in the audience shouts, "AOL?") "AOL?! Do I look that old to you? Remind me to make an appointment for Botox after this.

"Anyway, my job was to fix computer problems whenever the rest of you did something you weren't supposed to do at work." (Pause, a few laughs.) "Whenever a computer would freeze or start acting up, I was the one that would show up. Ninety percent of the time, the problem was a download from a—" (—air quotes—) "'questionable website'. Yeah." (Point to an overly enthusiastic guy in the front row.) "This guy knows.

"The main culprit was usually..." (Hold out hands encouraging audience to respond.) "Porn. Yeah. Or games. You know you fucked up when you have to call me because you were looking up words like spread *and* sheets—but not *spreadsheets." (Laughter.)*

"I tried my best to be professional whenever I was called to fix something, but I'd have to ask, 'Sir, did you download something called Wild Beach Safari?'" *(Mild laughter.) "That one was NOT a game." (Big laughter.)*

"But I got out of the business after a few years. I thought, 'Here I am, making good money, having consistent working hours, being treated like a royalty by high-level executives just for removing porn from their computers and helping them to find the dickpics they

accidentally saved to a company server, when I could be making shit money while standing here trying to entertain all of you and hoping no one throws a beer bottle at me.'" (Audience laughs.)

I grip the microphone in one hand while I pace around the stage. My button-down shirtsleeves are rolled up to the elbows, and I'm sweating a bit, which I hope the audience doesn't notice.

I'm on the stage for another ten minutes, telling jokes and stories and engaging with the audience. I make a few mental notes on what's working—and what isn't—and try to remember things to work on for next time. There's a pretty good crowd for a Sunday night, and they seem to be really enjoying themselves, their laughter loud and genuine-sounding. No one heckles me or throws anything while I'm onstage, so I call it a win.

There's something really invigorating about performing. It's the thrill of it—the adrenaline rush that comes from standing up here with no armor, no props, no musical instruments. Me and a microphone, that's it. The only one who can decide if I succeed or fail is me. And the only way for me to succeed up here is to make people laugh.

As soon as I say *thank you* and step off the stage, I hurry to the bar, sidestepping a woman who clearly decided the two-drink minimum was just a jumping-off point and is laser-focused on me. Misjudging her sense of balance, she stumbles like a newborn foal and lands in the arms of her friend, who's nearly as lit up as she is. The fall seems to have taken them both by surprise, giving me enough time to slip past them and making it to the corner of the bar.

I take a seat on the stool next to Charlie—who could easily be mistaken for a 1980s-era NFL linebacker, broad and beefy with a thick mustache—while Hugo, the regular Sunday night bartender, sets a glass of water in front of me.

"Nice job," Charlie says, patting me on the back. "Funny stuff."

His stern face shows no hint of amusement, which isn't surprising. In all the time I've been performing at his club, I've never seen Charlie laugh, not even once.

"Thanks, man," I say, hoping he doesn't notice I'm still a little out of breath after being onstage.

"Drink?" he asks.

"No thanks. I gotta go. Next time."

"Next time." Charlie nods and gives me a forceful clap on my shoulder before disappearing into the crowd.

I chug my entire glass of water in one go, feeling my pulse tick up rather than slowing down. I'm no longer in front of the bright lights, but the air in here feels at least ten degrees warmer than it did only a few minutes ago. I tug at the collar of my shirt and look around, hoping no one's watching me. Luckily, everyone's focused on the stage, waiting for the next performer. *I need to get out of here.*

I make a quick dash toward the back door of the club and push it open, desperate to get out into the fresh air. When the door closes behind me, I lean against it, willing my breath to go back to normal. A breeze hits the sweat on my back and neck, which helps to cool me down. My hand is shaking slightly as I rake my fingers through my hair, knowing it's going to cause short waves of dark brown to stick up in all directions.

Squeezing my eyes shut, I take a few more gulps of air and slowly count down from fifty before my breathing begins to even out. I peel myself from the door and slowly make my way toward the subway station.

Once I'm on the train, I finally feel the muscles in my shoulders unclench and I let my body relax, grateful that this hadn't been a full-on panic attack, but a small mental fire alarm.

I tip my head back and let it rest against the glass of the subway car as it clanks and lurches toward Queens. Pulling my phone out of my pocket, I see a text from my manager.

Hannah: Don't forget the photo shoot tomorrow. TMG photo studio, 9:30 a.m.

A second text contains the name of the person I'm supposed to meet along with the address of the studio. I'll have to get from Queens to Midtown Manhattan during morning rush hour. *Great.*

CHAPTER 2

AJ

9:12 a.m.

Forty-two minutes late.

Where is he?

I pace around the photo studio, looking at my watch every two minutes, and doing my best to ignore the uneasiness in my stomach.

Clutching my clipboard, I adjust my glasses and flip through pages of notes for today's photo shoot. In the stack are headshots of today's subject—Diego Ximénez, an up-and-coming actor—along with his measurements and clothing sizes sent to me from Hannah, his manager. The stack also contains notes and sketches detailing every photo we're planning that will eventually grace the pages of the eight-page feature in *The Modern Gentleman* magazine, or *TMG*, as it's commonly known. In the last thirty minutes, I've looked at this stack at least two dozen times.

Diego is thirty-three and starting to break out as an actor. He and his friend Maximo—or Dax and Max, as they call themselves—created a series of low-budget short comedy videos on YouTube called *Mexican't* four years ago. The show is based on their own experiences as two friends, both Mexican-Americans—one straight (Max) and the other gay (Dax)—living, working, and dating in New York City. It had a modest following but was mostly unnoticed by the mainstream until the two had a stroke of luck that most content creators can only dream of. Action-movie megastar Paz Alvarez watched a few episodes of their show on YouTube and raved about it all over social media, causing *Mexican't* to suddenly go viral. Capitalizing on his enormous fame, Paz helped Max and Dax develop the videos into a TV series and signed on as executive producer, bringing it to one of the top streaming services, where it's set to be released a handful of weeks from now. The web series starred Max and Dax, but for the television version, Max decided to focus on writing while Dax focused on acting. For this fashion feature, *TMG* wants to capitalize on Diego's rising-star status.

When I'd asked about having the two of them together for this shoot, I was told that with all of the newfound attention, Max doesn't like to be in the spotlight, preferring to work behind the scenes. He recently moved to Los Angeles to pursue more opportunities for script writing.

I walk around the studio, checking in with everyone while simultaneously trying not to look increasingly irritated—a feat that's getting more and more difficult by the second. I have to force myself to smile and not look like I'm internally panicking at the thought that our talent has either been in a terrible accident or has completely blown off the shoot. I'm trying not to think about how much it will cost the magazine if we have to reschedule, not to mention the disappointment I'll face from my bosses if today is a failure. It's nothing new. These are the thoughts I have before every photo shoot I work on. That part of being an art director doesn't get any easier with time or experience. The talent being late, however, certainly doesn't help.

Jürgen, the photographer, is all set up, and he and his assistants pass the time by doing light tests. The gray seamless backdrop has been placed so that the flash will hit it in a way that will give a dramatic fade-to-black look. For the tests, the photo assistants are making goofy poses to mimic glamorous couple photo sessions that were popular in the 1980s. I stifle a laugh when I see them.

Jaan, the hairstylist, and Anya, the makeup artist, are catching up on the latest gossip over coffee. In the dressing room, Sydney, the clothing stylist, is arranging the assortment of watches, wallets, sunglasses, belts, and other accessories on a long table while their assistant, Lira, meticulously steams dress shirts on the clothing rack. Everyone in the studio is cool as a cucumber. As chill as a penguin on an iceberg. As calm as, well, you get the idea. The only one who's not cool or chill or calm is me.

I check my phone again. No new messages or missed calls from Diego's manager. My annoyance is turning to dread with every minute that passes.

Where the fuck is he?

9:25 a.m.

Fifty-five minutes late.

I'm still pacing when I hear the buzzer at the front door of the studio. The receptionist, who's been scrolling through her phone and looking bored at the front desk, buzzes him through. Seconds later, Diego Ximénez strolls in as casually as if he were arriving at a house party—sunglasses on, phone to his ear.

I want to wrench the phone from his hand and shout at him for delaying the shoot for close to an hour, but I'm a professional and I can't give in to an impulsive act of anger, even if he deserves it.

Everyone looks at me, waiting for some signal of what to do as Diego continues his call. Eventually, he turns to me and his eyes catch on mine (I think—he's still wearing those goddamned sunglasses), and he says a quick goodbye to whomever he's talking to.

Diego pockets his phone and removes his sunglasses. His eyes are a greenish gray with long, dark lashes and faint lines in the outer corners. His hair is a thick, dark brown and just a little longer than the most recent photos I'd seen of him online. He's also sporting what was once a five o'clock shadow but is now a ten o'clock-the-following-Tuesday shadow that covers his square jaw. I was expecting him to be clean-shaven, but I like this look. We can work with it.

"Sorry," he says to everyone and no one.

Where have you been? You're almost an hour late! It's not like we've all been here sitting around waiting for you. Not like the magazine has to pay everyone, including the studio, overtime if we don't finish on time. That's what I *want* to say. What I actually say is, "Mr. Ximénez, thanks for coming. Let's get started."

He nods, but he doesn't apologize for being late.

Immediately, everyone on set surrounds him and introduces themselves, ready to get down to business. Upon hearing each person's name, Diego repeats it, as if committing it to memory. He's gracious and kind, laughing and joking around, putting everyone at ease right away.

Before I have a chance to introduce myself, he smiles at me—not a fake, business-lunch smile but a stunningly genuine one. He holds his hand out for me to shake, but as I open my mouth to speak, one of the photographer's lights falls with a clatter and I rush to the set to make sure everything's okay.

When I return, Diego is perusing the craft services table. He picks up a bottle of water and opens it. I try not to look too impatient while I wait for him to take a long drink, downing almost half the bottle at once.

"Mr. Ximénez," I say, hoping to keep him moving. "Let's get you into hair and makeup." His skin is smooth, with a light olive complexion that complements his dark hair. At least it should be a fairly quick grooming session before he's ready to photograph.

As I'm leading Diego toward Sydney to get him dressed in the first outfit of the day, he stops midstride.

"Sorry, I didn't catch your name," he says. "Are you AJ Bond's assistant? I was told he's the one in charge, but I haven't met him yet."

Diego looks at me with wide eyes, and I can tell he's not trying to be insulting. Still, I can't help but be irritated. I furrow my brow and take a slow, calming breath. *I am a professional. I will keep my cool. I will not blow up at him.*

"*I'm* AJ Bond," I say in a brusque tone. "I'm the art director at *TMG*." I can feel my jaw clench as I say it.

I can see from the way his smile drops that I've made a huge mistake. Technically I've said nothing wrong; I *am* AJ Bond, after all. But I'm pretty sure I've shamed and embarrassed him, and only moments before we start an all-day photo shoot.

"Oh, shit! I'm so sorry!" Diego exclaims, his face contorting into a guilt-laden grimace. He runs a hand over the back of his neck.

I quickly try to smooth it over. "It's fine. It's my fault. I don't think I properly introduced myself. And anyway, you're not the first to mistake me for an assistant. Don't worry about it."

I was going for light and breezy, but my voice comes out a little too flat. Diego's frown deepens.

It's not a lie. I get mistaken for assistants or interns all the time. I've been called *kiddo* or *buddy* on set more often than I care to count. I have the youthful face of a twentysomething despite being thirty-two years old, and I'm not dressed at all like I belong in the fashion world. Today, like most days, I'm dressed in a black T-shirt, hoodie, jeans, and sneakers. When I first started at the magazine as an intern several years ago, I used to try to follow fashion trends I'd seen in the magazine, but as I've moved up through the ranks, my style has taken a U-turn into emo college student territory. At some point, I realized that being comfortable, especially on photo-shoot days, is more important to me than being stylish. I mean, it's not like *I'm* the one being photographed.

I expect Diego to laugh or to say something mildly condescending—that's what usually happens in situations like these. Instead, he rubs his hands together and says, "Okay, boss. Tell me what you want me to do."

I nod in relief.

"Did your manager give you the call sheet with the information about the concept of the shoot?" I ask.

"No. She gave me the address and your name, but she didn't say anything about what we're actually doing other than it's a fashion shoot." Diego's face grows serious. "Please tell me I don't have to wear a hot dog costume or be covered in body paint or anything like that."

The crew laughs, and Diego smiles like he's thrilled to have a captive audience.

I try to force a smile, but with every passing minute with this man, my frustration only grows. It's not unusual for the talent to show up late, and honestly, he's by far not the worst celebrity to deal with.

Still, I'm tempted to tell Diego that the first shot is to pelt him with water balloons. Or that he'll have a live tarantula crawling on his face. Thinking better of it, I decide to keep my mouth shut.

Normally, the celebrity photo shoots are directed by Takashi, *TMG*'s creative director, but he's been on leave for the past few weeks taking care of his partner. It's a huge responsibility to fill in for him, and this shoot is a great opportunity to prove to the editorial board that I'm capable of a lot more than the small photo shoots I usually work on. If Takashi were to leave *TMG* at some point, filling his role would be my ultimate dream job. But that's a long way off. For now, I'm trying to do my best to make Takashi proud. Starting things off with the talent being nearly an hour late is not good, so I need to keep today's shoot on track.

I usher Diego to the tall director's chair that's positioned in front of a lighted mirror, where Jaan sprays his dark hair with water while Anya begins dabbing his face with makeup.

As they're working, I stand next to Diego's chair, flipping pages on my clipboard and leaning in to show him the list of photos and sketches, giving him an idea of what he'll be asked to do.

He nods, looking over each shot on the list, asking a few questions as we go. Being so close to him, I can't help but notice how good he smells—clean and fresh, like he washes his hair with some sort of scented shampoo. I'd expected him to smell like one of those stereotypical men's body sprays or heavy cologne, so the citrusy scent is surprising.

I also notice that he's bouncing one leg and fidgeting with the hem of his sweater, and I wonder if he's nervous. I can't explain why, but I find all of these details both surprising and endearing. I have a sudden urge to place my hand on his knee to steady his bouncing leg. But no, that would be unprofessional. Besides, I've also had the urge to punch him on the arm for being extremely late, so keeping my hands to myself is probably the best course of action.

Once he's finished with hair and makeup, I send him off to the dressing room while I chat with Jürgen. Ten minutes later, Diego steps out looking like—well, like he should be on the pages of a men's fashion magazine. When I catch sight of him, dressed in a beautifully tailored navy-blue suit over a crisp, white button-down shirt and black tie, a gasp nearly escapes my lips.

Being momentarily stunned isn't a highly unusual reaction the first time a model or celebrity steps onto the set all dressed up and ready to be photographed. After all, *TMG* is in the business of making people look good. *Still...*

Diego's hair has been tamed into submission with hair products, the minor flaws in his skin erased by the magic of makeup. Even his beard is a little tidier.

Something about the way he looks—amazingly polished and handsome, yet a little self-conscious—makes my stomach flutter. It's probably just secondhand nervousness for him. *Has to be.*

With an unsure look on his face—eyebrows pulled together and tension lines around his mouth—he smooths his hands over the lapels of his jacket.

"How do I look?"

CHAPTER 3

DAX

I'm standing in a room, surrounded by strangers and wearing expensive clothes that aren't mine. I wait helplessly as they all stare at me, some of them with smiles, some with frowns. Well, most of them are smiling. Only one person is frowning: AJ Bond.

I could've sworn he almost smiled when I came out of the dressing room, but in the next instant, it was gone, replaced by a stony face—not angry, just *nothing*.

AJ isn't meeting my eyes, but I can tell he's not intentionally avoiding my gaze. With one arm folded across his chest and the other tapping on his bottom lip, he's focused, slowly looking me up and down, scrutinizing my hair, my face, my clothes. I know this is his job and it's not personal. But this? This is agony.

I should be used to this. Well, not *this*, exactly. I've never been part of a photo shoot quite this big before. But I should be able to handle the pressure of being judged by strangers. I do stand-up comedy, for god's sake. Except, when I'm on the stage with a mic in my hand, *I'm* in control of the room. The audience's eyes are on me, and I can decide when to make them laugh. A really talented comic can make it look effortless, but that doesn't mean it's easy. It's definitely not.

Getting to the point where I feel comfortable performing in front of people has taken a lot of practice—especially when I'm also trying to manage my anxiety. I don't have stage fright—I'm okay with being in front of an audience. It's the interactions with people either before or after I'm onstage that can cause the anxiety to really ramp up. Like, the adrenaline of going onstage temporarily intensifies my anxiety, sometimes causing me to have a panic attack. The frustrating part is that the panic attacks are so inconsistent. I don't get them before or after every show, or even at most shows. They only happen once in a while, but it's enough that I'm on edge every time I'm performing, waiting for the warning signs to appear—the way they had last night.

Shit. I hope I don't have a panic attack today. That would only make things worse, since AJ already seems like he's in a foul mood. I don't even know what I did to cause him to scowl at me when I came into the studio this morning. I even showed up a little early. And, okay, maybe insulting him right off the bat didn't help, but that wasn't entirely my fault. Maybe he ate a bad breakfast burrito before coming in today.

I'm not normally so insecure, but this is my first really big magazine feature. And as AJ looks me up and down with agonizing slowness, taking in every detail of my appearance, I'm increasingly unsettled. My go-tos in stressful situations are to either make jokes, or sneak away for a few minutes alone, and I don't think AJ would appreciate either of those. So for now, I have to just stand here.

While AJ assesses me, the only thing I can do is stare back at him too. I'd been too flustered when I first arrived to really take him in. But being stuck here watching him work, I don't really have a choice.

He's taller than me by a couple of inches. I'm five foot ten, which isn't short by any standards, but he must be at least six feet, if not a little more. He has brown hair that has a coppery shine when the light hits it. It's short around the back and sides and longish and wavy on top, messy, like he's been running his hands through it.

AJ's eyes are a rich brown and would be unremarkable except for the long lashes and full eyebrows that frame them. His dark-rimmed glasses give off a sexy-smart vibe. His whole frame is long and lean, just on the edge of being lanky. He looks young—younger than I'd expect for someone in his position—maybe twenty-seven, if I had to guess.

Is he cute? Maybe.

Okay, yes.

I feel bad for inadvertently insulting him earlier, but seriously, when I'd pictured an expert on men's fashion, that image looked nothing like the guy standing in front of me. This guy looks more like he showed up to watch an indie band play a secret concert than to take charge of a high-end fashion shoot.

AJ continues tapping his chin with his finger, then finally nods.

"Looks good," he says, but not to me. He's speaking to the style team standing around me, watching AJ like they're presenting a cow to be judged at the state fair. *I guess that makes me the cow?* "But not that watch, it's too techy for this suit. Let's switch it out for something more classic."

He turns to chat with Jürgen for a moment before curtly directing me to have a seat on the lone stool that's been placed in the middle of the backdrop in front of the camera.

"Alright, I'm going to do a few test shots," Jürgen says to me in a strong German accent. "*Eins, zwei, drei,*" he says, which has me furrowing my brow. I have no idea what he said, but the camera clicks as soon as he finishes. He says it again. *Eins, zwei, drei.* Click. And again. *Eins, zwei, drei.* Click.

Ah, it must be German for *one, two, three*?

"What should I do?" I ask, because all I'm doing is sitting awkwardly on the stool and trying to figure out what to do with my hands. I place them on my knees, but this doesn't really feel like something a fashion model would do.

"These are test shots," AJ says to me. "You don't need to do anything. Just relax."

I nod. *Relax? Yeah, sure.*

Jürgen and AJ are concentrating on a computer monitor that's set up on a rolling cart on set, navigated by a young man with tattoo sleeves. I'm assuming the photos are showing up on the screen as Jürgen shoots. The two confer quietly before AJ looks up at me and says, "Okay, Diego, we're ready."

The photo assistants hustle around the set at Jürgen's instructions, making last-minute adjustments to the lights and reflectors. The stylists descend on me for one last touch-up, armed with tools like lint rollers, a puffy makeup brush, a comb, and one giant can of hair spray.

"Dax," I say loudly in the general direction of AJ. I can't see him because Jaan is shielding my eyes while he sprays my hair.

"Sorry, what?" AJ calls.

"Dax," I say, louder this time. "It's my initials: Diego Alejandro Ximénez. Actually, it's Diego Alejandro Ximémez Ibarra—you know us Mexicans love long names. You can call me Dax." I cough after inhaling a small cloud of hair spray. The style army retreats, and I'm left alone in front of the camera again.

"Okay, Dax." AJ shuffles through the papers on his clipboard as he approaches me. "Let's have you start off with a casual look, like this." He shows me the clipboard and I do my best to imitate what I see. Jürgen gives me instructions on where to look and how to turn my face before he lifts the camera to his eye and begins. He gives me directions every few seconds as the light boxes burst a blinding light with every shot.

"Chin up."

"Face toward the light."

"Relax your shoulders."

"Eyes on me."

"Chin down."

"Less smile."

"Bigger smile."

I try my best to follow Jürgen's instructions, and try *not* to be distracted by AJ, who's frowning while he looks at the computer monitor. After several shots, AJ stops Jürgen, then asks the stylists to come in and do some touch-ups to my hair, fix my collar, and cinch the back of my shirt a little more.

When the stylists are done, Jürgen raises his camera and begins again. I'm not feeling entirely comfortable, but I try to relax, hoping the tension I feel isn't coming through in the photographs. After a few more shots, AJ stops Jürgen again and asks him to come over to the monitor. AJ isn't smiling, and a deep vertical crease has formed between his eyebrows.

Not good. A tight knot forms in my stomach.

All I can do is wait while AJ and Jürgen talk quietly and point at the screen. Eventually they pull Sydney into the conversation. None of them seem happy with what they see. *Shit.*

I internally debate coming over to see what they're looking at, but I know that'll only make me more self-conscious, so I don't. I can't even think of anything funny to say to break the tension. Something tells me AJ wouldn't laugh anyway.

I pace around the set until I notice a wadded-up tangle of black gaffer's tape on the floor. Picking it up, I squeeze it into a tight little ball, then start kicking it around like a hacky sack. At first I do small kicks bouncing it off the toes of my shoes, but then I notice the photo assistants watching me. They start clapping and cheering me on with whoops of encouragement. Before long, I've got the tape ball up in the air, using my elbows, knees, feet, even my head to keep it aloft. Just as I manage to kick it high above my head, I catch AJ's eyes on me, arms crossed. As the tape ball comes down, I give it a little bounce with my elbow before I hold open the breast pocket of my suit jacket and let it land perfectly inside.

Everyone on the set claps and cheers, so I take an exaggerated bow. AJ has straightened up from the computer and his arms are still crossed, but he's not frowning anymore. He's smiling.

CHAPTER 4

A J

"Can I have everyone gather around, please?"

During the first set of shots, I knew something wasn't working, but couldn't put my finger on exactly what. But after Dax's little tape-ball hacky-sack show, things finally click into place. With the whole crew assembled, I stand on a wooden box to make an announcement.

"We're going to change the direction of the shoot. It's feeling too stuffy and formal and it's not revealing Diego's—sorry, Dax's—personality. This shoot needs to be more fun."

When I'm done giving the rundown of changes from the original concept, the crew disperses, rushing off to make the proper adjustments.

Twenty minutes later, the backdrop has been switched to a bright blue, Jürgen and his assistant are resetting the lights, Sydney is adjusting Dax's tie, and Jaan is doing some last-minute styling of Dax's hair. Dax is still dressed in the same suit, but he looks much more at ease.

I'd asked one of Jürgen's assistants to run to the vintage store down the street to buy an assortment of cheap, old-school toys. She came back with two bags full of things like bubble guns, a foam football, a Slinky, a Rubik's Cube, and a few other toys of a similar style. I pull out the foam football and hand it to Dax, instructing him to throw it in the air, toss it from hand to hand—basically play with it while we photograph him.

Once we start, something incredible happens: the nervous energy that Dax had been carrying seems to melt away. He relaxes and starts getting into it—and dare I say, having fun?

I watch the computer monitor as the photos appear a moment after the shutter clicks. Each one looks incredible. Dax may be inexperienced with this type of photo shoot, but he knows how to move so that the camera captures him at his best.

I stand beside Jürgen as he shoots, giving Dax some suggestions on what to do and words of encouragement when something is really looking good. Dax seems to be taking it all in, listening to my direction or happily responding to my praise.

The next several shots go much the same way—the background colors changing between each shot, Dax wearing different but equally sharp and flattering outfits, and me giving him new props to play with. He kicks around a mini soccer ball the way he did the tape ball, pulls a Slinky in all directions, and spins a yo-yo, flicking it from his finger toward the camera.

When we break for lunch, I walk around, checking in with each person on the crew to make sure everyone's happy about how things are going. I'm about to check on Dax, but I see him in the corner, eating his lunch while pacing back and forth and talking on the phone. I give him privacy and finish my own food while going through my notes for the final few shots of the day.

I'm feeling good about the new direction, but a little twinge of doubt sticks in the back of my mind. André, *TMG*'s editor-in-chief, almost always trusts my judgment when it comes to changing plans for shoots. But normally, Takashi is the one handling photo shoots of this scale. On smaller shoots that I usually work on, Takashi would be the one to officially approve—or disapprove—of such drastic changes.

I hope I haven't let them all down with this one. It's a risk, but one that I hope will pay off.

"That's a wrap! Thanks, everyone," I call out after the last shot of the day. I take the View Master from Dax's hands while Sydney and their assistant help him out of his suit jacket. He takes his time heading back to the dressing room, making sure to thank everyone with handshakes, casual pats on the back, or even a couple of friendly hugs.

While the crew is busy packing up and saying goodbyes, I grab a bottle of water before pulling up a chair beside Jürgen, who's sitting at the computer, to look over the day's work.

He's scrolling through the last set of photos, and we point excitedly at ones that seem to stand out among the rest. This is one of my favorite parts of the job: finishing a great photo shoot and poring through hundreds (or thousands) of photos to pick out the perfect shots for the magazine.

Sydney pushes a rolling rack filled with garment bags out of the dressing room, their assistant rushing behind with a stack of at least six shoe boxes in her arms.

"Hey Syd," I call. "I think I'm going to get dinner at Lowell's down the street after this. Wanna come?"

"Oh, man," they reply. "My boyfriend is cooking tonight. I really wish I could join you. *Really.*"

I know exactly what they mean. Sydney's boyfriend likes to try out exotic recipes he finds on the internet, some with more success than others. In fact, from what Sydney says, most of the recipes are a testament to how strong their stomach is for enduring these meals.

"Good luck," I say. "Oh, and could you send me the list of credits for the clothes and accessories once you have them typed up? André will want them by the end of the week. Please?" I make a little praying hands gesture to Sydney.

"Of course. It'll take me a couple days to return all of these clothes, but I can get it done by Thursday at the latest."

"Great! You're the best," I say.

I spend the next twenty minutes helping to load equipment into cars, saying goodbye, and thanking everyone. I look around for Dax, but he seems to have left quietly. It's not surprising; a lot of celebrities prefer a quiet exit. But I'm a little disappointed that I didn't get to say goodbye to him. I'd wanted to tell him how happy I am with the way everything turned out, and to let him know that André would most likely be calling him soon to ask him some follow-up questions. I guess I'll have to email his manager to let him know.

After chatting with Jürgen for a few more minutes, I walk him to the front door of the studio with a plan to see him in a day or two at the office to review the entire photo shoot. I head back inside, pick up a large black garbage bag, and start cleaning up the remaining trash—which isn't really necessary since a cleaning crew usually comes in after big shoots, but it's not in my nature to leave a mess for others to clean up. And I find it relaxing, the feeling of bringing closure to the end of a long day in the studio. I'm going over the events of the day in my head as I make my way around the studio, paying little attention to anything outside of my immediate surroundings.

The dressing room is the area that almost always ends up being the messiest, usually littered with lots of stray bits of tissue paper, masking tape, and plastic bags. I absentmindedly start picking up a ball of crumpled paper that looks like it had once been jammed into the toe of a shoe when a movement in the corner of my eye causes me to turn around and nearly jump out of my skin.

CHAPTER 5

DAX

"Aaaagh!"

I hear a shout and bolt upright on the little couch in the dressing room. My mind is scrambling to figure out where I am and what the hell's happening. I whip my head around to see AJ Bond standing in the middle of the room, trash bag in one hand, his other hand on his chest.

"Holy shit! You scared me," he says, his voice a little shaky. He quickly rights himself. "I—sorry. I thought you left a while ago."

"Oh, uh...yeah," I say, slightly embarrassed. "I was relaxing a bit and I guess I dozed off."

AJ's standing there, looking at me like he's waiting for something. Not sure what else to do, I keep talking. "It was so quiet here, and I guess I wanted to have some time to relax before I had to leave. It's hard to find a few minutes of peace in this city. Know what I mean?"

As if he's a robot being rebooted, AJ finally blinks. "Uh, yeah, of course. That makes sense."

He begins tidying the room again while I check the time on my phone.

"Nice job, by the way," he says, picking up an empty water bottle. "I think we got some really good photos today."

"Thanks. I had fun." I run a hand through my hair, which I'm sure looks ridiculous after all the products Jaan used. I can't see it, but I can feel it standing up in all directions.

As if needing to fill the silence, my stomach makes an embarrassingly loud growl. While it's loud enough for AJ to hear, he doesn't comment.

"Hey, did you say you're going to a restaurant nearby after this? Ludlow's or something?" I stretch and try to force my body awake. I think I only dozed for a few minutes, but my body feels like I'm coming out of an eight-hour deep sleep.

"Lowell's, yeah." He continues to pick up bits of trash and deposit them in the bag he's carrying. "It's a few doors down from here. It's nothing special—burgers, fries, pub food—but it's good. I usually stop by there after photo shoots."

"That's cool." I look down at my hands, then back up to AJ. "Mind if I join you?"

I didn't really mean to invite myself, but I'm hungry and my brain is still a little fuzzy. And, to be honest, I'm a little curious to see if AJ's as buttoned-up outside of work as he is on set.

"Oh. Uh..." AJ stops what he's doing. I can almost see his wheels turning, trying to come up with a quick excuse to get out of it.

"I mean," I cut in quickly. "If you want company, that is. If you don't, I totally understand. It's been a long day, hasn't it? And anyway, there's nothing wrong with eating alone at a restaurant. I actually like it sometimes. In Europe—" *God, stop talking.*

"Sure," he says, probably to shut me up. "But I want to finish cleaning up first, so give me about fifteen minutes. Feel free to hang out here, and I'll come and get you when I'm done."

"Y'know what?" I slap my hands on my thighs—harder than I mean to, causing a sharp sting—and stand up. "I'll help you."

"Oh, no." AJ shakes his head. "You don't have to do that."

"Oh, please. If my mom knew I was in here napping while someone else was cleaning up after me, she'd hit me with the chancla." I cross the room, taking the trash bag from AJ's hands.

"Besides," I say over my shoulder, "I'm starving, and you don't want to see me when I get hangry."

Lowell's is a modestly sized pub, by Manhattan's standards anyway, with a dark wood bar and black leather booths. Lining the back wall are shelves filled with dozens of old, leather-bound books, and the clientele all look like they shop in the same store as AJ—black shirts and jeans. No wonder he likes this place.

As we enter, AJ waves at the bartender, a huge, muscular tank of a man.

"Hey man, good to see you," AJ says. "Is the back corner open?"

"Yup, it's all yours," the bartender replies. AJ leads us to the back of the restaurant, where we sit in a high-backed booth with leather seats. Looking around, I can't help but notice we're almost completely hidden here. This must be the table where he brings celebrities after photo shoots.

Once we're seated, AJ looks at me, then fiddles with his watch while his eyes dart around the room. I tap the table with my fingers and shift under the weight of this uncomfortable silence. I can't tell if he's annoyed that I'm here with him or if he's like this all the time.

"So, uh..." I start. But I can't think of anything. His gaze flicks back to me and he waits expectantly. "This place seems...neat." Internally, I wince. *Neat? What am I, a grandmother?*

AJ doesn't acknowledge that I've just uttered a word that no one under seventy would use. He's either being polite or ignoring me and trying to get through this dinner with minimal conversation.

"Yeah," he finally replies. "I like it." Then more silence.

He clears his throat. I blow out a long breath. He checks his watch. I cross and uncross my legs. *God, why did I invite myself to dinner?* Before either of us can say—or not say—anything more, a waitress with tattoo sleeves and a pixie cut appears at our table and sets down two glasses of water, breaking the silence between us.

"Hi, hon," she says to AJ with a distinctive Southern drawl.

"Hi, Georgie, how've you been?" He responds so casually, not like he was sitting here having the world's most awkward staring contest only five seconds ago.

"Oh, the same." She sighs, and from her expression, I don't think *the same* is necessarily a good thing. "What can I get for you and your... friend?" She perks up a bit, acknowledging me.

AJ gestures toward me. "Georgie, this is Diego, uh, Dax Ximénez. He's an actor. We wrapped up a shoot in the studio a little while ago."

Georgie's eyes widen and she visibly lights up. "Ah, good to meet you." She shakes my hand with both of hers—a handshake sandwich.

"I'm always telling Bond to bring in some of those handsome men he spends all day with in the studio. But he never does." She puts her hands on her hips and gives AJ a look of mock contempt. Then she gives me a little nudge with her elbow. "Until now."

AJ shakes his head, but he's fighting back a smile.

"So, you want your usual?" she asks, putting a hand on AJ's shoulder.

"Yeah, please. And an IPA."

"Sure thing." Georgie nods without writing anything down. "And for you?" She turns to me and I realize I haven't even seen a menu.

"Oh, uh..." I'm famished and don't want to put off ordering. Flustered, I blurt out, "I'll have what he's having."

How bad could it be, right? I hope it's not fish, or something with mushrooms. Or worse, a salad. *Shit. I may have made a huge mistake here.*

"Sure thing," she says. I casually smile and take a sip of my water as she walks away.

AJ raises an eyebrow at me. A single eyebrow. I wish I could do that, but I've never been able to. I shrug as if to say, *What?*

"*I'll have what he's having*? That's so *When Harry Met Sally* of you." His eyes are inscrutable, but there are two lines bracketing his mouth like parentheses, and I can tell he's trying not to smile.

"What do you mean?" I ask. "Like that movie from the eighties?"

AJ's face falls and the line between his eyebrows reappears. "Wait. Have you not seen *When Harry Met Sally*?" he asks, a disbelieving frown on his face.

"No?" It comes out more like a question.

"How can you not have seen it? You're an actor!" I'm pretty sure this is the most worked up I've seen AJ all day.

"That doesn't mean I've seen *all* the movies. It came out before I was born."

"But it's a classic."

"Yeah, still no."

"Fine." AJ shakes his head like he's disappointed in me. "But surely you've at least seen that famous scene where Meg Ryan fakes an orgasm at Katz's Deli?"

"Uh, no." I whip out my phone and start to pull up YouTube. "But I'm gonna find it right now."

"No." AJ puts a hand over mine, and I freeze before my eyes flicker up to meet his. I feel like I've touched a live electrical wire. He pulls his hand away quickly and I detect a faint blush creeping up on his cheeks. *What the hell was that?*

AJ takes a sip of water, then clears his throat. "I'm just saying," he says, looking down at the table, "that you should watch the whole thing, not an out-of-context clip. It's a brilliant movie and one of the best rom-coms ever made."

I narrow my eyes at him. "Why, Mr. Bond, are you secretly a romantic?" He can't hide his blush now, and I can't hide my amusement at the fact that he's shared a tiny little bit of himself with the guy he's been frowning at all day. *Point Dax.*

"Well," he replies in a measured tone, "given that I only met you this morning, I'd say that everything about me is a secret as far as you're concerned, wouldn't you?" *Touché.*

Georgie comes back with two longneck beers and sets them down in front of us. "Your food should be out soon," she says, walking back toward the kitchen.

AJ picks up a bottle and I take the other, holding it out for a toast. We clink our bottles together before taking a sip. I nearly gag, realizing right away that I've made a poor decision ordering the same drink as AJ. It's absolutely awful—bitter and a little sour. I try my best to keep a straight face, but I can't help but wince.

"You don't like IPAs?" he asks, eyeing me.

"This? Uh, it's fine. It's good. Just a bit..."

I don't know why I'm trying to convince him that I like this. It's like what I'd imagine skunk's spray would taste like. I bring the bottle to my lips again, then stop.

"Nope. No. This is awful."

Shaking my head from side to side, I set the bottle down on the table and push it toward him. I suck down mouthfuls of water to wash away the taste, then flag down Georgie to order a fruit-flavored hard cider in a can. AJ's mouth turns up at the corners, and I think he's trying to suppress a laugh. When his eyes catch mine, I can't look away. They look more whiskey-brown in this light and seem to sparkle in the warm atmosphere of the bar.

The air in here suddenly feels like it's humming with electricity. AJ's gaze remains on me for a three-second eternity before he finally speaks. "Tell me about your show." So I do.

I tell him about Max and *Mexican't*: how the show is based on our own lives, how we'd been discovered, and the whirlwind that took us from working as IT specialists to making silly YouTube videos on the weekends to having our own television show. I tell AJ about how we I met—we'd both worked for the same company for a couple of years when one night at a work happy hour, we'd started talking and realized how much we had in common. Case in point: being children of Mexican parents, we'd both grown up fearing three things: El Cucuy, La Llorona, and La Chancla.

"Okay, you have to tell me what those are," AJ says.

"Well, El Cucuy is basically the boogeyman, but much scarier, like horror-movie scary. La Llorona is an urban legend about a dead woman's ghost who supposedly roams around lakes and rivers crying out and searching for her drowned children. It's a story that's told to kids to keep them from wandering off."

AJ's face is frozen in a half-engrossed, half-horrified expression. "And the third one?"

"La Chancla. That's the scariest one of all." I take my time, sipping my water and rubbing my hands together. AJ lifts his beer to take a sip, but stops, watching me expectantly.

"A chancla is a shoe."

AJ tilts his head like a dog hearing a high-pitched whistle. "A...shoe?"

"Well, it's more of a sandal," I say. "Or a flip-flop."

"I don't get it. What's so scary about that?"

I lean in and motion for him to do the same, which he does obediently.

"It's not scary. Until you do something to piss off your mom. Then it's a weapon." AJ eyes me suspiciously.

"If I came in after curfew or gave my mom any sass, she'd whip her shoe off and smack me on the arm or leg or wherever she could reach. And not a little tap." I reach over and give AJ a little tap on the arm to demonstrate. "She'd use the flat side and smack me hard enough to leave a red mark."

"You're lying," AJ leans back, folding his arms.

"It's true, ask any Mexican." AJ shakes his head in disbelief. "Last week, my mom took her shoe off and threw it at me. Can you believe that? I'm thirty-three years old and my mom is still hitting me with her chancla."

I expect AJ to comment on the fact that I live with my family, but he doesn't. Instead, he does something so unexpected, it takes me by complete surprise. He laughs. Not one of those kind, professional, *yes yes, you made a funny joke* laughs. This is a genuine, head-thrown-back laugh—the kind that would've allowed me to count all of his teeth if I'd wanted to. After spending most of the day under AJ's silent glower and the rest of it in uncomfortable awkwardness with him, I feel ridiculously proud of myself right now. It shouldn't make me this happy—it's literally my job to make people laugh—but for reasons I don't feel like examining too closely, I let myself bask in pride.

Georgie returns to the table balancing two plates and a can of hard cider on a tray. I smile widely when I look at the food that's been set down in front of us. AJ's "usual" is an old-fashioned grilled cheese sandwich and fries. And not the fancy sort of grilled cheese either. This one is straight out of middle school—thick white bread, grilled perfectly with lots of butter and that weird American cheese "food product" that turns to plastic as soon as it cools.

I don't bother with manners. I pick up my sandwich and take a huge bite while AJ is still unwrapping his utensils.

"Oh. My. God." I moan as I chew.

It's as good as I remembered. Maybe even better. Out of the corner of my eye, I see AJ pick up his beer and lean back, taking a slow sip. He's making the same face he'd made earlier today when he caught me kicking around the tape ball on set. He's amused. Again.

"Good?" he asks with a slight smirk on his face.

"Mm-hmm," I reply through a second mouthful. I gulp and take a drink of my cider. "I haven't eaten a grilled cheese like this in years."

"It's my guilty pleasure," AJ says, finally picking up his sandwich and taking a bite. "Actually, that's not true."

"Oh?" I say, trying not to stuff another bite into my mouth too quickly and risk an embarrassing choking/Heimlich situation.

"Yeah, I don't feel the least bit guilty about it. It's a little reward to myself after a long day in the studio. This is how I unwind before I head home."

I suddenly feel a pang of something. Guilt? Self-consciousness?

"Do you mean *long day* as in *bad day*?" I ask cautiously.

"No, no." AJ shakes his head. "It was a good day. Just long." He doesn't seem to want to elaborate, so I don't push.

We eat without talking for a few minutes and I finish off my food way too quickly, leaving me sitting in an awkward silence while AJ chews almost as slowly as my abuelita.

"Tell me who it was!" I plead to AJ over the increasingly loud music.

"I can't!" he replies, nearly shouting.

"Why not?"

"Privacy." It comes out sounding like it should be followed up with *duh*.

I give him a little *pshhh* and wave my hand. "At least give me a hint."

"Nope." AJ shakes his head. "I've told you too much already."

We're two drinks in and laughing and talking like two old friends. He'd shared some of the most interesting tidbits he's witnessed from behind the scenes of celebrity photo shoots. But professional that he is, he refuses to give me any hints as to who the stories were about.

"You can't give me that spicy nugget and not tell me who it was," I say, but AJ refuses, taking another sip of beer and laughing.

"Alright, fine." I fold my arms and make an exaggerated pout.

AJ finishes off his beer, then makes the universal gesture for *another round* at the bartender.

"I'll get this one," I say, pulling my wallet out of my pocket.

AJ looks horrified when his eyes land on my hands. "What is that?"

"It's a wallet," I say, looking down at the thing in my hands that *technically is* a wallet. It's so old and worn-out, it requires a strip of duct tape down the middle seam to hold it together.

"No, no, no. That *thing* is not a wallet. That's a disaster waiting to happen."

"What are you talking about?" I answer him in a tone that's a tad too defensive. I hold it close to my chest, as if it can hear AJ badmouthing it.

"I can imagine you taking that out of your pocket and having it explode all over the subway platform."

"That's only happened once," I say nonchalantly, then tap on the seam of the wallet. "Hence the tape."

"Okay, well, as someone who works in fashion, I can tell you, it's time for a new one. You're a celebrity, or at least, a soon-to-be celebrity. Why are you carrying that old thing around, anyway?"

I drop my gaze to my wallet and look at it with fondness. Then I see at least four different emotions wash over AJ's face in a matter of seconds. First, offense at my hideous wallet, then surprise, then understanding, and finally, regret.

"Shit, Dax. I'm sorry. Does it have sentimental value to you?"

"Kind of." I put my wallet back into my pocket. "My sister gave it to me."

"Is she...?" AJ winces as he lets the question go unfinished.

"Oh, she's fine. Great, actually. She gave me this wallet years ago. She keeps telling me I need a new one too, but I haven't found the perfect replacement. So until I do, I'm gonna keep using this one." I pat my pocket.

"Well, I can help you with that," AJ says cheerfully. My eyes snap to his and I cock my head to the side. "I mean, since I work in fashion, I have connections. I can find one for you that you'd like."

"Oh, thanks, but that's not really necessary."

AJ nods, then shifts in his seat and drops his gaze to his hands. *Is he disappointed that I refused his help?*

"I only meant that I don't really need anything expensive or fancy. But that's really nice of you to offer."

AJ shrugs. "It's cool. The offer stands if you change your mind." Then, without warning, he stands up from the table.

"I'll get the drinks," he says, walking toward the bar before I can say anything else.

I can't tell quite what to make of AJ. If I weren't almost certain he's not gay, I might be interested. I mean, he's definitely good-looking, even if he's a little younger than the guys I usually date. He didn't correct me when I'd casually asked about a girlfriend. Instead, he'd simply said he isn't in a relationship at the moment and left it at that. And when he got up from the table and was talking to Georgie a little while ago, he handed her something that might've been his number, so I'm fairly sure he's straight. Although, the way he blushed when he put his hand on mine... No, I'm reading too much into it.

Still, I'm intrigued by him. It's like he has two sides to his personality that don't quite match up. On the one hand, he's smart and confident, and even, dare I say, funny. At the shoot today, I was impressed by how his knowledge and confidence made everyone on the set listen to him, despite the fact that he was probably younger than most everyone there. He wasn't shy on set. When something wasn't working, or when he needed anything, he wasn't afraid to speak up—assertive, but not in a boorish or demanding way. And despite being obviously under pressure, he was generous with positive comments when he was happy with something.

But the other side of AJ's personality coin is introverted and quiet. When we were between shots, while the set was being changed or I was in the stylists' chair, he didn't say much, seeming to prefer to flip through the pages on his clipboard or observe everyone else around him. Not to mention his awkwardness when we first arrived at the restaurant.

Half an hour later, we're in the middle of a game of *Get to Know You* where we take turns asking each other questions. They'd started out pretty banal—favorite TV show, favorite music—but they've become more personal (and more interesting) as the night has gone on—or more specifically, the more we've had to drink.

I tell him about my family, about how I'd moved back in with them after I decided to quit my IT job to pursue acting and comedy full-time. I'd had apartments in the city over the years, but I moved back home to save money. And a lot of the money I'd made at my old job went toward helping my parents cover expenses they'd built up over the years while taking care of my younger sister, Camila. I'm doing well enough now that I could get my own place again, but my family is happy to have me there, Cami especially. And I'm happy to be there.

Cami's ten years younger than me and has a developmental disability. She's smart and has low support needs, but sometimes she has a hard time with separation, especially from me. This morning, I was ready to leave the house when Cami began crying and parked herself on the floor by the front door. It took fifteen minutes to calm her down and reassure her that I'd be back tonight. Luckily, I still managed to make it to the shoot on time.

I don't tell AJ about this morning. He'd seemed to have a burr in his saddle about something, so I avoid bringing it up.

AJ doesn't have any siblings, and from the sounds of it, he doesn't have much family at all. Growing up in a close, Mexican-American family, I can't imagine not having a built-in support system around me. Not that my childhood had been perfect. There'd been a few years when I was figuring things out about myself—those had been really hard, not only for me, but for my whole family. But I can't imagine not having anyone around me to lean on for support.

AJ and I had attempted to talk about sports, but we both failed the Bro Test miserably. The only sport I'm even semi-interested in is soccer, but that's only because my dad likes to watch Mexico play and I like watching with him.

AJ was a bit cagey when I'd asked him if he'd played sports as a kid. He simply said no, that his mother wouldn't allow it, then followed it up by saying he was more interested in art and reading anyway.

"Okay, my turn," I say. "What are your biggest fears?"

"Failure and horses." He answers, almost too quickly, like he'd anticipated the question. "But I think it was *my* turn."

"Fine, but we're coming back to that one. Horses? I need to know more." I gently nudge his foot with my own and notice that he doesn't move his foot away.

"Alright. What about you?" AJ asks, leaning in. "What's your biggest fear?"

"Uh..." I slide my hand over the back of my neck, pulling lightly on my hair. "Standing up in front of a room full of people and having them watch me while I attempt to entertain them." I give an uncomfortable little laugh and look around the room before fixing my eyes on AJ's hands which are folded neatly on the table. When I bring my eyes up to meet his, I realize he's watching me, most likely trying to figure out if I'm joking or not.

Waiting for him to state the obvious, I give him the palms-up *go ahead* gesture.

"I'm not going to state the obvious," he starts. "But, do you want to talk about it?"

I sigh and lean against the back of the booth, trying to decide how much I want to say. *Making people laugh makes me feel good and being on the stage gives me a sense of control. But when I'm going through a stressful period in my life, sometimes I get panic attacks. And a lot of times, those panic attacks are triggered by things like strangers wanting to talk to me after a show. Coming down from the adrenaline rush of doing a comedy set can sometimes trigger anxiety.*

Nah, too much.

"Not really," I say. "It'll sound weird."

AJ nods, not pressing me on it, which I appreciate. It's not something I want to get into with someone I've only met this morning.

When I'd started doing stand-up a couple of years ago, it was after *Mexican't* was taking off and we were in talks to develop it into a show. Max and I were still working as IT consultants and we'd gone to a bar for a drink—which happened to be on an open-mic night. They were running short on acts, so Max dared me to get onstage and try my hand at stand-up. I only agreed because I'd had a few drinks and my judgment was a little cloudy. Okay, *a lot* cloudy. I wasn't very good—mostly because I had nothing prepared—but I made some jokes, told some funny stories. I don't recall anything I said that night, but I remember the feeling of being onstage—the thrill and the pride I felt when the audience laughed. I was hooked. Of course, I threw up immediately after I got off the stage, but that was from all the gin and tonics. Probably.

I don't do stand-up consistently. Sometimes I do two or three sets in a month, sometimes I don't do any. I could be booking bigger venues, but RockPaperScissors is my safe space, my comfort zone. I'm not sure how well I'd do anywhere else, at least not until I get my panic attacks under control.

"Okay, okay. My turn," I say, taking a much-needed sip of my drink. I tap my chin with my finger as if deep in thought while AJ watches me expectantly. I know what I want to ask, but I'm not sure if he'd take it badly or not. But since we're both feeling the effects of a few drinks, I go for it.

"What was your deal this morning?"

AJ gives me a questioning look, the line returning between his eyebrows. "My *deal*?"

"Yeah, you know. You were there with your clipboard like…" I fold my arms and furrow my brow, giving him an overexaggerated stern look, clearly mocking him. "You were like an angry school marm. Wait, is *marm* right? It sounds weird when I say it out loud."

I expect AJ to get upset or at least deny it. Instead, he takes a long sip of his beer, then uncrosses his legs, kicking my knee in the process. I'm not sure it was unintentional.

"These kinds of photo shoots are stressful," he says matter-of-factly. I wait for him to elaborate, but he doesn't.

"I dunno," I say. "It was like everyone was having fun but you."

AJ lets out a sigh. "There's a lot of pressure with photo shoots, especially one like today that's going to end up being multiple pages in the magazine. Hiring a whole crew costs a lot of money. Every person who was at the studio was there because they were hired by me. That, plus the cost of the studio, renting equipment, all of it—it's not cheap. So the publishers and editors expect the final product to be perfect. It's my job to make sure everyone is staying on task and doing their best possible work."

I shift in my seat. "But it seemed like everyone was doing a good job and you said you thought we were getting some good photos. You could've loosened up."

"The change in direction first thing this morning was a big risk." AJ pauses and takes a sip of his beer. "I'm still not sure how André is going to like it. I mean, I think he will. I sent him some shots this morning and he said he did. But it's pretty different from what we'd originally planned."

"Yeah, but if it's better, what's the problem? Why the stress?"

"Photography is subjective. What I think is good, other people might not. I've been doing this job a long time, so I think I've got a good handle on what my bosses are looking for, but I don't always get it right. That's why I'm so meticulous about planning the shoots and sticking to the plan. Going into it, everyone knows what to expect and there's very little room for surprises. Unexpected surprises can be very expensive and time-consuming to fix if they don't go well."

"So what about today?"

"Well, if the plan isn't really working, I have to be able to switch things up and make a quick decision that will hopefully have better results. Ultimately, getting the best photos possible is the goal. Well, the best photos while also pleasing the editors, advertisers, and the readers. And today, I felt like our original plan wasn't giving us the best results. It's stressful to me when that happens because I feel like I've failed somehow during all the planning I've done. Like I should've known."

I can see from the deep line between AJ's eyebrows and the way his mouth is drawn tight that he's making himself stressed thinking about it.

"Did I do something—" I can feel a panicky feeling rising in my gut.

"No, no." AJ interrupts me, putting a hand on my arm. It sends a shock of warmth through my body, but he quickly pulls it away. "It wasn't anything you did."

"What was it then?" I ask, only slightly relieved.

He thinks about it for a long moment, then says, "It's hard to describe. It wasn't any one specific thing. It wasn't feeling authentic to who you are. The shots were feeling stiff, like you were modeling for a menswear catalog rather than a fashion magazine. When you started playing around with that ball of tape, I realized that the shoot should've been more playful, more colorful. Once we made the switch, it seemed to fit your personality much better. You were more comfortable, like you were having fun. It was authentic, and that isn't something we can manufacture. I mean, you can act like you're having fun, but it doesn't come across in the same way as *actually* having fun. And the crew liked the changes too. Everyone was into it. That's what made it great. It's what we should've done all along."

"So what happens now?" I ask. "After you get the photos from the photographer?"

"Well, I'll look through everything we did today and pick out the best six or seven. Then I'll lay out the pages in a way that makes the photos look their absolute best." AJ is sitting up straighter, his eyes almost seeming to light up as he speaks.

"Heh, you make it sound so easy."

"Well, I wouldn't say it's easy, but it's the part of the process I love the most."

AJ is smiling now. A real, genuine smile. Seeing him become so animated when he's talking about his job is surprising. And surprisingly endearing. I can tell he loves what he does. When he was on set today, every person there listened to him, respected his opinions. Although I don't pay much attention to fashion magazines, based on the few photos I saw at today's shoot, it's clear he's really good at what he does. I can see why his bosses trust him.

I'd been so busy watching him, I don't realize he'd stopped talking.

"Is something wrong?" AJ asks, his face turning serious.

"Uh, no." I clear my throat. "When you were talking about your job just now, it was so, I dunno, passionate? You're...cute."

Ugh, I made it weird, didn't I?

My cheeks suddenly feel like they're on fire, but thank god my olive skin makes it hard to tell when I'm embarrassed. AJ, on the other hand, has a flush creeping up the sides of his neck—most likely because of the weirdly intimate comment I've made.

"Uh, yeah. I mean, the job has its ups and downs, but I like it." He shifts uncomfortably, and all of the ease and friendliness of the last couple of hours slips away like air escaping from a deflating balloon—I can almost hear the *pfffftttt* noise. He scrubs a hand over the back of his neck and looks anywhere but at me.

I hadn't meant to make him uncomfortable. Maybe he thought I was trying to flirt with him? I'd really meant it as a compliment.

I glance around the bar, which has gotten quite a bit more crowded since we first walked in. AJ finishes off the last of his beer and starts drumming his fingertips on the table.

"Maybe we should..." I motion with my thumb toward the door.

"Yeah." He slides out of the booth and picks up his hoodie and bag while I look around for Georgie. He must realize what I'm doing because before I say anything, he says, "It's already paid for."

"Oh." I shove my hands in my pockets. "Thanks, man. You didn't have to do that."

"I didn't. This counts as a business expense." He pauses. "Well, except for the drinks after dinner. But I already paid for them." He gives me the smallest of smiles and starts heading toward the door.

Once we're outside, a blast of cool fall air fills my lungs. I hadn't realized how warm I'd been, but I'm suddenly grateful to be out of the stuffy, overcrowded bar.

AJ fidgets with the zipper of his hoodie while I spend way too long adjusting the strap of my shoulder bag. He straightens, putting his hands into his sweatshirt pockets, venturing a glance at me. I can't stand this weird energy anymore. I have to say something, anything. But as I open my mouth, AJ speaks first.

"You did great today. I won't see the photos for a couple of days, but based on what I saw, they're gonna look really good in the magazine." He pauses and opens his mouth, then shuts it again looking like he's thinking carefully about what he's about to say next.

"Well, it was nice meeting you," AJ finally says. "Thanks for your time today."

Wait. That's it?

I make one stupid comment that he might've misinterpreted as a come-on, and he reverts back to the uncomfortable, uptight person I'd met at the beginning of the day? I thought maybe we were becoming friends. *Guess not.*

AJ extends his hand like we've wrapped up a business lunch. I mumble something that sounds a bit like *yeah* before taking his hand, but unlike the casual touches from earlier that felt friendly, almost affectionate, this one feels cold and empty.

"Bye, Dax," he says, then turns and heads down the street.

CHAPTER 6

AJ

"Sam, am I an asshole?" I ask.

"No. Yes. Well, sometimes." My friend Samantha—who happens to be my ex-girlfriend twice over—is seated across from me.

"Ugh. He must think I'm such a jerk." I tap my mostly empty coffee cup on the table.

I'd been sitting alone in the Wright Media building's café, mentally beating myself up for the way I left at the end of last night.

I hadn't wanted Dax to join me for dinner, but when he asked to come along, the way he looked at me with puppy-dog eyes, I couldn't say no. He'd been friendly to me and everyone else all day, despite the rocky start to the morning, so there was no reason for me to refuse. Still, I'm an introvert and being around people all day takes a lot out of me. I had been looking forward to sitting in the corner alone, eating my grilled cheese and mindlessly scrolling on my phone, then going home.

But what started out as awkward turned into one of the best nights I'd had in a long time with someone who was so fun, so open and honest. A person who'd been a complete stranger at the beginning of the day. And someone I could even see myself becoming friends with.

Then I'd gone and acted like I'd been so put off by his comment, I left him standing alone on the sidewalk.

Sam spotted me brooding at the table and joined me, likely sensing I needed to talk. So for the past five minutes she's been patiently nodding and listening to me.

"Yeah, he probably thinks you're an asshole," she says, drumming her manicured nails on the table. Sam has never been one to sugarcoat anything to avoid hurt feelings.

"Thanks," I say, not thankful at all.

Sam and I dated for two and a half years while I was an intern at *TMG* several years ago. She was my first serious girlfriend, the one I'd thought I'd end up marrying—not because we were head-over-heels in love or anything like that. We'd sort of become fixtures in each other's lives, and that's how I'd thought love worked: you meet, you have fun with someone, you have sex, you spend enough days and nights together that you get used to each other, then you get married. The end.

But somewhere along the way, she'd decided that *used to each other* wasn't what she was looking for. She'd wanted L-O-V-E—the kind that gives you hope, inspires you, makes you want to be better for the other person. Sam and I didn't have that. We never had and we never would with each other. So she broke up with me. I'd like to say I was heartbroken, but I wasn't. Truth be told, neither was she.

Three years later, we ran into each other at our company holiday party. Wright Media, who owns *TMG*, also owns a dozen other magazines including *Waves*, the high-profile music and entertainment magazine that she'd been dying to work for while we were dating. When we reconnected, it felt like old times. Except that she's gotten a writing job at *Waves* and I'd been slowly working my way up at *TMG*.

Maybe it was nostalgia, maybe we'd both had too much to drink, but whatever it was, something sparked between us that night at the party, and we'd ended up getting back together. The second time around, it only lasted four months before we agreed that we're better off as friends.

We're not the call-or-text-every-day kind of friends, but working five floors apart in the same building means that at the very least, we pass each other in the lobby or in the café at least once a week.

"He made an innocent comment that he probably didn't mean as anything but a funny observation. And as far as he knows, you took it as some sort of pickup line. Then you clammed up and left."

"I didn't clam up." She's right, of course. I did.

She cuts me with a knowing gaze. "Bond, that's what you always do when you're uncomfortable. And having someone pay attention to you, *really* pay attention, makes you uncomfortable."

I fidget, fighting the urge to burrow under the table.

"So, do you think he thinks I'm a jerk?"

"Well, given the evidence, he might think you're—"

"An asshole?" I'm trying to be helpful here.

"I was going to say a homophobe."

Oh. Shit.

"That's not—I'm not—" I can't finish my thoughts.

I make an audible groan and feel an unpleasant taste rise up in the back of my throat. What if he tells my editor? Or worse, what if he goes to social media and blasts that *TMG* has a homophobic art director? It would be completely inaccurate, of course, but it would still be Out There, and once something like that gets out, it can't be taken back.

"I know," Sam says. "But does he know that?"

I look at her blankly, trying to remember if we talked about dating or relationships last night. *Had we?*

"I'm not sure," I say. "I mean, he may have asked something about me having a girlfriend. If it came up, it was only briefly. I should talk to him."

I run my hand across the back of my neck, feeling the prickles of sweat starting to form. "I don't even have his number or email."

"How did you get in touch with him before? When you were setting up the photo shoot in the first place?"

"His publicist got in touch first. Then I went through his manager to arrange everything, and she gave him the messages."

"So give his manager a call and ask for his number," Sam says, nudging my arm.

"What do I say? *Hello, I think I might have inadvertently offended your client by making him think I'm a homophobic jerk. Can I please have his direct number?*"

"No, dummy." Sam rolls her eyes. "You call up his manager, tell her something that makes it seem urgent, but something that she'd want handled without her. Like...I dunno, he left something at the shoot that he would want back ASAP—a wallet, maybe—so you'd be willing to go wherever he is and drop it off. Then call him up and ask him to meet you for a drink or coffee or something."

"I can't apologize over the phone, can I?"

"Nope. He needs to see your sincerity in person. That *I'm sorry I fucked up* face you're so good at." It's a face Sam knows well.

"Ugh. I hate when you're right."

"I know. Now call his manager." She pushes my phone toward me.

"I will, thanks."

Sam doesn't move.

"I'm all set here," I say, hoping she'll catch my meaning.

She shakes her head and leans back in her seat, looking like she's trying to get even more comfortable. "No way. I'm invested now. I want to see how it plays out."

"Don't you have work to do?" I ask, growing more exasperated by the second.

"It can wait." Sam smirks.

Three minutes—and one small lie about a forgotten wallet—later, I have Dax's number written on the side of my coffee cup—neither Sam nor I had a spare scrap of paper to write on.

"Okay, you can go now." I give her an exaggerated shooing motion and she finally relents, leaving me alone at the table.

I decide to text Dax first, because if he's like the rest of the modern, smartphone-carrying world, he won't answer a call from an unknown number. Also because I'm a coward.

> AJ: Hi Dax, this is AJ Bond. Do you have a few minutes to chat?

To my surprise, three dots begin dancing on the screen immediately.

> Dax: Bond? I don't remember you. Be more specific.

I roll my eyes and begin typing again.

> AJ: Art director from the photo shoot yesterday.
> Dax: Nope. Doesn't ring a bell.

He's messing with me, isn't he? Or is he trying to give me the brush-off? My money is on the first one. Otherwise he'd ignore me, right?

> AJ: Here, try this.

I swallow my pride and take a selfie with an exaggerated scowl on my face. Before I have a chance to reconsider, I send it to Dax. I stare at the screen, my heart inexplicably beating faster, as I wait for a response. When his reply finally comes, I realize I'm smiling at my phone like a teen with a crush. *God, way to be cool.*

> Dax: Ah yes. I remember that face... Too well.

Relief. But, the *too well* makes me think he might not be so happy to hear from me. Now what? I hadn't thought about what I'd say to explain my sudden change of mood last night. I can't very well leave him with the impression that I'm a jerk who was offended by him calling me cute.

>AJ: Is it okay if I call you?
>Dax: It's actually not a good time.

Shit.

>Dax: I'm on the subway. Bad reception.
>Dax: Since I have you though, I'm heading to an interview and looking for some pro tips to make myself look taller on the radio. Got any?

I laugh, then look around self-consciously.

>AJ: I was gonna say that's my specialty, but I think you're joking, right?
>AJ: Actually, I'd like to talk to you. It's about yesterday. How about coffee later? Or a drink? Dinner? Whatever. My treat.

After a long, agonizing pause, he finally answers.

>Dax: I have a dinner thing but I could meet you after. Maybe 9-ish?
>AJ: Ooh, is "dinner thing" code for a hot date??

Another long pause. *Why did I even ask that?* While I'd meant it as a joke, an unexplainable thought in the back of my brain is hoping he'll say no.

>Dax: Kind of.

Oh.

Dax: It's a blind date set up by a mutual friend. I cheated and looked the guy up online. He's a DJ from Staten Island. [eye roll emoji]
AJ: There's nothing wrong with DJs. And there's nothing wrong with Staten Island either.
Dax: You only say that because you're not from there.
AJ: You might have a point there.
Dax: His DJ name is Blue Dragon and he ONLY wears booty shorts and sunglasses during his sets.
AJ: No headphones?
Dax: Okay, booty shorts, sunglasses and headphones. That's it. Well, maybe shoes, but I don't know. It's going to be a disaster.
AJ: You never know, it could work out. Opposites attract and all that?
Dax: Trust me, it won't.
AJ: I think you're being too hasty in judging him.

Dax texts me a screenshot of an ad for DJ Blue Dragon's Electric Beach night at some bar in Red Hook. The guy has hair that defies gravity with its long, high swoop in front, very orange skin that's covered in at least half a pound of body glitter, and the tiniest pair of sequined hot pants I've ever seen on anyone. *Oh Dax.*

AJ: Wow.
Dax: I know, right? I'm glad I met you because I need a new friend to replace the one who thought this was a good idea.

At this seemingly innocuous comment, I have to bite my lip to keep from grinning from ear to ear.

AJ: What neighborhood will you be in? I'll find a place nearby to meet up afterward.

Dax: East Village.

AJ: Text me when you're done with Dragon Man. Unless the two of you decide to...

Dax: Stop!! I'll see you later.

CHAPTER 7

AJ

At 8:27, my phone buzzes on the table where it's sitting next to the barely touched bottle of warm beer I ordered half an hour ago.

I'd lingered at the office after-hours, distracting myself by taking care of some of the tedious tasks that had been on my to-do list. I'd been too wound up trying to think of a way to apologize and explain whatever it was that had made me leave so abruptly last night. The problem is that I still don't know myself.

The place I've chosen to meet Dax isn't seedy enough to be called a dive bar, but certainly isn't catering to the young people looking to have an Awesome Night Out. There are only a dozen or so patrons in here, and the bartender seems thoroughly bored. She must be at least fifty and has made only the bare minimum of attempts at being friendly toward the customers. She's here for one job: to serve drinks. Nothing more, nothing less. At the moment, we're both half-watching a hockey game on the muted television in the corner while the music seems to be a loop of a handful of overplayed pop songs.

I'd sent the location to Dax half an hour ago, then considered sending a follow-up text but eventually dismissed the idea. He knows

I'm here waiting for him. So when my phone buzzes, I jump—almost too eagerly—to check it. I'm disappointed to see it's from Sam wondering how things turned out with Dax.

> AJ: No news yet. Waiting for him at the bar.
> Sam: I like this side of you, Bond.
> AJ: What side?
> Sam: The one who's completely flustered over a new friend. You're usually trying to avoid meeting new people. It's CUTE.
> AJ: Oh, you're funny now?

I shake my head, but something about her comment strikes a nerve. She's right. I tend to stick with the few friends I have, not really feeling the need to add anyone new to my comfortable little circle. Even at work, I get along well with pretty much everyone, but there are very few people I'd want to hang out with socially after-hours. It's not that I'm opposed to making new friends, but I don't seek them out either.

Sam is one of the few who, despite our history, doesn't mind hanging out with an introvert who can talk for hours about magazines and books and music. It's not that I'm shy—when I'm working, I can be as assertive as I need to be. I just don't like making small talk for the sake of filling the silence. Of course, it's hard to get to know someone new without making some small talk, isn't it?

Except that last night with Dax, no part of our conversation felt like small talk. I told him more about myself than I'd ever told anyone at work, and some of them I've known for ten years or more. I even told him about my fear of horses, which is something not even Sam knows. But that's mostly because it's embarrassing to be an adult man with an irrational fear of something I'm not likely to see in New York City very often.

I've met celebrities over the years at my job, and I've never fretted about what they thought of me outside of the job. I never thought I'd see them again, and for the most part, I haven't.

So why do I care so much what Dax thinks of me? Or whether he wants to be my friend or not?

Unlike me, Dax isn't introverted or quiet. He's not overly gregarious, but he's an actor, a stand-up comedian, an up-and-coming celebrity. All day yesterday, I'd seen the outgoing side of him—the side that likes making people laugh. But last night after the shoot, I'd also seen an unguarded side to him. He was still funny as hell, but he seemed more quiet, more relaxed—like he wasn't trying to be "on," and just being himself.

That's the side of him I like—the part of him I want to get to know better, to maybe be friends with.

"Hey," a voice calls from behind me, startling me out of my thoughts. I must've really been in my head because I hadn't noticed Dax come into the bar.

"Oh, hey, Dax." I awkwardly half-stand up, not sure what to do with my hands. *Do I hug him? No, too intimate. Shake his hand?*

Before I can decide, he claps a hand on my shoulder, then pulls a chair out and flops himself down across from me, looking like he could use a stiff drink and a comfortable couch. Unfortunately, only one of those two are available here.

I sit back down, then stand up again.

"Can I get you a drink?" I ask. *God, Sam was right. Why am I so flustered?*

"Sure, maybe a cider?"

"I'm pretty sure they don't have those here," I say, gesturing around the room and giving him a wry smile.

"Oh, right. How about a vodka cran then?"

"Okay, sure. I'll...I'll be right back." I nearly stumble over my chair before heading to the bar.

When I return with his drink in one hand and a fresh beer in the other, I see amusement in Dax's eyes. His mouth is pulled tight like he's trying not to laugh at me. I catch my toe on a lump in the carpet and nearly spill both drinks before finally setting them down on the table.

"Fuck! Sorry," I say, wincing at my own clumsiness.

I take a seat before I make an even bigger fool of myself. When I look up, Dax isn't trying to hide it anymore. He's openly laughing at me.

"Dude, are you okay?" He puts a hand on my bicep and I feel a wave of warmth radiate through my body.

"Yeah. I'm just…" I let out a sigh. *What am I? Nervous?*

I run a hand over my chin, scrubbing over the end-of-the-day stubble that's starting to appear.

After a deep inhale, I say, "I asked you to meet me so I could apologize to you for yesterday."

"Okaaay," Dax draws out the word, but doesn't say anything else while he waits for me to go on. He eyes me from under his long lashes and I can feel myself tense as I start to speak.

"I'm…an introvert by nature and I don't usually talk a lot about my work, especially to people I don't know very well. I'm not what you'd call a natural self-promoter. Most people find listening to the details of my job to be, well, boring. I was excited that you were willing to listen to me ramble on about it. When you pointed it out, I got…I don't know, self-conscious?"

"Why?" Dax seems surprised. "I liked listening to you talk about your work. Yesterday was the first really big photo shoot I've done. It was interesting to hear how it all works."

"I guess I was afraid you were just humoring me by listening to me go on and on. That's why I got kind of weird and left." I hesitate. "I'm not so good with compliments. Or attention."

"Sooo…you got weird and left because you suddenly got shy?"

Shit. I can feel heat creeping up my cheeks.

"No—well, yes. I guess so." Dax starts to laugh. "Why is that funny?" I ask, frowning.

"It's funny because I thought you were upset that I called you cute. I thought you were offended, thinking I was trying to hit on you or something."

"No, that wasn't it at all. But afterwards, I did worry that you'd think I was homophobic or something." Dax cocks his head to the side. "Which I'm not," I add hastily.

"Didn't think you were." Dax sips his drink, then narrows his eyes at me. "Is that why you asked me to meet you tonight? To tell me you're not homophobic?"

I'm suddenly too hot, too uncomfortable in here.

"Honestly? Yes, at least that's part of it. I wanted to apologize if I made you think that. Trust me, I'm an equal opportunity conversation-ruiner." I try to chuckle, but it sounds stiff. I look down at the table, avoiding Dax's eyes.

"And the other part?" he asks.

"The other part is that I wanted to apologize for being a little moody with you in the morning. You did great at the shoot, even after I'd been a bit grumpy with you."

Dax drops his head back and laughs loudly. I look back up at him, trying to interpret his laugh.

"*A bit grumpy*? Seriously? Dude, you were staring daggers at me all day, or at least until lunchtime. I didn't know if you even knew how to smile."

Somehow, this makes me both cringe and laugh at the same time.

"No," Dax continues. "That's not true. I did see you smile. Just not at me."

Dax's observation, as true as it is, makes me feel unexpectedly ashamed.

"I know. I'm sorry." I rake a hand through my hair and look away. "When the first shot wasn't going well, I had a hard time shaking it off.

I mean, I told you about how stressful it can be to make big changes on shoots. And, to be honest, I was a little freaked out because you got there so late. I hadn't meant to take it out on you all day, though. But the shoot started going really well and then we got to talking at dinner—"

"Wait, back up. *What*?!" Dax interjects so forcefully, I flinch. "What do you mean *got there so late*?"

Is he serious? I give him an incredulous look.

"Dax, you were an hour late. I thought you'd blown off the shoot. I was worried that we'd have to pay everyone for the day and reschedule the whole thing."

"I wasn't late! I even got there a few minutes early."

"Eight-thirty," I say with narrowed eyes. "Your call time was eight-thirty. You showed up at nine-thirty."

He shakes his head vigorously. "No. My manager told me to be there at nine-thirty."

Dax pulls out his phone and begins furiously scrolling through his messages. When he finds what he's looking for, he shows me the screen. Sure enough, it says nine-thirty. He puts his elbows on the table and covers his face with his hands.

"Shit. I'm so sorry," he groans. "I had no idea. You and your crew must've thought I was acting like some entitled asshole."

"No, of course not." I try my best to sound sincere, I really do. Dax looks through his fingers and frowns at me. I can't lie. "Okay," I admit. "Maybe a little."

He flops his forearms on the table and drops his head onto them dramatically. "No, no, no, no, no. God, I'm so sorry." He lays a hand on my forearm, his head still resting on his other arm on top of the table.

The contact isn't meant to be anything other than friendly. I'd noticed yesterday that Dax is generous with little displays of affection—a squeeze of the shoulder, a hand on the arm. He gives these touches out freely, not meant to be anything other than a connection with another person. I've never been very comfortable with touching people—or with people touching me—unless I really know them well. And even then, it usually feels a little forced and graceless.

But with Dax, these touches feel like gifts—something meant only for me. And I feel compelled to reciprocate, even though I'd normally be uncomfortable with touching someone who I've only known for a couple of days. The strangest part about it is that I don't feel awkward about it with Dax. At all.

"Don't worry about it," I say, rubbing his shoulder. "You won them over with your charming personality."

He lifts his head a bit, barely enough for his eyes to meet mine.

"I mean, everyone on set loved you." I shrug. "It all worked out."

Slowly, he brings his head all the way up. His shoulders are slumped and he's clearly still distraught, but there's a hint of smugness in his eyes.

"Look, I didn't ask you to meet me here to make you feel bad." I nudge his foot with my own. "I apologized to you, you apologized to me. Let's start over, okay?"

Dax sits up straighter, takes a sip of his drink, then nods. "Okay."

I take a long drink of my beer and we sit in silence for a few moments. Somehow, the air around us feels lighter, like a thick fog has lifted.

"So...I'm charming, huh?" Dax lifts his glass to his mouth, covering his smirk.

I roll my eyes, but I can feel my cheeks warming. "You already know you are."

He takes a sip, but his eyes don't leave mine. Something about the way he's looking at me has me feeling nervous all of a sudden. Setting his drink down, he clears his throat.

"Okay, let's start over. What's your name?"

"Uhh...AJ?" I say with a questioning tone. "But that's not exactly what I meant about starting over."

"Yeah, no shit." Dax looks at me like I've said something incredibly stupid. "I mean, what do the *a* and the *j* stand for?"

"Ohhh." I get this question often enough, I should've realized that's what he meant. "Well, my first name is Aleksander. With a *k*."

Dax looks confused. "So...Kal-exander?"

"Not exactly." I try not to smile.

"Alexan-derk?" he asks, causing me to let out an unexpected snort of laughter.

"I've got it! The *k* is silent and it goes with the *n*, like *knock*, right? Alexa-k-nder." Only he actually pronounces the *k*, punctuating the hard sound on purpose.

I shake my head like he's a lost cause, then pull a pen out of my pocket and write my name on a napkin.

A-L-E-K-S-A-N-D-E-R

Dax makes a *huh* as he studies the napkin for a moment, then nods as if to say that it meets his approval.

"It's German," I say.

"Alright, *Herr Bond*. What's the *j* stand for?"

"I'll give you one guess."

Dax looks at the ceiling and twists his lips in thought.

"I'll give you a hint: my last name is Bond."

Dax's eyes go wide. "No fucking way!"

I make a little finger shooting motion at him. He opens his mouth, but I speak first. "Don't you dare call me that or make any James Bond jokes."

"You don't like it?" he asks.

"Not at all. Whenever someone finds out my middle name is James, they make some dumb Double-o-Seven comment like they're the first one to think of it."

"Got it," Dax says, like he's committing it to memory. "No James Bond jokes."

"Thank you," I say, not really sure if he's making fun of me or not.

"So why don't you go by Aleksander then? Or Alex?"

I take a sip of my beer and look away. "I was named Aleksander after my father. I don't want to share a name with him."

I can feel my voice bristle and I know I'm frowning. I can't help it. I hope I haven't ruined the mood like I did yesterday. But then something like understanding seems to pass over Dax's face and he doesn't say anything more about it. Instead, he cheerfully asks, "Wanna know what my middle name is?"

"It's Alejandro, isn't it? You told me yesterday."

"Oh right," he says. "But it's funny, Alejandro is the Spanish version of Alexander. But, you know, with a *j*."

"Jalexander?" I raise an eyebrow.

"Ha ha, funny guy," he says, shoving my elbow. "Actually, come to think of it, Diego is the Spanish version of James. Weird." He seems to say the last part to himself while he looks over my shoulder at nothing in particular.

"Meant to be," I chuckle, but I can feel my cheeks inexplicably warming. Dax pointedly looks at me, but says nothing.

"So, can I call you Kalexander?" he asks.

"You wouldn't dare."

"Wouldn't I?" Dax's eyes are full of mischief.

I roll my eyes. "Anyway, most people call me Bond," I say. "Even Sam, my ex, always called me Bond. Still does, actually. Never AJ."

"You're still friends with your ex?"

"Yeah, we decided a while ago that we work better as friends than as a couple."

"Do you see each other often?" he asks, and something in his voice tells me that maybe there's more to it than simple curiosity.

"Well, we work in the same building, so yeah. But it's usually just to catch up over coffee in the lobby café."

Dax nods, his brow furrowing ever so slightly.

"So, which do you prefer?" he asks after a beat of silence.

"Which what?"

"Which name do you prefer to be called? AJ or Bond?"

"Oh. Uh, Bond is fine."

"Yeah, but do you *prefer* it?"

No one's ever asked me that. I look at the ceiling for a moment before answering him. "I hadn't really thought about it before. I think I prefer AJ."

Dax nods and a grin spreads across his face. It's a look of pride—like a kid who's just won a spelling bee—and I can't help but smile at the ridiculousness of it.

We sip our drinks and continue talking about everything and nothing. Like yesterday, our conversation feels so easy, so comfortable. And suddenly, there's that warm, cozy feeling again—like we're old friends catching up, laughing as we remind each other of many years' worth of inside jokes.

We finish our drinks, then contemplate getting another, but decide we should call it a night. Dax has a podcast interview tomorrow, and I have to go to work in the morning. Besides, I'm thirty-two, not twenty-two, which means I don't bounce back from nights out like I used to. I'm still recovering from a slight hangover after last night's drinks with Dax. When I mention this, he seems surprised to find out we're nearly the same age.

We head outside and amble toward the subway station, both of us laughing as Dax tells me stories about his first few attempts at stand-up comedy. Truth be told, I can't imagine anything worse. I'd rather get a root canal than stand on a stage trying to make people laugh. Dax admits that he's not entirely comfortable onstage, but I don't believe him for a minute. He always seems so at ease no matter the situation, and he's funny without seeming to try.

"The first time I did stand-up," he tells me, "the second I got off the stage, I ran to the bathroom and threw up." I'm laughing and he is too, but when I actually look at his face, I can tell this isn't an exaggeration. A quick flash of something undecipherable flashes over his face, but it's gone in an instant.

"At least I haven't actually thrown up *on* stage," he says. "There was this one time," he starts, but we're interrupted when a bug flies in front of us, circles our faces a couple of times, and lands squarely in the middle of Dax's chest.

"Gaaah! The fuck!?" Dax shouts and waves his hands wildly in a swatting motion, not actually hitting anything. He quickly brushes over the front of his shirt to shoo away the offending visitor, but decides to flail around a bit and spin his whole body to make sure the bug is gone. I'm doubled over laughing—too hard to actually be helpful.

When he's sure the bug has flown away, Dax starts walking again, giving his shirt another brush-off for good measure. I'm a few paces behind, still wiping my eyes from laughing so hard. Dax stops and turns to frown at me.

The glow of the streetlights casts a warm shadow over his face and I'm immediately struck by how handsome he is. I mean, I was on a photo shoot with him all day yesterday—saw him in nearly a dozen different but equally flattering outfits, perfectly groomed and under the lights of the studio—so I already know he's handsome. But here on the street in casual black pants and a dark green sweater, he looks different. Like the person I'm here with today is the real, flesh-and-blood version of the one I met yesterday. Without the hairstyling and the makeup, he still looks like he could be on a magazine cover, but this version is simply...beautiful.

God, why am I being so weird?

"What the hell was that?!" Dax exclaims. "Did you see it? It was huge!"

I'm still chuckling when I catch up with him. "I'm pretty sure it was just a little beetle."

"Little?!" He's practically shouting. "That thing was the size of a Prius."

I can't help but laugh again. "Diego Ximénez, are you afraid of bugs?"

"*Afraid* is a strong word. I can appreciate bugs and all they do to contribute to the planet and all that." Dax waves his hand dismissively. "As long as they stay at a respectable distance. That one did not respect my boundaries." He looks at me, smiling.

"Man," I say, shaking my head. "Summer camp must've been a nightmare for you."

His smile falters, a dark expression falling over his face, and he slows his pace.

"Yeah, it was," he says on a long exhale.

Shit. Was it something I said? When he sees me looking at him—regret written all over my face—he gives me a smile, but it's tight-lipped and filled with tension.

"I'm sorry. I didn't mean to—" I don't actually know what I'm apologizing for, but I know I want to take back whatever I said to cause him to look like he's been sucker-punched.

"No, it's fine," he says, his voice wavering and sounding very much *not* fine. "I mean, it *was* the bugs…and the homophobic bullying." He shrugs and tries his best for a genuine smile. "Fifty-fifty. Well, maybe thirty-seventy."

"Jesus, I'm sorry." My chest feels tight, the weight of Dax's words stinging like a fresh paper cut.

"Thanks, but it's fine. It was a long time ago."

"Was it…bad?" *God, what a stupid question.* "I mean, of course it was. Forget I asked that."

But Dax doesn't seem to mind. "Eh, I survived. And luckily, I only went there for one summer. After that, my mom never made me go to sleepaway camp again." I get the feeling he's minimizing what he went through, but I don't push him on it.

We're quiet as we make our way to the subway station. There's an unintended dark cloud of tension that hovers over us as we walk, and I don't like that I've caused it.

It hadn't occurred to me that someone like Dax—kind, funny, laid-back to the point of being seemingly unflappable—could be the target of bullying and hate simply for being who he is.

"Which train are you taking?" Dax asks as we descend the stairs into the station, breaking me out of my thoughts.

"The Q. How about you?" I swipe my card and push my way through the turnstile.

"Q works for me. I can transfer before we get to the bridge." Dax looks like he's doing some mental calculations in his head to figure out the best route to get home. I don't know exactly where he lives, but I know it's somewhere in Queens, which is a long subway ride, no matter the route.

"Oh, how was your date with the Blue Dragon?" I ask when we reach the subway platform. It's a bit of a non sequitur, and I'm not sure I even want to know, but if I can steer Dax away from whatever memories I've apparently stirred up, then that's exactly what I'm going to do.

Dax seems to be trying to decide whether to say something or not.

"Ecstasy," he finally says, flatly. It's not the sort of tone I would pair with such a word.

"That good, huh?" I ask, playfully jabbing him with my elbow.

He lets out a humorless laugh. "No, the Blue Dragon. I'm pretty sure he was high on ecstasy when he showed up."

"Oh? How could you tell?" I've never been into party drugs or the club scene, so I don't really know how to spot someone who's high.

The subway train screeches to a halt at the platform and Dax and I step into the open car. It's fairly empty this time of night, so we sit on one of the long bench seats. It's loud and we have to sit close to be able to hear each other over the sounds of metal on metal as the train pulls out of the station.

"He kept calling me *darling*," Dax says. "But in that overly posh British way—and he's not even English." He makes a face that looks painfully proper. "*Daah*-ling."

I cringe.

"And he kept touching me, but like, petting me. It was weird." He demonstrates on my arm—although if he's intending to show how awful it was, it's not working. "The whole time, his pupils were really dilated, unnaturally so. And he was saying really weird things to me like, *I want to paint you in glitter and lick you up until all that's left is your soul wrapped in rainbows.* I have no idea what any of that shit means, but I don't want any part of it."

I try to muffle my laugh as Dax continues to regale me with tales of the Blue Dragon. With every bump and jolt of the train, I can't help but notice that our knees keep brushing against one another, causing a little spark of warmth up my spine. I also can't help but notice that neither of us makes any attempt to move away from each other, not even an inch.

"It's not funny," Dax says, but he's chuckling too. "The guy smelled like he bathed in vanilla and oranges."

"I like the smell of vanilla," I say unhelpfully.

"I do too, but it was so strong, it was like I was having dinner with a bag of potpourri. When we were saying goodbye, he hugged me so hard, some of that—whatever it was—probably rubbed off on my shirt." At this, Dax pulls the neck of his sweater up toward his nose. "Ugh, I can still smell it."

Dax tugs the neck of his sweater even more, indicating to me that I should smell it. "Here, check for yourself."

I'm not in the habit of sniffing other people for remnants of a bad date, but Dax is adamant, so I oblige him. I scoot over—just an inch or so—and lean down to put my nose closer to the neck of Dax's sweater. I inhale slowly and although I do catch a faint smell of vanilla, what I notice even more is the smell of, well, Dax. I'd caught the scent of fruity shampoo before, but it's not only that. There's something that's indescribably masculine.

The train lurches and my face nearly collides with Dax's chest. I reflexively put a hand on his chest—hard and muscular, in case you're wondering—to keep from face-planting into him. For a moment—one that lasts approximately four thousand seconds—neither of us moves. I don't even think Dax breathes.

"Sorry," I say, although it comes out as almost a whisper. I can feel my cheeks heat as I straighten up.

"Don't apologize." He gives me a playful smile. "That's one of the perks of riding the subway."

"What is?"

"The bumps. Someone could fall into your lap at any moment." He winks and playfully kicks my foot.

I laugh, but something pulls at my heart when he says it. *Is he flirting with me?* If he's not, it's definitely flirting-adjacent.

I finally decide he's not flirting. He's funny and charming and like this with everyone. I saw it first hand at the shoot yesterday. I mean, the whole reason we're even here on the train together is because he'd called me cute and I'd gotten weird, then apologized. I'm mistaking his acts of platonic affection as something more. But why am I so hung up on it? And why does it feel like disappointment to realize he's *not* flirting?

"So?" Dax clears his throat. "Did you smell it?"

I'm pulled out of my thoughts, which were on the verge of spiraling. "Uh, yeah, I guess I can smell it a little." I scrub a hand over my jaw, hoping I'm not blushing too much.

Dax shrugs. "I guess most of it has worn off by now."

"Yeah." I fidget with the sleeve of my sweatshirt. "So, how about a second date?"

Dax blinks at me.

"You and the Blue Dragon."

"Oh!" *What did he think I was talking about?* "No. He asked me, but I made it pretty clear that there will be no second date. It was obvious there shouldn't have been a first date." I feel an odd sense of relief when he says this. "He gave me his business card when I was leaving though. Said I should call him if I have an event I'd like him to DJ. This was *after* I told him there wouldn't be a second date."

"That's a little weird."

"Yeah. But it was *before* he asked me if I still wanted to go to his place and 'get properly fucked.'" Dax makes air quotes when he says this last part.

"Wait, let me get the order correct. He asked you on a second date and you said no. Then he gave you his card asking you to hire him as a DJ. Then he asked you if you wanted to have sex?"

"Yep." Dax nods, then shakes his head as if he's replaying the scene in his own head.

"Can I see his card?"

"Why?" Dax narrows his eyes.

"I dunno. Just curious. Wright Media hosts events with DJs sometimes. You never know." I put on my most innocent face.

"Fuck off," Dax says, chuckling.

"What? It's true." I can't hold a straight face for long and we're both laughing now.

"Ohhhh shit..." Dax suddenly stands and looks out the window.

"What?" I'm looking around to figure out what's happened.

"I missed my stop."

Sure enough, we're heading into the dark of the tunnel leaving the Canal Street station which is where Dax was supposed to transfer to a train that would take him to Queens.

Dax checks the map mounted to the wall of the train car. "This is gonna add another half an hour to my ride," he whines. Yes, he's actually whining.

"So come with me and get a cab from my stop. You'll get home quicker than if you try to backtrack on the subway."

Dax contemplates this, then nods. "Oh, yeah. Right." He flops back down next to me. "Thanks."

"You're welcome?" I shrug.

"Sometimes I forget I can actually afford to spend money on things like cabs." He's looking at the ceiling of the train car.

"That must be wild," I muse.

"What? Suddenly having a windfall?"

"Yeah. Well, no. Not *just* that. All of it. The fame, the money, going from a job behind a desk to...doing whatever you do every day."

"I guess. It really hasn't hit me yet. I mean, I'm not that famous yet. I'm starting to get recognized, but..."

I turn to look at him, but he's still looking at the ceiling. "But what?"

"It's a little scary, you know? To know that things are going to change soon, in a really big way. I'm not sure I'm ready for it. Part of me feels like I don't really deserve it."

"That's bullshit," I say a little too forcefully. Dax snaps his head toward me. "Seriously. You worked really hard to make this show happen. And you worked hard at your computer job for years and to help your family pay for your sister to get the help she needed."

Dax shifts in his seat, then looks down at his hands, which he balls into fists then releases, over and over. "My dad worked really hard," he says. "Still does. He's always done everything he could to make sure we had a house and food and clothes and all that. When Cami was young, my mom had to work two jobs to pay for medical bills and therapy for her. And that was on top of trying to raise two kids. If anyone deserves a windfall, it's them, not me."

I shrug. "Maybe *you're* their windfall."

He smiles—not a broad, beaming smile, but something more genuine. It's not quite wistful—maybe hopeful.

"Maybe so." He nudges my shoulder with his own, and I can't help but smile too.

We both turn and look out the window as the subway emerges from the tunnel, ascending the Manhattan Bridge. I've been in New York long enough to not have too many romantic feelings about the city anymore. I don't find it magical or beautiful like I did when I first moved here. Most days, it feels too crowded, too dirty.

Crossing the bridge on the train is one exception though. I'm in awe of the beauty of the city from this vantage point. Passing over the river, the subway track is high enough to see all the way to the Statue of Liberty on one side and far into Queens on the other side. I love it at night—seeing cars crossing the Brooklyn Bridge and the glittering lights of tall buildings stretching up from lower Manhattan—when everything looks so peaceful.

I rest the back of my head against the glass and stare out the opposite window, watching Manhattan get farther away as we approach Brooklyn. The low rumble sounds and gentle rocking of the subway nearly lull me to sleep.

Dax is quiet and I assume he's looking out the window too, but when I catch his reflection in the glass, I'm surprised to find him looking at me. When he sees my eyes on him, he turns back to look out the window, but it's slow, like he isn't quite fazed that he'd been caught. A wave of excitement jolts through me; I don't know exactly what to make of it.

We're still close enough that our knees continue bumping into each other, and I can't help noticing that it's not just our knees now, but our shoulders and elbows too. I don't know if it's deliberate on his part, and I could easily scoot over to make some space between us, but I don't want to—and apparently, neither does he.

Once the subway dips back underground and the magic of the bridge dissolves back into the grit and grind of the city, Dax turns his body to face me.

"Hey, so you know *The Knightly Show*?" he asks.

"Yeah, of course."

How could I not? It's a nightly cable talk show featuring a variety of guests such as actors, politicians, musicians, comedians. The host, Graham Knight, likes to champion up-and-coming acts and is known for bringing widespread attention to deserving newcomers. It's only been on the air for a little over a year, but it's been extremely popular with young people.

"What about it?" I ask.

"They've asked me to be a guest in a couple of weeks." Dax chews on his lower lip, looking less excited and more apprehensive about it.

"Really? Dax, that's amazing! I hope you're saying you're gonna do it."

"Yeah, I said I would." He takes a long exhale. "I stupidly told them I could do a comedy set though. I only do stand-up in one little club, and even then, I don't do it that often. Why did I tell them I'd do it?" He says the last part to no one in particular.

"Can you change your mind? Go back and tell them you'd rather not do stand-up?"

"I dunno. Maybe. I thought it would be good to challenge myself, but now..."

"How long would you have to be onstage?"

"It's a four-minute set. Just me on camera talking for four whole minutes. And then an interview with Graham Knight after."

"You can do that. You'll be great. And four minutes? That's like...less time than it takes to get a fancy drink at a coffee shop. That's less time than it takes to make a decent piece of toast, at least in my toaster."

"You need a better toaster," he says dryly.

"Come on," I nudge him as we pull into the subway station near my apartment. We walk together across the platform and up the stairs, as I continue my list. "It's shorter than the time it takes to sing 'Bohemian Rhapsody'. It's less time than it takes for me to get dressed in the morning."

"There's no way that's true," Dax says, narrowing his eyes at me. "It takes you more than four minutes to put on a T-shirt, jeans, and a hoodie?"

"Well, okay. Maybe not. But it does take me longer than four minutes to take a shower." Dax gives me a sweep over my body with his eyes and I feel myself blush. "Look, you do stand-up all the time. You can do this. Don't worry."

"You know, telling someone with anxiety not to worry is like telling a deaf person to listen." *Anxiety?*

"It's not like that at all," I say. "But I get what you're saying. I've watched a few of your comedy sets on YouTube. You're funny and you're good at thinking on your feet. You'll be fine." I'm not sure that's what he wants to hear, but it's the truth. "I'll be on my couch cheering you on through the television."

We're walking in the direction of my apartment and Dax is quiet for half a block. I think he's officially dropped the subject, but then he speaks. "Would you come?"

"Come to what?" I ask, momentarily forgetting what we'd been talking about.

"To the taping. *The Knightly Show*? They told me I can invite a few guests to sit in the audience."

"Oh." I'm a little stunned that he'd ask me when we've known each other all of two days. "Sure, of course. When is it?" I worry that I sound a little too enthusiastic.

"In, like, a couple of weeks? I have to check on the exact date."

"Yeah, that sounds like fun."

"I don't know how fun it'll actually be. I've never gone to a show taping. But they start in the afternoon, so you'd have to miss a couple hours of work. If you can't come, it's totally fine. I don't want you to miss work for—"

"Stop." He opens his mouth, then shuts it again. "You've already invited me and I want to go. You can't talk me out of it now."

"Okay, okay." He smiles a little, but the look on his face is more relief than happiness. "I'll ask them to put you on the guest list."

"Great. And thank you—you know, for inviting me."

We turn onto my street before I realize that Dax had said he was going to call a car from the subway stop. We'd fallen into such easy conversation that neither of us noticed we'd walked all the way to my block. When we reach the stoop of my apartment building, I stop.

"Well, this is me." I point to the window on the top floor. "Actually, that's me."

"Nice," Dax says, looking up at the brownstone nestled among a row of identical-looking three-story buildings, all with small, fenced courtyards in front and exactly ten steps up to the front door.

"Yeah, I like it. I'm on the top floor, so I don't have to hear the neighbors walking around." I rock on my heels. Dax nods.

"Um, AJ?" He shoves his hands into his pockets and kicks at a nonexistent rock on the sidewalk. "Can I ask you something?"

My stomach does a somersault. "Sure. What's up?"

"Would you mind if I come in and use your bathroom?" Dax looks thoroughly abashed at having to ask. I can't put my finger on exactly what I feel at this moment, but I think it might be something close to disappointment. *Why? What was I hoping he'd ask me?*

"Oh," I say. "I mean, yeah, of course." Relief washes over Dax's face. "Come on." I bound up the front steps to unlock the door.

"I'm so sorry to impose," Dax says as he follows me. "I've had to go pretty much since we left the bar."

"Don't be sorry," I say, leading the way up the three flights of stairs. "I'm glad I could help."

"I'll call for a car as soon as..."

"Yeah, that's fine. Whatever." I try to sound breezy, but I'm caught up short when I realize I suddenly have butterflies in my stomach at the thought of bringing Dax into my apartment. I'm a bit of a neat freak at home, especially when it comes to the bathroom, so I'm not worried about it being messy. It's just some strange, unexplainable nerves that have been turning themselves over and over in my brain all evening.

Once we're inside and I point Dax in the right direction, I'm left standing in the hallway, unsure about what I should do. It's like I'm a guest in my own apartment, not quite feeling comfortable with doing all the things I'd normally do when I get home, which is entirely ridiculous.

I try to shake off the feeling by turning on a couple of lights and filling two glasses of water. Then I sit on a barstool at the tiny kitchen island that serves as a dining table since I don't have space for an actual kitchen table.

All of the casual ease I'd felt earlier is gone, replaced by the same nervous energy I'd been feeling before Dax showed up at the bar. My leg bounces rapidly while I wait.

When I hear the door to the bathroom begin to open, a ball of electricity forms in my stomach, rapidly strengthening as Dax emerges. He's typing on his phone—probably calling for a car—and ambling down the hall toward me looking far more relaxed than I feel at the moment.

"Okay, car will be here soon," he says with his eyes still on his phone. As he slides it back into his pocket, he stops and cocks his head at me, furrowing his dark eyebrows. "Are you...okay?"

Don't be weird. Be cool. Say something. I struggle to string a few words together.

"Me? Oh yeah. Good. I'm awesome." *Awesome?* The words come out a bit too fervently.

Dax nods but looks unconvinced. He continues to walk toward the kitchen, where I push a glass of water toward him across the island.

"Busy day tomorrow?" I manage to ask, my leg still bouncing.

"Yeah." He takes a long drink of water, and I can't help but watch his Adam's apple bob up and down every time he swallows. "I've got a few things going on. How about you?"

"Same. Lots to do." I shrug. "But, good news: Jürgen should be coming to the office tomorrow to bring the photos from the shoot."

Dax rolls his eyes and makes an *ugh* sound, clearly not excited about it.

"I apologize in advance for you having to look at a thousand pictures of my face."

"It's actually closer to three thousand," I offer unhelpfully.

"Noooo! Don't tell me that." Dax rests his elbows on the island and covers his face with his hands. I can't help but grin.

"Aw, come on. From what I saw on set, the photos are stunning. Trust me." I try my best to give him an encouraging smile.

"I do trust you, AJ." Dax stares at me for a moment too long, then blinks. "Uh, my car is five minutes away."

"Oh. Yeah, okay."

Dax rolls back on his heels. "I should go downstairs and wait." He gestures over his shoulder toward the door with his thumb.

I nod vacantly while my brain tries to untangle the mess of feelings that have been stirring inside me all evening. When I realize what he's said, I'm suddenly filled with a sense of urgency, like I don't want him to leave. I know I can't ask him to stay longer, but why am I so desperate for more time with him? *God, maybe this is why I have so few guy friends.* I chew on my bottom lip, not sure what to say.

"Well, thanks for letting me use your bathroom," he says, clearly oblivious to the crisis going on in my head. "You're a lifesaver."

As he starts to walk past me toward the door, I reach out and grab his hand, stopping him midstride. I can feel an actual rush of blood to my head, my heart pulsing in my chest so loudly I'm afraid Dax can hear it. I dare to look at his face and find his gaze locked on our hands, mine gripping his.

"AJ?" His voice is barely audible. His eyes meet mine and the look they're giving me almost knocks me off balance. They're dark, his pupils wide and black and full of questions, but also something else.

Curiosity? *No.* Desire? *Maybe.*

"I—" My mouth has gone dry despite having drank an entire glass of water. I swallow, hoping more words will come out. I feel like a skydiver in an airplane high above the earth, ready to jump but unsure if I'm actually wearing a parachute.

Whatever I was about to say, I don't finish. Instead, I tug Dax's hand, just a little—enough to let him decide if he wants to move closer to me.

He does.

He takes one small step toward me. Dax is a few inches shorter than me, but sitting on the barstool, we're eye to eye. I drag a slow inhale through my nose, then pull his hand again—this time with a little more force, bringing him close enough that he's now standing between my knees. I scoot forward, planting a foot on either side of him.

My breaths are shaky—which I'm sure he's noticed—but he doesn't say anything. In fact, he doesn't do anything but look at me. Waiting. *God, what am I doing?*

I sit up straighter, dropping Dax's hand and tentatively resting my fingers on his shoulder. The touch causes his breath to catch. He inhales, but he doesn't exhale right away. It's like time has slowed to a near standstill. My heartbeat is a deafening pounding in my ears.

I move my face close enough that we're almost nose to nose. Our eyes are open, but at this range, Dax's face is all fuzzy shapes and lines; the only thing in focus are his dark eyelashes.

"Dax," I whisper before sliding my hand under his jaw, rough with stubble. I gently pull his face toward mine and inhale. My lips graze his, a featherlight touch at first. When he doesn't pull away, I lean in, and then...

I'm kissing him. I'm kissing Dax, and *oh god*. I've jumped out of the airplane and I'm definitely *not* wearing a parachute, free-falling without knowing whether I'm going to fly or hit the ground.

Dax doesn't seem to be kissing me back, and I'm terrified I've made a huge mistake. I pull my head back—barely an inch or two—but when I do, Dax leans in and slides a hand around the back of my neck. He parts his lips and pulls my face close, barely brushing his lips on my own before we abandon politeness and press our mouths together hungrily.

"God, AJ," Dax whispers into my mouth before he glides his tongue along my bottom lip. When he presses his mouth against my own, hot and needy, a desperate moan escapes my lips.

We're both breathing heavily as we move together—my fingers combing through Dax's hair while he keeps a hand on the back of my neck, the other gripping my thigh just above the knee. I lean in more, scooting toward the edge of the barstool. He responds by stepping closer so there's only a whisper of space between our bodies, and I can feel the heat radiating from his chest.

For every second that Dax kisses me back, the nervous, antsy feelings I'd been holding on to slowly begin to uncoil themselves inside my chest and I feel like I can breathe again.

He pulls his head back, just enough to catch his breath, but doesn't loosen his grip on my leg. "Jesus," he pants. "You're really going out of your way to prove you're not homophobic, aren't you?"

"I wanted to make sure it was clear." I laugh, then slide a hand through the back of his hair and pull him close, tracing his lower lip with my tongue before I cover his mouth with my own. He makes a soft *hmm* sound that vibrates on my lips, sending goose bumps down the back of my neck. His hand slides up my arm, lightly tickling my inner elbow, leaving even more goose bumps in its wake. I shudder. *Holy sh–*

Buzzzzz.

The shock of Dax's phone breaks us apart like a bucket of cold water thrown over us. We stare at each other, trying to catch our breaths. I can't exactly say what I feel at the moment, other than dazed. And... happy?

Had I really just done that?

Once I blink back to life, I notice Dax staring at me. He's flushed and adorably rumpled, and I'm suddenly bursting with affection for this man. All I want to do in this moment is grab him by the shirt and pull him close for another kiss.

"My car is here," Dax says, looking pained as he says it. He also looks like he has a thousand questions on his mind.

"Oh, okay." I wish I had something more profound to say, but my brain is cabbage and I can't seem to string two words together. I barely pull myself together enough to say, "I'll walk you down."

We're quiet all the way to the building's entryway. It's not an awkward silence, but not quite *not* awkward either.

Before we get to the front door of the building, Dax stops, turning to face me. I'm expecting him to say that this was a mistake. To let me down gently. Or maybe, to kiss me once more before leaving? But he surprises me and chooses none of the above. "AJ?" His voice is soft, hesitant.

"Yeah?" I can barely get the word out, fearing what he'll say next.

And then, an impish grin spreads across his face, not unlike the ones I'd seen on the set of the photo shoot. There's a little sparkle of mischief in his eyes.

"You owe me a wallet," he says, then winks and walks out the door. There's a bounce to his step as he descends the stairs to the street and gets into the car, leaving me speechless on the stoop.

CHAPTER 8

A J

Despite getting approximately forty-two minutes of sleep last night, I'm feeling happy, maybe even a little bit giddy when I walk into the office this morning. All night, I couldn't get thoughts of Dax out of my head, not that I wanted to. No matter what I did to try to sleep, my mind kept going back to the taste of his lips, the citrusy smell of his shampoo, the feel of his fingers gripping my thigh. *God, that was good.*

I'd also thought of his smile, the way it lights up his whole face, like it was made especially for laughter. The laid-back way he carries himself, like nothing seems to bother him too terribly. And the way he makes our interactions feel easy, like we've known each other a lot longer than a couple of days.

Maybe I like these things about him because they're so diametrically opposed to myself. I'm sure he sees me as someone who's awkward, uptight, and altogether too serious. Honestly, he wouldn't be wrong with this assessment.

Still, what happened last night was most definitely *not* one-sided. The way he'd kissed me back tells me he must not be totally put off by my prickly personality.

I'm not sure how I'd gone from wanting to be friends with Dax to kissing him in my kitchen, but I don't care. Before I'd grabbed his hand, I hadn't thought of him in a romantic way. I guess it's possible I had and didn't realize it. It's been so long since I had romantic feelings for someone, especially when that someone is another man. *Was I just being impulsive?*

We hadn't made plans to see each other again, but given the way we left things, I don't think last night was the last time I'll see him. At least, I hope not. He'd invited me to *The Knightly Show* taping, so that was something.

"Bond?" André calls from his office, his posh London accent breaking me from my thoughts. I hadn't realized I'd been standing in front of the coffee machine with an empty cup still in my hand. *How long have I been here?*

"Yes?" I walk into André's office, decorated with black leather furniture with accents of cream-colored throw pillows and lamps. Everything in this office matches the aesthetic—not a single item out of place—while still feeling warm and inviting. It matches André's personality to a T.

"How did your photo shoot go a couple days ago? The one with Diego Ximénez?" André had been out of the office yesterday, so we hadn't had a chance to talk about it until now.

"Oh. Uh, it ended up going well." *Really, really well.* I hope André doesn't see the blush creeping up my cheeks. "Jürgen should be bringing the photos today or tomorrow. You saw the samples I sent you from the shoot?"

I already know he has. I'd sent him several photos throughout the day to let him know we'd had a change of plans. André doesn't like surprises.

"Yes, I liked the new direction very much. Good work."

"Thank you, sir."

André gives me the smallest smile and nods approvingly. But in an instant, his smile falters.

"Please close the door. We have a private matter to discuss."

Shit. How does he already know? I can feel the sweat prickle the back of my neck as I try to think how he could've found out about last night. Did Dax contact him this morning to complain?

"As you know, Takashi has been out on a leave of absence for... family reasons." I nod, relieved that he's not talking about Dax and me. "Unfortunately, his partner has received a rather grim prognosis and Takashi will not be returning to work. He and Louis will be moving to their vacation home in France."

My stomach drops. Takashi and I haven't always seen eye to eye on the magazine, but he's always been passionate about his work, and I've learned so much from him. I've only talked to Louis a handful of times, but he's always been so kind. My heart hurts for both of them.

I sit on the chair facing André's desk, my throat tight. "When will he be leaving?"

"Tomorrow." André looks down at his hands, then back at me.

"Will he be coming by the office for his things? I'd like to say goodbye to him."

"No. He had me ship him a few items. The rest will be left to the new creative director to decide what to do with it."

"Oh." I'm surprised. Takashi has always taken great pride in his thoughtfully curated collection of art and design books, rare magazines, and design-related tchotchkes—although Takashi wouldn't use that word—he'd always referred to his fancy knickknacks as collectible art pieces.

André clears his throat and leans on his desk. "I know it's sudden, but we need to keep things moving here. Naturally, if it were strictly up to me, *you* are the obvious choice to take over Takashi's position as creative director." My eyes snap up. This has always been my goal, my dream job.

"Thank you. That means a lot to me."

"I'm in your corner, Bond. I'll do everything I can to try to convince the board that you're the best person for the job. But it's not a done deal. Not yet. The board would like to explore all available options before making a decision."

André clears his throat and continues. "In the meantime, keep up the good work. You're good at thinking on your feet and recognizing when things need to change to ensure the best outcome. That's a quality that's hard to teach, but one that's necessary in this business."

"Is there anything I can do to, you know, push them in my direction?" I ask.

"Keep doing what you're doing and you'll be fine," he says. Not helpful.

"Thank you sir, that's so kind of you—"

"No need for all of that," André interjects, waving a hand. "Let me know when Jürgen delivers the photos." He rounds his desk, then sits in his fancy, ergonomic monstrosity of a desk chair and turns his attention back to his computer, all but dismissing me.

As I head back to my desk, my emotions are being pulled in all directions with the news of Takashi, the possibility of the promotion of a lifetime, and of course Dax. And all of this is happening before I've even had a single cup of coffee.

Deciding I need something better than a single-serve coffee from the machine, I grab my phone and head down to the building's café. On the elevator, I type out a text to see if Sam is free for a chat. I could really use a friend right now.

Once I'm back at my desk, coffee in hand—Sam hadn't returned my text—I decide I need a distraction, so I put on my giant, noise-canceling headphones that make me look like a helicopter pilot, crank up some music, and focus on my work. I try not to think about the fact that sometime soon, Jürgen will be dropping off photos from the shoot and I'll be looking at thousands of pictures of Dax.

An hour later, a hand on my shoulder sends me nearly jumping out of my chair. André is standing over me with a slightly irritated look, and I wonder how long he'd been trying to get my attention. I slide my headphones off and set them aside.

"Sorry. Couldn't hear you."

"Quite alright," he says. "Could you please come into my office?"

I stand, preparing myself for yet another emotional hit I'm about to take. It's like being told to flex your abs right before getting punched in the stomach. André leads me into his office and shuts the door.

"Everything okay?" I ask, feeling my palms start to sweat. I shove them into my pockets.

"Yes, quite alright." André rounds his desk, then sits in front of his computer. "I've just received an email from Diego Ximénez." *Oh shit. Oh shit. Oh shit.*

"Oh?" I do my best to seem nonchalant. Pulling a chair up to André's desk, he turns his computer screen to face me. I adjust my glasses and read the words, feeling a ball of nerves settle in my stomach.

10:05 a.m.
To: André Laurent
From: Diego Ximénez
Subject: Thank you

Dear Mr. Laurent,

 I am truly honored to be included in your magazine. As a kid, I always enjoyed reading your magazine but never thought I'd be lucky enough to ever see someone like myself on the pages. It's truly overwhelming. The photo team was a pleasure to work with, and I was impressed by the leadership and professionalism of your art director, AJ Bond.

Thank you again for everything. You're truly making my twelve-year-old self's dream come true.

All the best,
Diego Ximénez

For the second time in twenty-four hours, Dax has left me speechless. André eyes me for a long moment, then turns his computer back around.

"It sounds like he was very impressed with you," André says, a little twinkle in his eyes. "No surprise there, of course."

I shrug off the compliment like it's a bug on my shoulder. "I tried my best."

"This type of leadership is exactly what the editorial board is looking for in the creative director position. This email will be great to present to the board when we're talking about Takashi's replacement."

"Thank you, sir." I nod sheepishly. I'm relieved, if not a little surprised that Dax had taken the time to do something so thoughtful for me. He certainly didn't need to do it, and I don't think he knows how incredibly helpful it could potentially be for me. "That was really kind of him."

"Indeed," André says with raised eyebrows. I choose to ignore whatever I might be reading into his expression.

"Okay, well…" I make my way toward the door, but then stop. "You know, he mentioned something about needing a new wallet."

André looks at me with curiosity. "Did he?"

"Well, he didn't say he needed one. I saw the one he's carrying and it's…well, it's awful." André nods, so I continue. "What do you think about trying a little social media experiment?"

André cocks his head and gives me a quizzical look like he's never heard of such a thing. "An experiment?"

I tell André about Dax tagging along with me to Lowell's and how we'd been chatting and joking around. I leave out the part about lying to his manager to get his number. I also leave out the part where Dax came up to my apartment last night and we'd kissed each other until we were breathless. He doesn't need to know about that.

"So tell me about this idea," André says.

CHAPTER 9

DAX

Earlier this morning—and without really knowing why—I'd written an email to AJ's boss letting him know about my experience working with AJ at the photo shoot. Wanting to let André know what an exceptionally talented and smart person AJ is had been my only motivation. I'm a firm believer that if someone does a good job, they deserve to have others know about it. Okay, maybe a little, tiny bit was to get AJ's attention, but that was only secondary.

I hadn't expected any response from André, so it was a surprise to find an email from him waiting in my inbox an hour later.

> 11:07 a.m.
> To: Diego Ximénez
> From: André Laurent
> Subject: Thank you

Dear Mr. Ximénez,

Your kind words are greatly appreciated. We at Wright Media strive to give our talent the best experience possible. As you can attest to, photo shoots can be long and tiring for all involved, so it pleases me to hear that Mr. Bond made your experience a good one.

He mentioned that you are in need of a new wallet, and we at TMG would love to help with that. Mr. Bond can give you more details.

Thank you for your participation in the photo shoot. We're all looking forward to seeing the photos in the next issue.

Sincerely,
André Laurent

I hadn't planned on doing anything about AJ's little white lie about the wallet, and I certainly hadn't planned on his boss hearing about it. I'm not sure how much AJ told André, but it was enough that now he knows about my crappy wallet too.

I'd actually thought it was cute the way AJ had made up some stupid story in order to get my number from Hannah. She would've given it to him if he'd simply asked for it—without all the theatrics—but she'd been amused by the whole scenario. We both had.

I'd been having coffee with Hannah yesterday when AJ called. She put the phone on speaker so we could both listen, and we tried not to laugh when AJ explained that he'd found my wallet in the dressing room of the studio. She'd tried her best to sound genuinely concerned, but she knew it was utter bullshit, because I'd paid for her coffee fifteen minutes earlier. She played it off by acting concerned about my misplacing something so valuable, and that she might be breaking my trust by giving out my number without my permission.

I mouthed to her that it was fine to give him my number. He thanked her profusely and told her that the shoot had gone extremely well and that I'd been "amazing"—his words, not mine. Naturally, I wasn't going to argue.

At the time, I didn't have any idea why AJ was so determined to talk to me. Looking back, it makes sense why he hadn't wanted to ask Hannah to set up a meeting. He'd been ashamed and embarrassed by his own behavior toward me, both at the shoot and at the end of the night.

I didn't tell Hannah about either of those things. She isn't winning awards as the world's most organized talent manager, but Hannah is fiercely loyal and would gladly go up against anyone who so much as whispers one negative word about me regarding my sexuality.

She'd been my roommate and closest friend in college—the one who knew almost everything there was to know about me. We'd lost touch though, shortly after Hannah got married. When Hannah came out as trans, her wife promptly asked for a divorce. The whole situation had left Hannah utterly torn apart. She'd reached back out to me, desperate to move back to New York. My acting career was getting started, and she offered to be my manager in exchange for a meager salary. Of course, I'd hired her on the spot. She's been my manager for the past two years.

When I had made that little comment last night, I hadn't meant that AJ actually owed me a new wallet. I'd have been happy with letting things go after last night's turn of events—for lack of better words. I'd already told AJ that I didn't need his help finding a new one, and I meant it. I'm capable of finding one of my own, I just haven't had a lot of time, or motivation, to look. I have to admit though, I'm more than a little excited about whatever AJ and *TMG* have in store for me.

When he kissed me last night, I could tell it wasn't something he'd planned on—that much was clear from the wild-eyed look on his face as soon as he grabbed my hand. It was like he was onstage in a play and had never seen the script.

I hadn't seen it coming either. Hell, I'd assumed he was straight the night we'd gone out to eat after the photo shoot. But last night, he'd talked about Sam, his ex, and then he kissed me, so I guess I was wrong. Shame on me for assuming.

I can't say I was unhappy about any of it though. Earlier in the night when I'd been on my date with the Blue Dragon, my mind kept wandering to AJ and wishing I were having dinner with him rather than the vanilla-scented human disco ball in front of me.

Being around AJ the last two nights felt like hanging out with a close friend. I can't put my finger on it yet, but there's something about AJ that I find irresistible. He's like a walnut—a tough outer shell that takes some work to crack, but once it's open, it's like a treasure hidden inside.

He seems guarded with his genuine smiles and laughter, like he's being cautious about letting anyone see that side of him. It's a side of him I could see was there on the first day I'd met him.

At the shoot, AJ treated everyone with respect, and no one was considered beneath him. And while he'd been annoyed with me (for good reason, I now realize), he still treated me respectfully. He'd even helped clean up before the cleaning crew arrived at the studio, when he didn't have to. My mom cooked enough meals and cleaned enough houses in her lifetime that being disrespectful to service people, or anyone really, regardless of their job or status, is a huge dealbreaker for me. It makes me happy to see that AJ seems to value everyone he encounters as his equal.

I could be totally wrong. After all, I don't know him that well, but something inside me tells me I'm not. I guess that's why I find myself buzzing with excitement knowing that I'll be hearing from him again.

I check my phone, then my email on my laptop. Nothing from AJ. I wonder what details he's supposed to be giving me that André was referring to.

Today is one of the rare days lately that I don't have anything scheduled, so I've promised Cami that I'll spend the day with her doing anything she wants. I foresee us playing board games, watching *Encanto* at least once, and taking a trip to the ice cream shop, to name a few.

I shower and get myself ready, then take a quick peek at my phone and see a text waiting for me.

> AJ: Thanks for the email.
> Dax: Was it too much?
> AJ: No. It was really nice.
> AJ: And thoughtful. You didn't have to do that.
> Dax: I know. I wanted to.
> Dax: So about the wallet. You don't actually have to help me with that, you know.
> AJ: I know. I want to. [wink emoji]
> Dax: So what do I need to do?
> AJ: Nothing yet. Keep an eye on your social media.
> Dax: What does that mean?
> Dax: AJ?? What does that mean??
> Dax: AJ???????

Silence.

What's he planning?

I'm leaning over my desk frantically texting AJ when Cami walks in holding Battleship—the game, not the movie—in her hands. Her smile drops when she sees me.

"Hey, Diego, are you okay?"

"Yeah, I'm good." I sit up and attempt to run a hand through my hair. "Are you ready to lose?" I nod toward the game.

"You don't have to play if you don't want to." Cami clutches the box to her chest.

"Cams, I'm ready. Let's go." Following her down the stairs, I try to ignore the prickling sense of dread about what AJ's planning. He's a quiet one, but as the saying goes, the quiet ones are the ones you have to watch out for.

Cami thoroughly destroys me at Battleship, partly because she's really good at it, but mostly because I can't focus on anything for longer than a minute or two. I feel an overwhelming urge to check my phone to see if I have any new emails or messages from AJ. Nothing.

Cami wins a second round of Battleship, then two rounds of Mastermind. At this point, she sighs heavily and looks around, clearly tired of playing games that I'm making no effort to win.

"You're boring today," she declares as I quickly try to pull my thoughts back to the present. "I thought you said it was gonna be a Diego-and-Cami day."

"Sorry, Cams." I help her put away the game pieces. "You're right. It's our day, and I'm here for you. I promise."

"You don't have to hang out with me," she says softly, looking down at the floor. "I can find something else to do if you need to take care of whatever you have going on."

With anyone else, I might take her comments as passive aggression, but Cami's heart is too good for that sort of thing. Most likely, her suggestion is meant to give me an out if I don't want to spend the rest of the day with her. And although I know she means well, having her tell me she's fine with me not being mentally present after I've told her I'd spend the whole day with her makes me feel like the world's shittiest brother.

"Listen, Cams," I say, touching her chin to get her to look up at me. "There is one thing I need to do that's really important. And it needs to be done now." I lean in and whisper, as if I'm telling her a secret. "But I can't do it alone."

Cami's eyes go wide and she wiggles in her spot on the floor expectantly. "What is it?"

"You and I," I whisper, "need to take a walk down the block and get some ice cream."

Cami can't take the excitement. She claps her hands, then stands up so quickly, she nearly trips over her own feet. Before I've even fully stood up from my spot in front of the couch, she's already wearing her jacket and rain boots, even though it's not raining outside. She bounces on her toes as she waits for me to put my own shoes on and grab my keys. Before I shut the door, I pull my phone out of my pocket and leave it on the table beside the door, ensuring I won't be tempted to check it while I'm out.

We get to the shop, only to discover they're out of strawberry ice cream—Cami's favorite. So we walk two blocks farther to the rival shop, where we manage to secure a cup of strawberry.

Passing a playground on our way back, we decide to go in. Cami has always loved the swings, so we finish our ice cream on a bench, then spend a full hour swinging in the crisp autumn sunshine.

Sometimes Cami can get hyperfocused on something repetitive like swinging, especially if she's anxious or upset about something. Yesterday afternoon, I noticed she was unusually quiet when she came home after work. I didn't really pry into why—sometimes she has occasional spells where she walls herself off and doesn't like to talk to anyone, so I hadn't known anything was really wrong until now. I should've realized sooner, but I've been in my own head since last night.

"Diego?" Cami is swinging slowly and looking at the ground.

"Hmm?"

"Do people ever say mean things to you? Like when you're onstage?"

"Sure, sometimes. Why?"

Cami doesn't answer, just swings quietly. The air is cool today, but the city is trying to hold on to the last scraps of summer and not quite ready to give it up yet. It won't be long before pumpkin spice and oversized knitted scarves start to overtake New York City.

"Cams?" I know too well why she's asking and now not answering. "Did someone say something mean to you?"

She turns her face away from me and lets her feet drag across the ground.

"Someone at work?" My grip tightens on the chain of my own swing. "Who was it?"

"Nobody at work." Her voice is barely audible. "A customer and his friend."

I don't bother asking what was said—I'm pretty sure I can guess—and I don't want to make her recount the story to me when it's obvious she's already upset.

"Cams, don't ever let anyone make you feel like you're less because of your differences. They don't know you. They don't see how kind you are, how smart you are, or how wonderful and funny you are."

Cami nods, but doesn't look up. "What do you do when someone says something mean about you?" she asks.

"I'd like to say I can ignore it and never think about it again. Sometimes I can, but other times, I can't. It makes me upset, mostly because they're not directing their attacks at me, but at all the people who are like me. I have to try to remember that it's not personal. They don't even know me."

"But why do they say things like that?" I stop swinging and turn to face Cami. My heart breaks for her, and as much as I'd like to say that some people are just assholes, I don't.

"People who say hurtful things are doing it because they don't feel good about themselves. The only way they think they can lift themselves up is to put others down. And to be honest, all the time you've already spent thinking about them? They don't deserve it. They don't deserve a single second of your time. I know it doesn't make it easier to hear when it's happening, but you have to try to remember that, okay?"

Cami nods, then wipes her eyes with her sleeve. I slide off my swing and wrap Cami in a big hug.

"Love you, Cam," I whisper into her hair.

"Love you more," she replies. She cries softly for a minute before letting go, but not before wiping her nose on the shoulder of my shirt.

"Cam, gross!" I feign outrage, which makes her laugh. I love the sound of Cami's laughter, the way it warms my heart every time I hear it. It's one of the things that keeps me from being in a hurry to move out of my family's house.

My parents try, but they don't really know what to say when Cami gets bullied. I don't always know either, but being gay means I've had to deal with my own haters for years. Living in New York, it wasn't nearly as bad as it could've been if I'd grown up somewhere else, but that doesn't mean I haven't encountered hatred and bullying because of who I am. Cami knows all of this. That's one of the reasons we're so close—we've both had our fair share of insecurities and are still working on overcoming them.

"Can we go home?" she asks.

"Yeah, let's go."

―――

We arrive at home nearly two hours after we'd left for our ice cream adventure. Cami runs upstairs to her room while I linger in the entryway, picking up my phone from the table where I'd left it. My last three texts are still unanswered.

Unable to keep my curiosity at bay any longer, I type out a message to AJ.

> Dax: I can't take the suspense! What am I supposed to be looking for on social media? What's going to happen??

AJ: Sorry. I wanted to make you sweat a little before responding.
Dax: You want to make me sweat??? [eyebrow raised emoji]
AJ: No!!
AJ: Well, maybe?
AJ: Oh god. Delete that last text.
Dax: I can almost see you blushing.

I see the three dots appear, then disappear, then reappear again.

AJ: I was going to refute your assertion, but I'd be lying.

I laugh to myself. *Refute your assertion?* Who says that when they're trying to flirt? AJ apparently. He *is* flirting with me, isn't he?

Dax: Sounds about right. I already know you're a liar.
AJ: What does that mean?
Dax: Ahem, does Hannah and a story about finding a lost wallet ring a bell?
AJ: Fine. You got me there.
Dax: So what are you planning with my social media?
AJ: I can't tell you now. You'll find out soon.

I can feel a wave of nausea roll through me. And as if he's reading my mind, he texts again.

AJ: Don't worry, it's not bad. Just a little fun.

All I can do is shake my head and smile. I can picture AJ at his desk with a smug look on his face. I'm not sure what kind of chess game we're playing here, but I'm sure as hell not going to let him checkmate me.

CHAPTER 10

AJ

Readers, we need your help! We had a great time on the set with @NotTheRealDaxXiménez. Look for the up-and-coming star in next month's issue of @TMGMagazine. In the meantime, he told us he needs a new wallet, and we've made it our mission to help. Send us suggestions that you think would be perfect for Dax. #finddaxawallet
[behind-the-scenes photo of Dax at the TMG photo shoot]

When the post went live yesterday afternoon, it took a little while to gain traction, since Dax isn't quite a household name yet. But the idea is to try to generate some buzz and get people interested, and I'm hoping that by including readers, some of them will even participate in the quest for a new wallet.

I'd waited all evening for a follow-up post from Dax—or at the very least, a text saying he saw it—but so far, there's been nothing. On my way into the office this morning, I pass a few street vendors on the corner near our building—the kind that sell bedazzled T-shirts, sunglasses, flashy hats, and yes, even wallets. I pick out a blue-and-black camo-patterned nylon wallet and pay a whopping six dollars—highly undervalued in my opinion—and head inside.

I stop by the desk of our social media coordinator, Kiara, who's bouncing in her chair like she's been waiting for me.

"We've gotten some good feedback on the wallet thing so far," she says with far too much enthusiasm first thing in the morning. To be fair though, I'm almost as excited as she is, but I'm better at hiding it under a facade of nonchalance. At least, I think I am.

"Good," I say, pulling the wallet out of my pocket. "I found this one. Let's put it up this morning."

Kiara takes it from my hand with two delicate fingers like it's a piece of stinky trash. Her face is a combination of horror and utter disgust. "Where did you find *this*?"

"From the guy on the corner," I answer cheerfully. "You know, the one who blasts reggae music and sells those tie-dye T-shirts?" Kiara isn't amused. Not even a little bit. "It's perfectly fine."

"It probably has bedbugs."

"It does not," I snatch it back defensively. "And besides, it's not like I'm asking you to use it. Let's just take a photo."

Kiara obliges and snaps a few photos. When she seems satisfied with the results, I pull up a chair and work on the newest post with her. She hits the Share button, and the post goes live.

> Hey, @NotTheRealDaxXiménez, I think we've found a wallet for you. What do you think? #finddaxawallet

So far, I haven't heard anything from Dax, so I hope he's willing to play along. I get a knot in my stomach thinking that he might not actually want this at all. After all, he didn't respond to my last text yesterday telling him to watch his social media. And he hasn't yet responded to the post from yesterday afternoon.

Back at my desk, I try to settle my thoughts by working on planning photo shoots for the next issue. Without Takashi here, I've been not only doing my work, but also taking on a lot more of the creative duties that he would normally do. I love it, but I'm starting to feel even more pressure with the news that I could possibly take over Takashi's position.

I really shouldn't have started this whole social media game with Dax, truth be told. I should be focusing on work, but I couldn't help myself. I wanted to have an excuse to see him again. I can't remember the last time I did something impulsive to get the attention of someone I actually liked. Hell, I can barely remember the last time I really liked someone.

And then another thought hits me—one that makes the knot in my guts twist even tighter. What if it's not the attention from the fans or the magazine he's avoiding? Maybe it's me he doesn't want.

Once I allow that one seed of doubt to make its way into my head, it scatters like dandelion fluff, giving life to dozens of negative thoughts that take root like stubborn weeds.

As time crawls by without a response from Dax, I can't help but think of all the reasons for him to not want to see me again. After all, I'm a regular guy who makes average money and works in an office. I'm quiet, introverted, and, let's face it, not nearly as fun and charming as some of the guys he's probably met while in his actor circle. I'm certainly not as handsome, with my plain brown eyes, glasses, and my obvious lack of desire to set foot in a gym. Dax, on the other hand, isn't cute, he's gorgeous. Those green-gray eyes, long lashes, his kissable lips, and that body that's the right amount of muscular without being bulky.

And, let's not forget that I'm the one that kissed him, not the other way around. To be fair, he kissed me back, but maybe being an actor, it could've been about attention rather than actually liking me.

For two hours, I'm in a doubt spiral while trying to focus on the next issue of *TMG*. I don't notice Kiara standing beside my chair until she practically has to shout to get my attention.

"Bond!" She's clearly visibly delighted. "We've got a response from Dax." When my head snaps up and I smile too quickly, she tilts her head and narrows her eyes at me. I quickly right my face into its usual expressionless self, hoping I didn't give too much away.

"Oh yeah?" I go for slight interest rather than full-on elation.

Kiara pulls up the *TMG* account on her phone and thrusts it in my face. Under the original post is a response from Dax.

@TMGMagazine Thanks, but this one isn't quite my style. Try again. #finddaxawallet

I knew the first wallet would be something he'd hate, so his response wasn't surprising. Still, I'm not sure how to interpret his tone, but clearly he's willing to play along. Kiara and I type out a response.

@NotTheRealDaxXiménez No problem. We'll keep looking. #finddaxawallet

This time, it only takes a few minutes to start getting responses from readers. Kiara checks *TMG*'s other social media outlets and finds that a couple of readers have actually posted photos of their own. Kiara answers with her own brand of cheeky replies, and by the afternoon, the whole thing starts to take off.

We post a couple more photos of wallets that Kiara was able to borrow from Sydney, who's busy in the menswear fashion closet, where the racks and shelves of clothes featured in the photo shoots at *TMG* are stored.

Dax answers by telling us to keep trying, and he even replies to the readers who've submitted their own photos, which encourages even more fans to get in on the fun.

I can't help but keep checking my own phone to see if he's sent me any texts away from the eyes of the public, but there's nothing.

I'm having such a blast with Kiara that when Jürgen walks into the office, I'm caught by surprise. I almost hate to stop what I'm doing, but then I remember that I'm about to see the results of all of our hard work on the photo shoot.

Because my desk is basically a cubicle in a sea of desks, I lead Jürgen to one of the small meeting rooms, which is really just a small room with a circular table, three chairs, and a phone. Jürgen opens his laptop and scrolls through thousands of files to find the shots from Dax's photo shoot. He clicks around a bit, and then my heart skips when Dax's face fills the screen. The images are unretouched, but his smile—devilishly sly and handsome—causes a kaleidoscope of butterflies to flutter in my stomach. There's a sparkle in his eyes that seems to jump off the screen. His lips are full, the bottom one almost pouty—something I hadn't paid much attention to on the day of the shoot, but since the night I kissed him, I can't unsee.

Jürgen doesn't seem to notice my temporary lack of cognitive ability and keeps flipping through the images, pointing out his favorites and mentioning tone and exposure and whatever else. I nod along with a *yeah* and an *uh-huh* thrown in every now and then. When he finally realizes I haven't really said much, he stops what he's doing and turns to me.

"You don't like them?" He furrows his brows, a worried look filling his face.

"What?" I blink a few times. "No, I do. I'm... I love them. They're..."

"Good? Yes?"

"Yes. Great." I'm embarrassed by my stupidly simple answers, but I can't put my thoughts into words. He's captured Dax's natural good looks, but it's even more than that. As he clicks through the photos, I'm stunned by how acutely he's tapped into Dax's personality. In some photos, it's the charm and sense of humor with little hints of mischief. In others, inklings of vulnerability seem to seep through the cracks in Dax's outer shell.

I'm fighting the urge to reach out and touch Jürgen's screen—to trace my finger over Dax's lips and run a thumb over his cheek.

I wouldn't though, obviously. I hate when someone has the audacity to touch my own computer screen, leaving a fingerprint that I have to immediately clean or else I won't be able to stop fixating on it. Also, it would be just plain weird.

I'm struck by one particular photo—a close-up of Dax, a small, almost shy smile on his lips, holding the Rubik's Cube. I audibly gasp when I see it. The photo is a little more subdued than some of the other shots. It's the most honest, sincere photo I've seen so far.

Jürgen stops clicking through the photos.

"I know," he says. "This is one of the best ones."

"Yeah." My mouth suddenly feels too dry. I swallow a couple of times, wishing I had some water. I remember the moment Jürgen snapped that particular photo. I'd been busy talking to Sydney when I noticed Jürgen had stopped to adjust the settings on his camera. I looked up and saw that Dax wasn't looking at Jürgen but right at me. He'd been watching me while Jürgen was busy. I remember smiling at Dax—a genuine smile, not a forced, tight-lipped one—maybe, probably, for the first time that day. Jürgen had just called "*Eins, zwei, drei,*" and at the last second, Dax took his eyes off me and looked at the camera. The whole thing had only lasted a couple of seconds, but I felt like all the air had been sucked out of my lungs.

This was the shot.

"Too bad this isn't the cover story, eh?" Jürgen pats me on the shoulder.

"Yeah, that would—"

But before I can finish, André saunters in.

"Bond, why didn't you tell me Jürgen was here?" he says with a smile as he extends his hand to Jürgen. Before I can answer, he goes on. "Jürgen, it's been ages. Bond here says the shoot went fabulously. How are the photos?"

"They're gorgeous," I tell both of them. "Stunning." I don't normally go overboard with superlatives, and the words leave my mouth before my brain has time to edit them. André cocks an eyebrow at me, and I have the sudden urge to cover my face with my hands.

"Indeed," he says, drawing the word out, still eyeing me. He leans down and squints at the laptop screen, looking at the photo I'd been admiring. Jürgen begins excitedly clicking through a few of the photos he and I had marked as our favorites. André offers his thoughts on the photos before giving Jürgen a pat on the back and praising both of us for a job well done. We both breathe a sigh of relief once André is gone. I knew André would like the photos, but it's always a relief when I know he's pleased with the results of a shoot, especially one that's going to take up eight pages in the magazine.

Once Jürgen is gone and I'm left with the photos, I check back in with Kiara to see how our social media is doing.

"We've got more readers submitting photos. The whole thing is really doing well now that Dax is playing along." She shows me the posts that he's responded to and, sure enough, the more he interacts with fans, the more likes and reposts we get. He's thoughtful with his responses—they're funny without sounding like they're trying too hard to be funny, just like Dax. He's careful with his wording to make sure he's not hurting anyone's feelings. I can almost hear his voice in every response.

Then Kiara shows me a post from Dax's own social media account rather than a response to one of *TMG*'s posts. It's a selfie that looks like it must've been taken this morning. He's wearing a baseball hat with a few waves of hair sticking out from the sides. His eyes are only slightly visible under the brim of his hat. Dax is holding a coffee cup and smiling.

"He's really getting into it," Kiara says. "Here, look at what he wrote."

> Thanks to all of you for your help to find a new wallet. This has been such an incredible bonding experience. Keep looking and make sure to tag @TMGMagazine. #finddaxawallet

I stare at the post. He's holding a cup from Luxe Coffee, my favorite coffee shop in Brooklyn, the only location being around the corner from my apartment—and nowhere near Queens where Dax lives.

An incredible bonding experience. Bond-ing. That little line thrown in there as if it were meant to sound so casual. Yep, he's definitely trolling me. And I love it.

CHAPTER 11

DAX

I've been resisting the urge all week to text AJ. What started out as a bit of work-related flirting has blown up into something I don't think either of us expected.

TMG keeps tagging me in posts with a variety of wallets that have started out cheap and tacky, but have gotten increasingly nicer as the week has gone on. AJ isn't named in the posts, but I can tell he's had a hand in at least some of them.

In response, I've been dropping little Easter eggs in my own posts without naming AJ specifically to see if he'll take the bait and reach out to me. He hasn't yet, at least not personally.

I even took a selfie in front of his favorite coffee shop, which he'd pointed out when we walked by on our way to his apartment. I used the word *bond* in a couple of my comments. And yesterday, I posted something about being a man of exquisite taste, along with a GIF of James Bond. That one had earned me a snarky response that had AJ written all over it.

My favorite posts are the memes that have popped up with the hashtag: a nod to the George Costanza overstuffed wallet is my personal favorite, with *Pulp Fiction*'s "Bad Motherfucker" a close second. I'm having fun interacting with fans and am impressed to see that my followers have increased—and that more people seem to be interested in *Mexican't*'s debut. I hate to admit it, but AJ's little game has been good for me.

I don't respond to all of the posts, since I'm not sure what the endgame is here—I'm sure it can't last much longer. It's only been a week, but I don't want to overplay this little game and risk fans getting tired of it. I'm sitting on my bed about to cave and text AJ when I get an alert that I'm tagged in a new *TMG* post.

> Hey, @NotTheRealDaxXiménez, we found the perfect one! Come by the @TMGMagazine office to pick it up. Readers, stay tuned to find out how the story ends! #finddaxawallet

The post is accompanied by a picture of me from the photo shoot, a portrait this time. The magazine had been squirrelly about showing photos from the shoot up until this point, so seeing a portrait of myself from that day is surprising. It's not one of Jürgen's photos but a candid behind-the-scenes shot of me on set while the hairstylist, makeup artist, and clothing stylist all fuss over me. It's black-and-white, and everyone else's heads are cropped out, so it's just my face with a bunch of hands reaching in to do their respective jobs. I'm smiling but not looking at the camera in the photo, and I remember AJ taking several behind-the-scenes photos that day. He must've taken this one when I wasn't looking.

I open my messages to send AJ a text when I get another message, an email this time. It's from André asking me when I'd be available to come to the office. Their social media coordinator, someone named Kiara, wants to take a few photos of me with my new wallet. *TMG* hasn't posted a photo of this new wallet, and André's message is somewhat vague, so I don't know what to expect. I decide not to message AJ after all and to see what *TMG* has in store for me.

When I arrive at *TMG*'s offices at eleven o'clock the next morning, I'm greeted by a small group of a dozen or so people in front of the building. They're visibly excited when I approach the doors, so I oblige them by shaking hands and taking a few selfies with them.

As I'm standing with an arm around a woman who's smiling and waiting for her friend to snap a photo, I have a sudden sensation of falling. It only lasts a second, maybe two, but in that moment, I'm completely thrown off-balance—both figuratively and literally—like I'm on the bow of a ship during a storm. It's not the first time this has happened. It's been more frequent lately, and I'm certain it's related to my anxiety. I take a deep breath and force on a face of happy nonchalance, then say a few polite thank-yous and goodbyes before I head into the building.

Once I'm inside and through security, I spend a moment taking a few deep breaths by the elevators before pushing the button. I lean against the back of the elevator, lucky to have it all to myself, and take a few more calming breaths. Rubbing my sternum with the palm of my hand, I start counting down from fifty in my head. When the doors open on the twenty-fourth floor, I'm mostly back to my normal self, but the incident leaves me feeling unsettled, not knowing if or when it'll happen again. *Fuck*.

André is passing by the reception desk when he notices me walking in. He sweeps me into the office in a flurry of politeness.

"Mr. Ximénez, how lovely to see you." He goes in for an air kiss on the cheek. "We're so delighted you could come in on short notice. The whole event seems to have been a success. Thanks for playing along."

"Sure," I croak out, then clear my throat, which has become dry and tight. "I had fun with it." I follow André around the office as he continues talking.

"It was certainly unexpected that this would become a..." André stops midstride, making circles with his hands as if he's using them to help extract the right word. "A whole to-do," he finally settles on. His accent and demeanor remind me of a snooty English butler from a vintage sitcom—except that André is very nice.

He weaves his way around the desks and cubicles until we get to an office that's decorated with lavish furniture and expensive-looking trinkets. It's dark and there's no computer on the desk.

"This is our previous creative director's office," André tells me as he allows me to enter first. "Make yourself comfortable and I'll be right back." I sit on one of the leather chairs and wait, taking a few more deep breaths.

A minute later, André returns with two young women I haven't met. I stand and shake their hands as they're introduced as the social media team, Kiara and Jenna. Or maybe it's Gemma? Or Emma? I'm still recovering from my almost-panic attack and I'm not quite firing on all cylinders.

And then my heart leaps as AJ enters the room. I have to fight to keep from breaking out in an all-out grin. He's wearing what I'm learning is his usual work uniform—dark jeans, black T-shirt, hoodie, and red suede Puma sneakers—but he wears them so damn well, confident and tall, with his soft, wavy hair falling over his forehead. When his eyes meet mine, I can see lines at the corners of his mouth as he struggles to keep his face pleasantly neutral.

"Mr. Ximénez, good to see you again," he says, extending a hand for a very stock-photo-worthy handshake.

"Likewise," I say as I take his hand. It's been more than a week since we've seen each other, but his hand feels warm and familiar. Our eyes lock for a moment before André speaks.

"Well, thank you again for coming in, Mr. Ximénez, and for being such a good sport. Your interactions with fans really made it work."

"I should thank *you*," I say to André. "I had a lot of fun and it was great to connect with fans and build some excitement about the show. I honestly hope you didn't go to too much trouble by doing all of this."

I have to force myself to keep my attention on André and not look at AJ.

"Not at all," André says, waving his hands. "It really worked out well for all of us. A win-win." He says *win-win* as if he's never used the phrase before and he's workshopping it to this small audience. "You were such a delightfully willing participant, and we intend to make good on our promise of a wallet for you."

André hands me a gift bag that had been sitting on a small side table. As I take it, I notice AJ watching me from behind Kiara and Jenna/Gemma/Emma.

"Oh," I say in an almost startled voice. I don't know why it feels unexpected, since this is the whole reason I'm here.

"Should I...?" I gesture toward the bag.

"Yes, please do," André says. "Once you open it, Kiara will take a few photos to post on our social media, and then you'll be free to go." He smiles warmly.

I set the gift bag on the table and reach in, pulling out an excessive amount of tissue paper until I get to the black box at the bottom. It's square and flat with no distinctive branding on the outside. When I open it, I'm surprised. I don't know what I'd expected to find, maybe something garish and obviously expensive, or maybe one of the cheap wallets *TMG* had posted that looked like it came from a street corner vendor.

This wallet is simple, made with soft black leather. I run my finger along the outside edge, marveling at how exquisitely well made it is. Pulling it from the box, I still don't see anything in the way of branding. It's a basic bifold with pockets on the inside. When I open it, I find the main pocket is lined with a fabric that has stripes of bright pink, orange, and dark blue in varying widths, looking almost as if it's been hand-painted. The pattern is bold, but since it's only on the inside pocket, it's like a hidden surprise. On the back corner, the letters *DAX* are embossed in the leather in small, tidy letters.

Something about the simplicity of it, along with the colors on the inside, makes me feel certain that AJ picked this out for me. I can't imagine André or anyone else here choosing this specific design especially for me.

When I look up, the faces in the room are watching me expectantly. AJ is watching too, but with a gaze that carries far more weight. It's like he's pinned all of his hopes on this moment. His hands are shoved into his pockets down to the wrists, all of his earlier confidence dissolved.

Is it wrong that I find his nervousness around me absolutely fucking adorable? It's like he's always flustered around me, which is ridiculous. He's around celebrities all the time for work—though I'd hardly call myself a celebrity, at least not yet—but for some reason, he seems to be so easily ruffled in my presence. It's, well, cute.

"Do you like it?" André asks, but before I can answer, he says, "Bond can tell you a little more about it." He nudges AJ forward toward me.

"Uh, yeah." AJ clasps his hands together tightly. "The wallet is handmade by a man named Peter who lives in Queens." My eyes catch his when he says this. AJ knows I have a lot of pride for my home borough, and having something that's made there makes it all the more special.

"The leather and interior fabric are from Peter's home village in Africa. He drives a cab full-time and makes bespoke wallets on the side. All the profits he makes from his wallets go to his family. He sends them money and they send him materials." AJ fidgets with his sleeve and looks around the room while he talks, his cheeks blossoming into a bright pink.

"So anyway, I hope you like it." AJ shoves his hands back into his pockets and pulls his shoulders up like he's trying to make himself smaller.

I know I'm staring at him with heart eyes, but I can't help it. I want to throw my arms around AJ and tell him how much I love this gift. Well, let's be honest, I want to do much more than that. But we're in an office and everyone's watching me.

I must wait too long to respond because André speaks up. "Of course, if it's not suited to your taste, we have a lovely Tom Ford—"

"No," I say, clutching it to my chest like it's a baby bird. "I love it. It's one of the nicest things anyone's ever given me. It's beautiful." I'm looking at André, but in my periphery, I can see AJ shift his weight.

"Fabulous," André says. "Bond has a great eye for finding hidden gems."

Nailed it.

AJ's cheeks go from cherry-blossom pink to a full-on magenta all the way to the tips of his ears.

"Well." André looks at the two women. "Kiara, would you go ahead and take the photos you need so Mr. Ximénez can get on with his day?" Then he turns to address the room. "Great work to all of you, thank you."

André pulls AJ to the corner of the room, evidently to chat about other non-wallet-related matters. As I watch them, I notice AJ standing tall, head high, his arms and shoulders relaxed as he speaks. This is how he was at the photo shoot—calm and confident in his comfort zone. I'm not gonna lie, it's pretty sexy to see him like this, in work mode. But it's also so adorable to watch him get flustered and nervous, especially when it's because of me.

Kiara and Jenna (I overheard) instruct me through a variety of poses with the wallet while they take a couple dozen photos. Once they seem satisfied with the results, they give me hugs and thank me profusely before leaving.

When I look around, André is still in the corner, eyes locked on his phone, but AJ is gone. I hadn't noticed him leave the room. Realizing we're done and that the two women have left, André looks up from his phone.

"Well," he says. "Thanks again, Mr. Ximénez. You're lovely." He shakes my hand vigorously.

"Thank you, sir." I pick up the gift bag that had fallen on the floor and take out the box.

"Shall I get Mr. Bond to walk you out?" André tips his head to the side, slightly smirking.

"Yes, sure. If you don't mind." I fumble with the wallet a bit but manage to get it back into the box.

"Of course." André calls out to AJ across a set of cubicles, then leans one hip against the door while we both wait. When AJ returns, there's a sheepish grin on his face, which he turns away from André, squeezing past him and into the room.

"Bond, whenever he's ready, please walk Mr. Ximénez out."

"Sure." AJ nods.

André looks at a nonexistent watch on his wrist and declares he's late for a lunch appointment, despite it only being eleven-thirty. He looks quickly between the two of us, says a hurried goodbye, then shuts the door, leaving us alone. All alone in an office whose only window to the rest of the office is frosted glass, obscuring the view from any curious coworkers.

I watch AJ as he runs his hand over the back of his neck—something he seems to do a lot when he's nervous.

"So..." he starts. "Do you really like the wallet? I mean, if you don't, that's fine. We have another one you can have. Seriously. Don't feel bad—"

I take three quick steps to close the distance between us—maybe a little too urgently—before cupping his face and shutting him up. With a kiss.

CHAPTER 12

AJ

I've had plenty of kisses before—more with women than men, but that's hardly the point—and I'd always thought of myself as a good kisser. I'd even had some great kisses. But none of my previous kisses were even in the same ballpark as the one happening at this moment.

Dax's hands cup my face with a little more intensity than I was expecting. He's shorter than me, but he manages to pull me down close enough that our mouths are perfectly aligned. It's not hesitant or uncertain like the one in my kitchen—that one was more of a question.

With this kiss, there's no question of intent or want from either of us. We've both been hungry for this since that night in my apartment. We'd been playing chicken for the past week, both of us using the wallet game to test the waters, and neither of us making any sudden moves. Until now. And I don't want it to end.

Dax slides one hand around the back of my neck and uses the other to cup my jaw, somehow pulling my mouth even closer. He sucks my bottom lip, giving it a nip before gliding his tongue over the spot he'd just bitten. My breath hitches and my heartbeat is so loud in my ears, I'm sure he can hear it. Hell, everyone in the office can probably hear it.

When he runs a thumb across the tender spot on the underside of my jaw, I make an involuntary *uhhh* sound. I can feel Dax's mouth smiling against my own.

"Sensitive spot, huh?" Dax whispers, still half-kissing me.

"Uh-huh." I try to control my breathing.

Dax makes a soft *hmm* noise, then uses his thumb to lift my chin and lightly tickles the same spot under my jaw, but this time with his mouth. I slide my hands down Dax's chest, then move them down his sides, letting them rest on his hips. He instinctively pulls his body toward mine so that we're nearly chest to chest.

"Fuuuck," I whisper. My knees feel like they're about to buckle.

He dials down the intensity, softly tracing my lips with his tongue before breaking our kiss entirely, and taking a step back. I grumble in protest. We're both breathing like we've just finished a triathlon.

"Why'd you stop?" I ask, suddenly feeling self-conscious.

"Jesus." Dax adjusts his pants, and runs a hand over his mouth. I can't help but notice that he either has an erection or a very awkwardly placed crease in his jeans.

"Oh. I see."

"AJ, if we keep doing this, I'm not going to want to stop."

"Right." I suddenly realize I should do something about my own pants situation. "Um, that, uh, I mean, that was…"

My brain has glitched and words are beyond me. Dax smiles smugly. "I know. Me too." He turns and starts to gather his things while I stand here stupidly, not knowing what to do with myself.

"Hey, AJ," he says. "About the wallet." The abrupt subject change catches me off guard.

"Yeah?" My voice sounds ridiculously high. I clear my throat.

"You picked it out, didn't you?"

I nod. "I did."

"How did you get the guy—Peter?—to make it on such short notice? I mean, if he's making them all by himself on the side…"

"Well, I was hoping you'd like it and the promotion on social media would inspire him to turn it around quickly. And I *may* have contributed a little extra as a rush fee."

What I don't tell Dax is that having a bespoke, one-of-a-kind piece doesn't come cheap. The magazine was happy to pay for it in the name of a social media campaign featuring an up-and-coming star, but I'd been the one at Peter's door, asking him to turn it around for Dax in only five days. I'm certain the media attention Peter will get out of this will bring him enough new orders that it will have been worth the extra hours this past week.

Peter would've done it with or without the additional cash I'd given him out of my own pocket, but he's such an amazing human being that I didn't mind at all. To be honest, I would've paid for the whole thing myself if only to see the look on Dax's face when he opened it.

"Well," Dax says, happily invading my personal space. "I love it. I'm going to have to find a way to return the favor."

He reaches down and takes my hand, drawing small circles over my palm with his thumb. I'd have never thought something so simple as touching my hand could be so goddamn sexy, but I can feel my pulse quicken again.

"Bond?" Kiara gives a single knock on the door before turning the handle. In the fraction of a second it takes her to get the door open, I spring away from Dax, putting several feet between us, and do my best to look casual.

"Yes?" I ask, attempting nonchalance. "What's up?"

Kiara flicks her eyes between Dax and me. "Sorry, are you two—"

"No," I say, a little too quickly. And a little too loudly. "We're not—not at all. I mean, I'd never..." *Shit.*

My mouth won't stop. I can feel Dax's eyes boring into me.

"I-I was just telling Dax about Peter, the guy who made the wallet." Technically not a lie.

"Okayyyy." Kiara looks between the two of us again. "Good. That's actually what I wanted to ask you. Do you have Peter's business card? I'd like to include his contact info or website in our post."

"Sure," I say. "I have one at my desk. I'll get it for you after I walk Dax out."

"No need," Dax cuts in. "I can walk myself out." I'm suddenly alarmed when I see him giving me a look of reproach. My stomach drops.

"Great!" Kiara says to me, not seeming to notice Dax's glare. "I'd like to get the post online ASAP." Then she turns to Dax whose face has instantly taken on a friendly, fake smile. "Thanks again, Dax. I hope to see you again soon."

Kiara is all but blocking my path while Dax heads toward the door. Before I can follow him, Kiara tugs on my sleeve to guide me back to my desk for the card I promised her.

I dig through my desk drawer and hand her the card, then fast walk—I'm still trying to remain professional and not break into an all-out sprint in the office—toward the elevators. I push through the glass doors in time to see the elevator door sliding shut with Dax staring daggers at me from inside.

Well, fuck.

This whole thing had gone so well. Up until about sixty seconds ago.

I consider running down the stairs after him, but I'm on the twenty-fourth floor of an office building, not the third floor of a brownstone. He'd be two blocks away before I could make it to the lobby.

I press the button for the elevator, then pace back and forth until it finally makes its way up to my floor. *God, what had I done?* Stepping in, I bite my lip until it nearly bleeds as the elevator makes its way down to the ground floor. I pull out my phone and call Dax, but after one ring, it goes to voice mail. I type out a text instead.

> AJ: Hey, sorry about what happened upstairs. Please wait for me in the lobby.

When I get downstairs, I'm only about sixteen percent convinced Dax will be waiting. To my surprise, he's here, albeit with a scowl on his face.

"Dax." I'm nearly out of breath from practically sprinting from the elevators to meet him.

He's standing near the doors with his arms crossed over his chest watching me approach. I stop short.

"Dax, I..." I start, but I'm not sure how to finish the sentence. He raises his eyebrows expectantly but says nothing. I immediately feel desperate, like this is an all-or-nothing situation.

"I'm sorry." I step closer to him, but he steps back. He doesn't answer. "I panicked. If Kiara hadn't walked in—"

"No, AJ. Don't do that." His voice is sharp.

"Do what?"

"Don't blame Kiara for what you said up there. It wasn't that Kiara interrupted us. It was what you said after she came in."

"What did I say? I wasn't quite thinking straight after that kiss." I reach for him, but my attempt at flirting fails miserably. Dax sidesteps my hand.

"Come on, AJ. You could've stepped away from me when she came in. Instead, you acted like I was a fresh pile of dog shit. You nearly jumped over the table to get away from me."

"I told you, I panicked. I'm sorry."

"And then you said nothing's going on between us, in a way that made it sound like it was so offensive that she'd even think that. Which, by the way, I don't think she did until you started word-vomiting."

"I know, I'm sorry." I look down at my feet and try to swallow down the ball of anguish I can feel gathering in my stomach.

"Are you saying you're sorry because of what you said? Or because you're afraid to let people at work see you with me?"

"I—" I want to say it's because of the stupid things I'd said in a panic, but it isn't that, exactly. I'd been so consumed with the whole online wallet-related flirtation, I hadn't really considered what would happen afterward.

"I can't let my coworkers see us together. Not right now."

"Why?" he asks, then raises his eyebrows like he's suddenly realized something. "Are you...not out?"

"Well, no. That's not exactly it though." I look around, then move toward an empty corner of the lobby. Dax follows, but stays a few paces behind me.

Waiting for me to speak, Dax eyes me, almost warily, like he knows I'm going to say something I don't want to say almost as much as he doesn't want to hear it.

"I like you," I say with a sigh. "I really do. And to answer your question, I'm not out, but I'm not *not* out, if you know what I mean."

"No, I don't know what you mean," Dax says so quickly, he nearly cuts me off.

"I'm not really open about my personal life, especially when it comes to my sexuality. I'm not trying to hide it, I'm just not that close with anyone I work with."

"Okay... If you're not trying to hide it, then what the hell happened upstairs?"

I take a huge inhale and drop my chin to my chest.

"I'm up for a promotion. It's a huge deal, Dax. Like *dream job* big."

"That's great," Dax says softly and with more kindness than I deserve. I sigh.

"Yeah, it is. But the editorial board is watching me very closely. I can't mess this up. And starting to date someone I met on the set of a photo shoot..." I don't bother finishing the thought. A look of understanding passes over Dax's face.

"So, you don't want it to look like you picked me up on the job?"

"Exactly. I mean, if we'd met any other way, or any other time..."

"Then why did you kiss me in the first place? And why go through with all that stuff with the wallet?"

"I..." I can feel my cheeks reddening. "I wasn't thinking about work when I kissed you. It was impulsive."

Dax's eyes narrow and he takes a sharp breath.

"I don't regret it though." I quickly backtrack, hoping he knows how much I mean it. "I wanted it. I mean, the way you kissed me. Good lord, I almost had to take a knee."

I see one corner of Dax's mouth turn up for a moment. Then he frowns again.

"So, what do we do about this?" He gestures between us.

"I don't know." I scrub a hand over my face. "I like you. A lot. But I can't jeopardize this opportunity with my job."

Dax nods and looks down at the floor, his shoulders drooping. "Look, AJ," he says, bringing his eyes back up to meet mine. "I like you too. I think that's obvious. But I've done the whole *dating on the down-low* thing, and I swore I wouldn't do it again. I have a lot going on in my life, and it's only going to get even more hectic over the next couple of months. I'm starting to get recognized on the street. I can't be with someone who's scared to be seen with me. I understand your reasons, but given that we've only met a little over a week ago, maybe we should quit while we're ahead."

"What? Um, are you saying...?" I start, but can't finish my question.

"I'm saying I think we should shake hands and say goodbye. Maybe sometime in the future, we could try this again. When we're both in a more stable place with our careers."

My knees are about to give out, but for an entirely different reason than five minutes ago. Five minutes ago, when our mouths and our bodies were pressed up against each other, both of us ready to—

"AJ?" His eyes cut through my thoughts.

I nod, swallowing hard. "Yeah. I guess you're right."

He taps the toe of my shoe with his own, then turns to leave. "I'll see you around, AJ." His voice is soft, almost like he doesn't want me to hear it. I drop my gaze to the spot where he'd just touched my foot.

"Who knows?" I say, perhaps in a last-ditch effort to give myself hope. "Maybe in a few months, we can try this again?"

Dax gives me a small smile. "Sure," he says, and I have no doubt he's only saying that to humor me. In a few months, *Mexican't* will be out, and he'll be a big celebrity. He'll get recognized on the street much more frequently than he does now. And he'll be able to date anyone he wants. I feel like I've swallowed a brick.

"AJ?" Dax turns around, and I feel a little spark of hope in my chest. But my hope is quickly dashed when he says, "Thanks again for the wallet. Tell Kiara I'll make good on my promise to promote it."

I can't get any words out, so I simply nod. Dax turns and pushes through the heavy glass doors. Too stunned to move, I watch him through the lobby doors as he greets a few fans who are still lingering outside. Once he's shaken a few hands and taken a few more selfies with them, he heads down the street, not once looking back.

CHAPTER 13

DAX

Fuck.

To say that didn't go quite as expected would be a huge understatement. When AJ chased me down in the lobby, I'd been hoping he'd apologize and then everything would be fine. I wasn't expecting for things to end before they even got started.

I get it though. He has his career to think about. I'd be wary of starting a relationship with someone if I thought it might derail my career the moment it was starting to take off too. I'd be an enormous asshole to push him to jeopardize this opportunity at a promotion for me, a person he barely knows. I know how much he loves his job and how much he wants to get the creative director position—he'd told me as much the first night we met.

Still though, it stings like a fresh slap.

I know it hurt him too. I could see it all over his face when I'd told him we should call it quits. AJ should never play poker—he can't hide his emotions for shit.

I can feel my hands start to sweat and my pulse is starting to ramp up despite the fact that I'm sitting still. After my visit to the *TMG* office, all I'd wanted was to go straight to the subway and get myself home. I hadn't counted on being accosted by more fans outside the building and being "on" for another few minutes after I'd left. To be fair, the fans were nice and seemed genuinely excited.

I'm sitting on the bench in the subway station—the ones that I'd usually avoid like hot garbage because they're so full of germs—acting like everything is cool when, in fact, everything is *not* cool. My brain is trying to give me a panic attack and I'm trying like hell to fight it before the train comes.

I take a few deep breaths and try to focus on the wall across the platform. Maybe I'll go back outside—the cool, fresh air usually helps to calm me down. When I attempt to stand up though, I feel like I'm in a carnival fun house—the kind where the floors are full of slopes and angles and the walls seem to bend in ways that make me feel like they could close in on me at any moment. I casually sit back down again before anyone notices me. Thank god I'm still mostly anonymous, because I'd hate to get recognized right at this moment.

If I can make it onto the subway, I'll be fine. It's a long ride to Queens and I can probably get myself back to normal by the time I get to my stop. But I don't trust myself to be able to get on the train without falling on my face, or worse. I'm sweating through my shirt as the feeling of utter helplessness threatens to swallow me. I'm beyond grateful that the subway is running slow today.

Realizing I still have the gift bag in my hand, I pull out my new wallet. I run my shaky fingers along the edges and feel the soft, smooth leather under my thumbs. AJ had done this. For me.

Opening the wallet, I carefully examine every detail, hoping to distract myself enough to calm me down. When I get to the main pocket, I stare at the striped fabric lining, mindlessly counting each stripe while continuing to focus on my breathing. My heartbeat begins to allay, and I can't quite feel it pounding against my chest anymore.

I continue to inspect the wallet, thumbing the inside pockets, until I notice there's something tucked neatly into the corner of the main pocket. It's a paper from a fortune cookie that says:

A smile is almost always inspired by another smile.

On the back, handwritten in blue ink, is a note.

You make me smile.—AJ

My head drops into my hands, and I sit there for a full two minutes before I look up. I'd had my fingers in my hair, and now I can feel it sticking up all over. Tucking the fortune back where I'd found it, I put the wallet into my pocket instead of back into the gift bag.

I pull out my phone and scroll until I find AJ's contact, then stare at the selfie he'd sent me the first time we texted each other—the night he first kissed me. In the photo, his arms are crossed and his brows are furrowed, giving me that same stern look he'd had on the set of the photo shoot.

Looking at his picture makes my chest ache. But we'd both agreed that we shouldn't date right now. I know it's for the best, but damn, it sucks. I don't want to break things off completely though. I hope we can still stay in touch, maybe even be friends? And maybe when things settle down for him at work and *Mexican't* begins airing, we could try again. I have to hope.

I type out a quick text asking if we can talk, then send it before I can think twice.

When I hear the familiar roar of the approaching subway train, I try standing up again, relieved to find I've gotten my sea legs back. I think maybe I can make it onto the train and get home after all.

———

"Mijo, is everything okay?" Mom puts her hand on my forehead as soon as I walk into the house.

"Yeah, I'm fine," I tell her. I'm honestly not sure that I am, but I don't want to alarm her.

She narrows her eyes at me. "Diego, did you have another one?" *Ugh*. I can't hide anything from her.

"Yeah, but I'm okay now." I sigh warily.

"Go lie down and I'll make you some hot chocolate."

I roll my eyes. "Mamí, I'm thirty-three years old. You don't have to make me hot chocolate because I had a panic attack."

"Cállate. I'm fifty-three years old *and* I'm your mother. If I want to make hot chocolate for my son, that's what I'm going to do." She shoos me away and although I don't want her to fuss over me, I'm not ashamed to say that what I want more than anything is to lie down on my bed and have my mom bring me hot chocolate.

An hour later, I realize I must've fallen asleep. My eyes are blurry and there's a cup of room-temperature hot chocolate on my desk. It's still early in the afternoon, but I feel like I could go to bed and sleep through the night.

My panic attacks have been coming on more often and more intensely in the last couple of months. They hit me fast, and every time I have one, I'm left feeling so exhausted afterward.

There's no question that they've been brought on by the stress of all of the media attention. It's not something I'd been prepared for at all, and it's barely getting started. The thought that this is only the beginning makes my pulse quicken. I decide to avoid thinking about it for now, downing my warmish chocolate and ambling downstairs.

I'm on autopilot the rest of the day—sending a few emails, scrolling through my social media accounts, having dinner with my family—until I can finally go to bed.

I check my phone for a response from AJ. Nothing. Maybe tomorrow.

When I wake up the next morning, I'm feeling a thousand percent better. Still no response from AJ, but I'm determined to not let it get me down.

I shower, eat breakfast, then breeze through an online interview for an entertainment website my publicist had set up for me. I'd been looking forward to this interview because it's one of the few that Max actually agreed to be part of. He's reluctant to be in the public eye, so despite the interest in having the two of us appear together for press events, he's resisted, only granting interviews to a few lucky media outlets.

After the interview has wrapped and the host has logged off, Max and I stay on the call to catch up.

"So, how've you been?" Max asks.

"Good, staying busy." My voice is a little too high and cheerful.

"Dax." Max eyes me suspiciously. "How have you been?" Max speaks slowly, enunciating every syllable.

I let out a sigh and roll my shoulders. "I've been okay. I have days when I feel like I have a hundred things to do and places to be. And then I have days when I have nothing to do at all. There's no routine."

As I say this, I realize that this could be why I've been feeling so unsettled. Maybe it's part of why I've been having more panic attacks lately. I put a mental bookmark in that thought.

"I've been getting recognized a little bit," I continue. "More than I used to when our show wasn't as well-known. So that's new. I don't mind it, it's just...new."

Max nods. "And the anxiety?"

I let out another sigh, this one louder and heavier. "I've been having more panic attacks. Not all the time or even every day. But more."

"You know..." Max starts.

"Yeah, I know. Therapy, blah, blah," I say in a dismissive, almost mocking tone. I know I'm being an asshole, but I can't deal with talking about it. "I'm managing fine. Things will get better once the show is out. It's only this beginning part with all the interviews and photo shoots and all that."

"But this is the part that's the most stressful. This is the time when a professional could really help you."

"No," I say firmly. "Besides, Whitney thinks it wouldn't look good for my brand to be starting therapy right before the big premiere."

Max takes a slow inhale and rolls his eyes in obvious annoyance. I can feel his disdain seeping through the computer screen. "Dax, do you even hear yourself? Your 'brand'? You're a person, not a new line of cologne."

"She's a publicist. That's her job," I say defensively.

"Whitney is all about image. She doesn't give a shit about your mental health."

On the advice of the network, I hired Whitney a few months ago to increase the public's awareness about *Mexican't* and to help me shape my public image. So far, it's been a rocky relationship. She's been getting the word out about the show and has helped to get me booked for interviews, podcasts, and online articles. I have her to thank for the *TMG* feature and my upcoming spot on *The Knightly Show*.

But Max is right. Whitney's extremely goal-oriented, to the point that she often doesn't consider that I'm an actual person and not a product in need of better shelf placement in a store.

As the show gets closer to launching, the tension between me and Whitney has only increased. The one time I brought up a conversation I'd had with Hannah about therapy for my panic attacks, Whitney quickly dismissed the idea, saying that it's not a good look for an up-and-coming celebrity to already have mental health issues that require medical attention. A nagging feeling in the back of my head told me she was wrong. But at the time, I was looking for any excuse to not seek help, so it was easier to ignore Hannah and use Whitney's advice as the reason.

"She's not doing a very good job if she's ignoring your needs," Max says.

"I'm fine, Max. The only needs she should be focused on are promoting the show and me." *God, I sound like such an arrogant jerk.*

This is the part of so-called fame that has never appealed much to me. I'd be happy making the show and letting the public think whatever they want based on my own actions, not on the machinations of someone I've hired. But that's not really how the business works.

Max shrugs. We've been over this before, and neither of us is going to change our minds anytime soon. I'm too stubborn to listen, and I'm sure Max is too tired of me dismissing his advice, so we let the subject drop.

"Oh, by the way," Max says. "How was the photo shoot? The one with *TMG*? I saw a few teaser photos on social media with that little wallet game. Very cute."

Heat prickles up my cheeks, although between my complexion and the subpar video quality, I don't think he can tell. I run a hand over my mouth.

"Oh, reeeeally?" Max says, despite the fact that I've said nothing. "Do tell."

Fuck. Am I that obvious?

Moving my laptop to my bed, I prop a pillow against the wall and make myself comfortable while I start telling Max all about the photo shoot and segue into the whole AJ story, concluding with our agreement to go our separate ways for now. Max is supportive and agrees that it was probably the right call, the bastard.

Before we hang up, he tells me that I shouldn't push AJ too much. If he's not ready for his coworkers to know, I can't force him. I need to give him the time he needs to get his job figured out. I know this already, but I don't really want to hear Max confirm it.

"He'll come around," Max says. "Or he won't. Either way, you need to focus on yourself. Make sure you're prepared for *The Knightly Show*."

What Max doesn't say is that I need to make sure I'm prepared so it's less likely that I have a panic attack in front of the cameras.

He gives me some more words of encouragement, and we make a plan to chat again soon. He'll be coming out here for the premiere of *Mexican't*, so at least I have that to look forward to. And knowing I'll have my best friend next to me at the premiere makes me feel... what? Safe? Comforted?

God, maybe I do need therapy.

CHAPTER 14

AJ

You know who's a real jerk? Time, that's who.

I've dated here and there, but I've mostly been single for the past three years. I'd been content being alone, focusing my attention on work. But at the precise moment I find someone I really like—who also seems to really like me—it coincides perfectly with the biggest opportunity of my career, making it the one reason I *shouldn't* date him. So, yeah. Fuck time.

It's been five days since I last saw Dax after he came by the office to pick up the wallet. Not that I'm counting. (I'm totally counting.)

Maybe, I thought—or hoped—he'd call or text. But he hasn't. To be fair, I haven't reached out either. After I told him about the possibility of a promotion at my job, we'd both agreed that it would be best if we stepped back, and that's exactly what I've done. It seems he's done the same.

I suppose I could reach out and see if he wants to get together as friends, but I know myself. Once I see him, I'll want more. I won't want to just be friends. And then we'll be right back where we are now.

It shouldn't be that hard to stop seeing each other. We weren't really seeing each other anyway. After all, it was only a couple of kisses, wasn't it?

I need to put Dax out of my mind and concentrate on the job. My priority should be trying to impress the editorial board enough to promote me to the creative director position. It doesn't help that in addition to all my other tasks, I've been working on the eight-page fashion layout featuring Dax. My heart feels heavy whenever I look at the photos.

I finish a draft of the layout and send it to André for his feedback, but all I get is a brusque reply.

Looks great.
André

Weird. Usually when I send him a first draft of a feature, he sends me notes with edits or suggestions. André's been out a lot lately, either in meetings that take up most of the day or out of the office altogether, and I'm not sure what to make of it.

Feeling the need to talk everything out, I text Sam to see if she's free for coffee. When I arrive in the lobby café, she's already there with two cups on the table.

"How'd you get here so fast?" I ask in lieu of a standard greeting.

"I was in line when you texted," Sam says.

I flop down in a chair and fold my arms on the table, burying my face in my forearms.

"Uh, you okay over there?" Sam asks, poking me in the elbow.

"Perfect, why?" I ask without lifting my head.

"No reason." She sits back in her chair and...what? I don't know because I haven't looked up. "How's Dax?"

I respond by making a groaning noise, although it's muffled by my sleeve so it's more of an *uuurff*.

Sam sits quietly for another few moments before saying, "Well, this has been fun," and sliding her chair back to stand up.

"Wait, don't go." I finally lift my head. "Please." My voice comes out more whiny than I'd prefer, but Sam doesn't seem to mind.

"Talk to me, Goose," she says, resting her elbows on the tabletop.

"Are you seriously quoting *Top Gun* to me?" I ask. Sam shrugs. "Anyway, you're Goose, not me."

"Nope." Sam sips her coffee. "You're definitely a Goose."

"I am, aren't I?" I muse. "Goose could play the piano though, so—"

"AJ, you're stalling. Tell me what's going on."

So I do. I tell her about the night I kissed Dax in my apartment (to which she responds by going for a high five that I leave hanging), the wallet-inspired online flirting, and the post-wallet kissing in the office (another unrequited high five), all the way up to the part where Kiara walked in on us and I acted like a complete jerk (to which she responds with an over-the-top grimace).

"I apologized and he forgave me, I think," I tell her. "But we decided that dating would be a bad idea, at least right now."

"Why?!" Sam says, her eyebrows shooting up in surprise. "Are you afraid of people knowing you're into a guy? Because I can tell you, no one would care about that."

"No, that's not it. I don't talk to anyone at work about who I date. André's the only one who knows about you and me."

"Okay, so then what *is* the problem exactly?"

"The problem with dating Dax is that I met him on the set of a photo shoot."

"And that's an issue because...?" Sam makes a circular motion with her hands.

"Because it looks totally unprofessional to date someone—especially a celebrity—that I met during a photo shoot."

"Hmm." Sam taps her fingers on the table, not looking entirely convinced.

"I'm trying to make a good impression on the editorial board. André's been trying to make the case to them that I'm the best candidate to take over Takashi's job. How would it look if I'm directing a photo shoot and I immediately start dating someone we're featuring that I met on the set?" I don't wait for her to answer. "It makes me look like a creeper who cruises photo shoots like I'm at a singles bar."

"And you told him all of this?" She narrows her eyes at me.

"Yes," I sigh. "Well, not exactly in that way, but yeah."

"How did he react?"

"He said he understood. Said he wouldn't do the 'dating on the down-low' thing. He looked hurt though. But he's actually the one who suggested we shouldn't date." Bringing up this conversation again hurts like a stubbed pinky toe.

"Probably because he didn't want to force you to choose him over your career."

The comment thuds in my stomach like a heavy weight, and I squirm uncomfortably in my seat.

"Well, it doesn't matter," I say with finality. "What's done is done. I don't want the editorial board to think I'm a star fucker, and now they won't."

Sam thinks about this for a moment, then shrugs. "I guess."

"You don't agree?"

"I don't think they'd care. None of them really pay that close attention to anyone's personal lives. If you did that kind of thing all the time, maybe they'd notice. But you don't."

"But—"

"Seriously. Have you ever hooked up with someone you met on a shoot before?"

"Well, no."

"Bond, when it comes to your job, you're the most serious person I've ever met. You're extremely meticulous. You organize every part of your work down to the most minute detail. When you're on set, you freak out whenever something doesn't go exactly to plan." The more Sam talks, the more I want to sink down in my chair. She's not wrong.

"You're always trying to please André and Takashi. Hell, you don't even drink at office parties for fear you'll do something unprofessional. You're wound tighter than a…" Sam stops midsentence to think. "Well, tighter than something that's wound really tight. I bet the people in your office would love to see you loosen up for a change. They'd probably be so happy to see you and Dax together."

"Won't it look bad that I met him on a shoot when I was supposed to be—"

Sam holds up a hand to stop me. "Listen to me. I guarantee that no one at the magazine cares where you met Dax. Hell, half the couples who work in the building met each other at work." I'm sure it's not true, but she makes a good point. I could name at least half a dozen couples who met while working for the company.

I open my mouth, then close it again.

Sam sits back in her chair and gives me a contemplative look. "Unless…" She trails off.

"Unless what?"

"Unless you're scared of having all these feelings for Dax and you're using the whole 'it's not professional' line as an excuse to push him away."

I open my mouth to speak, but nothing comes out.

"Maybe because he's a man? Or because he's a celebrity? Perhaps both?" Sam seems to be taking a lot of pleasure in trying to analyze me.

"Oh, please," I counter, accompanied by an enormous eye roll. It's not a great argument—nor is it the most mature thing to do—but it's the best I can come up with.

Especially when there's a chance she could be on to something—and by chance, I mean to say she's almost certainly correct.

I like Dax. I like him a lot. More than I've liked anyone in a long time. After Sam and I broke up, I put myself on a dating hiatus—one that turned out to be remarkably easy to stick to. I found that putting all my time and energy into work made it really easy to ignore the parts of my life that hadn't been empty when I had another person to share them with.

The second I realize this, I drop my head into my hands. "Fuck, Sam. You might be right."

"I usually am."

"Were you like this when we were together?" I ask.

"Yes," she says dryly. "But back then, you didn't listen to me like you do now."

I lift my head and smile at her.

"Speaking of jobs, don't you have work to do?" Sam asks.

"Yeah. I should get back."

My phone buzzes, and I jump too quickly to check it. I see a note that's popped up on my screen and I slump back down in my seat.

Reminder: Knightly Show taping, 1:00 pm, Cole Theater

I swipe the reminder away, then glance at Sam, who's giving me a quizzical look.

"What was that?" she asks.

"What was what?" I pocket my phone.

"You looked at your phone and then got this wistful look on your face."

"Wistful? *Pssshh*."

"What was it?"

I sigh. "It's a reminder that Dax's *Knightly Show* taping is this afternoon. He invited me a couple weeks ago. Before we..." I don't finish my sentence.

"You're gonna go, right?"

"Um, no."

"Why not?"

"Because we decided that we shouldn't date."

"He didn't uninvite you to the show, did he?"

"I guess not. We didn't talk about it."

"And you're not mad at each other, right? You didn't have a fight?"

"Well, no. But—"

"There you go," Sam says, like suddenly everything is clear. "You have to go! What's the worst that could happen?"

"I could show up, have Dax tell them he doesn't want me there, and I get escorted out by security."

Sam rolls her eyes. "Or maybe he'll be happy you're there and you'll talk things out."

I don't say anything. I don't want to get my hopes up.

"Fine," she says, clearly exasperated. "I can't make you go. But I'm telling you, as your friend, I think you should go. No one's saying that if you start dating, you have to announce it to the world. You can take things slow, you know."

"I don't know." I run a hand across the back of my neck, raking my fingers through the hair that's grown a bit too long.

"Trust me," Sam says. "A little bit of effort goes a long way."

"How do you know so much about relationships anyway?" I ask.

Sam shrugs. "Personal experience."

"Is that a jab at me?" I ask suspiciously.

"I would never." Sam winks at me, then strolls away from the table and toward the elevators.

The rest of the morning drags by, and I can't stop thinking about Sam's words. I'm in the office kitchen, reheating my leftover pad thai and numbly scrolling through my phone, when I pass a post from *The Knightly Show*'s account. It's promoting tonight's guest: Diego Ximénez. I try to ignore it and move on, but I stop, flicking my thumb over my screen until I'm back to the post. I stare at the photo—a promotional shot of Dax on the set of *Mexican't*—and, god help me, I actually do feel wistful. Sam was fucking right.

Before I second-guess myself, I abandon my lunch and run out of the kitchen and down four flights of stairs to the Wright Media fashion closet, where Sydney is busy working with an intern.

"Syd, I need your help," I tell them, still out of breath from sprinting down the stairs. "Can I borrow a casual outfit? It's an emergency. I have somewhere to be and I don't want to show up in this." I gesture over my own outfit of faded jeans with worn-out knees, a T-shirt, and a hoodie, my standard uniform. At least I'm wearing decent-looking black Chelsea boots today instead of sneakers. Sydney runs their eyes over me with a slight sneer.

"I don't know," they say through a sigh. "We're pretty busy today. What's the occasion?"

I briefly consider making up an excuse, but I don't want to lie. So I go with frank honesty.

"I screwed things up with someone that I really want to have a relationship with and I need to try to patch things up."

"Bond." Sydney says, almost impatiently, while carefully putting a shirt on a wooden hanger. "I can't—"

"It's Dax Ximénez," I blurt out, then cover my mouth, not really believing I actually said that out loud. Sydney's eyebrows shoot up. I try to give them my most pathetic, pleading look.

"From the photo shoot?" they ask.

"Yeah, but please don't say anything yet. It's kind of...uncertain at the moment."

"Of course. It's your business to tell, not mine."

"Thanks. Anyway, he's going on *The Knightly Show* and invited me to the taping today. It starts at one. You know I wouldn't ask if I weren't desperate." I put my hands together in a prayer pose. "Please?"

Sydney hands the hanger to the intern who's been pretending to be far more interested in shoeboxes than in our conversation.

"Fine. We have some past-season stuff you can wear. Come with me."

Ten minutes later, I leave the building wearing black pants—more fitted than I usually wear—a white button-down shirt, and a charcoal-gray cashmere sweater. Sydney had told me to change my socks, but I said I didn't have time, so they'd thrown a balled up pair into my bag while I was busy trying to shove my other clothes into my messenger bag. I'd given up on taking my clothes with me and told Sydney I'd pick them up tomorrow.

I do an awkward speed-walk through the lobby and out to the street, where I'm lucky enough to catch a cab that's dropping someone off in front of the building.

Once I'm in the car, I breathe a sigh of relief until I realize I have no idea what I'm going to say or do when, or if, I see Dax. I don't care. I need to talk to him. And if this fails, I'll be sad, of course, but at least I'll know I tried.

When the cab drops me off at the television studio, there's already a long line of people I assume are waiting to sit in the audience. There's still half an hour before taping is set to start, so I head to the back of the line, hoping Dax hasn't had me removed from the guest list.

A petite, no-nonsense woman with a clipboard and a headset is at the front of the line telling the people to have their tickets ready to be scanned. She repeats the announcement three times as she works her way down the line.

"The tickets have all been claimed. If you don't have a ticket, please exit the line."

"Excuse me," I call to her. She looks prematurely exasperated at whatever I'm about to ask. "I believe Dax, uh, Diego Ximénez put me on a guest list? I mean, he invited me, but I'm not sure—"

"Name?" she asks curtly.

"Diego Ximénez?" I say, immediately realizing my mistake.

The woman levels me with an annoyed look. "No, *your* name, sir." The *sir* sounds like a curse when she says it.

"Oh, AJ Bond." I feel my palms start to sweat.

She flips to another page on her clipboard, then adjusts her glasses, but doesn't soften her tone. "Follow me."

The woman leads me to the door, where I'm handed off to another PA, a young man who escorts me down a corridor and through another set of doors to the set of the show. It's smaller than I'd expected, but having spent a good amount of time in studios for photo shoots, it shouldn't be a surprise. There are at least a dozen or more people running around with headsets getting things ready.

I'm led to a row of seats in the front of the audience section. There are four seats with a white sheet of paper affixed to them with the words *Guest: Diego Ximénez.*

"Have a seat," the PA says, then hurries away. There aren't many people in the audience yet—only me and a couple of other people who are busy looking at their phones.

I check my email, typing out a couple of quick replies, then wonder if I should send Dax a quick good-luck message, or at least let him know I'm here. Before I can decide, the same production assistant who walked me in approaches.

"Excuse me, sir." I look up. "You're Mr. Ximénez's guest?"

"Um, yes?"

"Please come with me," he says.

"Okay...?" I say, drawing it out like a question. I'm bracing for him to escort me to the door, telling me to leave the premises at Dax's request. He doesn't.

Instead, he says, "Mr. Ximénez requested whichever of his guests is the first to arrive. That's you."

"Oh!" I stand up so quickly, I nearly collide with the young man. Slinging my bag over my shoulder, I follow him as he speedwalks away from the set.

I'm led down another confusing set of doors and hallways until we reach a door with a sheet of paper reading *Guest: Diego Ximénez* printed on it, exactly like the one on my seat in the audience.

He knocks softly before pushing the door open. "Mr. Ximénez? Your guest is here." The PA gestures for me to enter, then shuts the door as he leaves.

The dressing room is painted a light shade of gray with accents of navy blue. There's a modern gray couch with navy pillows against the wall and a sleek steel-and-glass side table nestled in the corner. On the other side of the room, there's a larger table in the same modern style, this one filled with packaged snacks, a variety of bottled drinks, a pitcher of ice water that's dripping with condensation, two glasses, and a vase filled with flowers. A television is mounted on the wall, but it's switched off.

At the far end of the room, there's a rolling clothing rack with a couple of garment bags hanging on it, both unzipped but not entirely removed from the hangers, like someone had started to open them but stopped. There's a folding screen that I'm assuming is meant to create a private changing area.

The only thing—or rather, person—I don't see in the room is Dax. The room is eerily quiet as I step farther in and set my bag on the floor.

"Dax?" I call softly. No response. Then I notice a foot in a black sock sticking out from behind the folding screen. As I approach, I realize it's Dax. *What the hell is he doing?*

Cautiously, I move closer until I finally make my way around the screen. I find Dax sitting in a chair wearing socks, boxer briefs, and nothing else. He's staring vacantly at the floor. He has one elbow resting on his knee, cradling his head, while the other hand is balled up in a fist that's dropped between his knees. He's sweating and his breathing is fast, faster than it should be.

Shit. Shit. Shit.

I remember him casually mentioning that he has anxiety and occasionally gets panic attacks, but he'd brushed it off as easily as saying he sometimes craves milkshakes.

"Hey, Dax," I say softly, but he doesn't move. I pull up a chair and arrange myself so that I'm sitting directly in front of him, scooting close enough that my knees are on the outsides of his. Tentatively, I reach out and touch his hand—the one in a tight fist—and stroke the back of it softly with the tips of my fingers. I lean in close until my forehead is resting on the top of his head and breathe.

I take long, loud inhales through my nose and similar exhales through my mouth.

In and out. In and out. Over and over.

Is this the right thing to do? Is this even what he needs? I don't know, but it's all I can think of at the moment.

In and out. In and out. Over and over.

I don't say anything, I just breathe. I can't say for sure how long I do this—one minute, five minutes, who knows—but slowly, ever so slowly, his breathing starts to match my own, and his fisted hand starts to relax. Once his fingers are loose enough, I lace them together with mine. I say nothing, do nothing, until I'm sure Dax is back in control of his body.

He takes one long inhale and sits back on the chair, rubbing his eyes with his free hand. He slowly drags his hand down his face and looks at me as if he's only just realized I'm here.

"Hi," I say quietly, giving him a small smile. Dax pulls his other hand from mine and rubs at his sternum.

"Fuuuck. Sorry, hi." His voice is low and rough, like he's been swallowing sand. He clears his throat and shifts in his chair, his knees bumping into mine. I stand, unsure whether he wants me this close, or even if he wants me here at all. We haven't spoken since the day we kissed in the office.

I don't know exactly what I should be doing, so I decide to give Dax a little space. I go to the table of snacks and pour him a glass of icy water, then bring it to him.

"Thanks," he whispers, then takes a long, slow sip, holding the glass with a slightly shaky hand.

"So…" I say, taking the glass from Dax and setting it on the floor. I'm not sure how to phrase what I want to ask him. I don't want to risk upsetting him even more. With a soft voice, I say, "If you want, I could go talk to someone in production. See if they can give you a little extra time? Or, if you don't want to do this…" I trail off.

He looks up suddenly. "No, don't do that. I'm okay." His tone is a bit defensive. "I mean, I'll be okay."

I nod and sit back down in front of him, this time with my legs to one side so I'm not crowding him. I don't ask if he's sure and risk agitating him further. Dax takes my hand and squeezes it, eyes laser-focused on mine.

"Thank you," he whispers.

I'm a deer in headlights, caught in the intensity of his gaze. Dax's eyes are locked with mine for the space of a few heartbeats before he looks around the room.

"I need to get ready," he says, sounding resigned to his fate.

"Well," I say, clapping my palms together. "Then the first thing we should do is get you dressed." I expect Dax to object, but he doesn't. I don't know if he actually wants my help, but he doesn't push me away, so I stay.

Walking around the room, I survey the clothes in the garment bags and see a few pieces of clothes strewn over a chair I hadn't noticed earlier.

"What are you gonna wear?" I ask, not looking at him and instead unzipping one of the bags on the rack.

"I don't know." Dax sounds weary. "I couldn't decide and I started overthinking things and I spiraled from there."

I don't give Dax time to think about what's just happened. We need to keep things moving forward now that he seems to be feeling better.

"Well," I say cheerfully. "You're lucky I'm here. This is my specialty."

"I am," Dax says, getting to his feet. "Lucky you're here, that is."

He joins me next to the rolling rack and I'm suddenly aware of how close he is. Our shoulders lightly brush together and our fingers momentarily graze one another. It's a closeness that feels different than it had a couple minutes ago. The tension in the room had been thick, like a heavy fog. But now, the fog is dissipating and the air between us feels lighter, yet intimate, charged with electricity.

I'm also acutely aware that he's only wearing boxer briefs and socks. When I'd first discovered him sitting here alone, of course I'd noticed his lack of clothing, but I was too scared about what was happening to Dax to take a good look at his body. Getting Dax to calm down had been my only focus. But now, it takes a huge amount of effort to force myself to keep my eyes on the clothes in front of me.

Once I start pulling pieces out of the bags, I'm able to focus. I may not be a professional stylist, but I've worked in men's fashion long enough to pull together an outfit suitable for most occasions. *Speaking of which, why doesn't he have a clothing stylist here to help him?*

I push the hangers around, flipping through several button-down shirts with loud prints, a salmon-pink blazer, a few brightly colored T-shirts, and a variety of other clothes that look like they'd been pulled for someone else entirely. They're all expensive pieces, but nothing that looks like it's even close to what Dax would choose for himself. If he's going to be in the public eye soon, he's going to need some serious fashion help.

"Dude, where's your stylist?" I joke. When he doesn't answer, I turn around to find him staring at the floor.

"Dax?" *Shit.*

"Sorry. I, uh, I asked my publicist to have her friend—who's a fashion stylist—pull some clothes for me. This is what she gave me."

He gestures to the garment bags. I frown. *These came from a stylist? Who did they think they were dressing?*

"When I saw what she'd brought me, I told her I wasn't comfortable wearing any of that." Dax gestures to the garment bags with a sneer of disgust on his face. "Then she told me I could dress myself if I didn't want her help, and she left. That's what caused me to..." He trails off. If I'm going to help him, I need to keep things moving forward.

"Here." I toss him a pair of dark-blue jeans. They're nice and look like they'll be fitted enough they won't look too sloppy, but not so tight as to be able to make out any obvious bulges.

Dax disappears behind the screen like he's suddenly become shy. I almost tell him that he doesn't have to be modest on my account, that I've seen plenty of guys wearing even less while changing on the set of photo shoots. But he doesn't need to hear that right now. Or ever.

"And let's try this." Removing a black button-down shirt from its hanger, I hand it to him. The shirt looks nice, if it weren't for the ridiculously large pink heart in the center. I continue looking for something to wear over the shirt, but can't find what I'm looking for.

"Do you have any plain sweaters in here?" I ask, rummaging through the bags.

He steps out from behind the screen, buttoning the shirt. I have to drag my eyes away from the exposed part of his chest.

"No." He slumps his shoulders like the question has defeated him.

"Okay, no problem," I say in my best reassuring tone, although I have no idea what to give him to wear. But then I look down at the sweater I'm wearing. It would be perfect for this outfit. Without a second thought, I pull it off over my head and hand it to him. "Try this."

Dax looks temporarily stunned, but I give him a *hurry up* gesture and he slides it over his head. I help him arrange the collar of his shirt so that it aligns with the neck of the sweater. He looks at me with eyes that are begging for approval. I take a few steps back, put a finger on my chin, and tilt my head to the side—the same stance I take when I'm working on a photo shoot.

"Well?" Dax asks in a hopeful tone. "Do I look okay?"

I smile. "You look great." He really does.

The sweater, which had been a little loose on me, stretches perfectly across his own chest, showing off toned pecs, biceps, and a lean waist without being too tight. I'd seen how well clothes fit him at the photo shoot, of course, but I'd been looking at him simply as a body on which to put clothes and not as Dax, the man I'd come to have such affectionate feelings for.

"AJ?" Dax asks. How long had I been staring at him? I shake my head to clear my thoughts.

"You look good. Really good. How do you feel?"

"I actually feel okay." If he'd said this ten minutes ago, I wouldn't have believed him, but I do think he's feeling much better. He has more color in his cheeks, which I hadn't noticed had been pale when I first found him sitting in the corner.

A soft knock on the door startles both of us. The door opens a crack and a different PA sticks his head through the door. "Mr. Ximénez? Five minutes, then I'll take you to hair and makeup."

"Thank you," Dax responds.

Once the door is shut, I turn back to Dax.

"Do you have other socks?"

"No. What's wrong with these?" I look down at his feet and frown. They're black and plain, like the kind that come in a pack of six.

"There isn't anything wrong with them, per se. But when you're sitting down with Graham Knight after your set, we'll be able to see your socks. You need something more colorful."

Dax gives me a doubtful look. I scan the room as if some socks will magically appear on the table among the snacks and bottled juices. My eyes zero in on my laptop bag.

"What are you doing?" Dax calls.

"One sec," I reply from the couch, where I'm rifling through my bag. I pull out the socks that Sydney had given me before I left.

"Comin' in hot!" I call to Dax as I toss him the colorful ball.

He catches them and unballs the socks, then gives me an *are you serious?* expression. I hadn't had time to look at them before, but now I see why Dax is making that face. They're an orange-pink color with an argyle pattern.

"Really?" Dax says, sounding put out.

"Yes, really." I'm bent over the pile of clothes, trying to clean up the small mess I've made with all the clothes. I look sideways at him.

"Trust me, okay?"

He relents and puts on the socks, then his black monk strap shoes.

Once he's dressed, Dax steps in front of the full-length mirror and examines himself. He looks gorgeous, and more importantly, he looks confident again and mostly back to his normal, laid-back self. I hope I've done enough to help him so that he'll be able to get through his comedy set.

While Dax is fidgeting with his watch, I sidle up next to him. We look at each other through our reflections in the mirror. The heat of his body is radiating from him, and I want so badly to wrap my arms around his waist, but I resist. Instead, I let my arms drop to my side. Dax adjusts the collar of his shirt, then drops his hand so that our knuckles brush. On instinct, I move my hand toward his and wrap a finger around his pinky and instantly feel him squeezing back. We stay like this for a few moments before he turns away from the mirror to face me.

"AJ," he says. "About the other day—" I hold up my hand.

"Let's talk about it later, okay? You've got a show to do."

"Well, at the very least, I should thank you."

"For what?" I ask.

"For helping me."

"Oh. Well, I didn't do anything. I helped you get dressed, but that's not much."

"It was to me." Dax takes my hand in his. "You literally gave me the shirt off your back."

"I know," I say in a playful tone. "Now I'm gonna have to wear something from your stylist when I sit in the audience. So thanks for that."

Dax smacks my arm and I chuckle, sending a warmth through my chest from this seemingly trivial little interaction.

"Oh," I say. "Sorry if the sweater smells like me. It's October and not really cold enough for cashmere. Plus, I practically ran to get here."

"It does smell like you," Dax says, putting a forearm to his nose and sniffing. "But I like it. It's like having your arms around me." I can feel my cheeks heat all the way up to my ears.

I turn to face Dax and stare into the beautiful sea of his green-gray eyes. What I want most in the world is to kiss him. I grip both of his hands in mine, bringing them to rest against my chest.

"Dax, can I, I mean, is it okay if—" I don't get to finish my question.

"Mr. Ximénez?" A PA opens the door and pokes his head in. This time, I don't drop our hands or spring back at the interruption.

"We're ready for you in hair and makeup." The PA holds his clipboard tightly to his chest. He looks between us but seems thoroughly unimpressed, like he walks in on a scene like this every day.

"I'll walk you down there," he says to Dax.

"Thanks," Dax says. I press a light kiss to his forehead, then let go of his hands.

"Should I go back to my seat?" I ask.

"Sure," the PA says. "Or you can stay here through the whole show if you want. Up to you."

"Is that okay if I go back to my seat?" I ask Dax, hoping he's not interpreting it as me fretting over him.

"Yeah, I'm good. Thanks."

"Break a leg," I say with a wink. Then I lean close and whisper in his ear, "I'll be the one in the front row cheering the loudest."

Dax smiles. It's not the big, full smile I've seen him give me before, but it's enough to convince me that he'll be fine.

The PA speaks into the walkie-talkie clipped to his vest, and within seconds, the young woman who'd been on line-control duty earlier arrives to escort me to my seat.

"We'll be starting in about five minutes." She says this while walking with Olympics-worthy speed through the corridors and back to the studio.

"Have a seat. Turn your phone off." Her voice is curt and she gestures to the only unoccupied seat in the whole audience. The paper with Dax's name printed on it is still taped to the seat. With a thunk, I set my bag on the floor and take out my phone to switch it off.

Once I sit, I notice the two people to my right looking at me. One is a woman of about fifty with a round face and dark hair. Her eyes are the same shape as Dax's—his mom, without a doubt. She gives me a warm, friendly smile but doesn't speak, and I wonder if Dax has told her about me.

Between his mom and me is a young woman who, based on what Dax has said, could only be his sister. She's unabashedly staring at me and beaming.

"Hi," I say with a small smile. "You must be Camila."

"Cam-ee-la." She corrects my pronunciation. "But you can call me Cami. Everybody does." She's squirming in her seat like an excited puppy.

"I'm AJ," I say, offering my hand. She takes it in both of her hands and holds it tightly.

"Hi AJ. Diego told us he invited a friend. He said you're nice. But he told me this morning that you might not come. He tells me things like that so I don't get surprised. You're really tall. Are you older or younger than Diego? I'm younger than him. Ten years younger. How old are you? He said you work at a magazine. That must be fun. What do you do there?"

She launches questions and comments at me like tennis balls, and I can barely keep up. I keep smiling, but not in the forced way that I'd expect myself to do. Her friendly demeanor is infectious and I like her instantly.

Dax's mom leans over and touches Cami's arm. "Mija, let's give Diego's friend some space." She gently removes Cami's hands from mine and sets them back in her lap.

"Oh, sorry." Cami looks thoroughly embarrassed. "I get excited."

"No, don't be sorry. It's great to meet you."

She grins sheepishly. I look past her at Dax's mom.

"Hi," I say, nodding instead of reaching over Cami to shake hands.

"Hi. I'm Alma, Diego's mother."

Her smile is warm and reaches all the way to her eyes, which have wrinkles in the corners from years of joy-filled, smile-worthy moments. Dax has this same smile. It's not the one he shares when he's posing for pictures or interacting with fans. It's one that's heartfelt, filled with sincerity, like it's a secret that he's only sharing with you. He'd smiled at me like that when I'd left him in the dressing room. My heart fills with warmth at the thought.

Once Dax's mother turns her attention back to Cami, I finally acknowledge the other set of eyes that's been boring like lasers into the back of my neck. I slowly turn to the woman on my left.

She has her hair pulled back in a tight bun on top of her head. One of her perfectly groomed eyebrows is cocked up in an arch that would make any villain jealous.

"Hi?" I say in a questioning tone. "AJ Bond." I put my hand out toward her. She takes it in a tight grip and I nearly yelp from the pressure.

"Hannah Jackson." She pauses, either for recognition or dramatic effect.

"Of course, Dax's manager. It's a pleasure to meet you."

She continues to eye me, and I squirm. She finally lets go of my hand, and I can feel a rush of blood returning to my fingers, which had been squeezed like a dishrag.

"How long have you been working with Dax?" I ask in my most friendly tone while trying to discreetly rub my poor hand.

"Two years. But I've known him since college."

"Well, I want to thank you for putting me in touch with him when he, uh, lost his wallet." She knows I'd lied about it. Dax must've told her when the whole social media wallet game had started.

Hannah surprises me by tossing her head back and laughing. "The wallet!" I don't know exactly why she's laughing, but I join in, albeit uncomfortably.

"Listen, AJ." Hannah stops laughing as abruptly as she'd started. "Dax is one of my oldest and closest friends. He's loyal to a fault. He's one of the few people that stuck by me at a time in my life when I needed it the most." Her eyes cut to me. "Did he tell you anything about me?"

"No, he didn't." I pause. "Knowing Dax, I'm sure he knew it wasn't his story to tell."

Hannah nods and gets a look in her eyes as if she's a hundred miles away. "That sounds about right." She sighs, then snaps her eyes back to me. "Look, Dax is a grown man and he can make his own choices."

"I agree," I say, not sure where she's going with this.

"I want what's best for him, and that includes him being with the type of person who sees him for who he is. Not some star fucker who wants him for his potential fame and money. And not someone who's in it to satisfy their curiosity, scratch an itch, or whatever. Do you know what I mean?" She narrows her eyes.

"I do." I nod slowly. "But I promise, that's not—"

"I know, I know. I'm not saying that's what *you're* doing. I hope for his sake that you're here because you really like him. *Him.*"

"Of course. I really do like him." I nod again, more enthusiastically this time.

"Good." She says, before turning her attention back to the stage as we wait for things to get started.

Okay then.

"My friends, please welcome the co-creator and star of the upcoming show, *Mexican't*, the enormously talented Diego 'Dax' Ximénez."

Graham Knight steps away from the camera and it pans over to the section of the set that's set up with a single microphone and a stool with a glass of water, illuminated by a spotlight.

My stomach is in knots. It feels like I'm at the top of a roller coaster at the precise millisecond before plunging into the first descent. I hold my breath and resist the urge to cover my eyes with my hands, hoping to god Dax isn't having another panic attack. I don't care if his jokes aren't that funny, if the laughs aren't sidesplitting. I just want him to be okay.

When Dax walks out onstage to cheers and applause, I can tell right away that I don't need to worry. He's smooth and confident, not second-guessing his words or movements. He looks about a million miles away from the person I'd seen only a little while ago. Dax also looks, well, hot. There's no other way to put it. The clothes look great on him and are the perfect mix of nice, but casual—dressed up, but not trying too hard. There's no hint of sweat on his face and his dark waves of hair have been tamed, but not confined to a shell of gels and hair sprays.

Relief washes over me. Next to me, Cami is bouncing in her seat like she might launch herself up and in front of the cameras at any second. Dax's mom beams with pride. Hannah claps and cheers enthusiastically, and that hard exterior she'd had before the taping began cracks. She looks so proud to be here to cheer her friend on.

Dax waves to the audience and takes the microphone off its stand. He looks our way, but I doubt he can actually see us past all the lights and off-camera production crew.

Then he raises the mic to his mouth and begins to talk.

The show wraps and the general audience files out, while the VIP guests, myself included, mingle in the studio's greenroom. There are a few other people in here—guests of the band that performed after Dax's set and a couple of friends of the host. The room is decorated in much the same style as the dressing rooms, but with a broader assortment of snacks and drinks.

Cami and Alma are chatting with Hannah, while the band and their friends are sipping complimentary mocktails and taking selfies. I'm standing with my back against the wall taking in the scene. If there'd been a dog or cat in the room, I'd be in the corner petting it within seconds. It's pretty much exactly how I am at a party.

When Dax enters the room, Cami nearly tackles him and gives him the tightest bear hug I've ever witnessed. She squeezes him with all of her strength, shutting her eyes tightly. Once Cami releases him from her death grip, he kisses her cheek. She's practically buzzing with excitement. Dax looks much more relaxed than he did earlier, even when he'd calmed down before I left him in the dressing room. I breathe a sigh of relief.

Dax's mom gives him a hug and a kiss on the cheek, and I'm caught off guard by the sweetness of the moment. I feel a tug of longing in my heart for a moment like this with my own mother. She lives an ocean away, so I don't get many opportunities for hugs from her—not that I would even if she lived close. She's never been an affectionate person. My eyes suddenly begin to sting, and I have to blink several times while I look at my phone to distract myself from watching what's clearly an intimate moment for Dax and his family.

Feeling like a voyeur, I decide I should leave them to celebrate as a family. Maybe I'm being a coward. If it weren't for the panic attack earlier, Dax might not have wanted to see me at all.

As I'm slinging my bag over my shoulder, I glance Dax's way. In addition to his family and Hannah, the band and their VIP guests are gathered around him, showering Dax with praise for his performance and taking photos with him. He's halfway across the room and surrounded by people, but his gaze is fixed on me. When our eyes lock, I stop in my tracks. The sight of this man who's just struggled through a really intense moment, then smashed his performance that will be broadcast nationally in a matter of hours, overwhelms me.

"AJ?"

I blink and Dax is in front of me. When did that happen? His brow is furrowed, head cocked to the side, wordlessly asking me a question.

"Hmm?" I say.

"Are you okay? You looked like you were having a moment." Dax's smile is playful but warm.

"Yeah, I'm..." What? *'Happy to see you'* doesn't begin to cover it. I have the urge to give Dax a hug that might rival Cami's. "You were amazing. No. You *are* amazing."

Dax raises his eyebrows in surprise and I can feel heat rising to my cheeks. *God, I sound like such a fanboy.* I worry he's going to laugh at me, but he doesn't. Instead, he leans toward me and puts his lips close to my ear.

"Give me five minutes. Don't leave." The words are barely audible as they leave Dax's lips. Then he gives me a quick kiss next to my ear, leaving my entire body covered in goosebumps.

He goes around the room—shaking hands and patting backs—saying goodbye to everyone. I follow Dax, his family, and Hannah out of the studio and back out onto the sidewalk, where the air has gotten chillier in the hours since I'd been in the studio. As Dax hugs Hannah, I see her eyeing me over his shoulder. It's not quite threatening, but not quite *not* threatening either. She says a quick goodbye to me—making sure to give me an extra firm handshake—then gets in a cab and is gone.

A car pulls up, apparently having been called for Dax's family. Dax gives his mom and Cami another round of hugs before ushering Cami to the car. But before she gets in, she makes a U-turn and comes back to hug me, almost as tightly as she'd hugged Dax.

"Bye, AJ," she says.

"Bye, Camila," I say, making sure I get the pronunciation right. "It was fun sitting next to you today."

His mom says goodbye to me, then escorts Cami back to the car. Dax puts the garment bags into the trunk, and I'm expecting him to give me a quick goodbye before going home with this family. But he doesn't.

He leans into the open door of the car, says something I can't quite hear to his mom, then shuts the door. Watching the car drive away, Dax and I are left alone on the sidewalk.

Turning to me, a smile slowly spreads across his lips.

"Mind if I join you?" he asks.

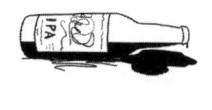

CHAPTER 15

DAX

I hope I haven't been too presumptuous in assuming that AJ would want me to come with him after the show. I was afraid my panic attack in the dressing room had scared him away for good, but he stayed. And he's still here now.

The other side of that, of course, is that I hope he doesn't feel like he has to take care of me or walk on eggshells now that he's seen that side of me. In the past, the guys I've dated have fallen into three distinct categories: the ones who can't deal with my anxiety and leave, the ones who give me pitying looks and tiptoe around me, and the ones who try to fix me. It's the whole reason I try hard not to reveal my anxiety to people I'm dating. But sometimes, like today, life happens, and there's nothing I can do about it.

Sure, AJ had taken care of me, but he didn't treat me like I was going to fall to pieces. Afterward, he didn't look at me like he felt sorry for me. And he hadn't left. So does that leave him in the third category? I guess time will tell.

"Where are you headed?" I ask, still standing on the corner in front of the studio with AJ.

"I was actually thinking about getting dinner," he says. "I abandoned my lunch in the microwave at work, so I haven't eaten since breakfast."

"Thank god. I'm starving." I realize I haven't eaten since dinner last night, and even then, I'd only picked at my food, too nervous to eat a full meal. "Let's go."

We walk a block or two in silence, the only conversation consisting of AJ asking if I want whatever type of food is offered at each restaurant as we pass.

"Chinese? ... Brazilian? ... Pizza?"

We're nearing Times Square, and the bright glow of the lights mixed with the onslaught of people—most of them tourists—begins to make me feel exhausted. I'm hit with a sudden feeling like I'm dragging a hundred-pound bag of wet sand behind me. My legs feel leaden. I'd barely slept last night due to nerves about today, and once the adrenaline of the show—and let's not forget my massive panic attack—had faded away, I'm left utterly wiped out.

Realizing I've slowed to a near stop, AJ slows to match my pace. He doesn't ask what's wrong or if I'm okay, though I know he wants to. He stays right next to me.

When it's clear I'm having trouble making decisions, AJ finally stops.

"What sounds good to you?" AJ's voice is gentle.

I look around, taking in my options: crowded pizza shop, crowded Mexican restaurant, crowded seafood restaurant...

"Actually, I don't care what we eat," I say, feeling resigned. "I just want to go somewhere quiet. Is that okay with you?"

AJ nods. "Of course it's okay." He puts a hand on my shoulder and gives me an affectionate squeeze. "Whatever you want."

"Sorry I'm not very good company."

"Dax, don't you dare apologize." AJ nudges my chin up to look at him. "You've had a huge day. You shouldn't feel like you have to be *on*."

"I know, but I invited myself to go with you, and now I'm acting like a wet blanket. I should be celebrating, but I'm so tired after this day. It's all hitting me at once, you know?" I can feel myself starting to talk faster, my words coming out without my permission. "I wasn't thinking when I asked to come with you, only that I wanted to spend more time with you tonight. You know, since we didn't really get a chance to talk earlier. And—"

I expect AJ to do or say something incredibly sweet, maybe to kiss me. Instead he laughs and shakes his head, then steps around me toward the curb and puts his hand up for a cab.

"Where are you going?" I ask, trying not to sound too desperate. *He's leaving. Of course he is. I've scared him off.*

A taxi slows to a stop in front of us. AJ turns to face me, then reaches out with gentle hands, and I think he's about to cup my face. Instead, he carefully adjusts the collar of my shirt, and at the brush of his fingers against the underside of my jaw, the gesture somehow feels much more intimate.

"*We* are getting in this cab and going to my apartment. We're going to order takeout and eat dinner sitting on the rug in my living room. We'll have a beer, or at least I will. I bought some of those fruity cider things that you like. Then we'll kiss each other goodnight and go to sleep. Okay?"

Holy shit.

This may be the most effective *let's go back to my place* line in the entire history of *let's go back to my place* lines. A moment ago, I could barely take another step, but I'm suddenly energized all over again. Telling me he'd bought me some fruity cider things shouldn't be the sexiest thing he's said to me all day—and that includes him telling me I'm amazing not that long ago—but yet, here we are. When did he even buy them?

I practically push AJ into the cab and shove him over to get myself in as quickly as possible. We end up in a tangle of legs and arms as he tries to scoot over. Once we're on our way, I lean into AJ, sliding my hand up his thigh while trying to maul his neck with my mouth.

He casually turns his face away and takes my hand in his, effectively cockblocking me in the back seat.

"Seat belt," he whispers to me. *Damn him.* I should've known he'd be too uptight for taxi cab shenanigans.

Trying not to feel rejected, I flop back to my side in a huff, buckling my seat belt as loudly as I can, then fold my arms like a petulant child. AJ reaches over and practically forces my hand away from my chest and laces his fingers through mine. I lean back against the seat, rolling my head to the side to face AJ. He's looking out the window as we speed through the streets toward Brooklyn, his thumb softly stroking my knuckles in small circles.

AJ's gentle touches and the rhythmic rocking of the car must have lulled me to sleep before we crossed the bridge, because the next thing I know, he's gently nudging me awake. Without a word, I clumsily roll out of the cab and follow him into his building, then up the stairs to his apartment.

We do pretty much exactly what AJ said we'd do: ordering pizza and eating on the floor, AJ with a beer and me with a fruit cider. We're both leaning against the couch, legs outstretched on the rug with the pizza box between us. We're using actual dinner plates instead of the cheap paper ones that came with the pizza because, well, AJ insists. Something about the grease soaking through onto the carpet or whatever. I'm too tired to listen. I'm also much too tired to try for witty banter. AJ seems to respect that, because he doesn't say much, so we eat in near silence. It's a comfortable silence, like we've done this a thousand times before.

When I've had my fill of pizza, I turn to AJ and notice he's stopped eating and is lazily sipping his beer. I set my plate on the floor and scoot toward him so that our shoulders are touching, our legs still on opposite sides of the pizza box.

AJ turns to look at me, and although he'd said he had no intention of anything happening between us tonight other than sleeping, his eyes are betraying him. They're dark and wanting. I catch him glancing at my mouth, then back to my eyes once, twice.

Without a word, I move the box to the side and scoot closer, our bodies touching from shoulder to ankle—well, my ankle anyway, his legs are longer than mine. I rest my head on his shoulder and let myself relax.

We sit like this for a minute before I take the beer from AJ's hand and set it on the floor. I reach up and comb my fingers through the short hair on the back of his head and stare at his profile, admiring how handsome he is. He's got a shadow of light stubble that lines his jaw. As my fingers comb through his hair, I watch his eyelids become heavy and start to close. He leans his head back, sinking into my touch. I lightly tickle his neck with my fingertips, causing him to shiver, his breath becoming shaky. A zing of excitement rushes through me and I sit up straighter, turning myself so that we're almost face-to-face. Placing a hand on his chest, I can feel his heart pounding beneath my palm.

He tips his head to the side so that his lips are lightly brushing my forehead.

"Dax," he whispers raggedly. Electricity tingles over my entire body at the sound of my name on his lips.

I'm still at a slightly lower angle than AJ, so instead of kissing his lips, I glide my mouth over the underside of his jaw, dotting it with kisses and warm breaths. His body responds instantly, hands moving down my sides with purpose. He grips my hips and pulls me with surprising strength over his legs so that I'm straddling his lap.

"Hi there," he says. From this position, I'm taller than him, so this time, it's AJ who's smiling up at me.

"Hi," I say. "Do you mind if I just..." I remove his glasses, folding them carefully and setting them on the couch behind us.

I don't kiss him yet. I look at his face, memorizing the exact shade of his eyes. I don't think I've seen him without his glasses until now. I must be staring stupidly at his face for far too long because he clears his throat.

"Uh, Dax?"

"Sorry, I'm... I was just looking at you. You're beautiful. Have I told you that?" I lean down and whisper into his neck.

AJ shifts like he's trying to hide his face, but since I'm basically sitting on him, the movement sends a jolt of heat through me.

"No," AJ says, gripping my hips tighter. "I don't think anyone's ever called me beautiful before."

"Shame." I press a small kiss to the corner of his mouth. "You should hear it more often."

AJ lets out a small sigh and pushes his hips up as he pulls me closer to him, causing unexpected—but not unwelcome—friction between us. My eyes go wide when I feel him stiffening against me and my own body responds instantly.

He leans in to kiss my lips, but I lean back slightly, just out of his reach. I lick my lips, then give him another chaste kiss, this time to the spot in front of his ear. I'm rewarded with another light thrust of his hips as he pulls me forward. When he tries to kiss me again, I lean away. Again. He makes a frustrated sound, and I press my face to his neck to stifle a silent laugh.

"You're enjoying teasing me, aren't you?" AJ is almost growling.

"Of course I am." I smile at him, but he doesn't smile back. The look in his eyes is pure want. The whiskey brown of his eyes is barely visible around his wide, black pupils. He removes a hand from my hip and takes my jaw in a soft grip, pulling my face toward his. It's not forceful or possessive but determined. He's moving with purpose.

And then his lips are on mine. The kiss isn't soft or timid. This is the kiss of someone who wants it, someone who's been waiting for it. It's not just lips, but tongues, teeth, breath. *God.* AJ isn't the only one who's been waiting for it.

I lean in, letting my whole body settle into his as we kiss. I hadn't realized I'd been sitting up on my knees slightly so as not to put my full body weight on AJ's lap. But I let go, sinking my hips into his and grinding lazily against him. He responds with a quiet but satisfying groan.

"You like this," I say, neither of us stopping the rhythm of our bodies against one another.

"Obviously." AJ is almost panting now. "Come here."

He slides his hands up my back and pulls my entire torso toward his so that we're chest to chest. I tip my head back, giving AJ an open invitation to kiss my neck. He glides his tongue over my throat, then moves upward, first nipping the underside of my jaw before pressing a hot, breathy kiss to the tender pulse point on my neck, leaving a trail of goose bumps in its wake.

"Jesus, AJ." I can barely speak.

I try to adjust myself, certain that at some point, I'm going to lose all sensation in my feet with the way my legs are folded to sit on his lap. It's a graceless move to get them out from under me, and as I'm stretching one leg out to wrap it around AJ's waist, I kick the beer bottle that I'd set on the floor next to him.

The sound of beer fizzing as it spills onto the floor is impossible to ignore. I'm hoping AJ will leave it, but I should know by now that he can't. I could tell he'd let himself loosen up a bit by eating on the floor, but this seems to be one step over the line.

"Shit," AJ says, wiggling out from under me, practically dumping me on the carpet next to him, and jumping to his feet with impressive speed.

"Sorry," I say. I try to get up, but my feet have nearly lost all sensation from the lack of circulation.

"No, it's fine," he calls from the kitchen. "It's mostly on the hardwood. But I need to clean it up before it seeps under the rug."

I'm rubbing my feet vigorously to try to get the blood back into them. I'm afraid if I stand to try and help, the pins and needles feeling will cause me to crumple back to the floor in a heap.

Towel in hand, AJ kneels in front of the couch and starts to wipe up the mess. He seems irritated, probably because he's having to clean up after me. Again.

Shit. This whole day has been AJ taking care of me.

"I'm really sorry," I say softly. "I can clean it up." I hold my hand out, offering to take the towel from him.

"Don't be sorry. I'm not mad, I promise."

"Are you sure?" I ask, not quite believing him.

"Yeah." He sits up on his knees and glances over at me. I must look like a child, sitting on the floor with my knees pulled up to my chest.

"It's just...it's a shame we had to stop. I was enjoying, uh, that." AJ's cheeks turn a slightly darker shade of pink.

"Mmm. Me too." I give him a small smile.

AJ goes back to cleaning up the spill, then stands, taking the towel and bottle to the kitchen. I'm finally able to get up without my legs turning to jelly, so I follow him. He turns, clearly surprised to find me standing so close. Leaning in, he kisses me on the cheek and rubs small circles on my shoulders with his hands.

"Dax." He says it so simply and so quietly. "In the second drawer of my dresser, there are T-shirts. And sweatpants too, if you want. Go make yourself comfortable. I'll meet you in bed in a few minutes."

"You aren't going to come with me? Help me get dressed?" I ask playfully before I have a chance to think about what I've just asked. He'd done exactly that, albeit in an entirely different context, earlier in the day. I hate to remind him of how much I'd needed his help as much as I hate to remind myself.

"Maybe pick up from where we left off?" I try to change the direction of his thoughts, and mine, as quickly as possible.

"I need to clean up the dishes and get ready for bed. Then I'll be in."

"Leave the dishes." I protest. "I'll help you wash them in the morning."

"Dax, this is an apartment building in New York City. If I leave food out, I'll get mice. Go lie down and get comfortable. I'll be in soon." He kisses me on the forehead and walks past me toward the living room.

"Fine," I grumble while heading to the bathroom. "Do you have an extra toothbrush?"

"Bottom drawer."

I open the drawer and find at least six toothbrushes still in the packaging. I pick out a pink brush and open it.

"Why do you have so many toothbrushes?" I call over my shoulder.

"I get them from my dentist every time I go. They're fine, but I have a specific kind I like, so I keep those for emergencies."

"Do you get a lot of toothbrush emergencies?" I'd meant it as a joke, but I don't think I want to know if the answer is 'yes'.

As if he can tell the direction of my thoughts, AJ stops washing and turns off the water.

"Dax, if you're asking if I have a lot of overnight guests, the answer is no. You're the first person to use one of my dentist-approved emergency toothbrushes."

He turns the water back on and continues washing the dishes. I smile to myself.

Once I'm dressed in AJ's T-shirt and sweatpants—both a little too small—I scurry under the duvet of his neatly made bed, lean back against the headboard, and wait for AJ. The chilly fall air that's seeped in through the slightly open window makes me shiver, so I reluctantly get up and take the blanket that's slung over the back of a chair and toss it onto the bed. I figure as soon as AJ joins me, we'll both warm up once we resume our earlier activities.

I burrow deeper under the covers, my face barely visible, and finally let myself relax thoroughly. Closing my eyes, I take a few deep, calming breaths. And I wait.

CHAPTER 16

AJ

I wake up early enough that the first rays of sun are barely starting to make their way into my room. The first thing I notice is that my glasses aren't on the table next to the bed where they usually are. The second is that Dax is gone.

He'd been exhausted last night, and I knew that the last thing he'd needed was to stay up even later, despite both of us being one-hundred percent into what we were doing before the spilled beer. I hadn't wanted to stop, and neither had he, so despite it being an accident, it was probably for the best that fate intervened and gave us a reason to. I knew that if I'd sent him to get ready for bed, it would be likely that he'd fall asleep before I got there. And I was right. I figured we'd have more chances to do…whatever we were heading toward last night.

When I'd finally gone to bed, the image of Dax curled up under a mountain of blankets, his hair a mess on the pillow, taking soft, even breaths was enough to pull at my heartstrings. I didn't dare wake him up. I resisted the urge to snuggle with him or even to touch him, only giving him a light kiss on the forehead before going to sleep on my side of the bed.

But now, looking at the empty side of the bed where Dax had slept, I wonder if not waking him up, not touching him, had been a mistake. Had he interpreted the gesture—letting him sleep—as rejection? Or had he simply changed his mind about me?

I haul myself out of bed and make my way to the living room, retrieving my glasses from the couch where Dax had set them last night. I look around for any signs of him. His clothes and shoes are gone, except for the gray cashmere sweater—the one I'd lent him yesterday. I check my phone, but no messages.

Well, shit.

I sink into a barstool and set my head in my hands, raking my fingers through my hair. A tightness begins to form in my chest.

Two minutes or ten minutes later—I really can't say how long—there's a rattling of keys in the lock of my front door, followed by a few choice expletives.

I don't bother with the peephole, since it's been painted over at least a dozen times—the landlord's version of apartment renovation. Flinging the door open, I find Dax trying to balance two coffee cups in one hand, keys in the other, and a small, but heavy-looking, white paper bag clutched between his teeth. For a moment, I'm stunned, then relieved.

"Help, please?" Dax says through clenched teeth. I quickly grab the bag, then take one of the cups of coffee. He follows me in, then tosses the keys on the kitchen island—which I promptly hang back on the hook by the door.

He's wearing my winter beanie, pulled low, nearly covering his eyebrows. He's also wearing my black hoodie that I should've noticed was missing from the hook on the back of the door. And my sweatpants.

"Good morning," he says, smiling brightly. When he's finally settled, he looks up at me and his smile drops. "Everything okay?"

I nod, exhaling. "Yeah. I thought…"

Dax's eyebrows furrow. "You thought I left, didn't you?"

"Yeah.." I scrub my fingers over the back of my neck, embarrassed for worrying about nothing. Of course he'd come back. Why had I thought he wouldn't?

"I did leave," he says, then winks at me. "To get breakfast."

"But it's so early. I thought you'd want to sleep in. You were so tired last night."

"AJ, you do realize we went to bed at nine-thirty?" Then he shoots me a pointed look. "At least, *I* did."

He opens the white paper bag and begins to take out what seems like an unnecessary number of food items wrapped in foil.

"I didn't know what you liked, so I got bacon, egg, and cheese sandwiches, and two bagels—one with butter and one with cream cheese."

I can't help but grin. "I'll take a sandwich." Dax smiles cheerfully and hands me one, then opens one of his own. "Thanks."

"I got you a coffee too, but I didn't know how you take it, so I just got it like mine, with cream and sugar."

"Thank you," I say, reaching out and taking a cup.

"Now that I think about it, I bet you like your coffee black, don't you?" Dax asks, pulling the cup back toward him before I can get a hand on it.

"Usually," I say, moving into Dax's personal space. I wrap my hand over his so we're both holding onto the cup. I lean in and put my mouth close to his ear. "But I like to treat myself now and then," I whisper. I bring the cup—and Dax's hand—to my mouth and take a sip of the warm, sweet coffee I didn't know I was craving until now.

"Mmm, sweet," I say, releasing his hand.

He sets my cup on the island before picking up his own coffee.

"Cheers," he says, raising his cup to me.

I sit on a barstool to eat while Dax uncovers half of his sandwich, the foil folded down to cover the half that he's holding. I try not to watch for dropped crumbs as he walks around, taking in my apartment in the light of day.

He looks at the books and knickknacks on the mantle of my useless fireplace, occasionally pulling something off the shelf then putting it back. He stares in awe at the bookcase that's completely filled with magazines, all neatly organized.

Dax gives me a sidelong glance. "Are you going to be one of those people who lives in the same apartment for forty years and collects so many magazines and newspapers there won't be any room to walk and you'll end up living in your kitchen?"

"A hoarder? No. I don't let myself have more than will fit on the shelf. When the shelves get too full, I get rid of some."

"But why so many?" Dax asks through a mouthful of sandwich.

"In addition to magazines being my job? Because I like them. Some I like to read, some I like to look at. Some have great photography, some have great design. I like them for different reasons."

This seems to satisfy Dax. Or maybe he doesn't feel like hearing me go on and on about magazines. To most people, it's probably a dull subject to talk about. Dax nods and moves on, taking another bite of his sandwich.

He stops and points to a framed photo on the shelf above the desk. "Is this your mom?"

I look up at the photo. "Yeah, that was taken in Mannheim, Germany. That's where she lives."

I remember when we took that photo. It was from when I'd visited her two years ago—the last time I saw her in person. She wasn't too pleased about the idea of taking a selfie with me. She's always had a hard exterior and didn't see the need to do anything that didn't serve a specific purpose or have a productive outcome. Photos of oneself for fun don't make sense to her. But I'd finally convinced her to take one, telling her that I wanted a recent photo to put in my apartment. I guess that had been a good enough reason. Her smile was hard and tight-lipped.

"It must be hard to be so far away from your mom," Dax remarks, still looking at the photo. "Are the two of you close?"

"No, not really."

"Oh, sorry." He turns to look at me, a look of regret, or maybe pity, washing over his face.

"Don't be." I say. "We get along fine, but we're not close. She's been in Germany since I went away to college. Mannheim is where she grew up. It's where I was born."

"Really?"

"Yeah, we moved to America when I was five." I'm quiet, and Dax lets the subject drop. He always seems to sense when I don't want to elaborate and I appreciate that he doesn't press me to keep talking.

I ball up the foil from my sandwich and toss it in the trash, then move to stand next to Dax as he continues to peruse the other photos on the shelf. I tell him about each one as he goes from one photo to the next. There's one of André, Takashi, and me in front of the Eiffel Tower—the one time I went to men's fashion week in Paris. There's one of me and my cousin Mia at the Statue of Liberty when she came from Germany to visit.

"Who's this?" Dax asks, pointing to another photo. "Another cousin?"

"No, that's Sam." It was about a month into our second try at a relationship. We'd taken a selfie in Prospect Park during a snowstorm.

"Sam? As in Sam, your ex who you're still friends with?"

"Yeah...?" I say, noticing a slight bristle in Dax's voice.

He's frowning but still looking at the photo.

"What's this for?" I ask, running a finger over the line that's appeared between his eyebrows.

"I thought..." He can't seem to get the words out. "When you talked about Sam, I didn't realize she was a *she*."

"I told you about her. Why do you seem surprised?" Now it's my turn to furrow my brow in confusion.

"You told me about your ex, Sam. You never said *her* or *she*. I assumed you meant *Sam* as in *Samuel*."

I twist my lips in thought. Had I omitted that detail? If I had, it wasn't on purpose. "Are you sure? I *must* have."

"No. That's something I'd remember."

"Oh. Well, I promise you, I wasn't trying to hide it. Is it a problem? That I've dated women, I mean?"

"No, of course not. Surprising, I guess." Then Dax takes a moment before speaking again. "Actually, that's not entirely true. That first night after the photo shoot, I didn't think you were gay. But then you went and kissed me the next day, so...?"

"I guess you could say I'm somewhere on the spectrum. I've had more experience with women—dating and sex and all that. But I've kissed a few guys too."

"So you're an 'I like the wine, not the label' kind of person?"

I laugh. "I guess so. I never really think about it in terms of what I call myself. I was with Sam for so long and then mostly with women after that. And for the last couple of years, I haven't really been with anyone." I shrug.

I know it seems like I'm being flippant about my sexuality, but I don't know what else to say. The truth is that I've always thought of myself as *mostly straight* but with an open mind if the right person comes along, but saying it out loud sounds too simplistic. Growing up, the portrayal I'd seen of bisexual people on television or in books was usually someone who was into men and women—and *only* men or women—equally. They'd go from one to the other like a pendulum. The label of *bisexual* didn't really seem to fit me. I didn't easily gravitate toward men the way I did with women, but I also didn't rule out men—or anyone for that matter—because of their gender identity.

After months, maybe years, of overthinking, I finally quit worrying about what label to give to myself and figured it was no one else's goddamned business anyway.

"So being with me isn't to satisfy a curiosity about dating a—"

"Comedian?" I ask, laughing. "Maybe a little."

He gives me a playful shove, and I pinch him on the arm.

"You know," I say, my smile dropping, "Hannah said something similar yesterday. She's worried that I'm 'scratching an itch' as she put it. Or that I'm some kind of star fucker."

"Are you?" Dax asks in a light tone, but I suspect there's some weight to it.

"Oh, please. I work at a fashion magazine. If I were interested in sleeping with a celebrity, regardless of gender, I probably could've done it already."

Actually, there's no *probably* about it. I've been propositioned a few times over the years. Some celebrities can get very comfortable (and very bored) on the set of photo shoots. But I don't say any of that out loud.

"Is that so?" Dax raises his eyebrows, either in mock suspicion or actual suspicion, I can't tell. I respond by pulling him to me and giving him a long, firm kiss. I pull my face back just enough to tip his chin up with my finger.

"Listen. I like you for you. You're funny and kind. And you have excellent taste in breakfast sandwiches." I slide a hand around and comb the short hair on the back of his neck with the tips of my fingers.

Dax sighs and burrows his head in my neck, pressing featherlight kisses along my collarbone.

"I don't know. You might have to do a little more work to convince me." He lightly draws a line from my hand to my shoulder with the tip of his finger, causing me to shiver. He does it again, this time with a bit more pressure on the inside of my elbow. Purely by reflex, I grab his wrist as I laugh from being tickled in such a sensitive spot.

"Oh, you're ticklish?" Dax's face turns from sweet to pure evil.

"No, I'm not." Yes, I am.

I back away from Dax, but he advances quickly, fingers curled and ready.

"Don't you dare," I say.

I bolt toward the couch, but Dax is fast and he manages to catch my arm. I flail wildly and pull away, making a beeline for my bedroom and tossing a pillow at him on the way. He sidesteps the pillow, but it slows him down enough that I'm able to make it into my room. He steps into the doorframe at the same moment I realize I've boxed myself in. No escape.

Showing no mercy, Dax charges at me, and I fall back on the bed. Despite being shorter than me, he's much stronger, and I'm no match for him when he tackles me. I don't make it easy though, kicking and squirming as he starts tickling my ribs and stomach. We're tangled together, wrestling, until he ends up straddling my hips and pinning my arms over my head.

"Mercy?" he asks, his breath barely above normal. Meanwhile, I'm panting like I've just run up five flights of stairs.

"Yes. Please."

We both stop laughing at the exact same moment. His normally green-gray eyes darken and we're both sweating from tickle-wrestling. He doesn't loosen his grip on my wrists.

I stare at him, helpless while he waits, watching me. *God, help me.* Looking up at him like this makes my brain nearly short-circuit. I can't reach to kiss him, so instead, I buck my hips under him, only once to gauge his reaction.

With wide eyes, he reciprocates with a roll of his own hips, grinding his body into mine. An embarrassing gasp escapes my lips. I thrust my hips upward again, and again, Dax responds in an equally satisfying way.

It's not long before we're basically dry humping on my bed, both of us fully clothed, searching frantically for gratification purely through friction. We're not kissing, but watching each other, turned on by each other's obvious want.

When Dax finally lets go of my hands, I make a valiant, albeit graceless, attempt to gain the upper hand by trying to roll him over and pin him. He laughs and pretends to be overcome by my strength, flopping onto his back. I act like this was a result of my own physical prowess, straddling Dax and flexing my biceps in triumph. I grab his wrists and press them into the mattress on either side of his head.

"Okay," he says in a low, gravelly voice. "You've got me. Now what?"

Triumph quickly dissolves when I realize I've made a huge error in judgment. I don't have the first clue of what to do. I want Dax to take the lead again. He doesn't.

When it comes to sex with women, I feel confident in myself to know what I'm doing. At least, I know enough to be able to satisfy my partner. I have Sam to thank for that—for being patient and willing to teach me.

But with Dax, everything feels new. Technically speaking, it is. I've kissed men, and even had a few sloppy hand jobs here and there, but those had been a long time ago, before I knew what it really meant to connect with someone on such an emotional level.

Sitting on top of Dax, I decide to go for it. In for a penny...

I make a few grinding movements with my hips. Dax seems to not be terribly put off by the effort, so I keep going. I release one of his wrists and reach between us, awkwardly fumbling to put my hand down his pants. I accidentally snap the waistband of his pants hard against his stomach while trying to maneuver my hand. I try again, my hand nervously shaking. I've lost all hope of trying to be sexy and focus on trying to not completely embarrass myself. I can tell he's watching me because he's gone stock-still.

I continue groping gracelessly until he brings one hand down and puts it on mine. I freeze.

"AJ?" Dax's voice is soft.

I don't move. I'm nervous and mortified, wishing I could bury my face in the pillow. I can't because, of course, I'm still straddling Dax.

I can barely even look at him, afraid all of my inexperience will show on my face. It's like I'm reliving the moment I'd first grabbed his hand in the kitchen—so far out of my comfort zone, hoping he'll give me some clue as to what I should do next.

He waits for me to look at him; I can feel my cheeks burning. When I finally meet his gaze, there's not any trace of judgment. His eyes are softer now; a small smile is on his lips.

"What's going on?" He uses his other hand, the one not still covering mine, and gently slides it over my thigh, not in a sexual way, but in more of a soothing way. I can't help but think of what a pathetic scene this must be from his perspective. But his face doesn't show even an ounce of pity. He looks...sweet. *Damn him.*

"What do you mean?" I ask, knowing it's a stupid question. Clearly there's something going on.

"I mean," he shifts under me, "you seem really nervous."

"I'm not!" I am. I totally am.

His face changes to something darker, like he's heard bad news.

"Is it that you've changed your mind about me? If you have, that's okay. Just tell me."

"No, that's not it. At. All." I make sure to emphasize each word.

Dax seems relieved. Then something else passes over his face. Something like...understanding.

"I know you said you have more experience with women than men when it comes to sex. But do you have any experience *at all* with guys?"

My face is already hot from embarrassment, and I'm not sure it can get any more red, but it's trying. I swing my leg over and flump down on the bed next to Dax.

"A little," I say, my voice sounding small.

I try to turn my head, but he puts a hand on my chin, preventing me from looking away. He's quiet for a long time before he finally says, "Talk to me, Goose."

I unexpectedly laugh out loud. "You know," I say, "Sam said the exact same thing to me yesterday."

"Yeah? I hope it wasn't while you two were in bed," he says. He's kidding, of course. I think.

"No. We were talking about you, actually."

"Oh, really?" Dax props himself up on one elbow.

"I told her about you and me. She's the one who convinced me to go to *The Knightly Show* to talk to you."

"Well, I should thank her," Dax says, and I don't think he's kidding. He goes quiet again. Seconds tick by and neither of us says anything.

"So..." Dax says.

"Hmm?" I ask, knowing exactly what he's waiting for.

"Look, if you don't want to talk about this," he gestures between us, "I won't make you. We should be able to be open with each other. You don't have to tell me your life story, but I'd like to know what's going on."

I sigh, then lie down next to him, stretching out on my back so I'm looking at the ceiling. And I start to talk. "I wasn't lying when I told you I've had a little experience with guys. But most of it was with one guy in particular."

"Ex-boyfriend?" Dax asks.

"Not exactly. It was this guy, Stefan. He was an exchange student from Germany when I was a senior in high school—back when I was still living in Philadelphia. So, yeah. It was a while ago." I turn my head toward Dax. "Don't do the math. It's depressing to know how many years it's been since then."

"Okay, okay. Go on."

"Stefan was the opposite of me in every way. Well, almost every way. He was cool, laid-back, outgoing, athletic. Everything I wasn't. I was a quiet, comic-book-loving, artsy nerd. Everyone liked him. Guys thought he was cool, girls thought he was sexy. On the first day of school, he sat next to me in calculus class. We were supposed to have a pencil, but Stefan only had a pen. I told him he could borrow one of mine, only I said it in German."

"Smooth," Dax says, and I laugh. "I didn't know you speak German."

"Yeah. My mom speaks English, but she only speaks to me in German, always has. Stefan was surprised, obviously. I think my classmates were too. I never spoke German at school.

"Anyway, after that, we became friends. He became my best friend. It was nothing romantic or sexual, at least not at first. I'd invite him to my house to study or to play video games, we'd hang out, sit together at lunch, that kind of thing. He was the only friend I'd ever had who was allowed to come to my house. My mom didn't want to be responsible for other people's kids, so she wouldn't let me have friends over. But she liked Stefan—you know, being German and all.

"And then one day, he told me he wanted to see some band that was playing in New York City. I had no interest in seeing the band, but it sounded like a fun adventure. I made up some lie about a senior class trip to see the Met. He'd told his host family he was going on a senior camping trip. We took the bus and stayed with some friend of a friend of his. I never knew exactly whose place it was.

"On the ride home, we were sitting together on the bus, talking, like always. And then Stefan started kissing me. At first, I was surprised. I'd never thought of him *that* way and I didn't know he thought of me like that. I thought I would, or should, feel weird about it, but I didn't. It felt normal—nice even. From there, we started making out with each other sometimes—mostly kissing and some light touching. We'd do it at my house after school, or we'd sneak off during study hall. And then one time at my house, my mom was working late, so we—"

I can feel Dax's eyes on me. "Go on," he says softly. "Or don't. You don't have to tell me."

"He gave me a, uh, a blow job." *God.* I can feel my face heating. "It was the first one ever for me. Him too, I think. I didn't give him one back. I just, you know, used my hand.

"The next day at school, we were talking by our lockers and he tried to kiss me. I asked him to stop and said we couldn't do that in school. I needed to figure things out for myself first. I said we could be together after school, but that I wasn't ready for people at school to know yet. To be honest, I was the most worried about my mom hearing about it. I wasn't sure how she'd react. Stefan acted like I'd slapped him. He said he didn't want to wait for me to get over my 'gay revelation', as he called it. And then he turned around and walked away. That was it.

"A couple days later, he started dating a girl that I'd told him I had a crush on—this was before Stefan and I started our...whatever you call it. I know he did it to spite me because he'd always look at me when he'd hold her hand or touch her. It didn't last. He went through a string of girlfriends, and a couple of guys too. They never lasted more than a few weeks. And he and I ended up avoiding each other the rest of the year.

"After our graduation ceremony, when everyone was still standing around, making plans for parties and all that, he walked right up to me in front of all of our classmates and friends. And he kissed me. Not like a peck on the lips either, a real kiss. Passionate as fuck. And then he left without saying a word. I guess he went to a graduation party or whatever, and I went home. That was that. I heard he went back to Germany a couple days later, and that was the last I heard about him."

"Well, shit," Dax says when I'm done. "That's not what I was expecting. At all."

"What were you expecting?" I finally roll over to face him.

"I dunno, drunken college party shenanigans or something."

"Well, I went to a small art school. It wasn't really a keggers and orgies type of place. Well, maybe there were orgies, but I never knew about them."

"Shame."

I laugh. "Since then, I've dated a few guys, but it's never really gone beyond kissing and hand jobs. Nothing meaningful. Not like this." *Oh shit. Oh shit.* I say it before my brain has a chance to edit my words. "I mean..."

But Dax already knows what I mean. And I don't want to take it back or imply that I don't mean it. I do. I hadn't quite planned on saying it out loud, at least not yet.

"I know," Dax says, then threads his fingers through mine. He leans over and presses a soft kiss to the corner of my mouth.

"Well. There you have it." I say it a little too loudly. "AJ Bond's complete sexual history with men. I can fill you in on the rest of my history with women, if you're interested."

"No thanks. I'm good," he says, sitting up.

"Where are you going?"

"Nowhere. I need to tell you this without getting distracted."

"Okay..." My stomach churns nervously over what Dax is about to say.

"I like you, AJ. I think you know that. This is meaningful to me too. But I don't want to push you to do anything you're not ready for. I won't. So if you want to be with me, we need to be open and honest with each other. You need to tell me what you're ready for, or what you're not ready for. Okay? I can be patient."

I nod like an obedient child.

"If we're...being intimate..." Dax says.

I snort-laugh.

"Okay, okay. If we're gettin' freaky..." He waggles his eyebrows and I laugh harder. He ignores me and continues. "And you start to feel like we're going too fast, do you promise you'll tell me?" The humor has disappeared from his eyes, leaving only sincerity.

"Yes. I promise." I pause for a moment. "But you have to promise me that you won't laugh or make fun of me the first time I try to give you a blow job. Or, uh, other things. I'll warn you now, it won't be great."

Dax leans over and kisses me. "It *will* be great because it'll be with you."

"Oh god, Dax." I cover my face with my hands. "If we're going for a record of how many times I can blush in a single day, I think this is a personal best."

Then Dax stretches out and rolls on top of me, bracing his upper body with his arms but letting the full weight of his hips and legs press me into the mattress. He leans down and rubs his chin, prickly with stubble, lightly over my cheek and whispers in my ear. "Let's see if we can make you blush a few more times before the day is over."

Of course, my cheeks fill with heat. Again.

CHAPTER 17

DAX

I have to admit, what AJ told me was a complete surprise. Okay, maybe not a *complete* surprise—it's been obvious since I met him that he's not totally at ease when it comes to being intimate with me. When we're talking or eating or hanging out, he's confident and relaxed, or at least as relaxed as AJ ever gets. But when things start heating up between us, I can tell he's into it but that he's not entirely comfortable. I'd been wondering why that seems to be the case, but now it makes sense.

I've always said I wouldn't let myself be used to satisfy some straight guy's sexual curiosity, and I still believe that. But I don't think that's what's happening here. At least, I hope not. I have to trust AJ the same way I know he trusts me.

I'm still lying on top of him, nuzzling his neck.

"AJ?" I ask. "What would you like to do right now?"

"Play chess," he deadpans without hesitation. "Obviously."

I have to roll to the side to keep from crushing him as I laugh. His dry sense of humor somehow gets me every time. AJ smiles like he's proud of himself. He does this every time I laugh—like he's accomplished a difficult task—and it's entirely too adorable.

"Oh really?" I say, pressing my hips against his thigh. My cock had lost interest while AJ and I were talking, but it's starting to take notice of what's happening again. "Well in that case, who gets to make the first move?"

"I'll be a gentleman and let you go first," he says. He shifts so his hips are against mine. I can feel his body starting to come back to life too.

We move slowly against each other, the first hints of friction causing us both to stop talking. I kiss AJ's temple, then his ear, then his jaw, giving a soft roll of my hips with each kiss. Each time, he responds with a pleased exhale.

Throwing my leg over him, I roll us both so I'm on top of him. I kiss him on the lips softly at first, keeping up the rhythm of my hips.

"Okay?" I ask.

"Yes," he gasps. "Better than okay." AJ starts to push his hips up in time with mine, our erections pressing together through underwear and sweatpants with each gentle thrust.

AJ slides his hands down my sides and tugs at my T-shirt. I sit up on my knees, grab a handful of shirt from behind my neck, and pull it over my head. While I'm at it, I pull AJ's off too. This is the first time I've seen him without a shirt, and I make sure to take my time, really getting a good look at him.

His upper body is lean but not skinny—that I already knew. He's more muscular than I would've thought though, which is pleasantly surprising. I guess it's hard to tell when he's always wearing T-shirts and hoodies.

He has fair skin, and a dusting of freckles dots his shoulders.

There's a light sprinkling of dark hair on his chest, and I'm surprised to find several tattoos on his torso and arms. It's not a lot—four or five that I can see. One nearly covers his shoulder and ends a few inches above his elbow. The others are small—one on his forearm, another under his collarbone, and one I'd seen before on the inside of his wrist. There's a hint of one that starts below his hip bone, but I can't tell how far down it goes. I'm sure they all have stories, reasons he chose to put them on his body, but I'm not really in the mood to listen to more stories. I'd prefer to do other things with AJ.

I also hadn't expected to find the little trail of dark hair from his belly button to below his waistband so goddamn sexy. I want to run my tongue from the top of it down to wherever it might lead.

I must be staring too long because AJ props himself up on his elbows to look at me, causing his ab muscles to tighten. *Good lord*. If it weren't wildly inappropriate, I'd be crossing myself and saying a Hail Mary.

"Is everything okay?" he asks.

"Uh, yeah," I say, my voice rough and low. "You're...you're fucking gorgeous." He blushes again. I give myself a mental high five.

"Well, stop staring and come here," he says.

So I do.

We're kissing again, grinding our hips together with increasing intensity. We slide against one another, and it's not long before our chests are slick with sweat and I feel dizzy with heat and want. I stop kissing AJ for a moment, pulling my head back so I can see his face more clearly.

"Is it okay if I take our pants off?" I ask.

"Yes, please," he says, breathless. "You can, um, take the rest off too. If you want."

I shake my head. "No. Not this time. I want to go slow with you."

He makes a frustrated noise. "Are you sure? I mean, we don't have to go *that* slow."

"AJ, have you considered that I might want to go slow too? Just because I've done this before doesn't mean I want to rush now."

"Oh." He sounds a little disappointed. "I guess I hadn't thought of that."

"I promise it'll be worth the wait," I say, pressing my forehead to his.

"I don't doubt that."

I playfully kiss the tip of his nose, then stand up, sliding my sweatpants off. Then, careful to leave his underwear on, I slowly remove AJ's pants. My erection is straining against the fabric of my boxer briefs, aching for relief. AJ is in a similar state, making my throat go dry.

I crawl my way up over AJ, leaving a trail of light kisses on my way up. I kiss his knee, his thigh, his hip, stomach, ribs, chest, all the way up to his neck.

AJ squirms under me, breathing rapidly. When he tries to reach down between our bodies, I grasp his wrist and hold it next to his head. His eyes widen and they've gone almost completely black.

AJ gives me a wry smile, then attempts to reach between us again, this time with his free hand. I'm realizing it's his way of asking me for what he wants. I grin and dutifully pin his other wrist to the mattress, leaving me to hold myself up by pressing my weight into his hands.

He starts moving under me, pressing his feet into the mattress and lifting his hips with even more determination. I might be on top of him, holding his hands down, but he's the one in control. I don't think he quite realizes it.

"Jesus, AJ," I whisper through heavy breaths. "For someone who claims to not have a lot of experience doing this, you're so good at it. So, so good."

The verbal encouragement seems to be exactly what he needs because he starts grinding his pelvis up against mine in earnest. I follow his lead, matching every thrust with one of my own.

I try to kiss him, but we're both breathing so hard, it's hasty and sloppy. I don't care. I'm so close, my cock achingly hard, and so wet at the tip.

"Dax." AJ's breath is heavy and hot in my ear. He squeezes his eyes shut and tilts his head back. "Fuck, Dax." His movements become even more frantic.

I kiss his neck hungrily, then bury my head in his shoulder, feeling myself come apart. My hips continue to move into his, even as I feel the warm, wet spot begin to spread between us. It only takes a few more thrusts before AJ explodes, accompanied by a litany of curse words that, to be honest, shocks me. I try not to react in the moment, though, for fear of embarrassing him.

After a few breathless moments, I roll off of AJ, releasing his hands. We lie on our backs, letting the cool air from the slightly open window blow over us.

"I'm definitely going to need to borrow some clothes to go home," I tell AJ, causing him to chuckle.

"That's fine. Help yourself to anything."

I turn my face toward his. "Was that okay?"

"Yeah." AJ is still on his back. He swallows and I watch his Adam's apple bob up and back down. "It was perfect. Thank you."

Probably deciding that one of us needs to make the first move to clean up, he stands, then opens the dresser, tossing me a pair of clean underwear.

"Where are you going?" I ask.

"To shower," he says with a hint of disappointment. "Unfortunately, it's a work day for me."

I frown. *Shit, it's Friday, isn't it?*

AJ pulls some clothes out of the dresser, then takes a shirt, still on the hanger, from the closet and carries the whole pile to the bathroom. He comes back one more time to kiss me before leaving again to shower.

I notice he leaves the door slightly open. An invitation? Maybe. I don't take the bait. *Slow,* I tell myself. *Go slow.*

I hear the shower run and eventually turn off. When he returns, he's fully dressed, hair still a little wet and clinging to his face. I stare openly and unabashedly. My body stirs a little, but decides it needs a little more time. I'm ninety-two percent sure that if I pull AJ back onto the bed with me, he wouldn't object.

My phone buzzes, forcing me to drag my eyes away from him as he towels his hair off. It's a text, one of several, I notice, from Cami asking when I'll be home. It's not a frantic message, not yet. But I know I should go home before she starts getting upset. I hadn't expected to not come home last night, and I'm sure the change of routine has Cami on edge. She's okay with me not coming home, as long as she knows before going to bed.

Mom doesn't have a problem with me staying out. I mean, I'm thirty-three years old, after all. But she doesn't like it when I do something to make Cami upset.

"I need to call my sister," I tell AJ. "She's worried."

"Oh, I'm sorry. I didn't mean to—"

"No, no. It's okay. I should've told her I wasn't coming home last night. She doesn't like me not being at home when she expects me to be. If I'd told her last night, she'd be fine this morning."

"Call her," AJ says. "I need to keep getting ready for work."

"Aren't you late?" I call to AJ's back as he walks away.

"Yeah," AJ says from the bathroom. "But I texted André before I got in the shower to tell him I'll be a little late. I'm not *that* late though. I mean, we both got up pretty early."

I hear him start to brush his teeth, so I call Cami.

It's only when AJ returns to the bedroom that I realize I can't very well walk to the subway with sticky underwear and massive bedhead.

"I can change quick so you can go to work," I say, swinging my legs over the side of the bed.

"No, it's okay," AJ says. "No offense, but you really *should* shower."

I frown at him.

"You know," he says. "In case some fans approach you on your way home. Also, you can't walk into your house smelling like, well..." He makes an awkward gesture that I think is directed at my crotch.

"Okay, but I can be quick," I say.

"Take your time. My door locks when you shut it. Shower, clean up, snoop around, whatever. Shut the door behind you when you're done."

"Are you sure you trust me alone in your apartment?" I ask playfully.

"Can I not?"

"You definitely can. I won't snoop, except to maybe see if you have any goodies in your nightstand." I wink at him.

"Sorry, but you'll be disappointed. I don't have any of the goodies you're looking for."

"That *is* disappointing," I agree. "We'll have to change that."

AJ laughs and shakes his head. He thinks I'm kidding.

I'm still sitting on the edge of the bed when he steps between my legs and leans down for a long, deep kiss. He smells like soap and tastes like toothpaste. I slide my hand over the back of his neck and try to pull him closer, but he steps back.

"I wish I could stay," he says, sounding truly disappointed. "I really do."

"Fine. Maybe I'll send you some sexy pics while you're at work."

"Don't you dare."

We both sigh at the same time. He kisses me on the forehead, then turns and walks out of the bedroom. He picks up his bag and keys, then opens the front door. I wait to hear it shut behind him, but instead, I hear quick footsteps coming back into the bedroom. Entering with determination, he puts a knee beside me on the mattress and leans down, wrapping one hand around the back of my head and pulls me in for one last kiss, deep and slow. He pulls away, then turns and walks out of the room.

"Happy snooping," he calls before he shuts the front door behind him.

As soon as he's gone, I take a selfie sitting on his bed with an exaggerated sad look on my face. I open our text thread, ready to send him the photo. I can picture him smiling when he sees it—the same way I'm smiling right now—while standing on the subway platform waiting for his train.

My heart thuds when I open the text chain. The last text I'd sent him—the one from the subway platform after we'd agreed that we shouldn't date—is there, but has a red notification: **Message failed to send**.

He hadn't gotten my text. That's why he never responded. I'd assumed that he'd shown up to *The Knightly Show* after seeing it. I'd thought he knew I wanted to try to talk things out. He hadn't.

He'd gone without having heard a word from me. He still showed up. For me.

I flop back on the bed with a ridiculous grin on my face.

CHAPTER 18

A J

Since the night after *The Knightly Show*, Dax and I have decided to give this thing between us a chance. I haven't told anyone at work, but I don't tell my coworkers anything about my love life anyway. It does feel a little surreal to be dating someone whose face I get to stare at shamelessly on my computer screen at work though.

For the past two weeks, Dax and I have tried to see each other when we can, even if it's only for a little while, despite both of us being extremely busy with work.

Saturday morning, we walk through the farmers market, where he buys me a ridiculously huge blueberry muffin, then spends the rest of the morning calling me *Marty McMuffin*. I buy Dax a cup of hot apple cider and a cider donut, then kiss him after every bite he takes so I can taste the cinnamon sugar and cider on his lips. As I'm paying for a bouquet of flowers for Dax to take home to his mom and Cami, he disappears, then returns a few minutes later holding a tiny potted cactus.

"It's cute, but prickly, to match your personality," he says, handing it to me. I pretend to be mad, but it only lasts a minute before he's making me laugh again.

As we walk, our hands graze, which turns into linked pinky fingers, which turns into hand-holding. The crowd here is mostly families with young children—not typically a late-show, YouTube series-watching crowd—so he doesn't get recognized, and I notice how relaxed he is, comfortable to be himself without being stopped by fans.

He has an interview scheduled for the afternoon, so we have to cut our day short, but we text well into the evening like we're a couple of teenagers.

On Monday, we meet up for lunch in the park near my office. Sitting on a bench basking in the autumn sunshine, we eat cheap deli sandwiches and share a bag of chips. Once Dax is finished, he leans back, stretching out his legs, and casually tosses some crumbs to a couple of hungry pigeons before I can stop him.

"Dax, no!" I try not to freak out when the number of birds multiplies in the span of mere seconds. He laughs like he couldn't care less that we're about to recreate a scene from an Alfred Hitchcock movie.

I don't like pigeons. There, I said it. They're gross and lazy and will pick at the most disgusting garbage they can find. Once they descend on us, I announce that I have to go back to work, giving Dax the last of my sandwich and leaving him on the bench to feed—and possibly get pecked to death by—the birds. He calls me a name in Spanish—an insult, no doubt—and laughs when I speed-walk away, then break into an all-out sprint when one pigeon nearly flies directly into my face.

Did I mention I don't like pigeons?

A couple days later, we go for an early dinner at a deli halfway between our neighborhoods, eating at a cafeteria-style lunch counter. Afterward, we take a long walk around the neighborhood, eventually sitting on an empty bench to enjoy the last scraps of the unseasonably warm day.

A few people stop us on the street, recognizing Dax from either *Mexican't* or *The Knightly Show*. I watch him carefully when people approach and can't help but notice that while he's cordial and friendly with fans, his shoulders are tense and his jaw is tight. Once he's said goodbye and they walk away, his body visibly relaxes—muscles, coiled like tight springs, releasing a load of tension. Not wanting to add to his stress, I decide to keep it to myself for now. Maybe I'll talk to him about it sometime in the future.

One evening, I invite Dax to my apartment for dinner, finally making good on my promise to introduce him to *When Harry Met Sally*. When I open the door, his breathing is fast and shallow—not surprising since I live in a third-floor walkup, although he doesn't usually get winded walking up a few flights of stairs. He has a slight glow of sweat around his hairline, and the collar of his shirt is loose, like he's been tugging at it. I take his hands, pulling him close to me. They're clammy, which surprises me since it's chilly outside.

"You okay?" I ask as he steps past me into the apartment.

"Yeah, of course," he says with forced nonchalance, not meeting my eyes. "You need an elevator in this building."

"You're sure? Because you seem like you—"

Dax shuts the door behind him, gently pushing me until my back is against the door, pressing his body against mine and kissing me deeply. It's not necessarily forceful, but not gentle either, making me forget whatever I was about to say. The kiss is hungry, almost desperate.

"I've been looking forward to doing that all day," he says, grinning slyly at me.

I can feel heat rising up from my toes all the way to the tips of my ears. *Well, that shut me up.*

We order dinner and sit at the kitchen island while we wait for it to be delivered. We chat a little, and while I'm in the middle of a story about work, Dax slides off his barstool and moves to stand between my knees.

"Go on," he says after I've stopped midsentence to stare at his lips, which are now at eye level.

"Uh, so I, uh, I had to go back to…" Dax is pressing tiny kisses to my ear, then down my neck.

"You had to go back to…?" Dax repeats, waiting for me to continue my story. He continues to kiss my neck, slowly making his way to my collarbone.

"Um…" I close my eyes and drop my head back, giving Dax full access to my throat.

"Fuck, I don't know," I whisper, swallowing hard. Dax rakes his fingers through my hair, then tugs, pulling my head to one side before kissing my neck hungrily. My hands slide up his sides, grasping his shirt to pull him closer.

The door's buzzer interrupts us, and I release Dax before running downstairs to get the food. When I return, Dax has set out spoons and napkins for each of us, and has even found the bottle of sriracha for our noodle soups. He's also set out a beer for me and helped himself to a canned cider. They seem like such simple gestures, but I can't help but feel grateful, both for the fact that he feels comfortable enough to make himself at home and for the fact that he's here with me at all.

Every time I'm with him, I'm surprised to find myself feeling like my relationship with Dax—an actor, a celebrity—could feel so normal. Here we are, in a small apartment in Brooklyn, eating takeout noodles, kissing, and talking about our day. Dax isn't at all the person I'd expected the first day we met on the set of the photo shoot. And every time we're together, I'm amazed at this fact all over again.

We settle into a comfortable intimacy, eating quietly at the island. When we're finished, Dax pushes me out of the kitchen and tells me to get the movie ready while he cleans up and puts the bowls in the dishwasher.

I carry my beer to the couch, sitting with my legs resting on the padded ottoman. When Dax finishes cleaning up, he stretches and lies down, resting his head in my lap while his feet dangle over the arm of the couch. I softly stroke his hair, occasionally winding a lock around my finger. He moans softly and wriggles like a cat getting comfortable.

The movie starts, but within fifteen minutes, I notice Dax's eyes are closed and his breaths are slow and even. Grabbing the blanket from the back of the couch, I throw it over him. I turn off the TV, leaving the apartment silent except for Dax's breaths and the muffled sounds of the city outside. I let my head drop against the back of the couch and close my eyes, not quite dozing, just letting myself enjoy the moment.

It's another half an hour before he wakes up looking dazed, his hair slightly disheveled.

"Sorry," he says looking at the TV. "Was I asleep long?"

"No. But long enough to drool on my leg." I point to the wet spot on my pants.

"Oh god." Dax covers his face with a hand. "I'd planned to come over here to give you a sexy lesson, and I end up drooling on your lap."

"That wasn't part of the lesson?"

"No, smartass." He smirks. "I do have a lesson that includes laps, but it doesn't include sleeping."

Well. "Oh?" I sit up eagerly. "Do tell."

Dax swings a leg over mine and arranges himself so he's straddling my lap while keeping his weight on his knees.

"Well, it goes like this." Without another word, he pulls my face to his and kisses me deeply, exploring my mouth with his tongue.

A hot, tingling sensation shoots up my spine, radiating out to every cell in my body. My hands are everywhere, trying to memorize the feel of him—the smooth planes and valleys of his chest, the tender skin of his neck, the hard lines of muscles along his arms and shoulders.

I run my hands under his shirt, feeling the warmth of his skin. He makes a soft *hmm* sound and lifts his arms, allowing me to pull his shirt over his head.

Dax pulls my sweater and T-shirt over my head in one swift move. The shock of cool air makes my nipples harden instantly. Dax rubs a thumb over one hard nub while kissing the other, lightly brushing it with his tongue.

I squirm under the weight of him, trying desperately to create some friction between us. He spreads his knees wider and rolls his pelvis into me, grinding our hips together. The movement goes straight to my groin, and I my jeans suddenly feel tight against my body.

Dax stands, gently pushing me back so I'm lying flat on the couch. He stares at me for a long moment, and a surge of anticipation rips through me, causing my breath to catch.

"Tell me what you want," he says in a near whisper.

I can feel my cheeks start to warm as I stare up at him. "Uh, what you were doing just now felt nice."

"No, AJ. Tell me what you *want*." His voice is gravelly and low. I think I might fall apart like this.

"Don't be embarrassed. I want you to tell me. I like it." He draws out the last part, and I almost lose my mind.

Well, here goes...

I raise myself up so I'm leaning back on my elbows. "Take your clothes off. All of them," I say.

He complies, pulling his socks off, then his pants and underwear. He's standing next to the couch, all muscular and hard and perfect. His eyes never leave mine. He just watches me while I stare at him. "And?" he asks when I've presumably been ogling him for too long.

"Um, touch yourself. Slowly." He takes himself in his hand and strokes himself lazily. *Oh god.* I pull the rest of my own clothes off in a matter of milliseconds.

"Come here," I whisper. Dax puts a leg over me, then straddles my hips again. He sits there like that, one hand still on his cock, waiting for instructions. I can't get over how thrilled—and terrified—I feel in this moment.

"Keep, uh, touching yourself." My face is burning, and I'm thankful it's dark enough in the room that he can't see how red it must be. He complies and I'm frozen, watching him.

"What else do you want me to do?" he asks. I can't do it. This is too much. The mix of arousal and embarrassment has me ready to explode. I shake my head.

"Do you want to stop?" he asks.

"No. I liked what you were doing. I..." I cover my face with my hand. "I want you to, you know, take the wheel."

Dax laughs softly, then leans down and kisses my forehead. In the next moment, his smile is gone, replaced by something darker. Want. And god, I want it too.

He takes both of our straining erections in one strong hand and slowly strokes them together. I writhe and buck my hips, gripping his thighs tightly. He rocks his pelvis and continues to stroke us both, his breaths coming hard and fast. I'm panting and biting my lip, trying to draw out this moment. But I'm quickly losing control. I couldn't slow myself down, even if I wanted to.

Dax slows, only for a moment, circling his thumb over the tip of my cock, and I moan. After another couple of minutes of this, I can't hold back any longer. The sensation is like a tidal wave nearing the shore, swelling and building strength until it's just about to crest. I let out a cry—and a few curse words—before exploding onto my stomach and into Dax's hand. He gives us both a few more hard and fast strokes before he's shuddering, coming onto my chest and stomach.

I lie motionless, trying to catch my breath, while my brain struggles to pull itself together again.

Dax leans an arm on the back of the couch, his head resting in the crook of his elbow, and smiles at me. "Jesus, AJ." He lets out a huge exhale.

"I'm sorry," I say.

"For what? That was so fucking good."

"I'm sorry about my, um, stage fright. I've never had someone ask me to tell them what to do." I swallow. "I guess I got shy."

"Hey, don't apologize." He runs a finger along my stubble-lined jaw. "I told you to tell me when you're not comfortable. And you did. That means a lot to me."

I sit up on my elbows. "Well, I'd like to try it again sometime."

"Yeah?" Dax grins at me.

"Yeah. You know what they say? Practice makes perfect."

Dax dips his head to kiss me on the tip of my nose. "I couldn't agree more."

CHAPTER 19

AJ

As I'm walking to the subway the following morning, I'm surprised to get a call from Dax. Not a text, but an actual phone call. I'm smiling before I even answer.

"Hey," Dax says cheerfully. "Sorry to call you so early."

"It's okay. You know you can call me anytime. What's up?"

"I forgot to tell you last night, my mom asked me to invite you to dinner at our house on Sunday."

"Dinner? With your family?"

"Yeah," he says, then adds quickly, "but you don't have to. If it's too soon, or if it's weird or whatever—"

"No, no. It's great. I'm just surprised, that's all."

"Well, don't feel obligated to come. She mentioned that she'd like to see you again. I can tell her—"

"Dax, I want to come. Tell her I'll be there. Okay?"

"Okay." I can't see his face, but I can tell he's smiling.

"Send me the address and time."

"Getting bossy after last night, huh?"

I laugh. "Bye, Dax."

It's early evening on Sunday, but the sky is already getting dark. I'm standing on the porch of Dax's family's house in Queens. It's a modest, two-story brick home nestled on a quiet street among similar sized houses. There's a small front yard and three steps up to the porch, which isn't as much a porch as it is a glorified top step with a few potted plants along the edge. Despite it only being October, there's a Christmas wreath on the front door.

I raise my hand to knock, but the door flies open before my hand makes contact. Cami lunges at me, grabbing me in a bear hug before I even know what's happening.

"Hi, AJ!" She squeezes me so hard I nearly drop the paper shopping bag I'm holding.

Dax's mom appears behind Cami. "Mija, let AJ come into the house." Alma puts a gentle hand on Cami's shoulder encouraging her to let me go, which she does reluctantly.

"Cami, go tell your brother that AJ is here," Alma says.

Cami turns on her heel and sprints away sing-shouting, "Diego, your boyfriend is here!"

Boyfriend. I smile to myself.

Alma puts her hand on my back to guide me inside. Just like with Dax, the touch doesn't feel like the touch of a stranger. It feels comfortable, like Dax's mom is someone I've known all my life.

"It's good to see you again," Alma says, giving me a warm hug. It's firm—not quite like Cami's hug—like being snuggled into a warm blanket on a winter day.

"Thank you for inviting me, Mrs. Ximénez." I say, sliding my jacket off my shoulders.

"Oh, mijo." She pats me on the shoulder, even though I'm almost a foot taller than her. "My last name is Ibarra, but call me Alma. Please."

"I'm sorry." Embarrassed heat rushes to my cheeks. "Dax didn't tell me." She smiles as she waves her hand dismissively.

"Let me take that for you." Taking my jacket from my hands, she hangs it on the coat rack that's already full of jackets, sweaters, and scarves.

I step farther into the house and am in awe of how much it feels like home. Not the kind of home I grew up in, but a place that feels comfortable, safe. There are pictures hanging on every wall, cozy-looking furniture filling the room, and knickknacks, some of which look handmade, crammed into shelves. The house smells like home cooking, and there's upbeat music coming from another room. I can hear Cami's laughter echoing down the hall. I've never been here, but I feel more at home in this house than I've felt anywhere else in a long time.

My ears perk up as Dax's voice floats down the hall, coming from the direction of what I assume is the kitchen, and I feel a flutter in my stomach.

"Cams, could you bring AJ in here?" he says. "I can't leave the stove."

"AJ!" I follow Cami's singsongy voice. "Diego is in here." Following the voices, I make my way to the kitchen, and I can't help but break into a wide grin. Dax is standing at the stove, humming to the music and stirring something in a pan.

"Hi," I say as I set down the shopping bag I'd been holding and press a kiss to his cheek. "What are you wearing?"

Dax looks down at himself. "It's called a mandil. It's a Mexican apron." I cover my mouth with my hand, trying to suppress a laugh.

"What?" Dax asks defensively. "I'm not too proud to wear it. I don't want to get grease stains on my sweater."

"It's not that," I say, chuckling. "It's just so...frilly." The apron looks more like a tunic that ties on the sides and has two pockets in the front.

It actually seems more practical than the aprons I'm used to seeing. But this one is pink with a floral pattern, loose ruffles hanging from the shoulders.

Dax, in defiance of my laughter, spins once, then gives me a polite curtsy. I pull him close into a hug.

"Diego!" Alma says as she enters the kitchen. I loosen my hold on Dax, but he keeps his arms around my waist. I'm still not quite used to being so open in front of, well, anyone. But I like it.

"You're going to burn the onions." She pushes him away from the stove. "¡Muévete!"

Dax hands her the wooden spoon and pulls the apron over his head, hanging it on a hook near the stove. He turns to face me and lifts his head, kissing me quickly on the lips.

"Bienvenido a mi casa." He holds up his arms and I grin even wider. I don't think I've stopped smiling since I walked in the door.

"What's that?" Dax points to the bag I've brought.

"Oh, just a couple of things," I say, picking it up and handing it to Dax. He pulls out a bottle of white wine (his mom's favorite brand), a six-pack of Dos Equis (his dad's favorite), and a plastic cake carrier, which I bought earlier today specifically for this occasion.

"What's in here?" Dax asks, removing the container from the bag.

"*Apfelkuchen.*"

If this had been a movie, there'd have been a record-scratch sound effect and the music would've stopped. Alma and Dax both freeze, staring at me, and I can feel my cheeks warming.

"Apple-fuckin'?" Dax asks.

"Diego!" Alma says sternly. "Don't make me use the chancla."

Dax cuts a knowing glance in my direction, then pointedly moves his eyes in the direction of her shoes, as if to say, *See? I wasn't kidding*. I snicker.

"*Apfelkuchen*," I repeat, more slowly this time. "It's a traditional German apple cake." I bite my lip and run a hand over the back of my neck. "I made it."

I glance up at Alma who gives me a small but knowing smile, like she's figured out a secret.

Dax stares at me in disbelief. "You made this?" he asks. "With your hands?"

"Yes," I say defiantly. "I *can* cook, you know."

"How was I supposed to know? We always get takeout when I come over." His face is still one of surprise.

"Okay, well, I don't know how to make that many things, but my mom taught me to make this cake when I was a kid."

My eyes unexpectedly sting with tears when I say this. It's something I don't think of often, but I've always kept the memory close to my heart. It was one of the few times I could remember doing something with my mom that was just for fun. Just for us. And one of the few times I felt like she truly loved me. I knew she loved me then, and I know that she still does, but she's always been so serious. She rarely laughed with me or even hugged me when I was a kid. The day she taught me to make the cake had been such an anomaly that sometimes it feels like it had been a dream, a story made up by a lonely kid to fill in the blank spaces that had been lacking color and warmth.

Baking the cake this afternoon had stirred up a lot of those old feelings—ones that had been locked away for so long—like blowing dust off a box full of old treasures.

I clear my throat. "It's supposed to be served with vanilla ice cream, but I forgot to get some on my way."

Dax's face lights up. "Well, it's a good thing the best ice cream shop in Queens is just down the block from here." He takes my elbow to lead me out of the kitchen. "Mamí, we'll be back in fifteen minutes."

"Diego, introduce AJ to your dad before you go," she calls as we walk out.

Dax takes one of the beers out of the pack, then ushers me into the den, where a man who looks to be in his mid fifties sits back on a recliner, eyes closed.

"Dad?" Dax puts a hand on his dad's shoulder, causing him to jolt awake.

He looks confused for a moment, then seems to pull himself together.

"Dad, this is AJ. My..." Dax looks at me, unsure. I nod. "My boyfriend." I can't help but smile when he says this.

"Ah." Dax's dad stands up. He's quite a bit shorter than Dax, with sandy brown hair and dark eyes. I don't see any resemblance between the two of them.

"Hi, AJ. It's a pleasure to meet you. Ray Ibarra."

We shake hands and I notice his grip is strong, his hands rough and calloused. My heart races as Ray eyes me, no doubt sizing me up to make sure I'm good enough for his son.

"It's nice to meet you, sir," I say.

Ray shakes his head. "No need to be so formal, mijo. Call me Ray."

"He can't help it," Dax says. "He's a *gentleman*." He says the last word in a terrible impression of a fussy London accent. He hands me the beer and gestures for me to give it to Ray.

"I brought you this." I hold out the beer, a little embarrassed, like I'm trying a bit too hard to get him to like me.

"Oh, thank you," Ray says, taking the beer from my hand and patting me on the shoulder. "Would you like one?" he asks, sitting back down on the recliner.

"Thanks, but not right now," I say. "I think we're going to walk down and get some ice cream." I gesture over my shoulder with my thumb. "But maybe when we get back."

"Okay, have fun, boys. Oh, and Diego. Don't forget to get something for your sister."

"I won't, Papí." Dax puts a hand on his dad's shoulder. "Bye."

We walk out into the chilly fall air, and I instinctively shove my hands in my pockets. As Dax and I start down the sidewalk, he tugs at my sleeve until I pull my hand back out of my pocket and take his hand. We interlace our fingers, and I'm struck by how tender this small bit of contact feels. At how *right* it feels.

As much as I'd like to take my time ambling down the street, hand in hand with Dax, the weather has turned downright cold and neither of us brought a jacket, so we hustle to get back to the warmth of Dax's house.

When we walk into the kitchen, Cami's waiting for us at the door. "Diego!" she says impatiently. "Did you get strawberry?"

"Yep, strawberry ice cream for you," he says, handing her the cup and kissing her on the cheek. "And vanilla ice cream for you." Dax hands the large container to his mom, then kisses her on the cheek.

"Thank you, cariño," Alma says. "Now go wash your hands. Dinner is ready."

The table is round and small, and it seems like it would be crowded, even with four people. Adding a fifth person means that Dax and I are elbow to elbow, our legs are pressed against one another. Next to me, Alma is dishing out food and handing out plates. Everything looks and smells amazing. I can't remember the last time I'd had an honest-to-goodness home-cooked meal.

"Before we eat, we must say a blessing," Alma says. She takes my hand without hesitation, and Dax takes my other hand. Everyone bows their head as Ray says a quick prayer in Spanish.

The meal is every bit as good as it looks. The food is spicy but not overwhelming, and the flavors are better than anything I've had in any Mexican restaurant. Throughout dinner, Cami and Dax taunt each other like children, while Alma gets up at least half a dozen times to get more tortillas, to refill drinks, to bring a serving spoon she'd forgotten, and to check that everyone has enough to eat. All the while, she asks me questions.

"AJ, where did you grow up?"

"Philadelphia," I say, swallowing a mouthful of rice and beans. "In the suburbs."

"So not too far then," she muses. "How long have you lived in New York?"

"Since I was eighteen. I moved here for college and I never left." The truth is that I couldn't have gone back, even if I'd wanted to. My mom had moved away, and my childhood home had become a home to another family. It hardly mattered though. I didn't keep in touch with anyone from my childhood, and so I had no reason to go back.

"So your family still lives there?" Alma's face is sweet and curious, and I internally debate how much I want to share.

"No, my mom lives in Germany. And my extended family too. I don't have any family here."

I expect pitying looks or more questions. Instead, Alma simply says, "Well, if you ever miss being with family, you're always welcome here."

She says it so easily, so freely. She's opening their home to me, welcoming me like family. I feel that familiar sting in my eyes I'd had earlier when I'd been thinking about my mom.

"Thanks," I say, then clear my throat. "I might just take you up on that."

Under the table, Dax squeezes my thigh, as if he can somehow feel a shift in my mood. I press my leg into his in response.

Thankfully, we move on to lighter topics while we finish our meal. When we're done, I stand, offering to help clear the table.

"Nonsense," Alma says, waving her hands at me. "The first time you're here, you're a guest. After that, you're family. Next time, you'll help." She gives me a little smile and a wink. *God, where do such good, generous people come from?*

Dax and his dad clear the table and begin washing the dishes while Alma puts the leftovers away.

"AJ, do you want to play a game with me?" Cami asks, leading me by the arm into the living room.

"Sure. What've you got?" I eye the stack of board games in the corner.

"Battleship, Mastermind, Cathedral, checkers..." She counts on her fingers while she names games.

"Battleship sounds good."

"Okay!" Cami bounces away to set up the game on the floor.

"AJ," Dax whispers conspiratorially. "Don't intentionally let her win. She's really good at games."

"Uh, okay." I nod, not sure I entirely believe him.

On our second round of Battleship, I'm getting beaten badly by Cami—she easily won the first round. Dax comes into the living room, settling on the couch behind Cami to watch. As I look at my game board, I notice Dax trying to give me indecipherable signals. When I lower my eyes at him, trying to interpret his hand movements, Cami turns around and punches him on the leg. "No cheating!"

It wouldn't have helped. She wins the second round.

"I think I'll let Dax take over while I go to the restroom," I say, getting up on stiff legs.

"Up the stairs on the left." Dax points me in the right direction, then slides over to take my spot on the floor.

Once I'm done in the bathroom, I head toward the stairs. As I pass Dax's open bedroom door, I peek inside, pretty sure he won't mind. It's nothing special, a bed, a desk, a dresser, and a closet. Standard stuff. The room is clean, the bed neatly made with a dark-green duvet and a fuzzy blanket folded and slung over a chair.

Above Dax's dresser are at least thirty or forty hand-drawn pictures. They're colorful, full of flowers, rainbows, and cute animals. I see Cami's name scrawled in the corner of each one. They vary in skill level, like he's been collecting her drawings over several years.

There's a corkboard above the desk with a variety of mementos and pictures: ticket stubs, flyers for comedy clubs, VIP passes to events. There's also a calendar with things like *Knightly Show* and *Good Morning LA interview* written among things like birthdays and dentist appointments. The high-profile events are given the same treatment as everyday events, none more or less special than another.

In the corner of the corkboard, I spot a picture that's been almost completely covered by other items. It's two boys, one taller—clearly older—and one shorter and chubbier, but both with the same eyes, the same smile. The boys are standing in front of a horse while a tall man stands behind them, holding the reins. I take the picture from the corkboard and adjust my glasses. The two boys look like younger versions of the man standing behind them.

"AJ?" Dax says softly from the doorway. He shuts the door behind him, then takes the photo from my hands and sets it on the desk without giving it a second glance.

"This is my room." He spins around as if showing off a grand castle. "Impressive, isn't it?"

I smile softly. "I like it. The whole house. It—" I'm slightly embarrassed at how weak my voice sounds. "It feels like a home."

"It is." Dax nudges me with his elbow. "It's *my* home."

"Smartass. I mean..." I sigh. "The place where I grew up never felt like home, not like this. It never had this feeling of..." I gesture as if to encompass the whole house. Then I shake my head. "I don't know what I'm trying to say."

"I get it." Dax takes my hands in his, stroking my knuckles with his thumb. The touch is so tender, I nearly sink into him. "Your house never felt like home?"

"Exactly. It always felt cold, like I was visiting the home of some distant relative. This place feels warm, comfortable."

Dax nods, keeping his eyes on our hands. "That's why it's hard to imagine moving out of here. I could afford my own place, but I love my family, and I think I'd miss them too much. I'd get lonely living alone. I've lived by myself before, in college and for a few years when I was working in IT. But the older I get, the more I want to be around the people I love."

"I want that too," I whisper. "I don't have as many of those people as you do."

Dax and I sit on the bed, the mattress dipping under our weight, which inadvertently causes us to lean into one another. I slide my hand around his waist and let my fingers rest on his hip.

"So, your dad seems nice," I say.

"Yeah, he's great. Not much of a talker, but he's a good man."

Dax is quiet for a little while and I don't think he's going to say anything more. Then he takes a breath and speaks.

"He's my stepdad, obviously. I call him *Dad* because that's how I think of him. He and my mom got together when I was fourteen. Ever since then, he's raised Cami and me as his own. He's always supported me and loved me unconditionally."

"And that guy in the photo?" I point to the photograph on the desk. "He's your…?"

Dax lies back on the bed. "That's my father. He owns a tequila distillery in Mexico. We haven't spoken in years."

I nod. The room is quiet, the only sounds coming from the TV downstairs. "And the other boy in the picture?" I ask after a long moment.

"My brother, Mateo." Dax's voice is flat.

"I didn't know you had a brother. You've never mentioned him."

"We don't really talk either. He lives in Mexico too. Helps my father run the distillery. Also, he's an asshole."

"I'm so sorry." I feel like I've accidentally opened a whole box of things Dax doesn't want to talk about.

"Don't be. It's fine. We used to be really close. He's my big brother, so of course I looked up to him. When I started questioning myself and my sexuality, I would try talking to him about it, but he'd get mad at me, saying I was just looking for attention. He'd tell me I needed to grow up and learn how to be a real man. I could tell I embarrassed him because the older we got, the more he'd say it. He wouldn't talk to me in school. Eventually, I stopped talking to him about anything personal."

"Oh, Dax." I rearrange myself so I'm leaning against the headboard, pulling Dax close to me, letting his head lay on my chest. I rest my chin on his head, inhaling the citrusy scent of his hair.

"When I was in seventh grade," he continues, "I got a big part in a school play. I was so excited that I ran all the way home to tell my family. When I told them, my dad wasn't happy about it, especially when I said it was a musical. I even started singing a little bit of a song from the show. He yelled at me and got so upset he threw a bottle at the wall. I had no idea why he'd been so mad, but it scared the shit out of me. I ran outside in the backyard, and I could hear my mom and dad arguing. He kept saying it was her fault he had a 'sissy boy' for a son. He called the school the next morning and told them I couldn't be in the play. I didn't know about that until later. When I went to rehearsal after school, the director made up some flimsy excuse and recast my part."

I can feel Dax's shoulders tremble lightly. I make slow circles on his back with my fingers while he speaks. My chest is tight and there's a lump forming in my throat. I have to blink a few times to hold my own tears back.

"When I found out that my part had been recast, I came home and cried. My dad was home—and he was drunk, which was rare. He told me to quit crying. 'Man up,' he said. 'Real men don't cry.' That just made me cry harder." Dax takes a slow, shuddering breath.

"...And then he hit me. It was the only time he'd ever done that. I don't think it was that hard, but it was hard enough that I had a red mark across my face. I know I make jokes about my mom and the chancla, but this was different.

"I ran to Mateo's room and cried on the floor. I thought he would stand up for me, or at least be on my side. Instead, he said Dad shouldn't have hit me, but that he was right. That I needed to finally grow up and be a man. He said I was an embarrassment to our family. I didn't even know why, not really. I mean, who has themselves figured out in seventh grade? God, AJ, I was only twelve years old. Do you know how much that hurt?"

"Fuck, Dax." My jaw clenches as I think about what his father and brother must've done to him, and at such a young age. With my free hand, I grip the blanket in a tight fist to relieve some of the anger that's boiling in my blood. "How could he do that to you? How could he possibly think that was okay?" As much as I want to shout, I try to keep my voice calm.

"Mom certainly didn't," he says. "She took me to stay with my tía and tío in the Bronx for a couple of weeks. When I came home, my dad was gone. While I'd been away, Mom told him to leave, then filed for a divorce. I only saw him a couple of times after that, when he came back to get his things and to talk to Mateo. He told Mateo that he could come with him to Mexico as soon as things got settled. He didn't even say goodbye to me. Can you believe that? My own father." Dax lets out a long, shaky breath.

"Mateo left at the end of the school year and moved in with him. He finished school in Mexico, and now he's the VP of my father's company."

My head is swimming as I try to imagine what that time in Dax's life must've been like back then. "So you don't talk to either of them anymore?"

"I talk to Mateo once in a while. I used to call him every couple of months, but after we started *Mexican't*, he told me he didn't like that I was 'flaunting my gay lifestyle' by making a YouTube show that's based, at least partly, on my own experiences of being gay." Dax pauses for a moment, then smiles. "So when Max and I signed the contract to make the show into a sitcom—and on a streaming network where the whole world can watch it—of course I *had* to call and tell him the news."

"Obviously," I say, relieved that Dax seems to be trying to lighten the mood.

Dax chuckles softly, then shifts his body, somehow managing to curl himself into me even more. "Mateo has never told me outright to stop calling him. We don't say much when I call, but I think he likes knowing how Mom and Cami are doing. And even me. Maybe. We'll never be close like we used to be. He always blamed me for my parents' divorce. I suppose it *was* because of me, in a way, but I don't feel bad about it. Mom says it was a long time coming and that there were a lot of reasons, not just because of how he was with me. I don't know if she says that to make me feel less guilty, or if it's true, but it doesn't matter. We're all where we're supposed to be."

I'm at a loss for words. I can't understand how anyone who knows Dax could possibly feel anything but love and affection for him. How anyone who knows Alma and Cami could turn their backs on them. They all have such big, kind hearts. This is the kind of family relationship I could only wish for.

In a quiet voice, almost a whisper, Dax says, "When I'm a parent, my kids are never going to feel like they don't belong or that they're not loved for who they are. Ever."

While the thought of kids would normally send me into cold sweats, my heart swells at the thought of Dax as a father. I hug him tightly, kissing the top of his head and smoothing his hair.

We stay like this for a few minutes before Dax untangles himself from my arms and pulls himself upright, running a hand over his eyes to wipe away any remaining tears.

"We should go back downstairs," he says. "Before my family thinks we're canoodling in here."

"In a minute." I roll Dax over on his back and lie on top of him, resting my head on his shoulder and breathing into his neck. I can feel him inhale as if to say something, then he exhales slowly, like he's letting go of something heavy. I press light kisses to his ear, jaw, his lips. It's not meant to be sexy, just a little something to make him feel comforted, safe.

Wrapping his arms around me, Dax gives me a kiss that warms my chest and makes my toes curl. The stubble on his cheek gives me goosebumps when it rubs against my own clean-shaven face. I want so badly to tell him I love him. It's been on the tip of my tongue for the past week. If there's a right time to say it, this is it. My heart rate suddenly feels like it's doubling in speed as I open my mouth to say it. But at the last second, I chicken out—scared that he might not feel the same way, or that it's too soon. Instead, I keep kissing him.

CHAPTER 20

DAX

"Diego?" Cami knocks loudly on the door to my room. AJ quickly rolls off of me, and keeps rolling all the way to the floor, hitting it with a loud *thud*.

"Yeah?" I say, trying to hold back a laugh.

"Are you okay? What happened?" Cami asks through the door.

"I'm fine. AJ just fell off the bed." I can't hold it in anymore. I burst into laughter.

AJ's face is red and he's sprawled out on the carpet. Cami opens the door and finds me doubled over laughing and AJ on his hands and knees trying to get up. She rushes to his side and tries to help him which only makes his cheeks an even more intense shade of red.

"I'm okay," he says. "Thanks."

"What did you need, Cams?" I ask.

"Mom is serving dessert. Ice cream and apple-fluefel or whatever you called it. Come downstairs."

"Cami!" Alma's voice calls up the stairs. "Give the boys some privacy. They'll come down when they're ready."

"They're not doing anything," she calls back innocently. "AJ fell on the floor."

I laugh hard enough to make my eyes water while AJ buries his face in his hands.

"Cami, come down and get some ice cream." Alma's voice is firmer this time.

Cami rolls her eyes and leaves, pulling the door shut behind her. AJ kisses me on the forehead, then steps toward the door.

"You know," I say to AJ as I sit on the bed and try to give him my most seductive look. "We don't have to go down yet."

"Don't you want to try the apple cake? The one that *I* made?"

"Of course I do." I reach for his hand, but he pulls away. "But, in a minute?"

"It's cake, Dax. And ice cream. Ice. Cream." He opens the bedroom door. "Are you coming?"

I sigh, only a little disappointed. "Yeah, I'll be right there." Standing up, I notice the photo of Mateo and my father still sitting on my desk. I stare at it for a minute or two, and for the first time in years, I miss my brother—or more specifically, I miss the relationship that was lost when he left to live with my father. The feeling of loss hits me squarely in the chest and I can hardly breathe. I slide the photo into the bottom drawer of my desk under a pile of papers, where I won't have to look at it again.

Eventually, I make my way out of the bedroom and down the stairs. When I reach the bottom, I see AJ standing at the kitchen table surrounded by my family. He's smiling and laughing with them as he cuts the apple cake, while Mom scoops ice cream into bowls. Cami's already digging into her dessert with a spoon and giggling at something he's just said.

I lean against the wall and watch.

Dad and AJ are talking about work, though their jobs couldn't be more different. My dad wears jeans to work every day too, so I guess they do have that in common.

I don't know if it's because AJ held me tight while I unloaded a lot of emotional baggage on him that I hadn't thought about in years, or if it's seeing him fit in so comfortably with my family, but I feel a tugging on my heart at the sight of him. The sensation is almost overwhelming—in the best way possible. I knew from the first time AJ kissed me that I was in trouble, at least where my feelings were concerned. And I was right.

I'm in love with him, let me be clear about that. In such a short time, he's become so much more to me than I ever expected. I don't know what the future holds for us, and I know it might get messy, but he's worth it. If something happens and this doesn't work out, I'll be heartbroken.

As if he can sense my presence, AJ looks up to see me watching him from the doorway. He gives me a sweet, almost shy smile—the kind that makes me feel both completely helpless, and like I can do anything. It makes me weak and strong all at once. I have to grip the doorjamb for support.

"Cake?" he asks, holding out a plate for me.

After a full fifteen minutes of goodbyes, AJ and I sit on the top step of the porch waiting for the car he'd called.

"I hope you had a good time," I say.

"I'm not exaggerating when I say I had one of the best nights of my life. Except for Cami kicking my ass in every single game we played."

"I told you. She's really good at strategy games."

"Seriously though. This was amazing. You're really lucky to have such a close, loving family."

Something in the way his voice cracks a bit causes me to look at him. He's looking up at the sky, his eyes glittering by the light of a passing car.

"Are you okay?" I set a hand on AJ's knee.

He nods and wipes his eyes, pretending he's adjusting his glasses. "Yeah, it's...being here makes me feel homesick, I guess."

"That makes sense," I say. "You miss your family?"

"No, it's not that. I don't know how to describe it. I have this feeling of homesickness, but for a home I've never had. Like, I'm missing my family, but the way I wish they were, not the way they actually are. Does that make sense?"

"It does." I kick a small rock off the step with the toe of my shoe. "I mean, I've never felt like that exactly, but I think I get what you're talking about."

AJ doesn't say anything, just stares into the distance.

"What about your mom?" I ask.

"Growing up, she wasn't very...warm. She was always good to me, took care of me. But she wasn't around a lot. She raised me on her own, and she had to work long hours most days. She and my dad divorced when I was nine. She hated being in America, but she stayed for me. Once I graduated from high school and moved here to the city, she left. Moved back to Germany. I'm an only child, and I don't keep in touch with my dad, so I've been alone here for, well, a long time. I'm not complaining though. I have a good job, a nice apartment, good friends..."

"And an amazing boyfriend," I add with a laugh.

"Yeah, about that..." AJ turns to me and my stomach tightens.

"Too soon?" I ask. "I should've asked you first. I didn't tell my family you were my boyfriend, Cami made the assumption..."

AJ shuts me up with a kiss. His hand slides up behind my head and he pulls my face closer to his. I let myself melt into his touch, wishing this moment didn't have to end.

He pulls away for a moment and whispers, "I like it," before giving me a peck on the tip of my nose.

His car arrives and he presses one more soft kiss to my lips before he heads to the car carrying a bag of leftovers that mom insisted on giving him. When the car pulls away, I'm left with a full, happy feeling in my heart. I feel like I'm a million miles from the celebrity side of me—the one who breaks out in a nervous sweat around fans and is prone to panic attacks.

All I feel is love. Love for my family. Love for my home. Love for AJ, and love *from* AJ. He hasn't said it, but yeah, I can feel that too.

CHAPTER 21

AJ

"Dax?"

It's early on a Monday morning—earlier than I'd normally wake up. Especially since Dax is here in my bed and we'd spent most of the evening doing sexy things with each other.

He'd spent the last two nights here with me.

On Friday, we'd gone to a bar known for its large selection of old-school arcade games. While it started out fun, in retrospect, going there wasn't the best idea. The bar was full of young people, so it didn't take long for Dax to get recognized. Fans were trying to be sneaky while taking photos and videos on their phones. Once someone approached Dax to ask for a selfie with him, the floodgates seemed to open and there were several people who wanted pics with Dax. He said he was fine with it, but the unexpected attention had clearly exhausted him. He kept smiling, but his shoulders were rigid and his jaw had been clenched the whole time.

Once the attention receded, we tried to continue our earlier conversation, but I found myself on edge, constantly looking around the room. We ended up coming back to my apartment, although I can't complain about that. We stayed awake until after four in the morning talking and kissing before eventually falling asleep wrapped in each other's arms.

And last night, I had my first lesson in oral sex. I wouldn't say I was particularly good at it after one try, but I'd gotten the job done, so to speak. And Dax had been satisfied enough to reciprocate. Although afterward, he told me, "Blow jobs are like pizza: there's good pizza, and there's amazing pizza, but there's no such thing as bad pizza."

I think maybe he was joking, but I'm pretty sure he'd just compared my skills to Papa John's, which is the worst pizza I can think of. In a pinch though, I'd still eat it.

I feel Dax stir and I can tell by his breathing that he's awake. I draw circles on his back with my fingertip.

"Hmmm?" He mumbles but doesn't move.

"Can I ask you something?" My stomach flutters nervously.

Dax rolls over to face me. It's still dark outside, but the first hints of sunlight are starting to peek over the horizon casting a soft blue hue over my room.

"Sure, what's up?" His face is pressed into the pillow that he's hugging so I can only see one eye—one green-gray eye over the caramel-colored skin of his bicep. The duvet has slipped down, giving me a perfect view of his shirtless, muscled back. I shift, trying to not get distracted by how good he looks.

"Well..." I hesitate. "You know that thing that happened at *The Knightly Show*?" I chew on my bottom lip.

He reaches for me, stroking my hip and letting his fingers rest on the waistband of my underwear. "Did you mean the morning *after* the show?"

"No. Before the show." My eyes fix on his. "The panic attack."

"Oh, that." He pulls his hand away and flops onto his back, one arm covering his eyes. "What about it?"

"It was..." I try to find the right word, but my mind goes blank.

"What?" Dax sighs. "Go on, say it." Despite it being rough from sleep, his voice bristles.

"I dunno," I say. "Intense?"

Dax stays silent, still not looking at me. Rolling over, I put a hand on his shoulder, which is tense and rigid.

"And...?" Dax finally says.

"Well..." I'd thought about asking him before, but I hadn't been sure how or when to bring it up. Or if I should bring it up at all. "Have you ever talked to anyone about it?"

"What do you mean?" Dax uncovers his eyes, but keeps them fixed on the ceiling, his tone defensive.

"I mean..." I shift closer so that my arm is pressed against his warm body. "Have you ever talked to a professional, like a therapist?"

"No." He scoots just enough that there's a space between us again. It's only an inch or two, but it creates a valley between us that makes him seem miles away.

"It could help, you know?" I lightly stroke his shoulder with my knuckles.

"What would help is if you'd stop talking about it." Dax's comment hits me like a sucker punch.

"But I—"

Dax grips my hand and pushes it away, then sits up with a jolt. "Look, I'm fine. Let's drop it."

"I don't want to drop it," I say, softening my voice. "I care about you, and I think you need—"

"No, Bond." He's only called me Bond a couple of times. This one sounds like pure poison on his tongue. "What I need are people I can trust. People who support me and won't tell me what they think I need. I thought you were one of those people."

I can feel the conversation starting to slip away from me like water through my hands, and I'm unable to stop it. "I do. I am. I just...hated seeing you like that." I sit up, reaching for Dax, but he moves toward the edge of the bed, barely out of my reach.

"Like what? Nervous? Okay, yeah. I'll admit it. I was fucking nervous about going on national television. You would be too."

"Of course I would, Dax. But we both know it wasn't only nerves. In the dressing room, you couldn't speak. You could barely breathe. Hell, you didn't even know I was in the room when I first got there."

Dax hauls himself out of bed and starts to collect his clothes from the floor, swiping up each piece more aggressively than the last. Once he's gathered all of his clothes, he stops to look at me with a hard stare.

"Look." His voice is softer, but resigned. "It was one panic attack. It's over."

"But it wasn't just one, was it?" I keep my eyes on his, hoping he'll see the concern on my face. "There've been more."

"Jesus." Dax throws a hand up in frustration. "I didn't realize you were keeping tabs on my mental health."

"I'm not keeping tabs. I can see..."

"Don't do this," he says, cutting me off. The way he's looking at me is unsettling. He's like a wild animal that's been backed into a corner, trying to decide between fight or flight.

With a clenched jaw, he says, "I don't need another boyfriend who wants to fix me. I thought you were different."

I open my mouth, but nothing comes out. He shakes his head. "So, what? You want me to ignore it?" I finally ask, my voice almost pleading. "To see you struggle through the anxiety and panic attacks? I can't. I care about you too much."

"God damn it, AJ." Dropping the clothes to the floor, he sits on the corner of the bed, his head falling into his hands, and he looks...defeated. He's quiet for a moment, and I'm too scared to say or do anything.

And with what's possibly the shittiest timing ever, my phone buzzes. Out of pure habit, I turn to the table to look at it.

TMG Office.

What the hell? It's 7:45 in the morning.

When I look back at Dax, his eyes are narrowed, the softness is gone, replaced by stony anger. I press the button on my phone to ignore the call.

"Dax, I don't want to fight and I'm not trying to fix you. I want you to be happy."

"I *am* happy." He's up again, pacing back and forth across the room. "I have a fucking great life. I have a family that loves me, a career that's taking off, I have money, and up until a few minutes ago, I had a supportive boyfriend who liked me for who I am."

"I *do* like you, Dax. I fucking l–"

My phone buzzes again.

TMG Office.

Again. And again, I press the button to send the call to voicemail.

Dax shakes his head. "I should've listened to Hannah," he mutters to himself. "And not fall in love with a straight guy."

Straight guy? Love? What?

I was about to tell Dax I love him. It's what I should tell him now. But I don't. Instead, I say, "What's that supposed to mean?"

"Nothing."

"No, you said it. Tell me what you mean."

He turns to me and gives me a venomous look. "Have you told your mom about me?" I swallow hard and I can feel my cheeks flame.

"No." My voice is small. "But I barely talk to her as it is. I haven't spoken to her in a couple of months."

"You don't think that, I don't know, having a new boyfriend would be enough of a reason to call her?"

I don't have an answer.

"Have you told anyone at work that we're together? Have you told André?"

I flinch and look down at the floor.

"No? That's what I thought," Dax says.

"Dax, you're putting up walls."

He ignores me. "All you care about is your precious job and impressing your bosses. If you cared about me, really cared, you'd tell at least one person we're together."

"I've already told you, I'm keeping things quiet at work because I'm trying to get a promotion. Once the issue is out and things settle down…"

Dax laughs, but it's a bitter sort of laughter. "You're so fucking scared of what everyone else thinks of you. Of what they'll think of you if we're seen together."

"That's not true. We've been seen together in public. I'm not hiding this. You know that."

"I'd hardly call getting takeout and eating in your apartment 'public'. The few times we've been out, we go to places in neighborhoods where no one will see us. A deli in a Jewish neighborhood? That hole-in-the-wall restaurant by your work? Please."

"I was doing that for you." I stand, moving toward Dax, but as soon as I take a step closer, he faces me with a stance that's clearly defensive—chest puffed up and arms at his sides, muscles tight. I don't take another step.

"I see how tense you get when people recognize you. I thought if we went to someplace where people wouldn't approach you, you'd be more relaxed. I mean, look at how you reacted at the arcade bar the other night."

Dax scoffs. "I don't need you to make things easier for me. And I don't need therapy. I need—"

My phone buzzes again. *Fucking hell.*

"It's fine. Answer it." Dax gathers his clothes into a bundle and carries them into the bathroom, shutting the door behind him.

I sit on the bed and stare at the phone still buzzing in my hand.

"*Answer it!*" Dax shouts from the bathroom. And then, almost as an afterthought, he mumbles, "For fuck's sake."

I swipe the screen and hold it to my ear, not saying a word.

"Bond? It's MaryBeth." André's assistant speaks, without waiting for me to say anything.

"Hi," I finally say.

"Can you come in? Now?"

"Why?" A surge of worry bolts up through my stomach. "I told André last Friday that I was taking this morning off."

Dax and I had made plans to see a new exhibit at the MoMA this morning. Not that he'd want to go now anyway.

"They're making the announcement about the position today. André wants you to come in as soon as you can."

I sit on the bed. This is the big announcement I've been waiting for weeks to hear. Something in MaryBeth's voice sounds off, but I can't place it. I open my mouth to ask, but I don't get the chance.

"Take a cab if it's faster. Just get here."

"Okay," I say. "I'll be there as soon as I can."

When I hang up, I turn to see Dax fully dressed in the doorway.

"Gotta go to work, huh?" he asks, his voice higher, with an air of fake cheerfulness. When I don't answer, he shrugs casually. "Yeah, I gotta go too. Busy day."

A lie. I don't call him on it.

"Dax, can we please talk about this later?"

"Yeah, sure." He turns to leave, takes one step, then turns back. "You know what? No."

"No?" The word is like a slap in the face.

"That's right. No. I don't think there's anything else to say. I think maybe we rushed into something you're obviously not ready for. I'm a public figure, AJ. People recognize me. If you're not okay with people knowing about us, then we can't do this. I don't need someone who's not sure who they are or what they want trying to tell me how to live *my* life."

"That's not...I'm not..." I can't finish. I don't know what to say. A ton of bricks hits me in the pit of my stomach. My brain scrambles for any scrap of something to say to salvage this. I can barely breathe.

Dax's shoulders slump and he sighs.

"Go to work, Bond." He turns and walks out.

CHAPTER 22

AJ

The front door shuts behind Dax, but it's several seconds before the footsteps start to recede.

My heart feels like it's being seized in a vice grip, the pressure getting tighter and tighter. I'm still sitting on the edge of my bed, and wondering what the hell just happened.

Go. Run after him. Beg him to stop and listen.

I don't. What would I say? It doesn't matter. He's not going to want to hear it anyway. *Give him time to cool off. Call him tonight. We'll work it out.*

I debate whether I have time for a shower before I head to the office, but after everything Dax and I got up to last night, I realize I can't skip it. Fifteen minutes later, I'm cleaned up and heading out the door, speed-walking toward the subway.

When I step off the elevator into the *TMG* offices, I'm surprised to see MaryBeth waiting for me. She gives me a tight-lipped smile.

"Hey, Bond. Thanks for coming in. Sorry I kept calling you. André was insistent."

"It's okay. Where is he?"

My stomach is in knots as I look around the office. I notice the light in André's office is off. All of the lights in the offices are on motion sensors to cut down on electricity waste, so it's easy to tell when someone's not in their office.

"He's in, uh…" She points to Takashi's vacant office. It doesn't look vacant now.

Shit.

The door is closed, so I knock softly.

"Come in," I hear André's voice call. When I walk in, I see André sitting on the leather couch, a man in an impeccably tailored suit sitting in the chair opposite him. They both stand and wait while I close the door behind me.

My palms immediately start sweating, and I'm nervous, filled with the sense that I've walked into a job interview. And then before anyone speaks, it hits me.

I am.

This is the new creative director. Not me.

"Ah, AJ Bond, come on in." André ushers me over to the other man. "This is Dario Souza, *TMG*'s new creative director." André gives me a hesitant look, like he's holding his breath—waiting to see how I'll react.

I'm a professional. I won't get upset. At least, not here.

"It's nice to meet you." Dario's voice is light and friendly with a distinct Italian accent.

"Dario comes to us from—"

"*TMG Italia*." I finish André's sentence for him. "I know. I'm a big fan of your work," I say to Dario, shaking his hand. He seems unfazed by my compliment.

Dario is at least half a foot shorter than me, give or take a couple of inches from the Italian leather boots he's wearing. His hair is dark, gelled back to look like a sleek, aerodynamic helmet. His smile is warm but reserved, probably gauging my reaction to the news.

André continues. "We are lucky to have such talent in our midst, all present company included." He gives me an encouraging look.

"Of course," I say. "It's a pleasure to meet you." I attempt a genuine smile to hide my disappointment, but I know it must look forced.

We all look back and forth at each other in an awkward social standoff, no one moving for a long moment.

"Well, I'll leave the two of you." André says, clearing his throat and stepping toward the door. "The official announcement will happen later today. AJ, please see me when the two of you wrap up here." He smiles and walks out, shutting the door behind him.

At once, the weight of this moment—the announcement—hits me. I'm glad I didn't have time to eat before I came in, because I suddenly feel sick.

"Have a seat," Dario gestures toward the couch. "If you like, that is."

"No thanks, I'm okay." I'm standing stiffly in the middle of the room with nowhere to put my hands. I fold my arms across my chest, but fearing my stance looks too defensive, I unfold them and stuff my hands in my pockets.

"As you wish." He crosses the room and leans against the desk, crossing one ankle over the other, taking care not to scuff his boots.

"Mr. Bond, I've heard a lot about you in the last few days. Mr. Laurent—er, André—has been singing your praises. He says you're a highly respected member of the *TMG* team."

Here it comes, I think. *The part where an important new hire cleans house and brings in their own staff.* I stand a little straighter, bracing myself for impact.

"I understand that you were hoping to take over Takashi's role. To be quite honest, I didn't know about your interest in the position before I agreed to come here. As it happened, Lorenzo called me at a time when I was feeling stagnant in my job and I needed a new challenge. He and I go way back, so he knew all the right things to say to convince me to accept the job. And here we are."

Here we are, indeed.

Lorenzo, the president and CEO of Wright Media, can be kind but shrewd. As long as you're doing a good job, he's happy. Well, *happy* might be a stretch. Content, maybe? And as long as the magazine is doing well and staying within budget, he doesn't get involved in our day-to-day activities. I've only spoken to him a handful of times in all the years I've been working here, and even at that, I'm still not sure he knows my name.

"I'm going to be honest here," Dario says, moving to sit on the chair he'd been occupying when I first walked in. He gestures to the couch, and I give in, sitting down and clasping my hands on my lap like a kid who's been sent to the principal's office.

"I've seen some of the work you've done for the magazine. It's good. I'd like to say you do great work, but it's hard to know if you've reached your maximum potential or if you've been held back." I shift uncomfortably as Dario speaks, the leather of the couch letting out a mortifying noise like a defective whoopee cushion. "Don't worry. I've known Takashi for a long time and I have the utmost respect for him. André says you're very talented. I'd like to see that talent for myself before I make any decisions about changes within our team."

My eyes snap up to meet his. "Changes?" I ask.

"Well, yes. I'm not looking to replace anyone," he says, although when he says *anyone*, we both know he's talking about me specifically. "But I'd like to see what you're capable of."

"Uh, okay."

"When Takashi was here, he was working on the cover designs and major feature shoots, yes?"

"Yes, that's right."

"And you did the smaller photo shoots: product features, restaurant reviews, gift guides, that type of thing. Yes?"

"Yeah, I mean, up until Takashi went on leave. I worked on a big feature for December's issue. With Diego Ximénez." Saying his name out loud hits me squarely in the gut. I take a breath and hope Dario doesn't notice.

"Ah. Let's talk about that."

I shift from feeling like I'm in a job interview to feeling like I'm on the witness stand being cross-examined by a lawyer. I try to discreetly rub my sweaty palms on my thighs.

Dario crosses the room to his desk and pulls a folder from the top of a stack of papers. He sits down again and opens the folder on the coffee table between us. It's the layout featuring Dax that I'd been working on. The bold, bright colors accentuate Dax's beautiful face, which practically jumps off the page. The photos should make me smile, but right now, looking at them makes me hurt all over.

"Tell me about this shoot."

I push down my feelings and try to focus on the technical aspects of the shoot. Dario listens while I walk him through the entire process of the shoot, and about how I'd made the decision to switch things up when it was clear that the original plan wasn't working. He nods, but remains quiet while I tell him about the idea to change the direction after seeing Dax goofing off on set. When I'm finished, he smiles, but I can't tell if it's genuine.

"It was a big risk," Dario says. I clasp my hands together in my lap again, tightening my grip as Dario pauses, seemingly for dramatic effect. "But I think it paid off. It will look great in the magazine." I sigh in relief, hoping it isn't too obvious.

Then he straightens up and runs a hand over his already smoothed-back hair.

"I think you have potential, Mr. Bond. I'd like to see what you're really capable of in the coming weeks."

"Uh, sure," I say, unsure of what he's asking.

"I'm going to be in and out of the office for the next week while things with my apartment get settled. I won't officially start until then. But I'll be around—you know, meetings and whatnot. During that time, you'll continue doing what you've been doing since Takashi went on leave. I know you've discussed ideas for the upcoming issue with André. I'd like to be included in the planning process. And I'd like to see the layouts you have for the next issue."

"Of course," I say, feeling a tightening in my chest. *Great, a micromanager.*

"That's all for now," he says, standing up, effectively dismissing me. I stand too, but hesitate before moving for the door. Dario eyes me thoughtfully before speaking.

"Mr. Bond, I know this announcement must be a disappointment to you given that you were hoping to be offered the position. But I hope you'll see this as an opportunity for growth. Based on what André says about you, I think you'll be able to rise to the challenge."

Challenge? Is he challenging me to work harder to keep my own job? A headache begins to creep its way into my skull, starting behind my eyes. Unable to say anything more, I nod and walk out.

I stop by André's office and give him a brief rundown of everything Dario had told me. He'd been worried that I'd be disappointed and upset at not getting the job. And I am. But between my argument with Dax this morning and the news about the job, I don't have the energy to be upset. I feel numb.

I force myself to focus as André and I discuss details on the current issue and go over ideas for the next issue. I know I'm supposed to step up and prove myself, but at the moment, all I want to do is go home and curl up on my couch. And cry.

I barely make it through the rest of the day before going home and doing exactly that.

CHAPTER 23

DAX

I screwed things up. Overreacted.

Fuck. What have I done?

I'd lashed out at AJ, then stormed out. God, the look on his face when I was leaving—he looked so hurt, so completely crushed. I never thought I'd be the one to cause him to look that way. The second I'd closed the door, I regretted it. I didn't leave right away. Instead, I waited in the hallway, wanting to turn around and knock. Wanting to tell him I'm sorry. Or maybe I was hoping he'd fling open the door and find me there, then ask me to come back in and talk things out.

But I hadn't knocked. And he hadn't come after me.

On my way home, I can't help but think about my father, thoughts swirling like dark clouds forming a funnel that will inevitably become a tornado of angry and painful memories.

The thinly veiled insults. The hurtful nicknames. The disappointed looks. The night he and mom fought when I'd gotten the part in the school musical. That night, I'd sat on the swing and listened to the shouting, mostly from my father—Mom has never been one to shout. I don't know what she said, but I'd heard my father, clear as a bell.

He used words like *embarrassment, unnatural,* and *maricón.* Every word I overheard, I collected, never forgetting.

And then I heard it. *Therapy.*

It rang in my ears like gunfire. *"They have places we could send him to,"* he'd said. *"They could help him. Straighten him out. Fix him."*

I hated him so much after that. And hated myself for a while too, not fully understanding what I'd done to make my own father turn his back on me with such finality. There was no talking to him about it, no effort at understanding. So for a long time, I was convinced that eventually whatever it was about me that was so terrible, I'd eventually drive away my mother and sister too. Mom must've had a sense about what I'd been thinking back then, because she only became more affectionate, hugging me all the time and telling me things like *"I'll always love you, cariño."*

I can feel a heaviness in my gut. On the train somewhere between Brooklyn and Queens in the early light of morning, I feel like I'm going to be sick. I focus my eyes on a crack in the window. I stare at it and concentrate on my breathing, trying to swallow the painful feelings back down.

I know the therapy that AJ—and before that, Max—was talking about has nothing to do with the type of therapy my father was referring to all those years ago. But for some reason, my mind can't differentiate between the two. I've put them all into one folder in my brain, filed neatly away under the heading *No Way In Hell.*

A voice in the back of my mind keeps telling me that all they're doing—AJ, Max, Hannah—is trying to help. But the voices of my father and brother are louder. Telling me I'm soft, weak. Telling me that men don't cry. That men don't talk about feelings. That men shouldn't love other men. And the insinuation that I wasn't worthy of their love, or even acceptance, as I was.

When I get home, Mom is making breakfast for Dad and Cami's already at work. With heavy, dragging steps, I haul myself upstairs and lie down on my bed, too emotionally drained to even take a shower.

A few hours later, I finally manage to clean myself up and try to salvage what's left of the day. I answer a few emails and make a couple of calls, all while attempting to push any thoughts of my argument with AJ out of my head. As I'm hitting Send on an email to Max, my phone buzzes. My heart jumps at the thought that it might be AJ. Not only am I disappointed to see it's not him, but my stress level heightens at the name on the screen: Whitney. *God, not now.*

Things with Whitney have been tense, and she's the last person I want to talk to right now. But figuring she'd at least be a distraction from thoughts of AJ, I answer.

"Dax. I got you a spot on a morning talk show." No greeting, no asking how I'm doing. Straight to business.

"Uh...okay," is all I'm able to say.

"It's a local show. They want you to do a four-minute comedy set. But it needs to be clean, no swearing. Family-friendly. Then you'll stay for an interview after. And..." She hesitates.

"And what?" I'm irritated before I even hear the rest of it.

"Then they usually ask their guests to stick around and help them with the cooking segment."

If I'd eaten anything in the last few hours, it would be threatening to come back up. I'm okay with interviews about the show, but another comedy set? And an on-air cooking segment? I could push through them, probably. Maybe. But those are the kinds of things that could potentially trigger my anxiety. The way my panic attacks have been sneaking up on me lately, I start to sweat thinking about it.

"I don't know. The comedy set on *The Knightly Show* was a one-time thing. It's not really how I want to be presenting myself."

"Dax, that's my job. Let *me* worry about how to present you to the public."

"Can't it just be an interview about the show?"

"Listen, in this business, you have to be able to adapt. They liked what you did on *The Knightly Show*." Her tone oozes impatience. "What's the problem?"

"Well…" I run a hand over my neck, then pull at the hair on the back of my head, a nervous habit I've had since I was a kid. "It's just that with my anxiety—"

"Oh, *pssshh*. Come on, Dax." Whitney's dismissive tone grates on me. "I know it's not the type of press you usually do. But it'll be good to get your face out there in front of a different audience."

"What do you mean by different?"

"Oh, you know…housewives, soccer moms—upper-middle-class suburban women. *Wake Up, Elizabeth* is a really popular show with that demographic—"

"Elizabeth? As in New Jersey?"

"Yes. Look, you wanted my help getting your face out there in front of the public. That's what I'm *trying* to do."

"Alright, I'm sorry," I say, trying to shake off my irritation. She's right. She's just doing her job. "So, when is it?"

"It's tomorrow. You need to be there by six o'clock." *Is she fucking with me?*

"Wait, what?" I say, shaking my head, knowing I know she can't see me.

"It's tomorrow. I checked the calendar. Your schedule is free."

"I can't do it. I don't have any material ready." My face feels hot with a rush of adrenaline and nerves. "Can't we do it next week when I'm more prepared?"

"No. They had someone cancel at the last minute. We're lucky to get the spot. You can just adapt some bits from *The Knightly Show*."

I'm pacing up and down the hallway, trying hard to keep myself together. I take in a huge gulp of air before I speak again.

"I just did that show a few weeks ago. I don't want to go out there with the same material. And—"

"Listen," Whitney cuts me off. "You're not being very cooperative for someone who's trying to make a good impression on the general public. You're on the brink of becoming famous. You need this. So get over your nerves and do the fucking show."

For the second time today, I'm fighting a losing battle. But unlike this morning, *I'm* the one begging for the other person to listen to me.

Shit, was this how I made AJ feel this morning? Christ.

Before I can dwell on that thought, Whitney speaks again.

"I'll send you the address as soon as we hang up. And bring a couple changes of clothes. Stylish, but casual. Something like what you wore for *The Knightly Show*. You know, you really should hire Allyson, at least part-time."

Another conversation I don't want to have right now. Allyson's the one who provided the clothes for *The Knightly Show*—the ones I'd rejected, resulting in my major panic attack in the dressing room. The mention of my outfit from the show feels like a swift kick to the shin when I'm already down. I swallow hard.

Whitney had been angling for me to hire Allyson, who's young and trying to break into the business, as a celebrity stylist. I'm not opposed to the idea per se, but when Allyson showed up at *The Knightly Show* with two garment bags full of garish clothes that were so far from my own personal style, she insisted that my own clothing style was boring and forgettable. She'd clearly taken direction from Whitney that my "brand"—the one Whitney's been trying to cultivate—is someone who wears lavish, flamboyant clothes and aims to push the boundaries of gender fluidity—a Mexican Harry Styles, as I overheard her say once. The Dax that Whitney wishes for me to be is someone who buys into the whole luxury lifestyle—which I don't. At all.

After the whole *Knightly Show* mess, Whitney's still trying to get me to hire Allyson. I can't imagine why on earth Allyson would want to work with me on a regular basis after that. I push the thoughts away for now, since I have no intention of actually hiring her.

After another five minutes of back-and-forth with Whitney, I finally give in and agree to do the morning show, ignoring the feeling in my gut that tells me this is a terrible idea.

A few hours later, while going through my notes trying to cobble together enough material to fill four minutes, I think back to AJ encouraging me when I'd first told him I'd been invited to *The Knightly Show*. Up until now, I'd been so thoroughly distracted that I'd barely thought about our fight this morning. But the memory has me pulling at the loose thread until my whole sense of calm begins to unravel.

I sit on the floor with my back against the door—knees to my chest, head in hands—and take in long, heavy breaths. I'm not outright sobbing but quietly letting tears fall down my cheeks and onto my thighs.

I stay like this for god knows how long before finally remembering I have to get up at stupid o'clock in the morning to be at the television studio in New Jersey at six. Ignoring my mom's advice to eat something, I skip dinner and force myself to go to bed early. As I try to fall asleep, memories of our fight, uneasiness about going on live TV in the morning, and worries about having unrehearsed material for tomorrow swirl through my mind like a low-grade hurricane. Tropical Storm Dax.

My phone's alarm startles me awake, and I quickly realize I'm sweaty and shaking. My breaths are coming fast and my heart is pounding, making me feel like I'm being chased. *This is new*. I'd heard of panic attacks happening during sleep, but this is the first time I've ever experienced it.

I arrange myself so that my back is resting against the cool wall and tip my head back, closing my eyes.

After a minute, I reach for my hand-grip exerciser, which I use in place of a stress relief ball, and, keeping my eyes closed, I squeeze it while slowly counting backward in my head.

Fifty. Squeeze. *Forty-nine.* Release. *Forty-eight.* Squeeze. *Forty-seven.* Release.

When I get to zero, I'm not quite feeling back to normal, so I switch hands and start over again from fifty. I repeat the process once more, each cycle bringing me back to feeling a little closer to normal again.

Once I'm able to get ready—at least twenty minutes later than I should have started—I get in the shower. As the warm water cascades over my face and down my chest, I suddenly have a feeling like I'm completely off-balance, like the floor is moving underneath me. I manage to open my eyes and grip the wall to keep from falling. The sensation only lasts a second or two, but it freaks me the fuck out. I slowly sit down on the edge of the tub, letting the water continue to fall on me as I regain my composure. Moments later, I feel balanced again, but I'm on edge.

With a towel around my waist, I go back to my room, but instead of getting ready—which is what I really should do since I'm now running late—I sit on my bed, clutching a pillow to my chest and staring at a spot on the floor. My eyelids feel heavy and I know I should get up, but I can't. My body feels wrung out and the effort it would take to get up seems insurmountable.

Five minutes. I'll give myself five minutes to recover and then I'll get ready to go. If I hurry, I won't be too terribly late. After all, leaving at five o'clock in the morning means there won't be much traffic.

Just five minutes.

"Fuck, Dax! Are you kidding me?!" Whitney shouts through the phone so loudly, I'm afraid everyone in the house will hear. "I can't believe you missed your spot on a morning show! And all for a little bit of stage fright."

I slip on a pair of flip-flops, pull a jacket over my T-shirt, and take the phone out to the front porch. I pace back and forth while she reads me the riot act for missing my spot on *Wake Up, Elizabeth*. It's eight-thirty and I'd barely woken up ten minutes ago, lying on top of the covers of my bed and still wearing only a towel. My panic attack had taken so much out of me that I fell asleep hard and woke up to my phone buzzing nonstop on my desk.

"I didn't skip it on purpose! Jesus, Whitney," I tell her, trying my best to keep my own voice down. "And it's not stage fright. It's anxiety. I had a panic attack."

"So what? You get those all the time." Her dismissive air makes my blood start to simmer.

"Yeah, I do. Which is why I told you I didn't want to do the show in the first place."

"You should know how to handle them by now." She takes a condescending tone with me that sounds like she's talking to a small child. "You sit down, you take a few deep breaths, and you get over it. It's not that hard."

"That doesn't always work. This one was bad." I hate that I have to defend myself like this. Every time I bring up my anxiety, Whitney brushes it off and tells me that it's only nerves and that I need to get over it because, according to her, having a mental health issue doesn't fit with the brand she's trying to cultivate for me.

"Look, I don't care what you have to do to get through things like this. Take a couple shots of whiskey, take a Valium. Whatever. Man up and do it."

Man up.

I squeeze my eyes shut so tight my head starts to throb while memories of my father and brother start to swirl in my head.

"Don't say that," I say curtly as I sit down on the porch, the cold concrete stinging my skin through the fabric of my sweatpants.

"Don't say what?"

"'Man up.' Don't say that to me. Please."

Whitney scoffs.

"Look, I'll apologize to the producers. I'll go on when I have more time to prepare. After the premiere, I'll be more well-known, so it'll be a better time for me to go on."

"You'd better make good with them. They were able to pull something together without a guest, but they're not happy. What you do, or don't do, makes me look bad too, you know."

I place an elbow on my knee and run a hand through my hair, noticing how tight the muscles in my shoulders are. I blow out a long breath.

"I know, and I'm sorry to put you in that position. I really am. I had a bad feeling about it and I should've said no yesterday."

Whitney starts to speak, then stops. Then starts again. "Fine, well maybe I should've realized you couldn't handle it on such short notice."

It's exactly the sort of non-apology that I've come to expect from her. But it's the closest thing I'm going to get, so I let it go.

"Thank you," I say. She hangs up without saying goodbye. A moment later, she texts me with the contact info for the show's producer.

I make a mental note to call them later today, once I've had a few minutes to formulate a half-decent response. Then I go inside and crawl back into bed.

CHAPTER 24

A J

Bond, please see me in my office. —Dario

I see the sticky note on my screen before I sit down and make a beeline for Dario's office. The door is slightly ajar, but I knock anyway.

"Mr. Bond, come in. You may leave the door open if you like."

It's been nearly two weeks since it was announced that Dario would be taking over Takashi's job, and his office has undergone a complete face-lift. All of the decor has been updated to suit his own personal style. It's more in line with my own style, to be honest. Takashi's cold glass-and-steel aesthetic has been replaced with warm, muted tones and dark wood. I haven't been in here much since the day we met. Dario had been in only a couple of times while he'd been busy uprooting himself and moving across an ocean.

On the coffee table are printouts from the upcoming issue spread out haphazardly. We'd been finalizing the issue and are just making final edits before sending the magazine to the printer.

"Hi," I say, looking around at the mess. "Did you need something from me?"

"Yes, please have a seat."

As I sit on the couch, Dario picks up a printout from among the mess of papers. "I'd like your thoughts on something."

He hands me the color proof of the upcoming cover—the last one that Takashi worked on before leaving. On it is a photo of a muscular man in a tight-fitting sweater standing on a beach. His thick arms are crossed over his broad chest and he's giving a thousand-watt smile, teeth almost gleaming. I hate it. I had since the first time I saw it. André had fought Takashi on it, but Takashi dug his heels in. God only knows why.

As I hold the printout, Dario looks expectantly at me. I'm not sure what he wants.

"Uh," I say. Because I have nothing else queued up in my brain.

"What do you think of this cover?"

"It's about maintaining a workout routine over the holidays. It's a fitness story."

"I know what it's about, Bond. It says so right here." Dario jabs a finger at the text on the printout to illustrate his point. "I want to know what you think."

"Well, this is one that Takashi worked on before he left. I think he was trying to capture the feeling of..."

Dario shakes his head, exasperated. "No. I don't care what the thought process was. I want to know what *you* think about it." Noticing my hesitancy, he says, "Takashi isn't here. I'm not asking you to judge him as a person. I simply want to know what you think of *this*." Dario pokes a little too aggressively at the printout in my hand.

I inhale, then look at the printout. "I don't think it should be on the cover," I say. Dario cocks his head to the side and waits, so I continue. "Readers don't want a story about working out right before the holidays. Plus, if someone wants to know how to really get in shape, they'd pick up some other fitness magazine. That's not what *TMG* is known for.

It's a fine story, but it's not what will make people pick it up off the newsstand or to motivate them to look at it online. Also..." I hesitate.

"Go on," Dario says.

"The photo is a little cheesy for my taste. It looks like the cover of a catalog."

"Interesting."

Shit. He doesn't react to my comments beyond that one word. I'm not sure what he'd been expecting me to say.

"So...what would you have done instead?"

"The photos of Dax Ximénez are brilliant. They're really colorful and would jump off the page. Plus, his TV show is premiering soon. By the time the magazine comes out, the show will have caught on with audiences, so the timing of the cover would work out great. I mean, he's already being featured, so the cover would make sense." I can feel my cheeks heating as I talk. "Jürgen has one really stunning photo that would make a great cover."

Dario's mouth spreads into a slow smile. He nods at me.

"Okay, Mr. Bond. Let's see it."

"Sorry? See what?"

"Mock up a cover. I want to see it by two o'clock."

"Uh, okaaaay." I'm a little stunned at Dario's request. "Would you like to see a few options?"

"It's not necessary. I want you to choose the best photo and mock it up. I'd prefer you work on one you feel strongly about rather than waste your time on others that you don't feel are as good." Dario looks at the ornate clock on the wall. "You only have a few hours. Go to it."

I nod and hurry out. *What the hell?* How am I going to pull off a new cover in only a few hours?

I grab a coffee from the machine, put on my headphones, and get to work. I'd been so wrapped up in work since our breakup that I hadn't let myself think about Dax. But now, opening the folder with the thousands of photos from the shoot, my heart begins to ache. I take a huge gulp of coffee, feeling the burn as it goes down my throat. I can't get distracted. I need to focus.

I pull up the photo of Dax that had stopped me in my tracks when I was reviewing them with Jürgen—the one of Dax with the Rubik's Cube. That's it. No need to go through the other photos.

André gives me some new headlines to match the story, and I work on the cover for a solid five hours, barely moving from my chair except to get more coffee. Kiara picks up lunch for me, which I scarf down in five minutes. André walks by and I pull him in for his feedback. He gives me a couple of notes, then smiles as he walks away. *Weird.*

At 1:58, Dario pokes his head out of his office. "Mr. Bond?" I look up. "Do you have a printout of the cover you've been working on?"

"Yeah, I need to get it from the printer. Would you like to see it?"

"Yes, please."

I retrieve the printout and hand it to Dario as he's exiting his office. He looks it over, then nods once before hurrying out, notepad and pen in hand. He crooks a finger at me, indicating I should follow.

When he opens the door to the conference room, it's filled with several members of the editorial board. *Holy shit.* I've never met most of these people and had never dealt with the board directly. Dario holds the door for me to enter. I'm not sure what to do, so I stand against the wall near the door.

I see André seated in one of the chairs at the conference table. I furrow my brow and cock my head, but he just smiles back at me.

"Good afternoon, everyone," Dario says. "Before we begin talking about the next issue of *TMG*, I have a quick matter to bring up regarding the December issue. You've all seen the cover that had been put together by Takashi."

Dario produces the printout of the gleaming-toothed man, and everyone nods.

"After some discussion with Mr. Bond, *TMG*'s art director..." Dario gestures to me. I wave stiffly. "We decided to try another approach." The room breaks out in a low chatter.

"Isn't it too late to change it?" a voice from across the room asks. Lorenzo. *Be cool.*

"I've checked with the production manager," Dario says. "If we finalize it in the next two days, it will still print on time. Mr. Bond will present the proposed new cover and tell you a little about it."

I will? Is this a joke I'm not in on?

Everyone turns to look at me. When I look at Dario, he gives me a nod and gestures for me to stand beside him.

I clear my throat and move to the front of the room, holding up the printout of the cover: Dax's face. I try to channel some of Dax's charisma I'd seen when he was in front of the cameras on *The Knightly Show*. I look at the face on the printout and a surge of confidence washes over me. *This is my work and I'm goddamn proud of it.*

I give the board an explanation of why I think this cover is the better option. At the mention of newsstand sales and potential online tie-ins—an online-only Q&A, behind-the-scenes photos I'd taken, a list of Dax's ten favorite things to do in Queens—the board members light up. They nod and whisper to one another in what seems like approval.

Lorenzo speaks. "Provided we can stay on schedule, I like it." The rest of the room agrees. I look at André who's smiling at me like a proud parent. Dario gives me a little nod.

"Thank you, Mr. Bond," he says and I take that as a dismissal. *Thank god.*

Half an hour later, André walks by my desk.

"Great job, Bond. The board was impressed with you."

"Thanks," I say. I'm still trying to recover from the events of earlier today, but at André's words, relief washes over me.

"Since we've all committed to go with this cover, I'll need to talk to Mr. Ximénez again."

"Sure," is all I manage to say.

"I'd like to ask him a few more questions for the article. We could also record an online Q&A session in the studio at the same time. Kill two birds with one stone."

"That seems smart."

"Great. See if you can have him come in tomorrow. He's local, so let's hope he can do that. If not, a phone call would suffice for now and we could do the video later." I'm instantly hit by an emotional dump truck.

"Sure, but shouldn't MaryBeth make the call?" I ask. She's André's assistant, after all.

"She could, if that's what you'd prefer. But I thought you'd like to deliver the good news to Mr. Ximénez yourself." He gives me a warm smile, then turns and heads back to his office before I can protest.

My heart sinks at the thought of having to call Dax. What would I say? *"Hey, I know we broke up and you never want to speak to me again, but could you please come to my work so my boss can ask you some questions?"* Ugh.

I pick up my phone and scroll through my contacts. When the voice on the phone answers, I clear my throat to keep my voice from breaking. With a shaky breath, I speak.

"Hi, Hannah, it's AJ Bond."

CHAPTER 25

DAX

I wake up from a fitful sleep, sweaty and somehow more tired than I'd felt before I went to bed last night. I don't quite remember the details, but I can tell I've had another panic attack while I slept. *Jesus. They never used to be this bad.*

I hate it. Knowing that even when I'm asleep—the time I'm supposed to be the most relaxed—those feelings of anxiety can creep in and snatch the few shreds of peace out from under me.

By some small miracle, I manage to get through the day, trying not to think about anything that could trigger more anxiety. I go to the gym and push myself harder than usual, enjoying the burn of physical exertion. It helps me to focus and block out all the other noise in my head.

I catch Cami on her break and we have lunch at the restaurant across the street from her work. Then I head home, where I do a virtual guest appearance on a comedy podcast, which thankfully works out much better than the whole *Wake Up, Elizabeth* mess I'd caused almost two weeks ago. Once I wrap up the podcast, I'm finally able to truly relax for the first time today.

I'd had my phone turned off during the podcast, but when I turn it back on, I see a missed call from Hannah. I don't bother listening to the voicemail and call her back.

"Dax, AJ just called me." My shoulders tense at the mention of AJ, and I look up at the ceiling, trying to hold back the deluge of emotions that's suddenly threatening to spill out. "He wanted me to let you know that *TMG* wants you to come to the office tomorrow. You pick the time."

"I'm busy." I say in a more curt tone than I'd intended.

"No, you're not. You have no scheduled interviews and no appearances."

"Okay, well, what if I don't want to?" *Good lord, I sound like a spoiled child.*

"Look, AJ didn't tell me what happened, but he sounded a little off. Clearly something did happen though. Otherwise, he'd have called you, not me, to deliver the good news himself. You haven't told me what happened between the two of you, and that's fine, but this thing at *TMG*? It's big."

"What thing? What are you talking about?"

"They're putting you on the cover. The feature that you did, they're expanding it and doing more of a story. André wants you to come in to answer a few more questions, and then they're going to do a video Q&A for their website."

I rake my fingers through my hair. This is huge. Being on the cover of *TMG* will give me a massive career boost. But still...

"Dax? Dax!"

"Sorry. I'm here."

"Did you hear me? You're going to be on the cover!"

"Yeah, that's, um, that's great." My throat feels like I'm trying to swallow a stone.

"You don't sound that excited," Hannah says.

"It's great, really. It's just...a lot."

"I know. It's nothing you can't handle," she says in her most assuring tone. She's quiet for a moment before she says, "Will you answer one question for me?"

I sigh loudly enough that Hannah can hear it over the phone. "Okay."

"Did he hurt you?"

"What?"

"Did AJ do something to hurt you?" I can hear prickles of defensiveness in her tone.

"No. He—"

"Because if he did, you know I can throw a mean punch."

"Yeah, I know." I chuckle. "But please don't. It's not...it's complicated."

Only, it isn't complicated. I'm too ashamed and embarrassed to admit that the whole reason AJ and I broke up was because of my own stubbornness. The more I think about the whole situation, the more I realize I might have acted like a complete and utter asshole. I try to push the thought out of my head.

"Well, whatever happened with AJ, put it aside for now. He said he'd stay away while you're at the office, if that's what you want."

I shake my head, aware that Hannah can't see me. That's not what I want. But it's what I deserve for acting like I did.

I should find a way to apologize. Maybe going to his office is a sign, and a perfect opportunity to talk to him.

"Hannah? Tell AJ I'll be there tomorrow at eleven."

I step off the elevator at *TMG*'s offices and I'm greeted by Mary-Beth, André's assistant whom I'd met when I was here before. She'd also been the one to arrange the original interview with André before the photo shoot.

"Hi, Mr. Ximénez," she says. "You can come with me to André's office and he'll ask you a few more questions. Then we'll go down to the studio. Well, it's not actually a studio. It's an office that's been converted to a small studio. I heard it's going to be turned back into an office, but I'm not sure when. I guess that means we'll have to find a new place to do in-house interviews. Anyway, we're all so excited that you're going to be on the cover. Bond did a great job with it and it looks stunning. You're going to love it."

MaryBeth doesn't stop talking the entire time I follow her to André's office. She reminds me of Cami in that way. Normally I'd find it charming, but right now, it grates on me. I'm on edge about seeing AJ, and it doesn't go unnoticed when MaryBeth mentions his name. When I don't see him in the office, I almost ask where he is, but I bite my tongue. I'm here on business. Still though, I hope I can see him at some point while I'm here, even if it's only for a minute. If he even wants to see me, that is.

We step into André's office and I thank MaryBeth before she leaves, shutting the door behind her. There's a frosted glass panel next to the door, making it impossible to recognize AJ, or anyone else walking by.

"Mr. Ximénez, thank you for coming by on short notice," André says, shaking my hand. "We had a late change to the magazine—a change for the better. Our newly appointed creative director has really shaken things up since he took on the role."

He's got to be talking about AJ. That's the job he told me about—the one he'd been trying to land for months. I smile and even allow myself to feel a little bit proud of him.

"Ah, and the creative director..." My voice trails off, not sure where I'm going with my thoughts.

"He'll be in the studio when we do the video part. For now, I want to ask you a few more questions—follow-ups, if you will—to give the story a little more depth since it's expanding to a slightly larger piece."

"Sure, sounds good," I say, taking a seat in the soft leather chair.

Half an hour later, our interview is done, and André leads me across the sea of desks to a small office with a sign that says *Studio* on the door. There's a director's chair in front of a large shelf full of books and magazines, all neatly arranged. I assume this is where I'll sit. The whole setup isn't nearly as elaborate as the photo shoot, but it's supposed to feel 'casual and personal,' as André had put it.

Sydney, the stylist from the photo shoot, is here with a sweater for me to try on. It's black and looks like it's two sizes too small. When I put it on, Sydney assures me it looks great. I wish AJ were here to reassure me I don't look like some fucking meathead jock trying to show off my muscles in a too-tight sweater. *Where is he anyway? Shouldn't he be here for this?*

A hair-and-makeup stylist comes in and touches up my face with some makeup to keep me from looking like a sweaty mess on camera.

"Mr. Ximénez?" A voice behind me catches me off guard. I turn to see a petite man dressed in a suit and tie with shiny shoes and even shinier hair.

"I'm Dario Souza, *TMG*'s new creative director."

I shake his hand and smile, hoping to mask my confusion.

"It's a pleasure to meet you," he says. "I've heard good things about you."

Where's AJ? My eyes dart out the open door into the rest of the office, but I don't see him. "Nice to meet you," I say, trying to make my voice sound friendly.

And then it dawns on me. AJ didn't get the job that he'd been working so hard for. That's why they were calling him so much on the morning of our fight.

Perfect. Another reason to feel like shit for what I'd done.

"Well," Dario says, ushering me to the director's chair in front of the camera. "Shall we get started?"

I sit while everyone around me gets set up. I'm told that off camera Kiara, the social media coordinator, will be asking me a series of twenty questions picked at random from *TMG*'s social media followers and I'm supposed to give short, honest, and funny (no pressure!) answers.

Then Kiara will edit it down to a three-minute video that will go on the *TMG* website.

The questions are all over the place, but none of them are too hard to answer. I get the usual *"What are your favorite TV shows"* and *"Who are your influences"* questions. I'm making the staff in the room laugh, which feels great, especially given how I've been feeling the last few days.

And then, at question eleven, I look up to see AJ in the doorway, and my heart skips a few beats. His arms are folded across his chest, but he has a small, almost shy smile on his lips. I fumble over my words when I see him, but I manage to play it off in a way that makes everyone laugh. I force my attention back to Kiara, hoping to get my thoughts back on track.

The next time I look up, AJ is gone.

I shake hands and thank everyone when we're done. André leads me to the door, telling me something about when I can expect to see the magazine or whatever. I'm not paying attention. My eyes are scanning the entire floor for AJ.

"Mr. Ximénez?" André asks.

"Hmm?" I reply, finally bringing my attention back to him. "Sorry, what?"

"I asked if you'd like to say goodbye to anyone before you go?" A knowing smile plays across his lips.

"Oh, uh, yes. I'd like to say goodbye to AJ, if he's not busy."

"Of course." André leads me to AJ's desk.

Empty. *Well, shit.*

There's a sticky note on his screen that says *Lunch. Back soon.* The note is worn and is barely hanging on to the screen by a corner, like he'd written it a long time ago and uses it often.

"Well," André says, and I can tell he's almost as surprised as I am that AJ's gone.

I shouldn't be surprised. I'd made it clear after our fight that I didn't want to talk to him. Looks like I got what I wanted.

"I'm sure he'll be back soon if you'd like to wait," André offers.

"No, that's okay," I say. "I'll catch up with him later."

He gives me a sympathetic smile. If AJ hasn't already told him about us, André's figured it out himself—that much is pretty obvious.

"Well, thank you again." André walks me toward the elevator. Dario pokes his head out of his office—the one that should be AJ's new office—and waves.

As I'm stepping into the elevator, André calls out, "Check the café downstairs. They have a good selection of lunch options there. And you never know who you might run into." He doesn't wink at me, but he might as well have. Subtlety isn't his strength.

Following André's advice, I scan the tables in front of the building's café as I walk toward the front doors leading out of the building. I tell myself, *If I see him, I'll go over there. If not, it's a sign I should leave him alone.* I hope like hell I'll see him.

I crane my neck like a creeper to look at every table. And just when I think he's not there, I see him. He's tucked into a corner couch/table thing that looks like a giant red slug with a built-in tabletop. He's with someone else, laughing and bumping shoulders like they're sharing a joke or a secret. Their body language is far too intimate to be a coworker. She has dark hair that's pulled into a messy bun, and I immediately recognize her from the photo in AJ's apartment. Sam.

I'm not jealous. A lie.

I'm not worried that there's anything romantic going on here, not really, but I wish it were me sitting that close to AJ, sharing food and laughs.

But I'm not. Because I fucked it up.

Me. Not AJ.

I internally debate going over there and asking AJ to talk, but I'd be interrupting what looks like a moment of happiness with a friend, and I can't bring myself to interfere. There's a good chance that seeing me would only make his day worse. Besides, if he wanted to talk to me, he'd have stayed there after the Q&A. He'd stopped into the interview when he thought I wouldn't see him—when he knew I couldn't say anything to him. And then he'd disappeared before I finished.

My pulse ticks up, but I take a couple of deep breaths and keep walking, leaving the building and hopping into a cab before anyone recognizes me.

"Hi, I'm Dax Ximénez. (Audience applause, a few loud whoops.) Thank you. It's been a while since I've been here. As some of you may have heard, I've been a little busy." (A few laughs.)

In the last two days following the Q&A at the *TMG* office, I've written, then deleted, at least fifteen text messages to AJ. I still don't know what to say to him, or if I should say anything at all. Maybe he's already dating someone new. And even if he's not, it's possible he's over and done with me.

In an effort to get my mind off the mess I've made of things—not only with AJ, but with *Wake Up, Elizabeth* and with my own publicist—I'd called up Charlie at RockPaperScissors to see if he had room for me on tonight's comedy lineup. I knew he'd say yes, he always does.

I pace the stage, realizing I'm not only out of practice but that I hadn't prepared any material. I'd used my best bits on *The Knightly Show* and had been so wrapped up in promoting the show—and my relationship with AJ—that I haven't been writing anything new. I can make it work though—I'm good at interacting with the audience and coming up with some funny one-liners on the fly. I try to shake off the feelings of nervousness that seem to be creeping up on me, much like they had the last time I performed here.

I talk to the audience a bit, riffing on feedback from a couple in front who are clearly on a first date. I'm starting to feel good, relaxing while I have the crowd laughing along, until a man in glasses at a table near the stage reminds me just enough of AJ that it completely takes the wind out of my sails. It's not AJ, of course, but I can feel my thoughts starting to slip away from me like grains of sand falling through my fingers.

My breath quickens. *No, no, no. I can handle this.*

"So, I went on a date last night, and I had a good time with this guy. At the end of the night, I thought, I want to kiss him, but he's a good few inches taller than me. I'm not that short, but this guy is tall. So when I went in for a kiss..."

I stop talking for a moment. The crowd waits expectantly. I try to continue, but the lights of the stage feel blinding and hot. I take a sip of water.

What is wrong with me? I sigh and let my shoulders sag a bit.

"So when I went in for a kiss... Actually, the guy is—well, was—my boyfriend. We broke up a couple weeks ago." (Audience is silent.)

I remove the water glass from the barstool and sit down, hoping to hide—or at least delay—the anxiety starting to rise in my chest.

"To be clear, *I* broke up with *him*. I broke up with the best person I've ever met. Why? Because he told me he's concerned about my mental health. He thinks I should talk to a therapist about my anxiety." (Pause.) "Yep. I have anxiety. I don't know the exact name for the kind I have because, well, I've never talked about it. Sometimes it's mild, sometimes it's...not. And sometimes I get panic attacks that make me feel like I'm riding a mechanical bull and I'm trying to hold on for dear life." (Mild laughter.)

"So yeah. I broke up with him because he...what? He cares about me? He loves me? I don't know.

"I have some stuff in my past that makes me wary of therapy in general. I come from a culture that has a long history of believing in men being Real Men—machismo, as they call it. The culture is changing, slowly, but it's still there. I had one particularly toxic person from my past who said I'd go to hell if I stayed the way I was. Gay, that is. If I stayed gay. He said no one would respect me, no one would love me. He also said 'Real men don't need therapy.' The only exception was if the therapy was to set me straight. And when I say 'set me straight', of course I'm talking about conversion therapy." (Long pause.) "'Pray the gay away,' so they say. I couldn't—wouldn't—do anything like that to myself. And luckily, the people who really loved me knew the truth: that the problem was this one person, not me. NOT. ME." (Audience is silent.) "It took me a long time to fully believe that. To believe in myself.

"But I didn't tell my boyfriend that. I didn't tell him anything. Nope. When he suggested I see a therapist, I unfairly lashed out at him, then broke up with him. Why? Because I was ashamed. Embarrassed. I didn't want him to know that I'm not perfect. Or maybe I didn't want to admit it to myself. I didn't want to admit that I need help to learn how to deal with my anxiety. And I ruined the greatest relationship of my life because of it."

The audience is staring at me, silent except for one person who quietly coughs. I scrub my hand over my face. I can feel my breathing start to slow and my heartbeat returning to its usual pace, or at least normal for being onstage. The panic attack is subsiding. Relieved, I blow out a shaky breath.

"Sorry. I hadn't planned on coming up here and dumping out all of my shit onstage. But you're stuck with me, at least for the moment. And since I have you here, let me say this: if someone—a friend, a partner, a family member, whoever—if someone suggests that you see a professional because they're worried about your mental health, listen to them. Please listen to them. If you don't know why they're suggesting it, ask. I'm not saying you have to go through with therapy or whatever. I'm just saying, listen.

"I wish I'd taken my own advice. Trust me, listening is a much better alternative than losing someone you love." (Long pause.)

"Well, I'll let you get on with your evening of promised laughs. This was supposed to be a comedy show, not group counseling, right?" (Mild laughter.) "Okay.

"Oh, and I know you're not supposed to be recording on your phones, but I see you over there with your phone out. Fuck the rules, right? (Laugh.) "Well if this happens to make it to social media, I want to apologize to the loved ones I didn't listen to. Especially my boyfriend—ex-boyfriend. I'm sorry.

"Thanks for listening."

Everyone in the crowd sits in a stunned silence for a few seconds. I put the microphone back on the stand and pick up my water glass. Then, to my surprise, the audience bursts into applause. I look around, not knowing what to do. I'm relieved when Charlie comes up onstage and takes the mic.

"Well, that was unexpected," he says, partly to me and partly to the audience. He pats me on the back, and I can tell he's not sure what to say next. The applause starts to die down.

"Before I turn the mic over to our next comedian, let's give one more hand to Dax Ximénez." He turns to me and smiles. Actually smiles.

It's so rare that I think I might be hallucinating this whole evening. "Thank you, Dax. That was really brave of you."

The crowd cheers once more. Walking off the stage, I wave awkwardly before making a beeline for the back door without stopping at the bar.

Hugo, the bartender, holds back a few fans who try to follow me while he holds the door open so I can escape. When it shuts behind me, I hear his booming voice from inside.

"Alright, alright. He's taking a breather. He'll be back in five minutes. Everyone go back to your seats." Hugo knows I won't be back tonight.

The whole way home, I wonder how long it'll take for this to hit social media. For the news of my comedy show meltdown to make its way out into the world.

Let's be honest, I'm really wondering how long it'll take for AJ to see it. Or if he'll care at all.

CHAPTER 26

AJ

I thought I'd be fine seeing Dax in the office for his Q&A interview, but when I heard his voice in the office, I had to go into the copy room to keep from breaking down in front of my coworkers. I'd gotten brave and peeked into the studio, but the second he saw me, he fumbled his words. I felt awful, worried that I'd ruined the flow of the interview. Of course, he rolled with it and recovered flawlessly, but I knew I should leave so he could focus.

After that, I'd called Sam and asked her to meet me for lunch, where she got the full rundown on everything that had happened with Dax, with Dario, and with the job I didn't get. When I was done with my sad story, Sam told me all about her most recent dating disaster and her own gripes with work. We commiserated, taking the *"If you don't laugh, you'll cry"* approach. By the end of lunch, we were crying with laughter and I felt a hundred times better. That was last week.

Where Dax was concerned, I decided to give him space to figure himself out. Well, by *decided* I mean I've been begrudgingly taking Sam's advice to let him have some time to cool off and figure things out on his own. When he was here for the Q&A, I wanted nothing more than to run back upstairs, burst into the interview, and beg him to talk to me until we'd worked everything out. But I didn't, because Sam was right. He needs time.

Between filling in while Dario is adjusting to the new role and trying to prove to him that I belong here, I've been so focused during the day that I'm starting to let Dax fade into the back of my mind.

After the breakup, the hardest part of the job had been having to look at the photos of Dax again and again when we expanded the feature and put him on the cover. Every time I'd see photos of him, it was like a kick to the gut. But as the days pass, it's getting easier. The new cover and updated feature went to the printer, so at least I'll have a little bit of a break until the issue gets delivered to the office. How I'll handle seeing the issue in person and all over social media will be a challenge, so I try to put it out of my mind for now.

"Bond, you're sulking."

I'm sitting at a table at a crowded bar with Sam and some other mutual friends from college. I'd agreed to be Sam's wingman and help her meet a cute guy, but I'm not helping at all.

She's right. Well, I wouldn't call what I'm doing sulking. More like wallowing. I'd been itching to get out of my apartment so I'd texted Sam. When she invited me to hang out with some friends I hadn't seen in a while, I imagined we'd be at a quiet restaurant or at a low-key wine bar, not a dance club full of sweaty people on the hunt for a hookup.

"What do you think of that guy?" Sam asks, pointing the neck of her beer toward the bar. There's a man who could best be described as a Ken doll, with perfectly coiffed blond hair, blue eyes, and blindingly white teeth.

"Yeah, he's...handsome, I guess. Want me to talk to him for you?"

"Maybe. Or for you. We can see which one of us he prefers."

I roll my eyes. "He's not really my type. Besides, I'm not looking to hook up with anyone tonight." I eye the man again.

"Fine." She holds up her hands in surrender. "Maybe see if he's single then? For me?"

I don't feel like getting up to talk to some random stranger—and he may not be looking to meet anyone either—but I also know that the longer I sit here, the more I'll wallow. I'm also nursing the same warm beer I'd started with an hour ago, so it's a good excuse to go to the bar.

A few minutes later, I bring Mr. Handsome back to the table and introduce him to Sam. He's a dentist or physicist, or some other *-ist*. I wasn't really listening. He'd also told me his name, but I forgot that too. He seems nice though, and Sam's a good judge of character. If she decides it's not going to work out, she won't be afraid to let him know right away rather than drag it out. I try not to think about the fact that it's a lesson she learned after she and I were together for much longer than we should've been.

It only takes a couple minutes before Sam and Mr. Handsome abandon their drinks and hit the dance floor.

The rest of the group joins them when the DJ plays a Beyoncé song, leaving me to hold down a table for eight. I take a long pull of a fresh beer when I notice a petite woman in a curve-hugging black dress looking—more like staring—at me from the bar. I nod and give a half-hearted smile, then turn my attention back to the dance floor.

A moment later, the woman is standing in front of me.

"Hi. Mind if I sit?" she asks.

"Uh," I look around, hoping for something, or someone, to give me a reason to say no. Before I say respond, she plops down on the bench seat next to me. Much too close. I can smell her perfume, something floral, and although it's not unpleasant, I find it a little too strong. Immediately I think of Dax and how much I miss the light, citrusy scent of his shampoo.

The woman is pretty—beautiful, even—curvy, with dark red hair and red lips to match. She must be at least a foot shorter than me, if not more, but she makes up for a few inches by wearing alarmingly high heels.

"Why aren't you dancing?" She nearly has to shout over the music.

"Someone has to hold down the fort," I say, gesturing to the table.

She laughs like I've just told a hilarious joke. I shift uncomfortably. "I'm Ginger." She offers a hand to shake. "I know, I know...Ginger, red hair," she says, in a self-mocking way. She looks at me expectantly, waiting for a response.

Not sure if I'm supposed to laugh or not, I chuckle half-heartedly, then take another sip of my beer. She scoots closer and puts an arm on the back of the bench seat behind me, leaning in closer.

"This is the part where you tell me your name," she stage-whispers into my ear.

"AJ," I say with cool indifference while I stare at the table. I know I'm being kind of a dick, but I can't help it. Ginger certainly doesn't deserve my surly attitude.

"Well, AJ, would you like to dance?" I notice her leaning forward, arranging her body so that I'm able to peek down the front of her dress, should I choose to. I don't.

"No, thanks," I say. She frowns. "Uh, I just went through a breakup and I'm not really in the mood. I'm sorry."

"Ah, well, too bad for her," Ginger giggles. I shrug. *God, I wish one of my friends would come back to the table.*

She leans in again, this time pressing her thigh against my own. "Well, you know what they say: the best way to get over someone is to fuck someone else."

That's not exactly how the saying goes, but I decide not to correct her. It would be so easy to drown my feelings in beer and have a casual fling, but hooking up with someone would be just that: a hookup—purely physical and nothing emotional—and that doesn't appeal to me at all. And as much as Ginger seems into it, I wouldn't want to use her like that.

"Thanks, but I'm good. If I change my mind, I'll let you know." I take another drink of my beer.

Ginger gives my thigh a squeeze, then stands, smoothing her dress with a shimmy.

"I hope you do," she whispers in my ear, then saunters away without looking back.

When the song is over and the rest of our party returns to the table, I finish my beer, then put on my jacket, letting Mr. Handsome take my seat. I apologize to everyone, promising our friends that I'll try harder to keep in touch. Bumping and being bumped into, I finally make my way out of the club and head home.

The next morning, I wake to find two texts from Sam.

Sam: Thanks for the help, wingman. I have a date tomorrow night.

The second is a link to a video. I put on my glasses and click the link. The video that fills my screen is dark and poor quality. But I can tell right away that it's Dax onstage doing a stand-up set in a small venue. It must be that place he told me about, RockPaperScissors, I think? I can't tell when it was recorded, but it looks recent. It starts in the middle of a big laugh from the audience, making me curious about what he'd just said. I feel myself start to smile and a warmth spreads through my chest. Dax pauses while the laughter dies down, then he launches into his next bit.

"So, I went on a date last night, and I had a good time with this guy—"

My stomach plummets and I close the video as quickly as I can. *He had a date?*

Why did Sam send this to me? I'd just been starting to feel better, finally trying to move forward. And now this?

I delete the text and try to find something, anything, to distract me from thinking about Dax.

I wash and fold all of my laundry, sweep and vacuum the whole apartment, and grocery shop for the week. I don't answer my phone when Sam calls, knowing she's going to ask me if I watched the video. A minute later, she texts me, asking me exactly that.

Sam: Did you see the video of Dax?
AJ: Yep.
Sam: Well??? What did you think?

I didn't watch it and I don't plan to. But I know she'll keep asking about it, so I give the vaguest answer I can muster.

AJ: No offense, but would you mind not talking to me about him for a while? I'm trying to move on.
Sam: Are you sure?
AJ: Yes. Please.
Sam: [zippy-mouthed emoji]

It's one o'clock in the afternoon and I've run out of steam. I'm tired and sad, and the cold, drizzly weather outside only makes me want to curl up on the couch with a warm bowl of noodle soup and rewatch my favorite movies until I fall asleep.

Determined not to turn into a rom-com cliché, I pick up my phone and open my contacts. My stomach roils nervously as I press Send and wait. It rings three times before there's an answer.

"Hallo, Aleksander."

"Hallo, Mama."

CHAPTER 27

DAX

"You wanna tell me what the fuck happened last weekend?" Whitney is livid, shouting through the phone at me. I'm standing in front of the entrance to the subway, but even the noise of the street can't drown out her voice.

"What are you talking about?" I ask.

"You. The comedy show. The massive emotional dump you took onstage?"

"Fuck." I hadn't seen or heard anything about it after that night, and had been hoping it would quietly go away.

"Uh, yeah. Why would you do an impromptu set without telling me? You went up there and said a bunch of stuff that I specifically told you *not* to talk about. And you weren't even funny."

"How did you hear about it?"

"A couple people sent me a clip of it. It started popping up on social media yesterday." She fights to get her tone under control, but it's still laced with irritation.

"Oh." *Oh shit*. "I didn't know anyone was recording it. I guess there was someone with a phone out." I didn't think they'd actually posted it—I hadn't heard anything about it since the night it happened.

"Come on. You practically dared the people in the audience to put it on social media. Anyway, this is a disaster."

"Was it that bad? I mean, I know it wasn't funny, but I thought..." *I thought what? I don't know.*

"You *didn't* think. That's the problem. Maybe we can spin this by saying it was a form of method acting. Preparing for the role of a character with a mental health issue."

"I don't want to spin it. I was being honest. That was *me* up there."

Whitney makes a frustrated sound. "Look," she says. "I'm trying to get your brand out in front of the world. Your brand is someone who's outgoing, fun. Someone who came from humble, Mexican beginnings to become rich and successful. Not someone who lives with his family, dresses like they still shop at The Gap, and gets panic attacks every time things get a little stressful. That's not the brand I created for you."

Now it's my turn to be frustrated. "Do you even hear yourself? I'm not a brand, I'm a person! Why do you always have to talk about my 'humble Mexican roots' like I grew up in some poor, remote village? I don't want to lie to people and make them think I'm some rags-to-riches story. Okay, yes, I live with my family. I'm not ashamed of that. I don't wear expensive clothes." I close my eyes and take a long breath. "And yeah, I do have issues with my mental health. Maybe I shouldn't have spilled it like I did, but I don't want to hide it anymore. It's part of who I am."

"Great. So, first you flake on *Wake Up, Elizabeth*, then you pull this comedy show stunt. What do you expect me to do?"

"I don't know. I'm sorry. I'm not trying to make things harder for you. I wish you'd understand that the brand you're trying to mold me into isn't who I am. I'll never be that person."

"Well," Whitney starts, her voice flat. "If you expect to be successful in this business, maybe you should start trying to be that person. Because you won't make it far with the brand you have going on right now."

Every muscle in my neck and shoulders is tight. I make a fist, then flex my fingers, repeating the motion over and over to relieve some of the tension. It's a long moment before I open my mouth to reply, but Whitney speaks first.

"You need to make some serious changes, Dax."

I take a long, slow breath. "You're right," I tell her in a quiet voice.

"Good. I'm glad you're finally getting it. Your brand—"

"I think I'll start now," I say, cutting her off. "I really appreciate all you've done for me up to this point, but we both know this relationship isn't working."

"What the fu—"

I don't let her finish. "I need someone who understands me and who sees me as a person. I need to be able to trust that they'll always have my best interests in mind."

"Wait. Are you seriously firing me? After everything I've done to help you?"

"I'm sorry," I tell her. I'm not sorry.

"Fuck you, Dax. I'll go to my sources in the media and tell them all about you."

"I have nothing to hide. And, you signed an NDA. Besides, you know how this business works. Bad-mouthing me will make you look bad too. Do you really think a new client will want to hire someone who leaks deeply personal information about former clients to the press?"

When Whitney says nothing, I continue. "I'll pay you for the upcoming month while you look for another client."

"Fine," she huffs. "I guess we don't have anything else to talk about."

"I guess not. Bye, Whitney. And good luck."

"You assh—" I end the call before she can finish what I can only imagine is a beautiful and heartfelt goodbye speech. And then I head down into the subway station.

"Dax?" Hannah sounds annoyed, but not mad. "Did you hear me?"

We're sitting at an outdoor table in front of a coffee shop. It's too cold to be sitting out here, but I don't care. The fresh, fall air and sunshine feel good. And I'm hoping that by sitting out here in my winter beanie and jacket, no one will recognize me.

"No, sorry. I'm distracted."

"Is it about Whitney? Because I have to say, firing her was absolutely the right move."

"Oh, yeah. That was something I should've done a while ago. I guess I'm gonna need a new publicist."

"Don't worry about that. I know people. We'll find you someone who's a better fit."

"Thanks. That's good news," I say, exhaling in relief. My shoulders—which I didn't realize had been tense—begin to relax. "So, what was it you were saying?"

"I said André's assistant called. *TMG* was really happy with how everything came out. He said we should see the new issue soon."

"Oh, okay. Great." I try to muster up some enthusiasm, but I can't. I'm doing a thousand-yard stare over her shoulder.

"So... I saw the video," Hannah says between sips of her iced coffee.

"You too?" My focus snaps back to her. "Shit." Between being unprepared and fighting off a panic attack, I can barely remember anything I'd said. "How bad was it?"

Hannah reaches out and grabs my chin, turning my face to hers, eyes fixed on mine. "Dax, you sounded real. Fans and people on social media are praising you for speaking up about your mental health issues."

I shrug. "That's good news, I guess. Whitney made it sound like I ruined my career."

"We don't need to dwell on her. Your career will be fine." Hannah leans back and folds her arms, taking an excruciatingly long look at me.

"So, that's it, isn't it?" she says. "This thing with you and AJ. You broke up with him because he suggested you get help?"

Looking anywhere but right at Hannah, I fidget with the paper straw wrapper and nod. Her shrewd stare makes me shift in my seat. A fresh wave of guilt washes over me and I want to crawl under the table. Being the proper grown-up that I am, I don't.

"What should I do, Han?" I ask, almost pleading.

"Nothing." Her tone is bordering on unsympathetic and I bristle.

"What? I can't just do nothing. Isn't this the part where I'm supposed to make some grand romantic gesture?"

"Look, Dax." Hannah leans forward on the table. "You made a pretty goddamned big gesture already. You admitted you were wrong, you publicly apologized to him, you even said you loved him. It's his turn to decide what he wants to do."

"What if he doesn't see it?"

"He will. Trust me." She takes a long sip of her coffee and shakes the ice around the cup. Did I mention it's freezing outside?

After a long pause, she speaks again. "You have the premiere coming up. You need to focus on *you*." She pokes a finger in the meat of my bicep.

"You're right." I say, sipping my own coffee. "I just...I miss him so goddamn much, it hurts." My voice is so small, it's a wonder she hears me over the noise of cars and the general hum of the city.

"I know you do. And for what it's worth, I miss him too." I cock my head to the side and give her a puzzled look. "For you, dummy. The two of you are good for each other. He's not who I would've pictured you with, but I like him."

I smile smugly at her. In all the years I've known Hannah, she's never had many nice things to say about anyone I've dated. Her loyalty is strong, and in her eyes, no one I've ever been with has been good enough. So for her to admit this, it's huge.

"Still," she says. "If he hurts you, I'll fuck him up."

I chuckle, but I know it's true, and that's why I love Hannah so much.

"Oh! That reminds me." Her abrupt change of tone causes me to flinch.

Hannah hauls her giant purse onto her lap and starts digging through it. It's so full of stuff, it's practically overflowing. I don't know how she finds anything in there.

"Here." She thrusts a wrinkled piece of paper at me. "These are some names of therapists you asked me for. The second one is the person my friend recommended. The one at the top is the one I go to. She's great. She could probably see you tomorrow if you wanted."

"You didn't tell your friend that this was for me, did you?"

"Of course not. HIPAA and all that." Hannah waves a hand around dismissively.

"Han, you know that's not how HIPAA works, right? You're my manager, not my doctor."

"Whatever. Do you want this or not?"

"Yes, I do. Thank you." I snatch the paper from her like a child taking a toy from a sibling. I fold it, then fold it again until it's a tiny rectangle, then put it in my pocket.

"Dax," she says, then pauses, waiting for me to give her my full attention. "For what it's worth, I think it's great that you're open to talking to someone. I know it's hard at first, but it'll get easier, I promise."

I put my hand on Hannah's arm and hold it there for a long moment.

"Thank you. For...being my friend." As soon as I say it, I regret it.

Hannah breaks out in song, belting out the theme song to *The Golden Girls*.

"'*Thank you for being a friend...*' Sing it with me, Dax. Don't pretend you don't know the words."

"You're assuming that because I'm a gay man I must know the words?"

"Don't pull that shit with me." Hannah narrows her eyes at me. "We used to watch reruns in the dorms every Saturday night, remember?"

"Of course I do." I smile.

And there in front of the coffee shop, we sing. Loudly.

CHAPTER 28

AJ

"Bond, could you come into my office, please?"

I've just returned to the office from location scouting for our next big photo shoot. Dario is standing in the doorway to his office, arms folded across his chest and wearing perfectly tailored navy pants and a crisp, white button-down shirt. It's in stark contrast to my gray sweater, faded black jeans, and black boots.

"Sure," I reply, removing my bag from my shoulder and placing it on the floor under my desk. As I walk past a few other desks toward Dario's office, I notice a couple of building maintenance workers removing boxes and photo equipment from the mini-studio. I furrow my brow, but say nothing as I enter Dario's office.

"Please close the door," Dario says, and my body immediately tenses. His back is to me while he shuffles papers around on his desk. When the door clicks, he motions for me to sit on the couch. Sitting across from me, he crosses one knee over the other, but says nothing. His face is neutral, but not unfriendly.

"Uh, did you need something?" I ask hesitantly.

"Yes," he says. "How are things?"

I look around, trying to get a sense of what's happening knowing Dario wouldn't call me into his office to make idle chitchat.

"Good. Great. The issue is coming along pretty well. I was out doing some location scouting for the next fashion feature. I'd like to try out that new photographer whose portfolio I showed you last week."

Dario raises both eyebrows. "A new photographer for the feature? That's quite risky, isn't it?"

"Well," my voice cracks a bit and I clear my throat. *Shit.* "It is, but you saw her work. It's stunning. And she has a real talent with lighting. Plus, she's really open to direction." I'm nervous about Dario's reaction and I expect him to say no. But instead, he nods and smiles.

I know I'm still on a probationary period with Dario. He's been keeping tabs on me and the work I'm doing, and I can't blame him. I'm still nervous as hell when he's around, knowing that he could fire or demote me at any moment and bring in one of his former colleagues to replace me.

"If you have faith in this new photographer, I trust you."

Dario's words sound like they should be comforting, but they're not. I feel like it's a test. When I don't visibly relax, Dario speaks again.

"I've been watching you work for the last few weeks. You're doing a great job, Bond. I like what I've been seeing." I exhale, a little too audibly. "In fact, that's what I want to talk to you about."

My pulse quickens and I sit up a little straighter.

"Okay...?"

"Obviously, you're free to decide what you want to do from this point, but I'd like to talk to you first before you make any decisions."

"Decisions?"

"You're talented and you work very hard. Based on the work I'm seeing now and what you've done since Takashi left, I'm very impressed."

"Thank you, sir."

"Oh, *pssshh*. You know this already." He waves a hand in the air. "And since I've been here, I can tell that your creativity and talents hadn't been used to their full potential in the past."

I nod. "Riiiight…"

"Mr. Bond, do you know why Lorenzo asked me to come work at *TMG*?"

I shake my head.

"When I started at *TMG Italia*, the magazine was fine. It was good. But I wanted to make it better. And it did get better. But it was because we had a great team. I pushed everyone to work to their full potential. But that isn't exactly why Lorenzo brought me here. It's because I brought more to the magazine than pretty pictures and beautiful pages. Of course, I worked a lot on the photo shoots. But I also pushed for a lot more content online: interviews with actors, behind the scenes videos of photo shoots, dynamic, animated photos, exclusive content… I made ideas happen. Anything to give readers more reason to be engaged with us. I gave us a presence not only as a physical magazine, but as a brand by giving people so much more. That's why I'm here."

Takashi had been resistant to all of that. He'd always said that the magazine would speak for itself and that readers would follow because they could appreciate the photography, the written words. I'd urged him to go further. I'd shown him my behind-the-scenes photos and asked him if he'd want to show them online. But he'd said the shoots I worked on weren't the high-profile celebrities or cover shoots. He'd tell me that no one was interested in behind-the-scenes shots of people they'd never heard of, despite *TMG* touting them as the next big star.

Everything Dario is saying now is what I'd tried to get Takashi to do, or to let me try to do.

Dario gives me a moment to think about what he's said. He seems to know what I'm thinking. It's likely that André had filled him in on my efforts. I'd always complained to André after my ideas had been shot down by Takashi.

"Mr. Bond?" I blink back to Dario. "I don't intend to take any work away from you now that I'm here. In fact, I plan to give you more responsibilities."

"Like what?"

"I want you to take over the planning and execution of all photo shoots. Covers, features, celebrities, big stuff, small stuff. All of it."

I feel the back of my neck begin to prickle with sweat.

"Don't worry. I don't mean you have to do it all by yourself. We can restructure the art department as needed so that someone else can take care of logistics, bookings, scouting, rentals, all of the details that go into planning photo shoots. If you need an assistant, we can start the search tomorrow."

I blink in disbelief.

"You'll design the covers and features. Again, with support from the art staff. I don't want you to get burned out, so whatever you need, staff-wise, I'll make sure you have it. Your title will remain the same, but there will be a salary increase commensurate with your new responsibilities. Oh, and I've already asked that you have an office instead of one of those god-awful cubicles. I don't know how anyone gets any work done out there." Dario wrinkles his nose in obvious disgust at the mention of cubicles.

"Wow. Uh, I don't know what to say."

"I'll oversee the work you do, but I don't like to micromanage. You'll do your job, and I'll do mine. You, me, and André will work together on planning each issue, but as far as the art goes, it'll be up to you to make it happen. We'll make a plan for how we can tie in stories with online content as well. André will be part of that planning too."

I nod. "Of course."

"It's a big weight I'm putting on your shoulders. But don't feel like you have to carry it alone. I've done the job you're doing, so if you need my help with anything, I'm happy to step in."

I swallow, my mouth suddenly dry.

"I would like to see what you're capable of given the proper resources. I want to give you the space to really be creative." Dario pauses a moment. "Think about it. Of course, you're free to move on if you choose. But I'd like you to give it a chance. I think you and I could make a great team."

Ten minutes ago, I was sure he was calling me into his office to fire me. Three weeks ago, I'd been determined to dislike this man for taking the job I'd wanted away from me. For his shiny hair and his shiny shoes and his fancy title. But I don't dislike him. I'm finding that I like him quite a lot. And I'm actually excited about the prospect of these new responsibilities.

"Mr. Bond, I'm hopeful that this will be something that excites you, that challenges you. I see a lot of potential in you and I want to get you to the next level."

I nod. "Thank you, Mr. Souza."

"Dario, please."

"Thank you. Dario." I shut the door behind me as I leave his office.

Half an hour later, I return to my desk after telling André everything that Dario had told me. André had been worried about me since the announcement. And to be fair, I was disappointed. But now, I'm excited about learning from Dario and about the prospect of basically being in control of the look of the entire magazine. Before I'd left André's office, I told him I'd give the job six months to see how things go with Dario.

In the days since my meeting with Dario, work has been intense. I've been working nonstop: scouting locations for a big shoot next month, coordinating a couple of smaller photo shoots in the studio, and scouring through résumés to find a suitable assistant for me. I've never had an assistant and am not quite sure how I feel about it. But with the new responsibilities I'd been given, Dario is right, I need help balancing everything on my plate. And if that isn't enough, I've been trying to find time to move into my new office, the one that used to be the mini studio that Dario had promised me.

There's a new energy in the office that's palpable. Watching Dario work with confidence, not arrogance, has really shown me how much I still have to learn. As much as it pains me to admit, it's been for the best that he was hired.

Another item on the growing list of things that have impressed me about working with Dario is that he's a fierce advocate of work-life balance. He's been making sure I take breaks during the day and that I'm leaving at a reasonable hour at night. It's refreshing to not feel pressured to work twelve-hour days or feel guilty that I'm *not* working twelve-hour days. But now that I'm going home earlier, I don't know what to do with myself in an empty apartment in the evenings. I used to enjoy the quiet after all the bustle of activity at work. Now I find myself logging on to my computer or flipping through magazines and making notes for future photo shoots just to have some way to fill the quiet space—an emptiness that either I'd never noticed, or that had never bothered me until Dax came along.

In such a short time, Dax brought so much to my life: joy, excitement, companionship. These were things I'd failed to notice—or likely avoided noticing—were missing. Now, with Dario shooing me out of the office at a reasonable hour every night, I can't help but miss Dax.

Every day, the pain dulls a little more, like a cut that's still healing, but that doesn't mean it's not still there. Seeing his face on promotions for his show, or in press releases and social media posts, makes the wound hurt all over again. So I've been avoiding all social media since our breakup, even going so far as to remove apps from my phone—just until this feeling goes away. I was never much of a heavy social media user to begin with, and I'm finding I don't really miss it at all.

———

When I arrive at work on Thursday, I see a package from the printer propped against the door of my office. I open the box, and three copies of the newest issue of *TMG* tumble out and onto the table. Dax's face stares back at me, and those green-gray eyes and mischievous grin nearly knock the wind out of me.

André is hurrying past when he stops midstride and steps into the room.

"Oh!" He takes one of the magazines and flips through the pages, stopping occasionally to take a closer look at a particular page. Then he closes the magazine again, looking once more at the cover. I don't think I've moved since I opened the box.

"It looks great." André turns his head and finally seems to notice I've gone numb, still staring at the cover. I can feel him eyeing me, but I'm frozen, still holding the empty box. He clears his throat. "I have to say, the last-minute change to the cover was the right call. Well done."

"Thank you." I manage to croak out. "I...yeah. Thanks." André must notice I'm struggling, but he's too nice to say anything. I set the box on the table and turn away, hoping he doesn't see my eyes turn glassy with tears. "Well, I'll leave you to it then." André turns to go, but then stops, taking one of the magazines and making a point to look at the cover again.

"You know," he says, "the big TV show premiere is tonight. Red carpet and all of that."

"Yeah," I say, somewhat vacantly.

"Ah, of course you know. You'll be there, yes?" He raises a curious eyebrow. It seems like a strange thing for André to assume.

"I hadn't planned on it. I don't usually go to red-carpet events."

"Oh." He frowns.

I cock my head. "Why did you think...?"

"Because of Mr. Ximénez, of course. You aren't going together?"

"No. We're not..."

"Oh! I'm sorry." He looks disappointed. "I must've assumed incorrectly. I thought you two were, you know..." He waves his hand around, searching for the word. "...a couple."

I cross the room and flump down onto the chair in the corner of my office. André follows, sitting in the chair across from me.

"We were." I run my fingers through my hair. "How did you know?"

André seems surprised by my question. He answers with a laugh.

"I think the better question is, how could I not know? The way you looked at each other that day he was here to pick up the wallet. The wallet you had custom made especially for him. After a week of flirting over social media..."

I can feel my eyes widen and heat wash over my face. André doesn't seem to notice and goes on.

"You positively lit up when you talked about him in the editorial board meeting. I was so happy for you." I want to hide my face in my hands. "But...you said 'were'. Does that mean you're not still together?" His voice is full of concern.

I lean back and give André an ultra-abbreviated version. "We got to know each other after the photo shoot, and then we dated for a few weeks. We broke up though."

"Oh, I'm so sorry."

"Thanks. It was my fault. I pushed him too hard about, well, it's personal."

"Oh!" André's cheeks bloom with a pink hue, and he suddenly becomes very interested in the impeccable hem of his sleeve.

"No, not *that*. It's more of a—"

"Bond?" Dario pokes his head through the door. He looks at André, then at me. I must look awful because he seems taken aback. "Sorry, the door was open. I was just wondering..."

Dario's eyes zero in on the magazine that's sitting on the table.

"Ah, it's here," he says. "I was told they had been delivered this morning." He picks up a copy and studies the cover. "Great work. Bravo!"

"Thanks," I say, hoping my voice sounds more upbeat than I feel.

"I was sorry to hear the two of you broke up," he says casually while flipping through the magazine.

"Oh?" A look of bewilderment crosses my face. "You knew too?" I give André a sidelong glance.

"Oh, don't blame him," Dario says. "I figured that one out on my own."

I swallow hard. "But...how did you know we broke up?"

"Bond, I might not be a young man like you, but I do keep up with social media." He sounds almost exasperated.

"Social media? What are you talking about?" I feel a wave of unease ripple through me.

"The video," Dario says. "You haven't seen it?"

"What video?" André and I ask at the same time.

"Mr. Ximénez. He announced during a comedy show recently—maybe it was last week, I don't know—that he's been struggling with anxiety. And that he recently broke up with his boyfriend." At this, Dario raises an eyebrow at me.

I pause for approximately two seconds before practically leaping off of the couch and racing to my desk. I'm typing so quickly that I have to correct my spelling three times. Dario and André file in behind me, the three of us hovering over my screen.

I click on the first headline that pops up.

Comedian Diego "Dax" Ximénez Opens Up About Mental Health Struggles While Onstage At Comedy Show

I scroll past the story, picking up a few key words as I pass them—words like *anxiety* and *brave* and *courage*—and go straight to the link to the video. I click on it and realize it's the same one Sam had sent me. The one I'd made a point to ignore.

I watch the video in stunned silence. At some point, Dario and André quietly leave my office, though I'm not sure when. It's only when the video ends that I look up to notice the room is empty and the door closed. I click on the link and watch it again.

When the video finishes playing for the second time, I put my head in my hands and let myself cry. I don't even know why I'm crying. There he is, apologizing to me in front of this crowd—in front of the whole world. Acknowledging the things I was trying to tell him, that I only wanted to help. And saying he loved me.

I cry because I'm realizing for the first time the sheer magnitude of what his father had done to him when he was a kid. The verbal abuse, the insults, and the threats of conversion therapy. And his brother, who should've been in his corner, was just as bad, maybe worse. Worse because his brother was someone Dax trusted. He should've been there when Dax had no one else to talk to.

I get it now, why he'd broken up with me. He was ashamed and embarrassed. It had nothing to do with me. *Shit, why hadn't I called him?*

It takes me a few minutes to put myself back together. Then I practically sprint to André's office. He's on the phone when I come in. Holding up a finger, he promptly ends his call. When he hangs up, he looks at me expectantly.

"André, can you get me a press pass for the premiere tonight?"

A wide grin spreads across his face and he swivels his chair to face me.

"I think I can make that happen. I'll need a little time. Can you come by and pick it up in a couple hours?" His eyes twinkle like we're both in on a secret, though it's not a secret at all. He knows exactly why I'm asking.

I check my watch. "I'm not sure I can wait that long. I'll need to go home to clean up and change out of these clothes." André frowns. "I'm sure Sam's going. She always covers these events. Maybe I can have her come and pick it up?" I'm talking more to myself than André.

"Sam Charles?" André raises his eyebrows. He knows the story with Sam and me. She occasionally writes stories for *TMG*, so it was inevitable that it would come up. He also knows we're still friends.

"Yeah."

"Ah, lovely. Tell her I'll leave it at reception."

"Thanks, André. You're the best."

He sighs. "Yes, I know." His voice trails off as he swivels back to his computer.

I gather my things from my office and head toward the door, dialing Sam's number once I'm on the elevator.

CHAPTER 29

AJ

I show up at the theater and find Sam waiting for me by the security gate, slightly irritated with me. I'd had to sprint from two blocks away, and I'm out of breath. She hands me a press pass and we're escorted to the part of the red carpet reserved for members of the media. I feel completely out of place standing here with reporters and photographers working for every facet of media.

Once we're in the spot that's reserved for Wright Media, we wait. Sam scribbles notes on her notepad which she slips into the pocket of her dress, then queues up her phone's recording app. I fumble nervously with my phone, pretending to look like I'm doing something important but failing miserably.

Sam settles in, then looks at me, as if she's seeing me for the first time tonight.

"Bond, you look..."

"What?" I ask, looking down at myself.

"Handsome. You look handsome."

"You think so?" I smooth the lapels of my perfectly tailored charcoal-gray suit and straighten my black tie against the crisp white shirt underneath. I may dress like a college student most days, but working in men's fashion means that I have at least one black-tie-worthy outfit in my closet.

"Yeah, I mean, you look way better than most of the people here," Sam says, not quietly, gesturing toward the other members of the media. She's not wrong, most of them don't look like they're ready to be on the other side of the velvet rope. To be honest, I feel a little ridiculous in my suit.

"This is a big moment, Bond. Huge. Do you know what you're gonna do when you see him?" Sam asks, clearly trying to entertain herself while we wait. She knows I'm already nervous as hell. "I mean, you should at least have something ready to say to him when he comes over here."

"I was thinking about 'I'm sorry,'" I say.

"That's it?" She makes a snoring noise.

"Stop it, Sam. I'm already freaking out." I grumble. "I'll think of something." *I hope.*

"Well, keep out of the way when everyone else comes by. Some of us are here to actually work." Leave it to Sam to get back to business.

"Yes, ma'am," I say sarcastically. Sam rolls her eyes at me. I know she's not really annoyed that I'm sharing this space with her, I don't think. But I try to stay out of her way anyway.

The first wave of people comes by: producers, the director, a couple of supporting actors. They're followed by Paz Alvarez, the megastar producer who had been the one to bring the show to life. Max, *Mexican't*'s co-creator—and one of Dax's closest friends—walks by, answering questions from reporters and smiling for a few photos. It's clear that he doesn't enjoy being the center of attention. Still, he carries himself with an air of cool confidence. He stops in front of us, and Sam asks him a couple of questions. I could swear that I see a little spark of something flash in Max's eyes when he talks to her, but

I'm too nervous to really pay attention. As he's about to walk away, Sam pulls me by the arm.

"By the way, Max, this is AJ Bond, the art director from *TMG* magazine." She winks at me. *Damn it, Sam.*

"Uh, nice to meet you, Max," I say, shaking his hand. "I can't wait to see the show." *God, I sound so stupid.* It takes a moment, but then recognition crosses his face.

"Thanks, AJ. It's nice to meet you." His tone is professional, but his eyes give him away. There's a hint of a smile on his lips. He definitely knows who I am, at least by name. Dax must've told him about me.

Max moves on, and I have to fight the urge to pinch Sam on the arm. "Sam, what the hell?"

"What?" she asks innocently. "I just wanted to see if he recognized your name."

"No shit." I try to be mad at her, but I can't. "Do you think he did?"

"Oh, definitely." She smiles wickedly at me. "Now move." Sam pushes me back to my spot out of the way.

God, I hate red-carpet events. If it weren't for Dax, I wouldn't have the slightest desire to be here. And, come to think of it, I doubt Dax wants to be here either. He'd told me how much he likes working with Max to create the show and he likes acting. But I also know how much he loathes press events like this.

I can't help but think about how all of these cameras and reporters and attention will affect him. Is he having another panic attack? When all the other actors except Dax have shown up, I start to worry.

Before I can change my mind about it, I pull out my phone and type a quick text. We haven't spoken in three weeks, and even if he doesn't want to see me here, I want him to know I'm thinking about him. That I still care about him.

AJ: Remember to breathe.

After I send it, I look at my screen and cringe. I'm telling him to breathe? *Ugh.* I wish I could unsend it. But a few seconds later, three dots appear. I stare at the dots for an agonizingly long time, thinking maybe he's not going to answer after all. Then,

Dax: That's funny. That's exactly what my therapist said.

Is he joking? Mocking me? I can't tell. I stare at my phone, wondering if I should respond.

"Bond," Sam says, snapping my attention back. "Dax is here."

My heart feels like it's about to leap out of my chest. I can't see him from where I'm standing. The photographers are all holding their cameras up high, hoping to get a good shot of him approaching.

"He's brought a date," Sam says. And my heart plummets.

Fuck. What am I doing in this ridiculous suit, waiting here in the media corral? I'm about to duck out and walk away when Sam tugs my arm to stand in front of her.

I'm finally able to see Dax standing by the open door of a limo, and I momentarily stop breathing. He's holding a hand out to help Cami out of the car, then his mom. He turns and gives a little wave at the cameras and reporters.

He looks stunning. It's not an exaggeration, I'm actually stunned.

He's wearing all white: white suit jacket, white button-down shirt, white pants. The only things that aren't white are his shoes. The white of his outfit perfectly complements his radiant olive skin and makes all of his beautiful features stand out. His hair is wavy and neatly styled, and he looks like he's actually had a good night's sleep.

Before he heads to the media area, Dax leads his mom and sister to the entrance of the theater and speaks to someone with a clipboard and headset who's guarding the door. The security guard escorts Cami and Alma inside while Dax heads back toward the reporters and photographers.

As he stops and talks with a few people, I can't help but stare at him. He moves easily in front of the cameras, waving and smiling. It's his trademark "celebrity smile," beautiful and seemingly effortless, but not quite reaching all the way to his eyes. It's a glossy veneer that's covering the real smile that's underneath—the one that's reserved for the people he loves. The one he'd shown me dozens of times, before we broke up.

A ball of nerves forms in my chest when I see Dax getting closer, and I'm wondering (again) if this was a mistake. When I'd shown up at the video Q&A at the *TMG* office, Dax had been more than a little shaken to see me. He'd stumbled over his words. *Shit.*

I don't think he's seen me yet. It's not too late for me to take a couple steps back, then disappear into the sea of faces. I have a strong urge to do just that. But then my eye catches on his hand. He's finished talking to one reporter and moving on to the next when I notice it—clench and release, clench and release, clench and release—before he puts it into his pocket. His shoulders are starting to tense and he has a faint line between his eyebrows. I know those signs.

CHAPTER 30

DAX

I'm all dressed up, sporting a fresh haircut and looking good. I spent the morning at the spa with Mom and Cami, treating us all to massages and skin care treatments. And now, I'm being driven in a fancy car to the premiere of the television show I created with Max. I should be feeling great.

So why don't I?

In a few moments, I'll be surrounded by strangers who'll be taking my picture, shouting my name, and asking me questions. My leg bounces up and down and I stare helplessly out the window. How bad would it be if I jumped out at the next intersection and ran to the nearest subway stop?

I try to appear calm in front of Mom and Cami, who are gazing out the window and pointing excitedly as we get closer to our destination. We're about a block from the theater when my phone buzzes with a message. *Who the hell is texting me?* I pull out my phone and freeze.

AJ: Remember to breathe.

Seeing the message, along with AJ's face on my screen, my heart leaps and for a few seconds, I almost forget how to breathe at all. He remembered the premiere. He thought of me, most likely worried that I'm about to have a panic attack. Well, he's right about that.

The little note of advice is exactly what I need. It's also what Hannah's therapist—I guess she's also *my* therapist now too—told me to do. I can feel my heartbeat starting to get faster, but I try to ignore it.

Remember to breathe.

I type out a quick reply as we arrive in front of the theater. I momentarily forget about my anxiety as I wave at the journalists, then help Mom and Cami out of the car and escort them directly into the theater. They've both told me they're okay with being photographed a bit, but I've seen how cruel people can be and I can't help but feel protective of them and their privacy, so I arranged to have them taken inside first.

Once they're safely in the theater, I turn and head over to the media area, determined to get through the next few minutes of photos and questions as quickly as possible.

My breath picks up, and I start to worry that the anxiety is going to get the better of me right here in front of the cameras. I squeeze my hand and release it a couple of times, almost forgetting I'm surrounded by photographers. If I can get through this, I can go inside and calm down without all the media's eyes on me.

Remember to breathe.

I'm getting a lot of the standard questions about *Mexican't*, questions about my costars, questions about my clothes, all the usual things.

I'm also getting questions about that damned comedy show. About my mental health. About AJ, although thankfully not by name. I want to tell them to back off, that questions about my relationship are none of their fucking business. But, of course, I'd be a hypocrite. I'd opened myself up by telling the world about my anxiety and how it ruined my relationship. I can't very well take it back now.

I don't regret talking about my anxiety—it's actually turned out to be a good thing. It was the kick in the ass I'd needed to finally make the decision to go to therapy. And the support and love from fans—especially the ones who've said that they're seeking help for their own mental health issues, thanks to what I'd said that day—makes me feel overwhelmed, in a good way. I hadn't intended to become a public advocate for mental health, but it turns out that's what happened anyway.

Still, two therapy sessions can't magically cure panic attacks. And right now, I can feel this one trying like hell to make an appearance right here on the red carpet. I shove my hand in my pockets so no one can see me making tight fists to try to relieve some of the building tension in my body. It helps, at least a little.

Remember to breathe.

The mantra seems to be working, and the panic is subsiding, but I'd still like this to be over with already. Trying to see exactly how much more of this dog and pony show I have to endure, I look around and am completely caught off guard when my eyes land directly on AJ.

My heart pounds in my chest at the sight of him—and not *just* because he looks so good. I mean, *my god*, he looks incredible in a dark gray suit, his hair trimmed short in the back but falling in soft waves above his eyes, barely grazing the top of his glasses. I should've known that while AJ dresses like a college kid most days, he's capable of looking like, well, like he belongs on the red carpet, not on the sidelines.

It's not only how good he looks that makes my heart stutter. It's that he's here at all. He hates this kind of thing. And he really doesn't like to dress up when he doesn't have to. When our gazes lock on each other, he doesn't smile or wave. He *looks* at me. I mean, it's a laser-focused, intense gaze that burns a hole right into me. I can see it in his eyes—there's no question of exactly why he's here. He's here for *me*.

"Dax," someone calls from my immediate right. It's a reporter from some entertainment blog or something-or-other. I try my best to answer their questions, but I'm completely distracted. I thank them and walk away, making a beeline straight for AJ, passing a few other reporters on the way. If they're annoyed, I don't notice.

AJ's eyes stay locked on mine as I approach. My stomach is in knots when I stop directly in front of the velvet rope that separates us. A woman appears next to him, the same one he was with in the café in AJ's office building. Neither AJ nor I speak.

After a moment, the woman says, "Hi, Dax. I'm Sam Charles from *Waves* magazine."

I finally break eye contact with AJ to look at Sam. She'd clearly been waiting for AJ to speak first, but he seems to be frozen.

"Hi Sam, nice to meet you," I say, cutting a quick glance back at AJ.

"A couple of questions for you." Sam is poised and direct, but she has a slightly impish smile that she's trying to hide. I nod at her to go ahead.

"Dax, after being so open about your mental health issues and your relationship, have you and your boyfriend reconciled?"

I look at the phone in her hand and she makes a point of pressing the Stop button on it and turning it to face me so I know she's not recording. She puts it into her pocket for good measure. She smirks and almost winks, but stops just short.

"Off the record," she voicelessly mouths.

"Uh, no." Out of the corner of my eye, I can tell that AJ's watching me closely. "I hope to, but I'm not sure he wants to." He blinks a couple of times and something in his face seems to flicker.

"Is that person here this evening?" Sam asks, her face full of faux innocence. I try to hide my smile.

"I'm not going to answer that," I say. "Out of respect for his privacy, of course."

"Of course," Sam says. I look for relief on AJ's face, but it gives nothing away. It's entirely unreadable. "Thank you, Dax."

"Thank you, Sam." My eyes go to AJ, but he doesn't speak. He doesn't even move.

Well, I guess that's it then. Maybe I should've expected it. I get my hopes up when it comes to AJ, then have them dashed right in my face.

"Dax!" A reporter calls for my attention from my left. They're all waiting, and I'm standing here wasting everyone's time hoping AJ will say something, anything.

Realizing I can't simply stand here any longer, I start to walk away, my heart heavy in my chest. "Right, well, enjoy the—"

"No! Wait." AJ finally speaks up, a little too loudly. I'm tempted to say "*What the hell, AJ?*" But I don't. He chews his bottom lip and clenches his hands together. He suddenly looks...nervous.

Sam's professional smile turns into an all-out beam at AJ, then at me. "Dax, before you go, I believe my colleague, AJ Bond, has a question."

The other reporters are getting restless and I can hear them calling my name. I cut AJ a mischievous look. "Yes, Mr... Bond, was it?"

"Yes. Um," he starts, then stops. His cheeks flush red all the way up to the tips of his ears. He's flustered. He's so rarely flustered. I have to put a hand over my mouth to keep from grinning stupidly.

Sam gives AJ a sharp elbow to the ribs and he lets out an audible 'oof'. I like her.

"Yes Diego, um, Dax? AJ Bond from *TMG* magazine."

"I believe we've met," I say, and if I could raise a single eyebrow, I would.

"Right. Well, my question is: i-if that person, your ex-boyfriend, were to show up tonight to apologize for pushing you to see a therapist rather than giving you the space to figure things out on your own... Well, um, what would you say to him?"

I'm momentarily speechless. Is he seriously apologizing to me? And if he is, why? It was all my fault we broke up. *I* should be the one apologizing to *him. Fuck. I should be apologizing to him.*

I open my mouth to say something, but AJ speaks again.

"And, um, what would you say if that same person told you that he doesn't care who knows about the two of us...um, I mean the two of you? That he doesn't care if the whole world knows. He wants you to know that he's crazy about you. He loves you. Not *Dax Ximénez, the Celebrity* but Dax, the person. You."

I stare at AJ with wide eyes. My heart can barely take it. *This man.*

The reporters who are standing close to us seem to take notice of what's happening here, and I can feel their stares. The others that are farther away continue to shout my name, seeming irritated that I'm not moving on. I don't care.

"So, um..." AJ bites his lip. "What would you say?"

My lips curl up into a slow smile. I step closer to him and lean in. "Are you sure?" I whisper. He nods, and I notice that his eyes are glistening, holding back tears.

I run a finger up the lapel of his suit jacket, stopping in the vicinity of his collarbone. I gently tug on it (the lapel, not his collarbone), pulling him toward me but giving him the opportunity to pull back if he wants to. He doesn't.

AJ leans into me and whispers my name, his mouth so close to mine I can feel his breath on my lips. "Dax."

I lift my chin, and he brushes his lips over mine, timidly at first, like I might push him back. I slide a hand over the back of his neck and pull AJ to me, bringing our lips together in a tender kiss. It's not chaste, but not pornographic either. Just, sweet.

The kiss doesn't last long, but long enough that the media picks up on what's happening. I hear camera shutters and people shouting my name, other people talking among themselves excitedly. When we pull apart, AJ isn't looking around to see who's watching. His eyes don't leave mine. He leans in again, but this time his lips go to my ear. "I love you," he whispers.

"I hope so," I say, with a soft chuckle. "Because we just made a big fucking scene, and I'd hate to find out it was all for nothing."

AJ laughs, touching his forehead to mine, and it melts my heart.

"Come on," I say, taking his hand, pulling him toward me.

"Where are we going?" AJ asks, stepping around the velvet rope to join me.

"We're going inside. You and I are going to sit together and hold hands and watch the show. I might even let you kiss me a little bit more."

He smiles, almost shyly, as I pull him toward the theater's entrance. "What about the rest of the press people?" AJ asks, though he doesn't actually seem to care one bit about them. He grips my hand tightly, and I look over my shoulder.

"They all took pictures. They have their story. No one's gonna care what I have to say about the show after that." I don't know if that's true, but there's no way in hell I'm leaving AJ alone now.

He doesn't argue as we hurry into the theater hand in hand.

Once we're inside, I make Hannah scoot over so AJ and I can sit together. She doesn't say anything to AJ, just nods at him with a raised eyebrow. Mom and Cami—who's beside herself with excitement over seeing AJ—are one row behind us, so we keep our kissing to a minimum. We'll get our chance later.

Before the show starts, Paz, then the director, then Max all give quick little speeches, a few thank-yous, and a few shout-outs. Max asks me to stand up, which I do, waving to the guests in the theater. He doesn't ask me to speak, thank goodness. I would, but I'd rather get to the show so I can sit down and kiss AJ again.

The theater goes dark, and I take AJ's hand, lacing our fingers together, then rest them on our thighs which are pressed together.

When the opening credits start, it occurs to me that AJ told me he loved me. He'd actually said the words *I love you* while we were outside. And I'd made a joke in response.

I lean over and whisper in his ear, "I love you, Kalexander."

"Shhhh," he says. "That's my boyfriend on the screen, and I don't want to miss any of it. Also, don't you dare call me that."

Chuckling, I lay my head on his shoulder, and he brings our joined hands up to his mouth, pressing a kiss to my knuckles.

"I love you," he whispers.

CHAPTER 31

AJ

Dax and I are standing on the steps to my apartment, the air between us thick with the anticipation of finally being together again, alone in my apartment. Both of us are physically exhausted, but still wide-awake from all that's happened today.

We'd gone to an after-party hosted by the network, where some members of the press, including Sam, were buzzing with the story of the night: Dax's and my kiss on the red carpet. I'd already seen it show up on social media. And while I'm not even a celebrity, my name had been leaked—Sam denies being the source—and Dax and I have already been dubbed "Ajax." *Ugh.*

I couldn't be bothered with any of it. My focus was entirely on Dax. He introduced me to some of the people from *Mexican't*, and I tried my best to be a good and attentive boyfriend. It was a tall order when all I could think about was getting him back to my apartment.

It's not that I want to ravish him tonight. Or that I want him to ravish me. I mean, I don't *not* want that. We're both dressed up and looking pretty damn good.

But I also want to lie in my bed with Dax, kiss him all night, eat bagels and drink coffee in the morning, walk to the farmers market, sit on a bench and eat lunch, watch him possibly get pecked to death by pigeons—okay, maybe not that—and just *be*. Together.

We get inside the apartment and I've barely shut the door before Dax is pressing me against the wall, kissing my lips, my jaw, my neck. One of his solid thighs pushes its way between my legs and I can't help but grind against it. He grips my suit jacket and in one swift move, it's sliding down my arms and onto the floor. Smooth.

His hands glide down my chest before tugging at the bottom of my shirt, untucking it and pulling it free from my pants. My heart is pounding in my chest, and I already feel dizzy from the thrill of it all.

Dax kisses and nips at the underside of my jaw while he starts to unfasten my pants, urging a soft moan out of me. "God, I've missed you," I say through long, heavy breaths. I'm glad his leg is still firmly between mine, because it's the only thing keeping me upright while his kisses cause me to go boneless.

I start to remove Dax's suit jacket, albeit far less smoothly than he did with mine. It gets caught at the elbows and Dax has to help me out, sliding it the rest of the way down and letting it drop to the floor.

We continue kissing while Dax loosens my tie and starts unbuttoning my shirt, one agonizingly slow button at a time. I try to unbutton his shirt, but he pushes my hands away, clearly deciding to take the lead.

He finally pulls his leg away from between mine, and I'm left leaning back against the wall, hoping I don't collapse every time he presses his lips to a spot of newly exposed skin. He hums with pleasure as he kisses his way across my collarbone, between my pecs, and down my chest. He sinks lower, tracing a line with his tongue down the trail of hair to my pants, making me feel light-headed. He slowly starts to lower his whole body when it hits me what he's about to do.

"Wait!" I say, through heavy breaths. "Stop."

Dax freezes, almost kneeling on the floor but not quite. His hands are still on the waistband of my pants and his mouth is just below my belly button. It must look almost comical to see us frozen like this.

Dax stands back up. "What's wrong?" he asks. "Too fast?"

"No," I say quickly, still trying to catch my breath. "It's just that…"

"What?" Dax furrows his brows, his eyes full of concern.

"Um." I bite my lip. I can feel warmth spread up my cheeks. "You're wearing a white Dior suit."

"So?" Dax asks, seemingly caught off guard by my statement.

"Dax. It's a White. Dior. Suit." I punctuate every word. "You don't kneel on the floor in a suit like that." Now he's staring at my face and I can't tell whether he wants to laugh or…no. He's definitely laughing at me.

"Plus," I go on, "I'm assuming it's borrowed? You can't very well return it with stains on the knees, or um, elsewhere."

Dax tosses his head back and laughs, and it's my favorite laugh. The open-mouthed, full-body laugh that erupts from his chest.

"Okay, fine," Dax says once he pulls himself together. He holds out his arms like a scarecrow. "Undress me."

Okay then.

I carefully unbutton his shirt and take it off, hanging it over my arm. Then I pick up his jacket from the floor, brushing it off with my hand. I hang them both on the back of my desk chair, making sure they're not touching the floor. Then I remove his shoes and socks and place them by the door. When I unbutton his pants, he helps me take them off, lifting one leg, then the other as I remove them. Neither of us speaks while I do this. I purposely don't look at his face, knowing he's watching me with amusement. If I look at him, my face will erupt in a fierce blush.

Once his pants are off, I fold them neatly and set them on the seat of the desk chair with the rest of his clothes. When I'm done, I finally allow myself to look at Dax. He's standing in the middle of the room wearing only a pair of white boxer-briefs and trying not to smile.

I stare at him shamelessly. *God, he looks so good.* In our haste to ravage each other when we first entered my apartment, I hadn't turned on any lights. It's dark in here except for the orange glow of a streetlight below, streaming in through the window. The light casts shadows across the planes of his torso, accentuating the muscles of his abs and chest. His biceps and shoulders are big, but not bulky, and right now, he looks like a goddamned superhero. He patiently waits, letting me ogle him.

I start to take off my tie, but he stops me. "Leave it on," he says. Oh? *Ohhhhh.*

Dax leads me to the bedroom and lays down on the bed, leaning against the headboard. I kneel over him and he pulls my tie, bringing me closer. I kiss his forehead, then his temple, then his lips. I inhale the citrusy scent of his shampoo, and a different sort of warmth fills me—a familiar sense of home. My eyes prickle with tears of happiness.

Dax slides his hands up my thighs and grips my hips. "AJ, I missed you. So goddamn much. I'm sorry for pushing you away. For getting mad at you when I..." He drops his forehead to my chest, wrapping his arms around my waist, then sighs heavily. "I needed help. I still do. But I'm working on it. I promise, I'm working on it."

I'm still straddling his lap, but I sit back. "Why did you do it? The comedy show?"

He sighs heavily. "I don't know. I was upset. Mostly at myself. I knew you were right, I just didn't want to admit it. I didn't want to think about *why* you were right. I thought making people laugh would make me feel better. But I wasn't prepared. I had no material, nothing planned. That triggered a panic attack. I forced myself to talk through it, and, I dunno. Standing there saying all of it out loud somehow made the anxiety subside a little bit. I hadn't planned on saying...well, any of it. Hell, I didn't even know *what* I'd said until I saw the video. But I meant it. All of it."

I bury my face into Dax's neck, take a deep breath, and let a couple of stray tears fall. "I wish I'd seen the video sooner," I whisper into his chest. "I'd have gotten in touch with you. I…"

I don't want to tell him that I'd intentionally not watched it. I'd thought he was already dating someone after me, and I couldn't bring myself to think about it.

"I didn't know."

"It's probably for the best that we both had some time to think," he says. "At least, that's what my therapist says."

I sit up and look into Dax's eyes. "Are you really seeing a therapist?"

"Yeah," he says, not looking away, even though I can tell he wants to. "I mean, I've seen her twice. I like her, and I think she'll be good for me. She's already helped me. Or rather, taught me how to help myself—those are her words, not mine. She thinks I might need to see a psychiatrist about the panic attacks. It might be something medication can help with. But we're not there yet."

"Would you be open to that?"

"I don't know. Maybe." Dax is mindlessly tracing circles on my thighs with his thumbs. He pulls me close and rests his forehead on my shoulder. I can feel his warm breath on my chest.

"AJ?" His voice is so quiet, I can barely hear him.

"Hmm?"

"I'm not going to be perfect. I'm still going to have anxiety. I'll still have panic attacks sometimes. I'm learning how to minimize them and to manage them once they start. But I promise I'll keep trying. For you. Well, for me, but also for you. And for my family. And Max. And Hannah, and everyone else."

"That's all I want," I say. "For you. I'm not looking for perfection. Perfection doesn't exist. I want you to be you, whoever that is. Happy, sad, good, bad, funny, anxious, confident, sexy, messy, hangry...everything. And I want to be here for all of it. But you have to let me."

He lets out a long breath and I can feel him nod against my shoulder. "I'll try," he says.

And that's good enough for me.

We sit like this for a minute—or fifteen, I can't tell—arms wrapped around each other like vines, breathing steadily. I can't get enough of him: the smell of him, the feel of his chest against mine as it moves when he breathes, the sound of his heartbeat. My own heart is bursting with love and affection for him.

Dax is the first one to move. He slides a hand down from my waist and lightly smacks me on the ass. I bolt upright.

"So..." he says. "I'm sure you didn't invite me here after finally getting back together just so you could sit on my lap."

"No, I definitely didn't."

Dax shifts his weight under me. Then he leans back, resting against the headboard. "Okay then, what do you want to do?" He puts his hands behind his head like he's lounging on a beach chair.

I slide my hand down his chest and stomach, stopping just below his belly button. "How about we start with some mediocre pizza and see where we go from there?" I ask with a smirk.

"You know, I've been looking forward to some pizza all evening," he says with a glint in his eyes. "But as long as it's with you, it won't be mediocre. Besides, I'm a good teacher. Let's see what you've learned."

I start to kiss my way down his chest, trying not to smile the whole time I'm doing it because there's some Very Serious Business that's about to happen. I'm approaching his stomach, and his breathing gets heavier. So does mine. He's not rock-hard yet, but there's some definite tenting action happening down below.

"Hey, AJ?" he whispers.

"Yes?" My fingers pull down the waistband of his underwear a bit to expose more of his hip. I follow it up with a kiss to the spot I've uncovered. Dax exhales loudly. I think he likes that.

"Uh, when you said you wanted pizza a minute ago, you meant..."

I kiss a little lower. He doesn't finish his sentence. Instead, he lets out a low moan when I kiss the tip of his erection, still covered by the fabric of his underwear. I touch him, but I don't take his underwear off. Not yet. When I look up at him, his eyes are dark and he's intensely focused on me—or more specifically, my mouth.

He shifts again, pushing his hips against me, just a little. I kiss again, this time a bit lower but still covered by his underwear. He lets out a groan that makes my own cock stiffen.

I've never been good at making my partner wait—teasing and drawing out the foreplay, building anticipation. I guess you could say I've always been more of a 'let's get down to business' type of person in the bedroom. But I absolutely love seeing Dax get all worked up from some light, over-the-clothes kissing.

I'm very aware that I'm still fully dressed. My shirt is unbuttoned, and my tie is hanging loosely around my neck, but I'm still in my dress pants. When I sit up, abandoning Dax's body for a moment, he responds with a frustrated noise.

I unfasten the buttons on the sleeves of my shirt. Slowly. When I start to take my shirt off, he puts his hand on mine to stop me.

"No," he says. "Leave the shirt on. Leave it all on."

I raise an eyebrow at him. "Oh?"

"For now, anyway," he whispers with a grin. "You look sexy all dressed up. So fucking sexy."

"Well..." I say, drawing out the word. "Let me at least roll up my sleeves."

Dax sighs, almost impatiently, while I meticulously roll up one shirtsleeve, then the other. When I'm done, I lean over him, pressing a kiss to his lips before I scoot back and settle myself between his knees.

I've only done this a couple times before—and only with Dax—and we both know I'm not the most skilled at oral sex. Yet. But this time, I'm not worried about what he'll think of my blow job prowess, or lack thereof. I push away the thoughts of inadequacy and focus only on Dax. I want to make him feel as amazing as he does to me.

I trace the line above the waistband of his boxer briefs with my tongue while softly stroking my fingers up his thighs. Dax's breathing has deepened, and from this angle, I see the rise of his chest every time my lips graze his skin. His head is still resting against the headboard, and I can't help but notice he's watching me. Normally this would make me entirely too self-conscious, but this time, I'm not the least bit embarrassed. I'm surprisingly turned on knowing how much he's enjoying the view.

"AJ, if you don't fucking hurry, I'm gonna—"

"Fine." I make a show of rolling my eyes before I grip his waistband again, this time yanking his underwear all the way off.

I lick my bottom lip at the sight of his hard cock flat against his stomach, glistening at the tip. Dax moves a hand to grip himself, but I push it away.

"Nope," I shake my head. Then, in the lowest, sexiest voice I can manage, I say, "the only person who's allowed to touch is me."

"Oh god," he groans. "I love it when you say things like that." He reaches out, this time combing his fingers through my hair. "So confident. So fucking hot." I can't help but smile and preen a little.

Without another word, I grip Dax and slowly slide my hand down his erection, lowering my head toward the tip, licking the pearly droplet that's formed there. He's still watching me but his chest has stopped moving, like he's holding his breath.

Finally, I give into what he wants—what we both want. I take him in my mouth and suck, moving my hand up and down slowly as I do. Dax exhales loudly.

"Fuuuuuuuck," he moans. When I look up at him, he's not watching me anymore, his head tipped back and his back arching up.

I continue to stroke him, following my hand's movements with my mouth, guiding him in and out, stopping every few strokes to swirl my tongue around the tip, then running it down the length of him. Dax is panting and writhing on the bed, trying his best to keep his composure.

My own body is screaming for some attention, but I hold off. I want this moment to be all about pleasing Dax.

"I'm not gonna last long if you keep doing that," he says between heavy breaths.

"Oh, should I stop then?" I ask with a devilish grin. Dax doesn't answer, just makes a *hnngh* sound.

I sit up a little and start kissing the soft skin below his belly button. His cock is still in my hand, but I'm not doing anything more than holding it. He moves his hips up toward my hand, like he's trying to get friction from the movement, but I don't let him. With my other hand, I hold him down, not quite forceful, but with enough pressure that he knows I don't want him to move.

I continue to kiss and lick the area around his hips and inner thighs, grazing the stubble on my jaw dangerously close to the most sensitive parts of him, but stopping just short of where I can tell he wants my mouth.

"Okay, okay. I don't care if I don't last long. Just stop teasing me!" he pleads.

After a few more kisses to his inner thighs, and a nip at the very impressive v-cut of his abdomen, I wrap my mouth around him and go for it. My hand and my mouth work in sync, while I slide my free hand under him to squeeze his wonderfully firm, round ass. It must surprise him, because he involuntarily jerks his hips up from the bed.

After a minute or two of working Dax with my hand and mouth, I slip my free hand down until my thumb is able to reach the ultrasensitive spot behind his balls. As I work him with my mouth, I circle my thumb with a whisper-light touch, and he lets out a delicious moan.

Speeding up my movements, I can feel his body tense under me, and his breathing goes from rhythmic, lust-filled pants to ragged and desperate gasps.

"AJ, I'm close. I'm so close."

Dax grasps at my hair and attempts to push my head back, but I bat his hand away with my elbow. I tighten my grip on him slightly and slow my movements, gently coaxing his orgasm out of him.

For a moment, Dax stops moving and the tension in his body seems to relax before he pushes his hips up toward me and I can feel the warmth of his release in the back of my mouth while he groans and twitches. I slide my fingers down his length a couple more times, urging out every last drop before I take my mouth off of him.

"Jesus," he says while trying to catch his breath. "I...uh...fucking hell."

"Was that okay?" I ask.

"That was...the best goddamned pizza of my life."

I rest my chin on Dax's hip and smile up at him.

He pushes a lock of hair from my eyes and gazes down at me. "I love you so much, AJ."

Something cracks inside of me and I get an overwhelming sensation like I'm about to start crying. I don't know where it comes from, but I have to bury my face in the duvet to keep from bursting into tears.

"Come here," Dax whispers, pulling me toward him and arranging us so we're lying on our sides, face to face. He pushes his leg between mine and uses his strong arms to pull me close enough that we're chest to chest. "I love you," he whispers again and again.

Resting my head on his shoulder, I let a few stray tears fall onto him, but he doesn't say anything. Instead, he holds me close, stroking the back of my hair with his fingertips. The sensation nearly lulls me to sleep, especially after everything else that's happened today. Even my own cock, which was up and ready to party a handful of minutes ago, has decided it's done for the day. Dax seems aware that I'm okay with not getting my own turn at an orgasm, which I'm grateful for. His sixth sense about what I need or want never fails to surprise me.

Eventually, we both get up and shuffle to the bathroom, quietly taking turns getting cleaned up and ready for bed. We climb back into bed, wrap ourselves in each other's arms, and fall asleep surprisingly quickly. Normally, I have a hard time falling asleep like this, being so close to another person, but tonight, there's nothing I want more than to fall asleep touching Dax with every available inch of my body. Apparently, so does he.

I wake up to find Dax under a mountain of blankets, so many that I can barely see his face peeking out. Despite having at least one-third more muscle mass than I do, when we're in bed, he always seems to be cold. Sometime during the night, I'd given him my share of blankets.

"Stop staring at me," he says. He's lying with half of his face smushed into a pillow and his eyes closed.

"How did you know I was looking at you?"

"I can feel it," he says, still not opening his eyes.

"You know," I say, standing up and stretching, "I keep expecting to wake up and find a rotisserie chicken under the blankets instead of you."

"What?"

"How can you sleep under all of that?" I poke at the mound.

"It's cozy," he says, finally opening his eyes. Or at least the one eye that's not squished into the pillow. He pulls the blankets up even higher for good measure. "Anyway, *I* keep expecting to wake up to a pile of frozen fish sticks on your side. I don't know how you can sleep without all the blankets, *and* with the window open. It's too cold in here!"

I shake my head. Dax reaches an arm out of the blanket mound and takes my hand. "You're freezing!" he says. "Come here and let me warm you up."

He pulls me back to the bed and doesn't let go until I'm under the covers with him. We kiss and touch, snuggling until I'm too hot to stay put.

"Stay," Dax says.

"I can't," I say, pushing the duvet off my legs. "It's too hot."

He quickly pulls it back up like a vampire trying to hide from sunlight. "Where are you going, anyway? I thought André gave you the day off."

Actually, when André saw Dax and me together at the party last night, what he'd told me was that if I dared to show up at the office today, he'd send me home. Dario wholeheartedly agreed.

"It's my turn to get breakfast," I answer.

When I return twenty minutes later with bagels and coffee, Dax is wearing a pair of my sweatpants and a T-shirt and sitting on the couch looking at his phone. I love to see him in my clothes. Part of it is the intimacy of it. But also, the caveman part of my brain just likes when he wears things that are a little too tight on him so I can ogle.

We eat standing around the kitchen island, chewing in comfortable silence. When I'm done, I ball up the foil and try to throw it at the garbage from where I'm standing. I miss by at least a foot. It's no wonder I never played basketball.

"So what's on the agenda for today?" I ask, retrieving the foil ball from the floor.

"Actually, Max wants to go look at a couple of places while he's here. He's writing for the second season and wants to check some things out. For accuracy or whatever." I nod. "But that's not until later. We have the morning."

"Good," I say, smiling wickedly. Or as wickedly as I can—I can't help but grin like a dope seeing Dax here again.

I step behind him and wrap my arms around his waist, resting my chin on his shoulder. He sets the rest of the bagel on the counter and leans his head back, giving me perfect access to his neck. I kiss him softly all over his neck and throat, gently nudging him forward until I sandwich him between my body and the kitchen island.

"Mmmm, AJ," he softly moans. "I can't. I need to go home."

"Why?" I whine, my mouth still not leaving his throat.

"I need a shower. And clothes."

"You can shower here. And you can wear my clothes."

"Yours are too small," he says. "I can't walk around like this." He gestures toward the pants. "I'll get arrested."

"You've worn my pants before," I protest.

"Yeah, but with your hoodie covering me. Without it, they're bordering on obscene. There are old ladies in my neighborhood that would be offended."

"Oh please," I scoff. "They'd love to see you like this." I slide my hands over his torso. Dax laughs, wrestling himself out of my arms.

"Alright, fine," I say. "But you really should bring some clothes with you next time."

"When I left the house for the premiere yesterday, how was I supposed to know I'd end up here? I don't exactly carry an overnight bag with me all the time."

"Well, then bring some clothes to keep here." As soon as I say it, we both go still. I don't regret saying it, and I certainly don't want to take it back, but I'm surprised at myself for blurting it out like that.

"Really?"

"Yes, of course," I say. "I'm not asking you to move in with me. I'm just saying, bring some clothes over so you don't have to do a walk of shame when you leave here in the morning."

We're both leaning on opposite counters facing one another. Dax doesn't say anything, so I go on. "Look, I want to make room for you in my apartment. In my life. I want us to make room for each other. If you want that."

Dax reaches out and cups my face. "Of course I want that." He pulls my face toward his, gliding his tongue along my bottom lip. "Anything, mi amor."

Pretty soon, we're wrapped up in each other's arms again, kissing and pressing our bodies against one another.

Approximately eighty-seven kisses later, he pulls away from me, his lips flushed and warm. "I really should go home," he whispers.

"Okay," I whisper back. "Don't let me stop you."

Of course, I say this while slipping my palm down the soft skin of his abdomen and letting it wander below the waistband of his (my) pants. He's not wearing any underwear. Interesting.

"AJ..." He tries to protest, but trails off.

I double down by sliding my hand around to his ass and gripping it firmly, pulling his body closer to mine. Dax groans and circles his hips, grinding lazily into me, causing me to make a mortifying sound that can only be described as a whimper. The second time he does it, I pull back.

"I thought you said you have to go," I say innocently before I turn as if I'm going to walk away. *No way in hell I'm walking away.*

"Get back here," Dax says, grabbing my waist and pulling me toward him. He spins me so my back is against the counter. Then in one swift move, he yanks my track pants and underwear down to my ankles.

I should be bashful or embarrassed, but I'm not. The way he's looking at me—like he hasn't eaten for weeks and I'm a steak from Peter Luger's—makes my insides boil. I'm staring at him, awestruck. He looks so determined, so single-minded, like something carnal in his brain has been activated.

I think maybe he'll lead me to the couch or the bed, but he doesn't. He kneels down on the floor right there in the kitchen and gives me some real fucking gourmet pizza.

It doesn't take long for me to come, accompanied by a string of expletives and nonsense—*ohjesusIloveyouIfuckingloveyouDaxfuckohgodohgodfuck*. He smiles smugly at me, then finishes himself off while still on his knees. *God, help me.*

Afterward, he stands, rubbing his knees, which must be absolutely on fire.

"You see?" I gesture toward his legs. "You would've ruined your pants last night."

"Yes, yes. You were right." He kisses me and I can taste a bit of myself on his tongue. It's strange and thrilling all at once.

He leans into me, resting his head on my chest, and I wrap my arms around his waist. We're sweaty and sticky, but neither of us wants to let go.

Eventually, we pull ourselves apart and get cleaned up.

Dax leaves me to go home and shower before meeting up with Max. He'd invited me to lunch and location scouting with Max, but I wanted to let the two of them have some time to themselves without creating a third-wheel situation.

I stay home and take care of some of the chores and errands around my apartment that I'd overlooked—or more accurately I'd been too depressed and unmotivated to take care of—for the last few weeks. I make a plan to meet up with Dax and Max for an early picnic dinner in the park since the weather is relatively warm today.

A few hours later, I'm walking through the aisles of the market looking at cases of prepared foods and trying to decide what to bring for dinner for the three of us. I'm already carrying a bottle of wine and some cheese in my cart when my phone buzzes. It's a video call from Dax. I move to the frozen food aisle where it's mostly deserted.

"Hi," I say.

"Hey babe," he says cheerfully.

I cringe. "Babe? Is that a thing we're doing now?"

"I dunno." Dax shrugs. "Just trying it out."

"Well, don't expect me to call you that. I don't think my mouth is physically capable."

"Oh, your mouth is plenty capable." Dax smirks at me and my cheeks immediately flush with heat. I clear my throat.

"So, did you call just to embarrass me in public, or is there something you need?"

"Oh yeah." He makes his voice do that raspy, sexy thing. "There's definitely something I need—"

"I'm hanging up," I say.

Dax chuckles. "How do you say *prude* in German?"

"How do you say *fuck off* in Spanish?" A lady at the end of the aisle gives me an affronted look.

"Alright, fine," Dax says. "I was calling to let you know that you need to bring enough food for four people."

"Uh, okay. Is someone else joining us?"

"Uh-huh." Dax turns his phone around to show two people walking in front of him on the sidewalk. I can only see their backs, but I recognize Max right away. The woman he's with is tall, her hair pulled up in a messy bun. They're walking close enough that their arms and shoulders are brushing against one another. I instantly know her by the red backpack she's carrying.

"Is that Sam?!" I ask, loudly enough that she can hear me through the phone.

Sam's head whips around and she notices the phone in Dax's hand. "Is that Bond?" she asks. There's a bit of jostling with the phone and I'm not sure what I'm looking at until I see Sam's face taking up almost the entire screen.

"Bond?" She looks surprised to see me on the phone, but it's *me* who should be surprised to see *her*. "What are you doing? Why aren't you here with us?"

"Uh, I'm buying food for dinner. What are *you* doing? With my boyfriend. And his best friend."

"Oh, you know. Max and I got to chatting last night at the after-party." Sam tries for an innocent voice. "Which, by the way, you ditched within the first thirty minutes *with the star of the show*."

"It was forty-three minutes. And we had...business to take care of."

"I'll bet. Sexy business." I look around the aisle and notice another customer trying hard *not* to listen to our conversation. Or, more likely, she's just trying to look like she's not listening.

"Are you at Union Market?" Sam asks.

"Yeah..." Here we go.

"Can you get some of that vegan tofu salad that I like?"

"Sure."

"And some macarons?"

"Yep."

"And some of that bread with the nuts and stuff? You know the one."

"Sam!" I nearly shout into my phone.

"Sorry, here's Dax. See you later, Bond." She hangs up before I actually get a chance to say goodbye to Dax, so I text him instead.

AJ: What??
Dax: I know! Maybe we inspired them.
AJ: I guess so. I'm still shopping, but I'll see you at 5.
Dax: See you later, babe.
AJ: Nope, still not doing that.

The four of us are sitting on a blanket on the grass eating from paper plates and takeout containers from the market and drinking wine from paper cups. It's chilly now that the sun is setting, but none of us mind since we're all bundled up in sweaters and scarves. After we eat, Dax lays his head on my lap and gives me a rundown on some of the more interesting things they saw today while I gently stroke his hair.

Max scribbles ideas for the next season in a notepad and sneaks glances at Sam when he thinks we're not looking, while she scrolls on her phone—also sneaking glances at Max. Sam stands up and announces to the group that she's cold and that she'd like to take a walk to warm up. She pointedly looks at Max when she says this. He obliges her and they head off toward the paved path.

Dax is awake, but his eyes are closed as I rake my fingers through his hair. "Babe?" he says.

"Hmm?" I answer, only because I'm learning that Dax likes to troll me and the more I complain about something, the more he'll keep doing it. Also, I'm starting to like it.

"I want you to know that if you change your mind about being with me, you can tell me. I don't want you to stay with me because you're worried I'll think you're suddenly homophobic or whatever."

"That's ridiculous. What makes you think I'll change my mind?" I ask.

"I don't. But it's... You have the option to be with women and I realize that's, I dunno, easier?"

"What do you mean by that?" I still my hand and start to worry.

"You know what I mean. You being with a woman is more socially acceptable. It's not an option for me, but for you—"

"I don't give a fuck about what's socially acceptable."

"Well, the other thing is that if you're with me, people are going to want to know who you are. Your name is going to be out there."

I shift my legs under his head. "I hate to tell you this, but that ship has sailed. I'm not famous like you, but after the kiss on the red carpet, people know who I am. And anyone who knows me has heard about it. There's no going back in the closet now."

"I know, but you could still—"

"Dax, stop it." I move abruptly, causing Dax to sit up. "I don't want to be with anyone else. I want to be with you. Just you. Period. Okay?"

He nods like I've scolded him. I scoot closer so we're sitting side by side and wrap my arms around him, pulling him tightly into me. I push a lock of hair away from his ear and lean in close.

"I love you. I love everything about you. Okay?"

"You mean it?"

"Of course I do. I mean, most of the time, I feel like *you're* the one making a compromise by being with me." I hadn't meant to tell Dax that, but it's been simmering in the back of my mind since we first got together.

"Seriously?" Dax leans back, focusing his eyes on mine with laser-like intensity.

"Yeah, I mean, come on. You're gorgeous, funny, outgoing... You could have any guy you want."

"Well, that's bullshit," he says, almost angrily. "If you think being with a smart, beautiful guy who's good at his job and cares about the people he's closest to is a compromise, then you need to change your way of thinking about yourself."

"But—"

"No. Don't." Dax puts a finger over my mouth. "Can we agree that we're both pretty fucking great and it's by some miracle that we found each other? That even with both of us being absolute boneheads, we're here now, together again?"

It's my turn to feel like I've been scolded. "Yes, babe," I say in a small voice.

"Ha! You called me babe!" Dax throws his head back and laughs. "I knew I could break you!"

I shove him and he falls on his side, still laughing. I lie down next to him and wait until he's quiet again, then kiss him deeply. Out of the corner of my eye, I think I catch someone taking our picture, but I don't care. All I care about is Dax. That he knows how much I love him.

EPILOGUE: FIVE MONTHS LATER

AJ

"Dax, wake up." I give his leg a gentle shake. "Your family will be here any minute and you need to take a shower."

"Mm-hmmph." Dax turns and buries his face in a pillow on the couch. He fell asleep an hour ago after staying up late packing, then spending most of the morning in New Jersey doing his third guest segment on *Wake Up, Elizabeth*. When he'd called them to make up for missing his spot six months ago, he'd offered to come back once *Mexican't* started airing. After his first appearance, the hosts loved him so much, they'd asked him to come back for regular appearances.

Since he got back, he's spent the day trying to get everything ready before he leaves early tomorrow morning for New Mexico. He'll be there for eight weeks filming a part in a movie, a comedy set in the Wild West. He's not the lead, but he has a pretty significant part, so he'll be there for a while. It'll be the longest we've been apart, and though I know I don't have anything to worry about, I'm not looking forward to him leaving.

"Dax! Get up!" I shake his leg more forcefully this time. When I turn to head back to the kitchen, he reaches out and grabs my arm, then pulls me until I practically fall on top of him on the couch. He wraps his legs and arms around me like a starfish, pinning me in place.

"Whose idea was this party?" he asks, kissing the back of my neck.

"Yours." I suck in a breath when Dax playfully nips at my shoulder. "You invited them to come and see our place and say goodbye before you leave in the morning."

Dax makes a *hmm* noise into my ear and attempts to move his hands lower. I wriggle the top half of my body free, but I'm trapped from the waist down by his muscular legs. I really should start going to the gym.

"I need to check on dinner!" I protest when he starts tickling my ribs and stomach. I squirm and kick until we both end up in a heap on the floor. I manage to get away and dash back to the kitchen.

"Hey, before I forget," I call to him. "Hannah dropped off a couple more scripts for you to read."

"Oh yeah?" he asks with a yawn.

"Yeah. You're a wanted man, Dax Ximénez."

"As long as *you* still want me, that's all I care about." Smiling, I shake my head at him.

Dragging himself up to standing, he makes his way toward the bathroom, and I hear the shower start.

Dax moved in two months ago, which is sooner than either of us had planned on, but working on the second season of *Mexican't* with Max, plus the time he spent with me, meant that his schedule was all over the place for months, which was stressful for Cami. When I'd casually suggested that he move in so Cami wouldn't worry about when he'd be home, I was pleasantly surprised that he took me up on my offer. I haven't regretted it for a second.

The building's buzzer startles me, and I nearly knock over a stack of plates to answer it. Cami bursts in, throwing her arms around me like she hasn't seen me in months—I saw her on Sunday. In fact, I see

Dax's family every Sunday when we go to their house in Queens for dinner. It's become my favorite day of the week.

"Hello, mijo," Alma says, hugging me and kissing me on the cheek when she enters the apartment. "Please tell your mother thank you for the apple cake recipe she emailed me. I made it yesterday and it was delicious."

That's something I'll be forever grateful to Dax's mother for, and another thing I look forward to on Sundays. When I'd told Alma about my mom—about how we're not close and don't call each other very often—she'd given me a stern talking-to.

"Mijo," Alma had said. "She's your mother, your family. You might not be close, but you love her and she loves you. Your relationship will never get better if you don't try to keep in touch. A mother wants to know her child is doing okay. You need to call her. Every week. Will you please try to do this for me?"

Not wanting to disappoint Alma, I agreed. And I actually follow through, calling my mom every Sunday while Dax goes to the gym.

When I'd called her after Dax and I broke up a few months ago, I thought she'd be surprised to know I had a boyfriend. She'd hadn't been.

She said that back when I was in high school, she'd known there was something going on between Stefan and me. She told me she never said a word because I was an adult and it wasn't any of her business.

When I gave her the details of Dax's and my breakup, Mom told me that even though we'd split up, she was proud of me for caring enough about him to risk our relationship for the sake of his mental health. When she told me that, I broke down and cried. I don't think either of us had been prepared for my outpouring of feelings, but while Mom has never been one for big displays of emotion, she was surprisingly tender and understanding.

After that phone call, I tried to call more often, but it wasn't until my promise to Alma that it's become a regular occurrence. Sometimes we only talk for a few minutes, other times we talk for half an hour.

She asks about work, about Dax, about our relationship, and about Dax's family. I think she likes knowing that his family has taken me in like their own and that I'm not alone here.

In the past month, Alma and my mom have even begun sharing recipes over email.

"I'll thank her," I say. "Did you bring some leftovers?"

"Sorry, AJ. Dad ate the leftovers!" Cami tells me from the living room, where she's sitting on the floor pulling Battleship out of the bag that I can only assume is full of games.

I give a faux stern look at Ray, but he only shrugs. I get a beer from the fridge and hand him one, offering him a seat on the couch.

Dax comes into the room fully dressed and smelling clean and lightly fruity from his shampoo. After he moved in, his hair didn't have that same smell it used to. When I asked him about it, he said it was Cami's shampoo, but he liked it better than his own, so he kept using it. I asked his mom for the name of it so that I could make sure it's always stocked in our bathroom.

I stay in the kitchen looking after the food and Dax catches up with his dad while playing Battleship against Cami (she wins easily).

A few minutes later, Max and Sam arrive. Together. After filming wrapped for *Mexican't*, Max seemed to have reasons to keep visiting New York, and Sam coincidentally started needing to take lots of work trips to Los Angeles.

"Max!" Cami nearly tackles Max in a bear hug.

"Hey, Cams," Max says. "What are we playing?" He immediately takes off his jacket and shoes, sitting cross-legged on the floor to play games with her. I take Sam's coat and introduce her to Dax's family. When I return to the kitchen, I find that Alma has taken over the cooking duties. She shoos me away, telling me to go sit with Dax since he'll be leaving soon, and the reminder wrenches at my heart.

Since there's not a real dining room table, Sam and I eat at the kitchen island, Dax, his dad, and Cami sit on pillows around the coffee table, and Max eats standing at the kitchen counter talking to Alma while she buzzes around the kitchen, making sure everyone has enough to eat.

At one point, I stop eating and take a look around. I don't think my apartment has ever had this many people in here at once, but it doesn't feel crowded. It feels full. Full of happiness and life. Full of the people I love.

Once we say goodbye to Dax's family, leaving Dax, Sam, Max, and me, we sit on the floor and just relax. Sam is leaning with her back against Max's chest, and Dax lies with his head on my lap while I stroke his hair—something I've learned is one of his favorite things ever. It works out well, since it's one of my favorite things too.

We're out of wine and I offer to go down to the corner to get more. We shouldn't, but we're all trying to draw Dax's last night in town out just a little longer.

"I'll come with you," Max says while I put on my shoes. It surprises me since we don't spend much time alone with each other, but I'm happy to have company. I like Max a lot. He's quiet, but when he gets to talking about something he's interested in, he can talk for days—a fellow introvert. He's smart, really smart. He and Sam seem to complement each other well.

"Hey, AJ," Max says as we amble down the steps to the sidewalk. "I wanted to thank you."

"For what?"

"For getting Dax to talk to a therapist. And for, you know, sticking by him through it. I know it can't be easy for either of you sometimes."

"Oh, uh..." I run a hand over the back of my neck. "I love him, so sticking by him is a no-brainer."

"Yeah, but it *isn't* a no-brainer, is it?"

I don't reply. He's right, of course. It hasn't always been easy for us.

"Other guys he's dated have left when the anxiety got too intense. Or was too much of an issue. Maybe Dax pushed them away."

I chuckle a little. "Yep, he tried that with me. It didn't take."

Max laughs. "I'm glad. I think you're good for him. He seems better. Happier. Since we've been working together on season two, he hasn't been getting stressed like he did in the first season. The whole thing has felt...easier."

We buy a bottle of wine from the store on the corner, then make our way back toward my apartment.

"While we're on the subject of relationships..." I let my voice trail off. Max doesn't take the bait, so I continue. "You and Sam seem to be getting along pretty well." Max shoves his hands in his pockets without comment.

After a long silence, he says, "Sam told me about your relationship with her."

"Yeah. We're just friends though. You know that, right?"

"I do." Max is quiet for a moment. "But it's not weird for you to see us together?"

"No. You'd think it would be, but it's not. I love Sam, but not in *that* way. I think when we were young, I loved her as a good friend and kind of assumed that's how love was supposed to be. Or maybe I didn't think true, head-over-heels love was a real thing." As I say it, I realize it's true. "I do now, though."

Max nods. "Good. I'm happy for Dax. And for you."

"And I'm happy for you and Sam," I tell him.

We're quiet until we get to the steps of my building.

As I'm fiddling with the key, I say, "I suppose this is where I should say that if you hurt Sam, I'll hunt you down and hurt you or whatever, but she can do a good job of that by herself."

Max laughs at that, then gives me a sidelong glance. "I'm not worried about you hurting me," he says. I think that's meant to be an insult.

The night winds down and Sam and Max eventually go home, leaving Dax and me alone. I try not to think about how this time tomorrow,

I'll be here without Dax. The job has been keeping me busy, so I'm hoping that will distract me enough while Dax is gone.

For now, I want to savor every last second I have with him.

"So, wanna play chess?" I ask, waggling my eyebrows at him.

"Not really," Dax says, wrapping his arms around my waist. "I'd rather make love, if it's all the same to you."

Dax's hands slide down my chest and under the hem of my shirt. He glides them over my stomach and around to my lower back, just grazing the skin above the waistband of my pants.

"Heh," I chuckle. "It's not the same, but sex does sound better than chess."

Dax kept his promise to be patient and take things slow with me, and eventually, we'd gotten around to making love. Like everything else we'd done with each other, Dax was tender and sweet, letting me tell him exactly what I wanted, what I was comfortable with, and listening to what I needed.

I don't know whether it's the fact that we've had a few glasses of wine or knowing that Dax will be leaving in the morning, but tonight feels different. Like we're desperate for one last kiss, one last touch. We lose ourselves in each other, not holding anything back. When we move together, we don't take our eyes off each other, not wanting to blink for fear of missing a single second. It's incredibly sweet and utterly ridiculous.

Dax lets himself go, coming apart in my arms, whispering "I love you" over and over in my ear. I follow seconds later, biting his shoulder and letting loose a truckload of profanity and gibberish into his neck.

I keep telling myself that two months isn't long. He'll be back soon. And I've already made plans to visit him while he's in New Mexico. Still, I'm going to miss him like hell.

We're startled awake at five in the morning by the sound of my alarm clock. Dax showers and gets cleaned up while I lie in bed trying to get a few extra minutes of sleep. When he's ready, he sits next to me and kisses me on the forehead.

"I've gotta go, babe," he says, and even without my glasses, I notice his pained expression. I grumble but throw my arms around him, pulling him back onto the bed and kissing him.

"I'll come downstairs with you," I say when I finally let him go. I throw on a pair of sweatpants and an orange knitted cardigan (a gift from Dax's mom) and slip on a pair of checkered Vans. No one would ever suspect I work in fashion.

I help Dax with his bags, then stand next to him on the curb, a pit gathering in my stomach. We're quiet as we wait for his car, huddled together in the early morning light, arms around each other and Dax's head on my shoulder.

"Before I forget," Dax says, lifting his head, "there's a gift for you upstairs in our room."

"What is it?"

"I'm not telling. It's a birthday gift. Two, actually."

"Do I have to wait until my birthday to open them?" My birthday is a month away.

"No, you can open them when you go back inside. In fact, you *should* open them when you go inside."

"It's not alive, is it?" I ask. Dax shrugs mischievously.

When his car comes, we hug each other tightly, and I press my forehead to his. We both sniffle, trying to hold back tears.

"Love you, babe," I say, then shake my head. "Nope, *babe* still doesn't feel right."

I press a kiss to his lips while the driver loads Dax's bags into the trunk. "I love you, Dax."

A tear rolls down his cheek and I wipe it away with my sleeve.

"See you later, alligator," he says before getting into the car. He presses his fingers to the window, and I do the same while the driver rounds the car and slides into the seat. Dax mouths "*I love you*" through the window as the car pulls away. I watch until it turns the corner and is out of sight. With a heavy sigh, I turn and trudge back into the building and up the stairs.

When I get back to our apartment, I find a large gift bag tucked into the corner on his side of the bed. I dig through the tissue paper, then burst out laughing. In the bag is a large throw pillow with Dax's face printed on the front. It's the photo of him that appeared on the cover of the magazine—my favorite photo of him. The pillow is ridiculous, but it's so perfectly Dax. There's a note attached:

Babe,
This is for when you're lonely while I'm gone. It's for hugging only. No humping the pillow!!
Love,
Dax

I roll my eyes while stifling a smile and throw the pillow on the bed. There's another gift in the bottom of the bag—a small, flat, square box which I immediately recognize. When I open the lid, there's a beautiful black leather wallet inside, almost identical to the one I'd given to Dax. This one has a blue-and-green striped pattern on the lining. On the back, the word *BOND* appears in small, embossed letters. There's a photo tucked into the cash pocket—a selfie of Dax with Peter, the maker of the wallet.

Peter had a huge bump in business since Dax promoted his wallet six months ago, and since then, he's been able to rent a small studio and work full-time making bespoke wallets, even hiring an assistant. Peter emails me often to update me on how his business is doing, and to thank me for helping him.

There's also a note in the pocket. I brace myself for another sarcastic or silly note from Dax.

> Querido AJ,
> I'll miss you more than you can imagine. You've brought so much joy and love into my life—more than I thought was possible. You've filled all of the parts of me that I never knew were missing. And most importantly, your patience and encouragement have helped me to become the best version of myself. I'll always be grateful to you for that. I can't wait to come back home to you. I love you more and more every day.
> Siempre tuyo,
> Dax

I pause to wipe a tear away with the sleeve of my sweater. Swallowing the lump in my throat, I force myself to read the rest.

> PS: Use this wallet and think of me when you put it in your back pocket right next to your gorgeous ass. Love you, babe.

Aaaand there it is.

I should get ready for work since I'm already up, but I don't. Instead I lie back down on the bed, hugging my ridiculous pillow and smiling to myself while I count down the days until Dax comes home again. To our home. To me.

ACKNOWLEDGEMENTS

Writing this book has been such a strange and wonderful journey—one that I still can't believe I'm on.

First and most importantly, I want to thank you, reader, for taking a chance on me, and this book. When I started writing, I had serious doubts that I would ever finish it. The fact that it would find its way into the hands of people who actually want to read it, you know, without being paid to, is both surreal and amazing. Thank you.

To Amy Spalding, my developmental editor: I appreciate your guidance, your honesty, and your support. You urged me to keep trying at a time when I was sure I was going to give up for good. You gave me a strong foundation on which to build my writing, and for that, I'm forever in your debt.

Thank you to Peter Senftleben, for not only editing my book and helping me smooth out the rough edges, but also for going above and beyond to help me bring this book to life. You shared your valuable knowledge about publishing, offered spot-on suggestions to help me perfect the cover, and even helped me with the dreaded summary. Most of all, your kind words gave me the confidence in myself to believe this book could be something truly special.

Thanks to Rose Thomson for your attention to detail with regards to accuracy and writing about sensitive subjects. Your expertise and insight were extremely helpful in ensuring the characters were portrayed in a positive and thoughtful way.

A very special thank you to all of my bookish friends I've met online this past year. I am so grateful to every one of you who's liked, shared, or interacted with me. Your positive comments and encouragement continue to inspire me to keep going. You are my people!

To my parents: thank you for always being supportive and creating a loving, open, and welcoming home—not just for me, but for anyone who needs a place to feel safe. (Sorry I used the f-word so many times in this book.)

Finally, thank you to my husband for all of your love and support throughout this process. And for being willing to put up with all of my messiness—both literally and figuratively—for all these years. I'm in awe of your never ending patience.

ABOUT THE AUTHOR

Valerie Gomez is a wife, a mother, a Virgo, an introvert, a reader of books, a petter of dogs, a coffee drinker, a grilled cheese sandwich enthusiast, a wearer of sneakers, a lover of rom-coms, a maker of lists, an art director, a designer, an illustrator, a writer, a work in progress.

valeriegomezwrites.com
Instagram: valeriegomez_writes

Made in the USA
Middletown, DE
18 October 2024